The Wildflowers Quartet

A 4-in-1 Edition including
MISTY, STAR, JADE and CAT

V.C. ANDREWS® BOOKS

Flowers in the Attic
Petals on the Wind
If There Be Thorns
My Sweet Audrina
Seeds of Yesterday
Heaven
Dark Angel
Garden of Shadows
Fallen Hearts
Gates of Paradise
Web of Dreams
Dawn
Secrets of the Morning
Twilight's Child
Midnight Whispers
Darkest Hour
Ruby
Pearl in the Mist
All That Glitters
Hidden Jewel
Tarnished Gold
Melody
Heart Song
Unfinished Symphony
Music in the Night
The Orphan Chronicles
Runaways
Olivia
The Wildflowers Quartet

Published by POCKET BOOKS

The
Wildflowers Quartet

A 4-in-1 Edition including
MISTY, STAR, JADE and CAT

V.C. ANDREWS®

POCKET BOOKS
New York   London   Toronto   Tokyo   Singapore

Following the death of Virginia Andrews, the Andrews family worked with a carefully selected writer to organize and complete Virginia Andrews' stories and to create additional novels, of which this is one, inspired by her storytelling genius.

An *Original* Publication of POCKET BOOKS

 POCKET BOOKS, a division of Simon & Schuster, Inc. 1230 Avenue of the Americas, New York, NY 10020

ISBN # 0-7394-0554-3

PRINTED IN THE U.S.A.

Contents

Misty

Prologue

We were brought separately to Doctor Marlowe's house. My mother drove me herself because it was on the way to meeting her friend Tammy for their weekly window shopping and lunch with some of their girlfriends at one of the expensive restaurants near the beach in Santa Monica, California.

I think my mother believes she still has a chance to be discovered and put on the cover of a magazine. Even as recently as yesterday, she held a magazine with the cover beside her face and asked, "Don't you think I'm just as pretty as she is, Misty? And I'm at least ten years older."

Twenty years older was more like it, I thought, but I didn't dare say it. Aging is definitely considered a disease in our house. Minutes are treated like germs and days, months and years are diseases. My mother makes Ponce de Leon's search for the fabled Fountain of Youth a mere Sunday-school picnic. There's nothing she wouldn't buy, no place she wouldn't go if it held the possibility of stopping Father Time. Most of her friends are the same and have similar fears. I can't help but wonder if I'll become just like them: terrified of gray hair, wrinkles and calcium deficiencies.

If my mother wasn't going to Santa Monica today, she would have hired a car service for me as usual and mailed the bill to my father. She just loves sending bills to him. Every time she licks the envelope and closes it, she pounds it with a little closed fist and says, "Take that." I'm sure when Daddy sees it in his pile of mail, he grimaces and his wallet goes "Ouch."

I'm like a dart she throws at him now. "She needs new this; she needs new that. The dentist says she needs braces. She needs new school clothes. Here's the bill for her dermatologist visit, the one your insurance doesn't cover."

There is always another bull's-eye for Mom, who is punishing my father with my needs, whipping him with the costs of keeping me in designer jeans, straight teeth, and anything else she can buy. She pounces on a new expense and rushes to get the charges added up and sent to him ASAP, as she says. Once she sent a bill special delivery to his office even though he had days to pay it.

Daddy tries to keep the bills down, asking *why* sometimes and trying to find alternatives, but whenever he does that, Mommy waves his opinions in my face like a bullfighter with a red flag, crying, "See how much he thinks of you? He's always looking for a bargain. If he wants to find cheaper prices for the things you need, let him do all the shopping."

Daddy says he just wants to be sure I'm getting value for the dollars spent.

I'm so lucky to have such concerned parents. I have to count my blessings on my hands and feet, my nose and ears. Doesn't everyone wish their parents were divorced?

I couldn't help but wonder if the other girls who were coming to Doctor Marlowe's today had also been turned into whips their parents could snap at each other.

Jade's father's chauffeur drove her because it happened to be her father's weekend with her and he had a previous appointment. All of us members of the OWP, Orphans With Parents, just love to hear about "previous appointments." What our parents usually mean is "I've got something more important to do for myself than look after your needs. If I wasn't divorced, your father could help, but no, that's not the way it is. We're different. You're ... like some wildflower growing out of the garden, untended, left to fend for yourself most of the time, to pray for the right amount of rain and sunshine because no one's there to water and nurture you."

"I must have had blinders on when I married your mother," Daddy says. Mommy says, "I was on drugs. There's no other possible explanation for such a stupid act."

Did the other girls' parents say things like that in front of them? Sometimes I felt like I was invisible or something and my parents simply forgot I was standing there when they ranted and raved. Doctor Marlowe was right about one thing: I really was interested in hearing what the other girls' experiences were. That, more than anything, brought me here today. Oh, I know other OWPs at school, but without the therapy, without a Doctor Marlowe shining a light in the dark corners, they don't really tell you what's in their hearts. They keep it all locked up, afraid or ashamed that someone might discover just how lost and alone they really are.

Star's grandmother brought her to Doctor Marlowe's house. She told us later on that her grandmother was actually sixty-eight and had inherited all the new responsibility for her and her little brother just when she was supposed to be rocking herself on some porch and knitting sweaters for her grandchildren. And then suddenly, guess what? She's a mother again.

Cathy's mother brought her, but it nearly took a crowbar to pry the information out of Cathy's mouth. Maybe she's afraid to hear the sound of her own voice and admit to herself she exists. Very quickly she reminded all of us of a terrified kitten, rolling itself into a furry ball. I was the one who decided to call her Cat instead of Cathy and after a while, guess what? She liked it better, too.

I was unloaded at the doctor's home and office on a warm early summer morning in Brentwood. The marine layer of morning fog was just lifting to reveal a California sky the color of faded jeans. It was going to be another one of those perfect days we all took for granted in Los Angeles. By afternoon, any clouds would resemble puffs of meringue. The breeze would feel like soft fingers on your cheeks and hair, and car windows would become glittering mirrors.

We live in such a perfect world. Why were we so imperfect? In all our homes there were shadows in corners and whispers behind doors, no matter how bright and glorious it was outside. I used to think everyone else was at peace while we were pawns in silent wars. There were no guns fired, although sometimes we all wondered if there would be. The wounded and the dead were only hopes and wishes and the bombs were just words, nasty words wrapped in cold smiles or printed on official documents that floated into our lives along with the ashes from the fires that burned up our families.

It was easy to see that Doctor Marlowe had a successful psychiatrist's practice, I thought. Her house was an enormous Tudor on a sizeable lot in an area of prime real estate. There was just her and her older sister Emma, so there was plenty of space for her offices.

Why shouldn't she have a profitable practice? I asked myself. After all, she won't ever have a shortage of clients. Even the kids I knew who didn't come from broken homes had problems and many of them were in therapy either at school or privately.

Maybe it was an epidemic. Arthur Polk, one of the boys in my eleventh-grade class, said all this family dysfunction was a result of sunspots. He was a computer whiz and a science nerd, so some of my friends thought he might just be right. I thought he had a head filled with bees, each one a different thought buzzing, some stinging the others. Whenever I looked at him and he saw I was looking at him, his eyes seemed to roll like marbles in a teacup.

"Call me to tell me what time to come for you, Misty," my mother said as I opened the car door and stepped out.

"I already told you about what time to be here," I said.

"I know, but you know how I lose track of time. If I'm not home, remember, you just hit four and the answering service will forward the call to my cellular phone, okay, honey?"

"Right," I said slamming the door a little harder than necessary. She hated that. She said it jolted her nervous system. The way everything jolted her nervous system these days, I thought she was like a pinball machine that if shook too hard would go tilt. Her eyes would take on that gray glazed look of dead bulbs and she would get lockjaw.

I turned and headed for the arched entrance, hoping I wasn't the first to arrive. If I was, I might have to spend some time with Emma, who had a smile as phony as plastic fruit. All the while she spoke to me, I could feel her eyes searching my face for signs of some madness. She talked to me as if I was about nine years old, tiptoeing her questions around me and laughing nervously after everything I said or she asked. She was the one who needed therapy, I thought, not any of us.

Maybe that was why she lived with her sister. She was at least fifty and had been married and divorced years and years ago. She never remarried and from what I could tell was close to being a hermit. Maybe her husband had done something terrible to her. Jade, who I would discover liked to diagnose everyone but herself, decided Emma suffered from something called agoraphobia because she was afraid of being in public places. Maybe Jade was right. I saw that just stepping out the front door was enough to give Emma a panic attack.

Neither she nor Doctor Marlowe had ever had any children. Doctor Marlowe was in her early forties and had never been married. Was this one of those famous cases of a shoemaker with holes in his shoes? After all, she was supposed to be an expert in parenting and she had no one to parent. She wasn't so unattractive that no man would look at her. Maybe she analyzed every man she dated and they couldn't stand it. I laughed, imagining her making love and then explaining every moan and sigh.

Could a psychiatrist ever be romantic? I was eager to learn if any of the others had similar thoughts about her. Yes, maybe it would be fun to be together after all, I thought, as I jabbed the door buzzer.

My heart did little flip-flops. All of us had been here before, but never together until today, never for what Doctor Marlowe termed the start of special peer group therapy. She had decided we had all reached the stage where it might be of some benefit. To me the only interesting thing was none of us had met. Doctor Marlowe's technique was to tell us very little about each other. She said she didn't want us coming to the sessions with any preconceived ideas. All she would really tell each of us was each girl's name and whom she lived with since her parents had divorced or split up, or, as I like to think, came apart. It seems to fit better. That's the way I feel . . . like I'm coming apart, like my arms and legs are floating away and I'm left with just this sixteen-year-old torso searching for a way out of this nightmare house that has no doors or windows.

Anyway, a group of girls who had never spoken to each other was now supposed to gather in a room and share their pain and their anger and their fear, and that, according to Doctor Marlowe, would work miracles. I'm sure the others felt as I did: very skeptical and very anxious. *All the king's horses and all the king's men couldn't put Humpty together again.*

Go on, Doctor Marlowe, I challenged as I approached the door. Put us back together.

No matter how easy Doctor Marlowe made it sound, it was still going to feel like taking off your clothes and standing naked in front of the curious eyes of strangers, and most of what each of us had to reveal, we wouldn't reveal even to our parents, *especially* not to our parents.

Why?

Simple.

We hated them.

1

"Good morning, Misty," Doctor Marlowe's sister Emma cried from the circular stairway after their maid Sophie opened the door.

Emma wore one of her flowery oversize dresses. Her hair was cut with razor-perfect precision at her earlobes and her bangs looked painted over her forehead and glued down a strand at a time. She kept her hair dyed coal black, probably to smother any signs of gray; however, the contrast with her pale complexion made the skin on her round face look like tissue paper. She froze on the steps, waiting for me to enter as if she thought I might change my mind.

Sophie closed the door behind me. From somewhere deep in the house came Mozart's Symphony no. 40 in G Minor. I'm not an expert on classical music; the only reason I could identify it was because we were practicing it in the senior high school band. I play the clarinet. My mother thought it might ruin my orthodontic work, but Mr. LaRuffa, our bandleader, practically signed an affidavit that it wouldn't. Mother finally put her signature on the permission slip.

My father forgot to attend this year's big concert, even though I had brought my clarinet to practice while I was at his new home the weekend before. Ariel, his twenty-something girlfriend, promised to remind him, which I thought was amazing in and of itself. She looked like someone who had little mirrors in her brain reflecting thoughts, bouncing them back and forth accompanied by little giggles that reminded me of tiny soap bubbles.

No matter how obvious I was with my sarcasm, Ariel smiled. I guess Daddy was comfortable with her because she looked like a Revlon model and never challenged a thing he said. Whatever pronouncements he made, she nodded and widened her eyes as if he had just come up with a new world-shattering comment. She was quite the opposite of my mother, who today would challenge him if he said good morning.

Mostly, Ariel gave him sex. According to my mother and her friends, that's all men really care about.

"The doctor will be with you in a moment or two," Emma said as she stepped down the carpeted stairs, taking each step with the same precaution someone walking across a muddy road might take: tiny, careful steps followed by a tight grasp on the balustrade. I wondered if she was an alcoholic. She wore enough perfume to cover the stench of a garbage truck so it was hard to tell from her breath if she drank or not, but she had gained at least forty pounds since I had first started with Doctor Marlowe and when I told that to Mommy, she said, "Maybe she's a closet drinker."

It better be a walk-in closet, I thought.

"How are you today, dear?" Emma asked when she finally stood before me. She wasn't much taller than I was, perhaps five feet one, but she seemed to inflate like a balloon replica of herself, her heavy bosom, each breast shaped like a football, holding the flowery tent out and away from her body.

I wore my usual costume for these mental games with Doctor Marlowe: jeans, sneakers and white socks, and any one of a dozen T-shirts that annoyed my mother. Today's had a beached whale on the front with a stream of black liquid drooling from its mouth. Under it was written *Oops, another oil spill.*

Emma Marlowe didn't seem to notice what I wore, ever. She was as nervous as usual in my presence and pressed her thick lips together as she smiled so that it looked more like a smothered little laugh.

"The doctor wants you to go directly to her office," she said, her voice thin and high-pitched like someone on the verge of screaming.

That's a relief for both of us, I thought.

"Anyone else here yet?" I asked.

Before she could reply, the doorbell rang and Sophie, who was standing to the side like some doll on a spring, sprung into action. She opened the door and we all looked out at a tall, attractive black girl with braided hair. She wore a light-blue cotton sweater and a dark blue skirt. I immediately thought, that's the figure I hope I have someday when my stupid hormones decide to wake up.

"Oh, Star," Emma Marlowe said. She looked back toward the music as if she was hoping to be rescued. "Come in, come in," she added quickly.

Star? I thought Doctor Marlowe meant that was her last name when she told me that was the name of one of the girls. Misty was hard enough to carry around, but Star? Doctor Marlowe had left out a small detail, too, that she was black.

Star smirked. It was a clear look of disgust, the corners of her mouth tucking in and her ebony eyes narrowing. She stared at me. For a moment it felt as if we were both gunslingers in a Western movie waiting for the other to make the first move. Neither of us did.

"I'm sure the doctor wanted to do all the introductions, but this is Misty," Emma Marlowe said.

"Hi," I said.

"Hi." She looked away from me quickly and practically dared Doctor Marlowe's sister to try to make small talk.

Instead, Emma made dramatic gestures toward the office and stuttered.

"You two can . . . just . . . go right on . . . in."

We walked to the office. Neither Star nor I needed any directions. We had been here enough.

The room was large for an office. One side of it was almost a small living room with two large brown leather sofas, some matching cushion chairs, side tables and a large, round, glass center table. The walls were a rich oak panel and there were French doors facing the rear of the house where she had her pool and her garden. It was facing the west side so if you had an afternoon appointment, the office was as bright as a Broadway stage. Morning appointments not only didn't have the direct sunlight, but when dominated by overcast skies required more lamplight.

I always thought the moods we experienced in this office had to be different on brighter days. You carried your depression and anxiety like overly loaded suitcases into this office and hoped Doctor Marlowe would help you unpack them. Darker days made it harder, the depression heavier.

I used to believe bad memories were stuck to my brain with super glue and if Doctor Marlowe pulled one off, a piece of me went along with it.

Sometimes, Doctor Marlowe sat behind her desk and spoke to me while I sat on one of the sofas. I thought she might believe that if she was a little farther away, I would be more open. She did lots of little things like that to test me, and I couldn't wait to compare notes about her with my fellow OWPs.

I went right to my usual sofa and Star paused. I could see what she was thinking.

"Which one do you usually use when you're here?" I asked her.

She glanced at the other and then looked at me sharply.

"What difference does it make?" she replied. I shrugged. She remained standing.

"I always sleep on the right side of my bed. What about you?"

"Huh?" She grimaced and when she did, her eyebrows hinged and her ears actually twitched. I laughed. "What's so damn funny?"

"Your ears moved," I said.

She stared a moment and then she cracked a smile on her black porcelain face. Her complexion was so smooth and clear, it looked like a sculptor had put finishing touches on her just an hour ago in his studio, whereas I had little rashes and pimples breaking out on my forehead and around my chin practically every other day despite my high-priced skin specialist. Mommy blamed it on things I ate when she wasn't around. Doctor Marlowe said stress could cause them, too. If that was the case though, my head should be one giant zit, I thought.

"I know," Star said. "Everyone tells me I do that, but I don't even know I'm doin' it. I sleep on the right side, too," she said after a beat.

"And when you have to sleep on the other for some reason or another, it's a problem, right?"

"Yeah," she admitted and decided to sit on the same sofa I had taken.

"How long have you been seeing her?" she asked me.

I thought a moment.

"I think it's about two years," I said. "How about you?"

"Almost a year. I keep telling my granny I should stop, but she doesn't want me to."

I recalled Doctor Marlowe telling me one of the girls was living with her grandmother.

"You live just with your grandmother?"

"That's right," she said firmly. She looked ready to jump down my throat if I made any sort of negative comment. That was the furthest thing from my mind. Actually, I was envious.

"I never knew my father's parents. His mother died when he was very young and his father died when I was just an infant. My mother's parents live in Palm Springs, but I don't see them much. They're golf addicts. I'd see them more if I became a caddy."

"Caddy?"

"You know, the person who carries the clubs and stuff."

"Oh."

"One year I gave them golf balls with my picture on them so they could look at me once in a while," I told her, "but they wouldn't use them because they didn't like smacking my face."

Those eyebrows went up again, the ears twitching.

"Are you kidding?"

"Uh huh," I said. "I lie a lot."

She stared a moment and then she broke into a nice laugh.

"Oh," she said. "Yeah, I bet you do."

"Your name is really Star? It's not some kind of a nickname or something?"

She stopped laughing, those ebony eyes blazing like two hot coals.

"Your name's really Misty?" she threw back at me, turning her shoulder as she spoke.

"Yeah," I said. "My mother named me after a movie because she and my father couldn't agree on a name or relative to name me after. How did you get your name? And don't tell me your mother gave birth to you outside one night and named you after the first thing she saw."

Before she could answer, one of the prettiest, most elegant looking teenage girls I had ever seen stepped into the office. She had long, lush brown hair with a metallic rust tint that flowed gently down to her shoulders. Her eyes were green and almond shaped. Her high cheekbones gave her face an impressive angular line that swept gracefully into her jaw and perfectly shaped lips. Her nose was a little small, but also just slightly turned up. Of course, I suspected plastic surgery. She wore a lot more makeup than I would. Who put on eye shadow and liner for a visit to the therapist's? Actually, she reminded me of my own mother, the queen of overdress who single-handedly kept the cosmetic industry profitable.

The new girl wore a designer pants outfit and looked like she was on her way to some fashion show luncheon. I glanced at Star, who looked very disapproving.

"I'm Jade," the new girl announced. "Who are you two? Misty, Star or Cathy?"

"Misty. This is Star," I said, nodding toward Star. "We were just discussing how we got our names. Your parents in the jewelry business?"

Jade stared at me a moment and then glanced at Star to see if we were putting her on or something. She decided not, I guess.

"My parents named me Jade because of my eyes," she said. "Where's the good doctor?" she asked looking toward the empty desk impatiently.

"Getting prepared, I imagine," I said.

"Prepared?"

"You know, putting on her therapist's mask, sharpening her fingernails."

Star laughed. Jade raised an eyebrow, tightened her lips and then sat gracefully on the other sofa, crossing her legs and sitting back with her head high.

"I don't know if this is a good idea," she said after a moment.

"So why did you come?" Star shot at her.

Jade turned to her with surprise. The expression on her face gave me the feeling she hadn't really looked at her before this and just realized there was a black girl in the group.

"I was reluctant, but Doctor Marlowe talked me into it," she admitted.

"She talked us all into it," Star said, declaring the obvious. "Did you think we all just wanted to come waltzing in here and talk about ourselves to a bunch of strangers?"

Jade squirmed uncomfortably, gazed at her watch and looked toward the door. We heard footsteps and moments later, Doctor Marlowe appeared with a chunky girl who was about as short as I was. She looked older, though. Her dull brown hair lay straggly about her neck and shoulders as if someone had been running a rake through it. The loose gray pullover did little to de-emphasize her really ample bosom; she had breasts that nearly rivaled Emma's. She wore a skirt with a hem that brushed her ankles. Her face was plain, with not even lipstick to bring some brightness to her watery hazel eyes, pale complexion and bland uneven lips. Her mouth twitched nervously.

"Hello girls. Here we are. This is Cathy. Cathy, let me introduce Misty, Star and Jade," Doctor Marlowe added, nodding at each of us. Cathy merely shifted her eyes slightly to glance at us before looking down again. "Cathy, why don't you sit over there next to Jade," Doctor Marlowe suggested.

Cathy looked like she wasn't going to do it. She hesitated a long moment, staring at the seat as if it would swallow her up, and then finally sat.

Doctor Marlowe, dressed in a dark-blue pants suit, sat in one of the centrally placed cushioned chairs so she could face all of us. Usually, before a session ended, she would take off her jacket and walk about with her hands clasped behind her. Right now, she pressed her long, thin fingers together at the tips and smiled. My mother would notice that she wore no expensive rings and an inexpensive watch. Mostly, she would notice her fingernails were not polished.

Doctor Marlowe had a hard smile to read. Her eyes really did brighten with interest and pleasure after some of the things I said, but her face moved so mechanically at times, I suspected everything she did, down to her smallest gestures, was contrived for a planned psychological result. She kept her dirty-blond hair trimmed neatly at her ears. She wore silver clip-on earrings but no necklace. Her milk-white silk blouse with pearl buttons was closed at her throat.

Our therapist wasn't particularly pretty. Her nose was a bit too long and her lips too thin. Unlike her older sister, she did have a trim figure, but she was very tall for a woman, at least six feet one. Because her legs were so long, when she sat, the knees came up amusingly high. I think from her waist up accounted for only a third of her body; however, she had long arms so that she could sit back and nearly place her palms over her knees. Perhaps being so awkward had made her concentrate more on being a brain than a beauty.

My mother often commented about Doctor Marlowe's hairstyle and clothes, claiming she could do wonders with her if she had a chance to make her over. My mother believed in the miraculous power of hairstylists and plastic surgeons. In her mind they could even achieve world peace. Just get rid of ugly people and no one would argue about anything.

"I assume the three of you had a chance to introduce yourselves," Doctor Marlowe began.

"Barely," Jade replied, the words dripping out of the corner of her mouth.

"Good. I want us to do all the talking and revelations here together."

"I still don't understand what we're doin'," Star snapped. "We haven't been told much and some of us," she added glaring at Jade, "aren't exactly happy about it."

"I know, Star, but a lot of this has to do with trust. If we don't take small risks, we'll never make progress and get anywhere."

"Where we supposed to be goin'?" she demanded.

I laughed.

Jade's beautiful lips folded into a small smile and Cathy nearly lifted her gaze from the floor.

"Home," Doctor Marlowe replied, those eyes filling with an almost impish glee as she rose to the challenge. "Back to yourself, Star. Back to who you are supposed to be, who you want to be. Back to good weather, out of the storms, out of the cold angry rain, out from under those dark clouds," she continued.

When she spoke like this in her soft, therapist's melodic voice, she sounded so good, none of us could prevent ourselves from listening. Even Cathy looked up at her, as if she held out the promise of life and happiness and all Cathy had to do was reach for it.

"Away from the pain," Doctor Marlowe continued. "That's where we're supposed to go. Ready for that, Star?"

She glanced at me and just nodded.

"Good."

"This is going to be simple, girls. You're all going to do most of the talking. I'm really just a listener, and when one of you is speaking, the others will listen along with me."

"You mean we just sit here like potted plants? We can't ask questions?" Jade inquired.

"What do you all think? You set the rules. Can you ask each other questions?" she threw back at us.

"Yes," I said. "Why not?"

Doctor Marlowe looked at Star and Cathy. Star nodded, but Cathy looked away.

"Well, maybe we should just start and see how it goes," Doctor Marlowe decided.

"What exactly are we supposed to tell?" Jade asked.

"In each session, each of you will tell your story," she said with a small shrug. "I've scheduled four sessions in a row for this."

"Our story? I got no story," Star said.

"You know you do, Star. Each of you just start wherever you want. Here you are today. How did you get here?"

"My chauffeur brought me," Jade said.

"Come on, Jade. You know what I mean," Doctor Marlowe said.

Jade sat back, folding her arms, suddenly looking impregnable, defying our good doctor to uncork her bottle of secrets.

"So who's going to start?" Star demanded.

Doctor Marlowe looked at Cathy who turned even whiter. She glanced at Jade, passed her dark eyes over Star and settled on me.

"I'd like Misty to start," she said. "She's been with me the longest. That okay with you, Misty?"

"Sure," I said. I looked at the others. "Once upon a time I was born. My parents tried to give me back, but it was too late."

Jade laughed and Star smiled widely. Cathy's eyes widened.

"Come on," Doctor Marlowe urged. "Let's make good use of our time."

She gave me that look down her nose she often gives me when she wants me to try to be serious.

I took a deep breath.

"Okay," I said. I sat a bit forward. "I'll begin. I don't mind telling my story." I looked at them all and smiled. "Maybe someone will make it into a movie and it'll win an Academy Award."

2

"**I** really can start my story with once upon a time because once upon a time, I truly believed I was a little princess living in a fairy tale. My mother and I still live in this Beverly Hills mansion where I grew up. Some people would call it a castle because it's got this round tower with a high, conical roof. That part houses the main door.

"It's a big house. If it wasn't for the intercom, my mother would have a strained throat daily trying to call to me, and if I don't reply when she uses the intercom, she'll call me on my own phone. I've got call waiting so when I'm talking to someone, she'll call and say, 'Misty, I need you downstairs. Get off the phone. I know you're on it.'

"Of course, she's right. I'm usually on the phone. When we were a happy little family with smiles floating like balloons through the house, my daddy used to tell me I was born with a telephone receiver attached to my ear and that was why my birth was so difficult for my mother."

I paused and looked at Doctor Marlowe.

"I don't remember if I ever told you how much trouble I was for my mother when it came time for me to show my face. She was in labor over twenty hours. Sometimes, when she's reminding me about my difficult birth, it goes to twenty-four hours. Once it was twenty-eight." I looked at the other girls. "I told her that proves I didn't want to be here."

I threw my hands up and bounced on the sofa.

" 'No, no,' I was screaming in my mother's womb. 'You doctors keep your paws off me.' "

Jade and Star laughed. Even Cathy cracked a small smile.

"You've told me that, but not as colorfully," Doctor Marlowe said.

"Yeah, well it's true. She had to be stitched up afterward as well. I mean, she loves sitting there and describing it all in gruesome detail, the vomit, the blood, the pain, all of it."

"Why do you think she does that?" Doctor Marlowe asked.

"So, we are asking questions," I fired back at her. She laughed.

"Professional habit," she said.

"She just wants me to feel guilty and sorry for her so I'll take her side more against my father," I said. "She's always telling me how much easier men have it, especially in a marriage. Well? That's why, isn't it?"

Doctor Marlowe kept her face like a blank slate as usual. I didn't need her to agree anyway. I knew it was true.

"Anyway, I once thought I was a princess because I could have anything I wanted. I still get everything I want, maybe even more since their divorce. My mother's always complaining about the amount of alimony and child support she gets. It's never enough and whenever my daddy gives me something, my mother groans and moans that he has enough money for that, but not enough for decent alimony. The truth is I hate taking anything. It just causes more static. Sometimes, there's so much static, I have to put my hands over my ears!" I exclaimed.

I did it right then and everyone stared at me. After a moment the feeling passed. I took a deep breath and continued.

"Sometimes, I think about my life in colors."

I saw Jade raise her eyebrow. Maybe she did the same thing, I thought.

"When I was little and we were the perfect family, everything was bright pink or bright yellow. After their breakup and all the trouble, the world turned gray and everything faded. I thought I was like Cinderella and the clock had hit midnight or something. There was a gong and a puff and I was no longer a princess. I was a . . . a . . ."

"A what?" Doctor Marlowe asked.

I looked at the others. "An orphan with parents."

Jade nodded, her eyes brighter. Star appeared very serious and Cathy suddenly lifted her head and looked at me like I had said something that made a lot of sense to her.

"My father works for a venture capital company and travels a great deal. It was always hard for me to explain what he did for a living. Other kids my age could tell you in a word or two what their parents did: lawyer, doctor, dentist, pharmacist, department store buyer, nurse.

"My father studies investments, puts money into businesses and somehow manages with his company to take over those businesses and then sell them at a profit. That's the way he explained it to me. I remember thinking that didn't sound fair. Taking over someone else's company and selling it didn't sound right. I asked him about that and he said, 'You can't think of it like that. It's business.'

"Everything is business to him in one way or another. For him, that expression can explain everything that happens in the world. Maybe to him even love is business," I said. "I know this whole divorce is business. My mother is always calling the accountant or her lawyer.

"Mommy was vicious about getting every trace of Daddy out of the house. For days after he had left, she searched the rooms for anything that was evidence of his having lived there. She actually took all the pictures of the two of them and cut him out if she thought she looked good in them. She sold or gave away many nice things because they were things he liked or used, right down to the expensive tools in the garage. I told her she was just going to have to replace some of it, but she replied, 'At least it won't have his stigma on it.'

"His stigma? I thought. What had his stigma on it more than me? I looked like him to some extent, didn't I? There were times I actually caught her staring at me, and I wondered if she wasn't thinking I looked too much like him. How could she change that? Maybe she would have me go to her plastic surgeon and ask him to get my father out of my face.

"However, we had a big, soft chair in the living room, the kind that has a footrest that pops out and goes back until you can practically lie down on it. Daddy loved that chair and spent most of the time in it when he was in the living room. I know it sounds weird, but in the early days of their divorce, before my mother purged the house of everything that even suggested him, I used to curl up in the chair and put my face against it to smell the scent of him and pretend he was still there and we were still a happy little family.

"Then, she gave the chair to the thrift store one afternoon while I was in school. There was nothing in its place for a while, just an empty space. You all feel that sometimes, that empty space when you're walking with just your mother or your father and there's no one on the other side where one of them used to be? I do!" I said before they could answer. Suddenly, my head filled with static.

I closed my eyes for a moment until it passed and then I took another breath.

"For a long time after I was born, I had a nanny. My mother needed to recuperate from my horrendous birth and the nurse who came home with us turned into a full-time caretaker. Her name was Mary Williams."

I glanced at Star.

"She was a black woman. She was in her thirties when she lived with us and took care of me, but when I think about her now, I remember her as much older. She was with us until I was four and sent to preschool."

I laughed.

"I remember my mother making a big deal about getting too much sun on her face because it causes wrinkles. I thought Mary's brown skin was from a suntan.

Star shook her head with her lips tight.

"I was always asking questions, I guess. My mother tells me that when I was little, I wore her out with why this and why that. She would literally try to run away with me trailing behind her like some baby duck going why, why, why, instead of quack, quack, quack!"

Cathy's smile widened, but she had what I would call only half a smile . . . just her mouth in it. Her eyes remained dark, cautious, even frightened. She really is like a cat, I thought. Cathy the cat.

"When my father wasn't traveling, we would have great family dinners. Sometimes, I think that's what I miss the most. We have this dining room that goes on forever. You sit on this coast at one end and you're on the East coast on the other end."

Doctor Marlowe's blank stare brightened with a tiny smile on her lips.

"I was taught the best etiquette, of course, and my mother justified the effort by telling me I was going to be a beautiful young woman and mix with the best of society so I had better behave that way. Beautiful young woman. What world does she live in? Right?" I glanced at Jade who nodded.

"Anyway, I couldn't have been a more polite child. I always said please and thank you and never interrupted adults.

"Usually, Daddy brought me dolls from every trip he made, some of them from other countries. I had enough toys to fill a small store. My closets were stuffed with fancy clothes, dozens and dozens of pairs of shoes and I have a vanity table with an ivory oval mirror. I have the best hair dryers and facial steamers, the newest skin lotions and herbal treatments. Being pretty is a very important thing in my house."

I paused and gazed out the French doors for a moment.

"My daddy is a very handsome man. He takes good care of himself, too. He belongs to one of those fancy gyms. That's where he met Ariel, his live Barbie doll.

"Daddy has an even tan to go with his thick, flaxen blond hair. Lately, he wears it longer. My mother says he's trying to look twenty years younger so he can match his level of maturity. They both criticize each other like that all the time and I'm supposed to sit or stand there and pretend it doesn't bother me or else agree with one or the other."

I could feel my eyes grow narrow and angry.

"I can't believe how I used to think my parents were both so perfect. I thought Mommy was as beautiful as any movie star. She spent as much time on her makeup and her clothing as any movie star would. She never, even to this day, sets foot out of the house unless her hair is perfect and her clothes, shoes and jewelry are all coordinated. She complains about how my daddy tries to look and stay young, but she goes into a coma at the mere sight of a gray hair or the possibility of a wrinkle. She's had plastic surgery, or as she calls it, aesthetic surgery to tighten her skin under her chin and her eyes. I'm not supposed to tell anyone. She lives for someone to compliment her by saying how young she looks. Then she goes into this big act about how she watches her diet, only uses herbal medicines, has all this special skin cream and exercises regularly. She never tells the truth.

"It's funny how when you're little, you miss all the little lies. They float right past you, but you don't wonder about them much. For a long time, you think this is just something adults still do after being kids— pretend. Then one day you wake up and realize most of the world you're in is built on someone's make-believe. My parents lied to each other for years before they finally decided to admit it and get a divorce.

"Once, when I was about twelve, my mother found out that my father had had an affair with a woman in his company who had gone with him on a trip to Texas. He made some dumb mistakes with bills or receipts, something like that, and she was waiting for him when he came home, just sitting there in the corridor off the entryway with the evidence in her lap like a pistol she was preparing to turn on him.

"I was in my room on the telephone talking with my best friend Darlene Stratton when I heard something crash and shatter against the wall downstairs. She had heaved an expensive Chinese vase at him. There was a moment of quiet and then the shouting began. I had to hang up the phone to go see what was happening. I practically tiptoed to the top of the stairway and listened to my mother screaming about the woman and my father and his deceit. He made some weak attempts to deny it, but when she confronted him with evidence, he blamed her."

"How could he blame her?" Star asked, suddenly looking a lot more interested.

"That was when I first learned they were having sexual problems. He said she was too frigid most of the time and when they did make love, she was always complaining about the pain.

" 'That's not normal,' he said. 'You've got to see a doctor about it.'

" 'I did see my gynecologist and he said nothing was wrong with me. You're just looking for an excuse.'

" 'I don't mean that kind of doctor. You should see a psychiatrist,' he said. 'You make me feel like a rapist every time I want to make love.'

"She started to cry and he apologized for his affair, claiming some great moment of weakness after having had too much to drink.

"I sat quietly on the steps and listened. He said he had just been lonely.

" 'I swear I don't love her. She could have been anyone,' he said, but that only made my mother angrier.

" 'How do you think that makes me feel,' she screamed, 'knowing you would sleep with anyone and then crawl beside me in our bed?'

"He apologized over and over and also pledged that it would never again happen, but he begged her to see a psychiatrist.

" 'You're just trying to run away from blame,' she accused him again. 'You're just trying to make me look like the bad one here. Well, it won't work! It won't work!'

"She was coming up the stairs, so I snuck back into my room.

"For days afterward, it was as if they had both turned into mutes. If I didn't talk at dinner when we were together, no one did. They both used silence like a knife, cutting into each other's hearts, until one day my mother bought an expensive dress for an affair they were to attend and my father told her she looked terrific in it.

"Suddenly the floodgates of forgiveness were opened and they pretended they had never had an argument. It made me feel like I was living in a dream where people, words, events just popped like bubbles and no one could say whether they ever happened. Of course, I didn't know how serious the problem really was."

I paused.

Emma Marlowe came through the door with a tray upon which she carried a pitcher of lemonade and some glasses. There was a plate of chocolate chip cookies, too.

"I thought you might want this now, Doctor Marlowe," she remarked. She always called her sister Doctor Marlowe in our presence. I had to wonder if she did so when we were gone, too.

"Thank you, Emma," Doctor Marlowe said.

She placed it on the table, glanced at us all and flashed a smile before walking out.

"Help yourselves," Doctor Marlowe said.

I took a glass of lemonade because my throat was dry from talking so much. Star poured herself a glass, but Jade and Cathy didn't. Doctor Marlowe helped herself and drank with her eyes on me. I thought for a moment. My talking about my parents had opened closets stuffed with memories I had labeled and filed away, memories I had thought were buried forever.

"I remember the cards, so many cards, cards for everything. Neither of them ever missed the other's birthday or their anniversaries."

"Anniversaries?" Jade said. "How many times were they married to each other?"

"Not just that anniversary. They celebrated anniversaries for everything . . . first date, their engagement, stuff like that. Many of them were secret, but I could easily imagine what they were for," I said, looking at Cat. "Like the first time they made love."

Cathy turned a shade of pink.

"I also think they did get married twice," I added for Jade. "The first time, they did it for themselves and the second time for the relatives. They always talked about renewing their vows when they were married twenty years. They made it sound so romantic and wonderful, I was even looking forward to it. I was supposed to be the maid of honor, carrying flowers. I might just go to someone's wedding that day."

"What do you mean?" Star asked with a confused smile across her pretty face. "Whose wedding would you go to?"

"I don't care whose it is. Anyone's. I'll check the newspapers and just show up and watch them get married and imagine the two people are my parents and everything was as wonderful as they said it would be."

"But . . ." Jade uttered with a look of confusion.

"As beautiful as they said it would be!" I screamed at her. She just stared. Everyone was quiet. Tears were burning under my lids.

"Take another drink of your lemonade," Doctor Marlowe said softly. "Go ahead, Misty."

I drew in my breath and did what she said. Everyone's eyes were on me. I closed my own for a moment, counted to five and opened them again. Doctor Marlowe nodded softly.

"You want to stop?" she asked.

"No," I snapped. I drank some more lemonade.

"My mother still has those cards," I continued. "She doesn't want me to know she still has them, but she does. I saw them in a box in the back of her closet. There are lots of funny cards, cards my daddy sent her for no special reason except to say how much he loved her or how beautiful he thought she was and how lucky he was to have her."

I fixed my eyes on Doctor Marlowe.

"I've asked you before," I said, my voice dripping with rage, "but how can people say such things to each other and mean it so much at the time and just forget they ever said them?"

I saw she wasn't going to offer me an answer, so before she could ask her usual "What do you think?" I just looked away again and continued.

"When I was a little girl, I did think I might become as beautiful as my mother. People used to say I looked like her. We had the same nose or the same mouth. I've got Daddy's eyes. I know that, but that's okay because he has beautiful eyes. Mommy will reluctantly admit that too, even today. She doesn't want anyone to think that someone with her good looks would marry an ugly man. It's kind of a . . . what do you call it . . ."

"Paradox?" Star offered.

"Yes, paradox. Thanks. Anyway, what I mean is Mommy didn't mind my mimicking her, experimenting with makeup and trying to get my hair exactly as she wore hers. She took it as a compliment. I tried to walk like her, eat like her, talk like her because I thought that was what made my father fall in love with her and I wanted my father to always love me," I said.

"I asked my mother why I don't have a bigger bosom, and she told me I was fine because I was perky. Perky and cute, that's me. I feel like I'm twelve," I said.

When I glanced at Cathy, she looked guilty and actually folded her arms over her own large breasts. Like she could ever hide them, I thought. I sighed and went on.

Suddenly Cathy took such a deep breath, we all paused to look at her. Her eyes were directed to the ceiling and she had her hands pressed against her bosom like someone who was reciting a prayer. I looked at Star who shrugged. Doctor Marlowe sipped some lemonade and waited. I hated her patience, her damn tolerance and understanding. Where were her bruises hidden, her pain and disappointments? I felt like turning my rage on her. She saw the angry look in my eyes.

"Let's take a bathroom break," she said.

"I don't have to go," I said. I wanted to keep talking. I knew she was handling me. If there was one thing I hated more than anything, it was being handled.

"Well, I've got to go," Jade said and sauntered out as if she was a runway model.

Star looked over at me, then stood up.

Cathy's eyes narrowed before she looked down again.

And I sat back against the cushions of the couch and wondered what it was about this little group that made me able to share the deepest secrets of my put-away heart with them.

3

When Jade returned, she plucked a cookie from the tray and sat. Then she thought for a moment, leaned over and took the plate to offer one to Cathy, who gazed at them as if they were forbidden fruit.

"It's only a cookie," Jade said. "Don't consider it a life threatening decision."

Cathy gingerly took one off the plate and brought it to her mouth slowly, barely opening her lips.

"Girl, it's not poison," Star said sharply and took a bite from the cookie in her hand as if to prove it.

I looked at Doctor Marlowe and saw something in her eyes that told me she was very interested in how we behaved toward each other. For her, this was as much an experiment, perhaps, as it was for us.

She turned back to me and nodded. I looked out the window and made them all wait. After all, they had interrupted me, hadn't they?

"I know my father wanted more children. That was actually the first big fight I can remember," I began, still gazing out the window. Slowly, I turned back to them.

"This was before my mother started to have her problems with sex, I guess. My father didn't know my mother was on birth control pills. All the time she was pretending to be trying to get pregnant. One night he found them and went into a rage, but not right away. He didn't come charging down the stairs screaming or anything.

"My mother and I were downstairs watching television. She liked to do her toenails while she watched one of her nighttime shows and I was mimicking her as usual, doing my toenails, too.

"Suddenly, Daddy appeared in the doorway. He had taken off his tie, and his shirt was unbuttoned. His hair looked like he had been running his fingers through it all day.

"He stood there staring in at us quietly for a few moments. Mommy looked up at him and then continued working on her nails.

" 'Guess what I just found, Gloria,' Daddy said sweetly, so sweetly I thought it was something they had both been looking for a long time.

"Without looking at him, Mommy said, 'What?'

" 'I was looking for that designer belt I had bought you last year because I remembered you wanted the same one in a different color, so I opened the bottom drawer in your armoire to look at it and check the name on the belt and lo and behold . . .' he said still quite calmly.

" 'What is it, Jeffery?' she asked impatiently, raising her eyes reluctantly.

"He opened his hand and revealed the box of birth control pills. There were a number missing. I didn't really know what it was. I still thought it was something they had been searching for, maybe some important medicine.

"She stared for a few moments in silence.

" 'You had no right to go searching through my things, Jeffery.'

" 'So you're going to turn this around? Make *me* the bad guy?' He waited for a moment. Despite my age, I sensed that the silences between them were like those just before big explosions. I remember holding my breath and my little heart pounding as if there was a woodpecker in there trying to get out.

" 'What about your lie?' he continued shaking his head. 'Not deceiving me? Not pretending you were really as interested in having another baby as I was and making me feel bad that you weren't getting pregnant, so bad that I actually went to have my sperm count checked? That's not the big bad thing here? Birth control pills! You've been secretly taking birth control pills all this time?'

" 'Don't get so dramatic about this, she said nonchalantly, but I could hear the tiny cracking in her voice, a note of fear.

"He nodded, looked like he was going to turn and walk away, and then spun around and heaved the small pink box of birth control pills across the living room so hard that it smashed against the numbered print my mother had bought at a gallery on Rodeo Drive just a week ago and shattered the glass. The pills went flying all over.

" 'You idiot!' my mother cried.

"I was practically under the sofa.

" 'How could you lie to me about this? How could you do this?' Daddy cried.

"Mommy just went back to her toenails while he fumed in the doorway, his face so red, I thought the blood might shoot up and out of the top of his head.

" 'I didn't want to disappoint you,' she finally said.

" 'What?'

" 'I didn't want to tell you that I wouldn't have another child. I knew how much you wanted one, so I just kept them out of sight,' she offered.

" 'I don't understand,' he muttered.

"She looked up again.

" 'Look at me, Jeffery.'

" 'I am looking at you,' he said.

" 'No, take a good look, Jeffery. I used to be a size two and no matter what I do, I can't get back because my hips will be forever too big and no matter how hard I try, diet, exercise, personal trainers, whatever, it doesn't help. If having one baby does this to my figure, what will two do?'

" 'Your figure? Your figure! That's what you're worried about?' he cried.

" 'Oh, don't try to fool me, Jeffery. Men,' she declared, 'make their wives ugly and fat and then go looking elsewhere. Just like every other husband, you'll go looking at other women,' she said. 'If I don't stay beautiful,' she added practically under her breath.

"I remember I was shocked to overhear her say that having me ruined her figure. Daddy walked off. She finished doing her nails, picked up her copy of *Vogue* and walked out mumbling about how unappreciated she was.

"After she left the room, I remember I found one of those pills and thought if she could change things, go back in time, and use one of those little pills to keep me from growing in her stomach, she would. Even then, that young, I understood that. I took the pill and crushed it under my foot.

"What I didn't understand was that was the beginning of the end way back then."

I sat back and thought for a moment. No one spoke. Doctor Marlowe sipped some of her lemonade and waited.

Gazing at the floor, I went on talking like someone in a hypnotic state. I could hear myself, but I sounded as if I was talking through a radio.

"It's like you're living in this magical world inside a big balloon and slowly the air is leaking out. As time passes, the walls and the ceiling begin to close in on you. It gets stifling and all you want to do is break out."

I gazed at the others. They all looked lost in their own thoughts, each of them really looking sad, but not for me, as much as for themselves, I thought.

Doctor Marlowe looked pleased, very pleased about how everyone was. It was as if I had proven she was a good therapist or something. Great, maybe I'll get a certificate of achievement at the end of the session, I thought.

I took another deep breath. Why did I feel like I was lowering my head under water each time I spoke?

"When I was almost fourteen, it really began. My father's trips began to take longer and longer. I seemed to notice and care more than my mother did. He missed my birthday. He called from New York, but not until very late in the day. He asked me how I liked my present, but I sensed that he didn't know what it was, what my mother had bought.

" 'Was it something you were wishing for?' he wanted to know.

"The only thing I was wishing for was for them to love me and go back to loving each other, but I said yes and he was relieved."

I gazed at the others again. My eyes had a film of tears over them.

"We make everything so much easier for them when we tell them what they want to hear," I said, "but that doesn't stop it. It doesn't stop the static. Suddenly, there were more and more arguments. It was like some kind of disease infecting everything. Daddy never openly complained about the bills before. Now, he would toss them on the dinner table and question Mommy like some prosecutor, demanding to know why she needed this or that and always asking, when was it going to end?

" 'It's never going to end, Jeffery. It's called living,' she told him and that would set him off ranting about other husbands and wives, mostly about how other wives were more economical and efficient.

"They both seemed to look for reasons to complain. It was as if . . . a pair of magnifying glasses was suddenly put in front of their faces and they saw the little mistakes and blemishes in each other. One of Daddy's favorite topics was Mommy's salon bills. She also has a masseuse twice a week, facial treatments every weekend and, of course, the personal trainer. I didn't understand the comments he muttered under his breath, but he would say things like, 'Why are you making yourself so beautiful for me? It's just a waste.'

"She would cry and they would stop arguing for a while, Daddy looking like he felt just as terrible.

"I knew they weren't fighting because Daddy was making less money. Shirley Kagan told me that was why her parents eventually got a divorce, but Daddy bought a new car that year, an expensive one, a Mercedes, and he bought an expensive new big screen television set. More and more it seemed to me they were looking for the arguments, lifting stones to see what they could find that was wrong about each other.

"They even fought over food. Daddy complained about the choice of breakfast cereals. He hadn't cared much before. He only had juice, toast and coffee anyway, but there he was rifling through the food cupboards criticizing what Mommy had bought at the supermarket.

"Sometimes, they made me into a referee. They would both turn to me and ask my opinion. I felt like I was being held over a raging fire and if I gave the wrong answer, one or the other would cut the string and I'd fall into his or her rage.

"My mother started to say things like 'Your father's a narrowminded fool.'

"Daddy would say, 'I only hope you don't become like your mother.'

"I started doing badly in school. Often, in the middle of one of their arguments, they would both spin on me and complain about my work, my clothes, my friends. I think it made them both feel better to have me available. It was like I was a test target or something. On more than one occasion, I told them I hated them both and ran upstairs, hysterical, tears streaming off my face.

"Then one would blame the other for failing me and that became a whole new round of battling.

"The gray had come seeping into our house. I hated coming home and hated to go down to dinner when Daddy was there. I could feel the lightning in the house, that damn static, crackling all around me.

"What I really remember is how quiet it suddenly became. I didn't hear music or even the television going. We had become a family of zombies, shadows of ourselves, gliding along the walls, avoiding each other.

"When Daddy came home, Mommy wouldn't even greet him. He would say something like 'Hello to you too, Gloria, and she would mutter something under her breath.

"And then finally one day, on a weekend, Mommy and Daddy called me into the den and asked me to sit on the sofa. Mommy was seated in the cushioned, red leather chair and Daddy stood by the window. I remember every detail of that day. It had rained in the morning and the sun began to appear between thick, dirty looking clouds, puffs that looked bruised and stained. The whole world seemed to have turned angry. I had a little stomachache, some cramps that told me my period was getting ready to make its usual spectacular entrance. Lately, they had become more severe and less regular. The school nurse told me it might be due to stress. I think she was fishing for good gossip.

"Anyway, I joined them in the den. Daddy was wearing a dark sports jacket, no tie, slacks and his light brown loafers. Mommy had her hair perfect as usual, her face made up as if she was going to an evening affair. She wore one of her pants suits and matching thick, high-heel shoes. On her wrists and fingers was her usual array of expensive jewelry. She also wore her gold leaf earrings with small diamonds on her lobes. I remember thinking how well dressed they both were.

"I was wearing jeans and a sweatshirt with sneakers and no socks. My mother hated it when I didn't wear socks.

"I sat and waited. Finally, she looked at Daddy and said, 'Well, are you going to tell her or am I?'

"Daddy turned, threw a look at her that would have shattered her face if it was a fist, and then turned to me and softened his expression.

" 'Misty,' he began, 'you probably have noticed that this ship we're all on has been in some stormy waters lately. The old boat has been rocked and rocked and frankly, it's taking in too much water.'

" 'Oh God,' my mother said, 'just tell her and skip all these stupid comparisons. She's not a baby, Jeffery.'

" 'If you don't like the way I'm telling her, then you tell her,' he said and I realized they were even fighting over this.

"I knew what they were going to tell me. I felt it, sensed it, practically heard the words before they were spoken. I just dreaded hearing them from their lips because I would then know that it was really happening, that this wasn't all just some passing bad dream.

" 'What your father is attempting to tell you in his clumsy fashion is we have decided it would be better for all of us if he and I got a divorce,' Mommy stated firmly.

"I looked up at him and he looked down. Then I turned to her and said, 'Better for all of us? This is supposed to be good for me?'

" 'It can't be good for you to be in the middle of all this every day, every minute,' Mommy said. 'It's affecting your school work, too. We've already spoken to a counselor and he's assured us that your dramatic downturn is due to our marital problems,' she said.

"I remember being shocked by that. They had spoken to a counselor, told him about their personal problems, our personal problems? This had been started and had been going on for some time without my knowledge. Never before in my life did I feel more like a stranger in my own home than I did at that moment. Who were these two people? I wondered.

"I looked at Daddy and then at Mommy and thought how they had both changed. They were both trying to be younger, but suddenly they both looked so old and decrepit to me. What happened to my parents, to my beautiful parents who used to attract so many compliments?"

I paused.

"Where do people go when they change?" I asked the others. They saw I was really looking for an answer.

"What?" Jade asked. "Go? I don't understand."

I looked at Doctor Marlowe. This was something she and I had discussed before: my theory that people die many times before they're buried.

"The two people that were my parents were gone," I told Jade. "Those two people somehow died."

"I don't understand," Star said, her head tilted a little to one side. "You're parents are still alive, aren't they?"

"Not the way they were to me," I said.

Jade's eyes narrowed as she thought about what I was saying. Then, she nodded gently.

"I get it," she said. "She's right. My parents are different people now, too."

"Well, I'm still not sure what you mean. Maybe because my parents are really gone," Star insisted. She looked at Cathy, who pressed her lips together as if she was afraid she might comment.

"You will," Jade told Star.

"Oh, you know what I'll get and what I won't get? What are you, the therapist now?"

"Don't direct your hostility toward me," Jade said in a firm, take charge demeanor.

"Direct what? What's that supposed to mean?" Star cried, her eyes flashing.

"Girls, take a breath," Doctor Marlowe interceded. "Come on, everyone relax. Just sit back and think about what Misty has said. Just digest it all for a moment and later we can talk about it."

"I don't know what there is to talk about. It's dumb. Dead, not dead, gone," Star muttered but sat back with her arms folded. Her large dark brown eyes looked from Jade to me and then to Doctor Marlowe.

"Do you want to continue, Misty?" Doctor Marlowe asked.

"Okay," I said. I took a breath and continued.

"My parents were both looking at me, staring at me, waiting for my response to their announcement, I guess. 'What do you want from me?' I asked.

" 'We don't want anything from you,' my father said. What a laugh that was. They would never want more from me than they were about to want.

" 'We just want this to go forward with the least amount of pain for you. Your mother and I have agreed that you will continue to live here with her. I'm moving out. You won't lack for anything. We'll both see to that,' he said and then I did smile with disgust.

" 'I won't lack for anything? Is that so, Mommy?'

" 'Now Misty, you're old enough to understand all this,' she said.

" 'Am I?' I looked at Daddy and he suddenly seemed like a bad little boy to me. His eyes dropped and he lowered his head.

"I felt the tears building in mine, but I didn't want to cry in front of them," I wanted them both to think I didn't care about either of them at that moment."

Jade nodded, her eyes welling with tears. Cathy looked like she was chewing the inside of her cheek and Star stared at me with a look of pure terror on her face as if she was looking back at herself, I thought. I could just begin to imagine what her memories were like.

" 'Where are you going to live, Daddy?' I asked with barely a hint of emotion. I could easily have been asking him where his next business trip would be.

" 'Oh, I'll be nearby. I've found an apartment in Westwood,' he said with a smile as if that was it. That would make everything all right. 'You'll come stay with me on weekends,' he promised.

" 'When he's here,' Mommy quickly pointed out.

" 'I'll make sure I see you often,' he insisted over her infuriating eyes.

"I remember I felt like I couldn't breathe, like the air in my chest was so hot, it was better not to bring it up through my throat and nose, but it was so heavy, I had to take a deep new breath.

" 'When is all this going to happen?' I asked them.

" 'It's already happening,' Daddy replied. 'Our attorneys are in touch and I'm leaving this afternoon.'

"Where had I been while all this was going on? I wondered. They had spoken to counselors, lawyers. Daddy was leaving the very same day they told me. He was already packed!

"One day, they woke up in the morning, looked at each other and decided they were never again to be man and wife? Was that the way it worked?

"All the cards and all the promises, all the beautiful gifts and happy laughter, all the kisses and the hugs that each rained down upon the other were tossed into the wastebasket. I imagined every nice word they had spoken to each other, every pledge of love was sucked back into their mouths and swallowed.

"Only I was left remembering my happy heart beating at the sight of the two of them holding hands, walking on beaches and on streets together, kissing at dinner tables, embracing each other with me sometimes in between.

"Only I was left to recall the music and the singing, all the happy birthdays, the Christmas mornings, the New Year's wishes, the sound of laughter.

"I was alone, on an island of remember when's, looking out across an ocean where waves tossed and turned under cloudy skies.

" 'So that's it,' Mommy said. 'I'm sorry, honey, but we promise not to put you through any pain, if we can help it.'

" 'That's right,' Daddy said.

"I laughed."

Jade, Star and Cathy's eyes widened with surprise.

"That's right, I laughed. I laughed so hard my stomach began to hurt. The two of them, Mommy especially, looked at me with such surprise and confusion, I had to laugh harder. I actually folded up and fell to the floor.

" 'I don't understand what's so funny,' Daddy said to Mommy.

"She shrugged.

" 'Neither do I,' she replied.

"Look at them, I thought. They're finally in agreement again.

" 'What's so funny about this, Misty?' Daddy demanded with his gruff, Daddy face.

" 'Yes, tell us what you think is so funny,' Mommy said, her face in a frown, something she hated to do because it encouraged the birth of wrinkles.

" 'The promise,' I said.

" 'What?'

"They looked at each other and then back at me.

" 'The two of you,' I said, 'making promises to me now.'

"I dragged myself to my feet and wiped the hot tears from my cheeks. Then I gazed at both of them, both sitting there with disturbed faces.

" 'You know what a promise is for me in this house, Daddy,' I said. 'It's a lie in disguise.'

"Then I ran out of the den and up to my room and dove onto my bed.

"A little while later, I heard Daddy carrying his things down the stairs. Before he left, he came to my door and knocked, but I wouldn't respond.

" 'I'll call you in a day or two, princess,' he said.

"And you know what," I said to my three new friends, "I don't remember him calling me princess since."

4

"At first I tried to hide the fact that my parents were getting divorced. None of my friends, not even Darlene, ever thought anything was wrong in my home. It was actually quite the opposite. They all believed I still had the perfect little family. If they came over and didn't see my father, they just assumed he was on another one of his business trips.

"Darlene has two younger sisters and an older brother. She thinks I'm lucky because I'm an only child. Her brother is always criticizing her. She says he's afraid she'll embarrass him somehow, and her mother is always after her to set a good example for her younger sisters. She complains about her parents and her brother and sisters every time she calls me or I call her. Once, she even said she hated her family and she would rather be an orphan.

"People never know how lucky they are. I've been over at her house on holidays when they're all together, even her grandparents on her mother's side, and they have a great dinner and exchange gifts. Last Christmas Eve, Mommy and I went to a restaurant in Beverly Hills with my mother's two other divorced friends and throughout the dinner, all they did was congratulate themselves for no longer being under their husbands' thumbs. I took one look at them and thought, like these women ever were under anyone's thumb.

"For a while I hoped that my parents would get back together. I used to daydream about Daddy showing up one afternoon with his suitcases in hand and a big smile on his face. I even imagined the conversation.

" 'Hi Misty,' he would say. 'I guess the divorce didn't work out. We decided we really were too much in love after all and we would work out our problems because we realize what we're doing to you.'

"What was so wrong with that dream? People are always telling me I have to work out my problems. Teachers, counselors, coaches are always saying don't give up. Whatever happened to that idea?

"Anyway, Daddy didn't come home and after a while, it settled in like a lump of lead in my stomach that he would never come home again, at least to my home.

"Then, one day in school, Clara Weincoup, whose mother sometimes joins my mother and her clan for lunch, stepped up to my table in the cafeteria and turned her mouth into a foghorn, blaring out the news with, 'I heard your parents are getting a divorce.'

"It was like someone's mother or father had died. Everyone shut up and looked at me.

" 'Oh, are they?' I asked. 'I was wondering why Daddy packed all his things and left.'

"No one knew whether to laugh or not. Someone did giggle, but the others looked at me as if I had just broken out in gobs of pimples.

" 'I just wondered why, that's all,' Clara said in her singsong voice. 'I always thought your parents got along.' She wore these thick braces on her teeth with the rubber bands and had a nose with nostrils big enough to serve as tunnels of horror at some fun park. She was so immature. Samantha Peters told us she heard Clara still slept with her Ken doll."

"You're kidding," Jade said.

"So what did you say?" Star asked.

"I said, 'You don't have to worry about divorces, Clara, you'll never get married. Not with your personality.'

"Then the table roared. Clara turned the shade of dry blood and walked away. I got rid of her, but the news was out and I could feel the eyes of my so-called friends all over me, looking for differences."

"Differences?" Star asked.

"Don't you feel people look at you differently when they first learn your parents are getting or have gotten divorced?" I asked the three of them.

"I know what you mean," Jade said after a beat of silence.

I looked at Cathy. She shook her head.

"You can talk, can't you?" I asked her.

She looked at Doctor Marlowe for rescuing, but Doctor Marlowe didn't say a word.

"Yes, I can talk," she said in a voice barely above a whisper.

"Good, because I was beginning to wonder if you would be telling your tale in sign language."

Jade laughed again. We were beginning to look at each other more and more like two people do when they think similar thoughts, and I was thinking we might even become friends.

"I know divorce is no big thing these days. My school counselor actually said that to me! But I couldn't help feeling that I somehow looked different to everyone, now that it was being broadcasted on Gossip F.M. I know I walked differently with my head down, avoiding the looks other kids gave me. What I hated the most, I guess, were the looks of pity. I snapped so hard and viciously at my friend Darlene when she offered me sympathy that she practically ran away.

"I really felt miserable. My grades, which were getting pretty bad as it was, took another dive, so my counselor called my mother who decided she had better do something.

"Most of the serious conversations about my school work that I had in my house, I had had with my father. Daddy would call me into his office and ask me to sit and then he would get up and walk around his desk and begin with something like, 'I was young once and I wasn't any poster child for the best behaved by any means, but sometime along the way, I realized I had better get serious about myself or I would end up in Nowheresville.'

"That's a favorite expression of his," I explained, "Nowheresville. For a long time, I actually believed there was such a place and looked for it on the map."

Jade's smile softened. Star shook her head and leaned back while Cathy suddenly clasped her hands and planted them firmly in her lap. She looked like she was holding onto herself, as if she expected her body might just decide to go floating away at any moment. I couldn't wait for her story.

"Anyway, my mother, who hated serious conversations, tried to play the role of Daddy this one particular afternoon. I didn't know whether to laugh or feel sorry for her. She certainly tried to get me to feel sorry for her.

" 'I know what you're doing,' she said. She actually started by sitting behind Daddy's desk and then got up the way he always did. At least she knew the stage positions.

" 'You're trying to make me feel guilty about all this. You're punishing me,' she cried.

"My mother doesn't actually cry real tears. She grimaces a bit, but not too much because her beauty guru told her that scowling and grimacing will deepen wrinkles or even create them. It weakens the face in the same place so much, it makes grooves, she said. She told me this so I wouldn't grimace or scowl as much as I do.

" 'How am I punishing you?' I asked her.

" 'By embarrassing me!' she wailed. 'You're doing miserably in school just so the administrators will talk about you and call me, and then they'll blame it all on my problems with your father. I know about these things. I read an article in *Good Housekeeping*. Actually, the article was about stress and its effects on the complexion, but it included a situation like this as an example. Divorced women age faster if they're not careful!' she emphasized. 'It's a proven, cosmetic fact.'

"As my mother ranted and raved about my grades, the calls from the school, her stress and embarrassment that day, I suddenly realized how selfish she was and how selfish Daddy was. Neither of them were as concerned about my happiness as they were about their own. I made the mistake of telling my mother that and she nearly blew a false eyelash. Then she went into a list of her sacrifices that stretched from one side of the house to the other.

"The best one was the claim that she was still very much a young and beautiful woman, but she was holding off involving herself in any new romance for my benefit, until I, not her, had adjusted to the new situation. According to my mother, men, who had found out about her new unmarried status, were circling the house like a war party of Indians, waiting to shoot their Cupid arrows through the windows and into her mushy heart. In short, all these lonely days and lonely nights were my fault. Get with it, Misty, I chanted to myself, accept and enjoy their divorce so Mommy Dearest can start dating."

Jade laughed the hardest yet. Star's smile was a lot friendlier and Cathy suddenly looked like she was actually enjoying this. I glanced at Doctor Marlowe. Her eyes were darker, focused, her continually changing thoughts rolling together into a ball of rubber bands behind that intense scrutiny of the four of us.

I sat back, sipped some lemonade, and continued.

"Of course, Mommy felt she had to do something serious. I thought she might go as far as take away my lipstick, which she had chosen for me and which I didn't really use much, but she surprised me with the threat to take away my phone. I knew it was an empty threat because if there was one thing my mother hated, it was my friends or anyone calling me on her phone. She was the one who got my father to have my own phone installed when I was only eight.

" 'She can barely hold a thirty-second conversation!' he bellowed. 'Why does she need her own phone?'

"Mommy wouldn't argue with Daddy much. She would say what she wanted and then sulk until he gave in, which he most always did.

"It was funny, because when I did get the phone, I used to sit and stare at it and wonder who I should call. If I called anyone, I would ask how she was and what she was doing and the other person would answer in monosyllabic 'Okay. Nothing,' and then I would hang up. If my phone ever rang, I would practically jump out of my skin.

" 'If you're next set of grades aren't improved, the phone comes out of your room,' Mommy declared and felt confident she had fulfilled her responsibility. I could just picture her at lunch in a fancy restaurant proudly telling her friends how severe she was and how she had established new rules."

Even Doctor Marlowe risked a small smile. She knew my mother well and she knew I wasn't exaggerating all that much.

"I was at the point where I didn't care anyway. Many of my friends had stopped calling me. I knew it was my fault. I wasn't very nice to them in school or on the phone. Mommy was half right with her accusation. I was punishing her and punishing Daddy, but I was really punishing everyone I knew. Doctor Marlowe helped me to see that. Right, Doctor?"

"You made your own discoveries about yourself, Misty. I merely showed you the way," she said softly.

"A travel guide to Nowheresville," I retorted. Surprisingly, none of the three laughed.

"Is that really who you think I am?" Doctor Marlowe asked.

"No," I said. "But it sounded funny."

I looked to the others because I hoped they would understand even more than our trained psychiatrist.

"You reach a point where you can't stand yourself because you're so damn depressing to be with," I said. Now they all looked like they knew what that meant. "I suppose that's why I grabbed so fast at the first lifesaver tossed my way.

"That's how you referred to him once, Doctor Marlowe, remember, drowning in sadness and grabbing onto the first emotional raft that comes floating by?"

"I think it came from you," she said.

I shifted my eyes.

"Okay, okay. Our therapist isn't supposed to put things in our heads that aren't already there," I muttered.

Jade turned to look at Doctor Marlowe and Cathy did the same. Star simply nodded.

"His name is Charles Allen Fitch. Whenever he introduces himself, he always includes his middle name. He even prefers being called

Charles Allen, rather than just Charles. He thinks the added name makes him sound richer or more important or something. And you can't call him Charlie or Charlie Allen. He won't respond. He'll pretend he doesn't hear you. Even if one of his teachers does it, he'll keep this glazed, indifferent look on his face until the teacher realizes what's wrong and states his name correctly. Then, he'll turn and brightly respond. Good old Charles Allen Fitch.

"He's not bad looking. Actually, he's a very good looking, six-foot-one-inch boy with thick, mahogany-brown hair that he keeps perfectly styled and trimmed. He goes to the hairdresser's twice a month. What I love are his eyes. They've got these hazel speckles floating in green, and there's just something very sexy about his lips.

"He's in my class, but before my parents' divorce made the national news, he and I had said little more than a half dozen words to each other. I, along with all my girlfriends, just assumed he was too stuck-up. He comes from a very rich family. He told me the house he and his mother live in once belonged to Clark Gable's personal manager, who also managed other big stars.

"It is a big house, so big it makes my castle look small. They have a room they actually call the ballroom. His mother has a small army of servants to tend to her and his needs. Charles Allen's butler functions as his valet as well. You all know what that is?" I asked.

Star shook her head.

"The butler puts out his clothes every day and sees that everything is kept clean and pressed and his shoes are polished," I said. "Charles Allen doesn't even pick out what he's going to wear to school. Groden, that's his name, does it for him."

"You're kidding," Star said.

I raised my right hand.

"Swear. I saw the clothes laid out for him myself. Even his underwear.

"Anyway, one afternoon, just at the end of lunch, the bell had already rung, Charles Allen approached me and said, 'I can appreciate what you are going through. My parents are in the middle of their divorce, too.'

"That was all he said. I stopped and watched him saunter off. There's something about the way he holds himself that causes people to think he's a lot older than he is. When we were going places together, I always noticed that. He's got this air of confidence, this arrogance, I guess. Even the school's vice principal, Mr. Proctor, speaks to him differently, speaks to him as though he's speaking to an adult. Mr. Proctor seems to be aware of his own posture when he confronts Charles Allen. Most people are because Charles Allen is so correct he makes you aware of yourself. I guess even I was walking and standing better. I know I stopped slumping in my chair in class.

"You're all looking at me as if I'm nuts, I know, but he's got these eyes that fill with criticism. You can see your faults reflected. You even speak better."

Just talking about him now made me aware of my posture. I straightened my shoulders and sat up.

"Charles Allen has very good grades, of course. He's diligent, responsible, reliable, trustworthy," I catalogued, "all the things teachers tell us to be. He's a little stiff when it comes to sports, but he's the school's best tennis player. He has a serve that turns the ball into a bullet.

"Of course, it doesn't hurt that he has his own tennis court at home and when he was only ten was given lessons by a professional who had competed at the U.S. Open."

"Is he an only child?" Star asked.

"No. He has a brother who is five years older, Randolph Andrew Fitch, who works with his father in their commercial real estate business. His brother isn't married, but he has his own condo in Beverly Hills. When Charles Allen would tell me about his parents' divorce, he would claim his brother sided with his father, although Charles Allen told me right away that his parents were having what he called a civilized divorce. There was, according to Charles Allen, little animosity. Don't you just love his vocabulary? Little animosity," I repeated speaking a bit through my nose.

"'Everything is in the hands of their lawyers,' he claimed."

"Tell me about it," Jade said, twisting her mouth so that the corner cut into her cheek. "I think my mother's lawyer is after more than just his fee. He'd love to have my mother in his hands."

Star laughed. Cathy's smile of amazement lit her eyes. I saw her whole body relax. For the first time this morning, she actually looked happy.

"I didn't think Charles Allen would say anything else to me because of the way he had rushed off, but at the end of school that day, he was waiting for me in the hallway and he just started talking as if we were still in the middle of a conversation.

"'Although every divorce has to be different by its very nature,' he declared like some professor lecturing on the subject, 'I'm sure we share a great deal in common.'

" 'Excuse me?' I replied. Are we speaking the same language? I wondered.

" 'I knew my parents were going to get divorced one day. For years my father has had a mistress and my mother has known it but pretended not to,' he continued. 'Of course, I feel confident that she has had her assignations as well.'

" 'Her what?' I asked.

" 'Affairs,' he said with that dry tone. He has a way of lifting the right corner of his mouth when he's making a nasty comment. I called it his Elvis lip. He said he didn't know what I meant, but I knew he did. Charles Allen is very . . . sneaky," I said. "He'd probably call it subtle. As you can see, if I got anything at all out of knowing him, I got a better vocabulary."

"Were you in love with him?" Cathy asked. The words just seemed to leap out of her mouth. They even surprised her and she looked about with terror after she had said them.

I looked at the others and then quickly at Doctor Marlowe, who appeared very pleased about it.

"I thought I might fall in love with him. Why? Are you in love with someone?"

She shook her head quickly and looked down.

"Because if you want, I'll stop talking and you can tell us about it."

"All right, Misty," Doctor Marlowe said.

"I don't want to stifle anyone, Doctor Marlowe. If Cathy can't wait to tell us about herself . . ."

"Stop being mischievous," she warned.

"Am I being mischievous?" I asked Jade. She laughed and nodded.

"What do you think, Star?"

"I think if you're going to tell your story, tell it already. Afterward," she added, "we'll decide if you are mischievous or not. But if I had to vote now," she quickly added, "I'd say you had some of the devil in you."

All of us laughed, even Cathy, but her laugh was short, insecure, careful. Who burned the smiles off her face? I wondered.

"I didn't really think that Charles Allen and I would become an item just because we both had parents who were into divorcing. The gossip about Charles Allen was that he had an older girlfriend who was a freshman at the University of Southern California. What I found out was he had a cousin in her first year at USC, but there was nothing romantic about it.

"He has his own car, a BMW convertible. I learned later that he has a trust left to him by his grandfather on his father's side. I don't know how much exactly, but it's pretty obvious that it's a lot of money. He offered to drive me home. I thought why not and it started.

"On the way to my house we talked about our parents a little. It was easy to see he wasn't all that close with either his father or his mother. His mother is an elegant looking lady, tall and thin, but a little wide in the hips. My mother would blame that on her child-bearing and say, 'See, that's why I didn't want to have another.'

"Although Charles Allen's mother isn't as concerned about her looks as my mother is, she looked like she was the type who was never surprised."

"Surprised?" Star asked.

"What I mean is no matter what time of day anyone sees her, his mother would always be stylishly dressed. Charles Allen said she was involved in various charities and sat on the boards of a number of non-profit organizations. He thought it was ironic that she gave so much of herself to the sick and the downtrodden and so little to him.

"Like me, he had a nanny when he was little. After that, he was mostly cared for by maids and butlers and chauffeurs. He said his parents even hired people to play with him. One day, he said he felt as if his parents were doing all they could to avoid being with him. 'Keep me occupied and away from them,' he muttered, 'that was their motto.' "

"Don't they like their own son?" Star asked.

I shrugged. "I think they just don't like children, their own included."

"Rich people make me sick," she said.

"Poor people can behave just as poorly," Jade reminded her.

They looked like they could get into a real argument, so I quickly went on with my story.

"The second time we left school together, I went to his house and got the tour. His mother was just on her way out to a meeting. Charles Allen made sure to perform the proper introductions, however.

"Perform was his word. He told me he felt most of the things he did for and with his parents had always felt like little scripted acts.

" 'Mother,' he said, 'I'd like you to meet Misty Foster. Misty, this is my mother, Elizabeth Howe Fitch.'

"Wow. I take it that his parents are very formal," Jade said.

"That's an understatement. His father's name is Benjamin Harrison Jackson Fitch."

"I bet it takes him forever to fill out forms," Star quipped.

"He probably doesn't fill out anything," Jade returned. "He has lawyers who do it for him, I'm sure."

"Can I continue?" I asked them. They both zipped up their lips.
I went on.

"His mother offered her long, thin, bejeweled fingers. The moment
I touched them, she pulled them away as if I might be diseased. Charles
Allen told me not to be offended by that. His mother had a thing about
contact. She absolutely hated hugging and was an expert at the false
kiss."

"What's that?" Cathy asked. Star and Jade turned as if just remembering she was there.

"She kisses the air and not your cheek. Charles Allen said she even
kissed his father that way. He said he had never seen his mother and father kiss on the lips."

"No wonder he had a woman on the side," Star said. I nodded.

"How did Charles Allen kiss?" Jade asked with a sly smile and impish eyes.

"Not very well at first. He took me through the house that day, as I
said, and we played some Ping-Pong in the game room. There's also a
pool table and a hockey game in it. He showed me their gardens, pool
and tennis court and then, he took me to his room. It was as big as my
parents' bedroom, only his has a built-in television set and CD player,
and everything. You should see his closet. It's so organized, color coordinated. And his drawers, the socks, underwear, everything looks brand
new. Some of his things are even in wrappers!

"We sat and talked for a while about each other's home life. He
claimed he didn't see his father that often before the divorce, but now he
said it was more of an organized, scheduled meeting. Once a week, he
had to go to his father's office and give him a report about his school
work.

"I think what bothered me about his world was how formal everything was. All of his servants called him Charles Allen. His mother called
him Charles Allen and, although I never met him, I imagined his father
did, too. Everyone was so . . . proper. It made me uncomfortable.

"Anyway, toward the end of our little talk, which he called a tête-à-
tête . . . ever hear of that?"

Jade nodded, but Cathy and Star shook their heads.

"We were sitting on this small sofa in his room. He was on one end
and I was on the other. There was enough space between us to put another person, and toward the end of this little talk as I said, he paused,
looked at me with those heart-melting eyes and said, 'I've always wanted
to talk to you, but I never could think of anything to say until I heard
about your parents divorcing.'

" 'At least one good thing has come out of it,' I said and he laughed.

"Charles Allen has two definite kinds of laughs. One, sounds more like a robot, each sound perfectly spaced from the other and always the same amount, like ha, ha, ha. It's hard to explain, but his other laugh, what I call his real laugh, is soft. It makes his eyes brighten and does something cute in the corner of his mouth. You're looking at me as if I'm crazy, but you've just got to see and hear it to understand.

"Of course, I knew what he meant. He had always had a crush on me. For a moment I didn't know what to say, and then I said, 'I was always hoping you would speak to me.' Of course, that was a bright, white lie, but he obviously was pleased.

" 'Most of the girls in our school are vapid,' he said. I didn't know what vapid meant. I thought we had recently had it on a vocabulary test, but I hadn't studied for that test and I failed it.

" 'I know what you mean,' I said. It seemed like the thing to say, which pleased him again.

" 'I thought you might,' he told me. 'I bet there really isn't anyone with whom you care to share your feelings concerning your parents' divorce,' he added.

"Then he sat back and started to describe what it was like for him, really like . . . how he thought of his family in terms of this big, powerful train, and how it was running along efficiently and perfectly, but all of a sudden the chief engineer and his assistant got into a dispute and the train began to sway with its wheels screeching around turns for a while until it went off the tracks and came to a grinding halt. I didn't know what to say. It sounded . . . smart and yet, it sounded silly, too, until he added, 'Sometimes, I feel like jumping off the train. How about you?'

"Yes, I thought, I do. I want to run away. Maybe that was a good idea. I told him and he and I got into this great discussion about how we would live on our own. I actually began to think it was possible. He knew how to get some of his money. It sounded . . . romantic.

"Suddenly, he crossed the space between us and kissed me on the lips. It was sort of clumsy. He practically fell on my face.

" 'I hope you don't mind,' he said.

"I shook my head. He made it sound like he had just helped me with my books or something. Then he did it again, only this time it was longer and better.

" 'You're the first girl I've brought to my room,' he told me softly.

"I don't know . . ." I looked at Doctor Marlowe. She nodded so slightly to encourage me, only I could tell she was doing it, I thought. "I guess I wanted someone to say nice things to me so much, I would have welcomed the lips of Jack the Ripper. My heart started to beat wildly. We kept our faces very close, the tips of our noses practically touching. I closed my eyes and he kissed me again."

Cathy really began to squirm in her seat. She looked like she had sat on an ant hill. Doctor Marlowe's face took on a worrisome expression. Star stared at me with almost an angry turn in her mouth, but Jade just gazed with eyes that suggested boredom. Did she think I was some little teenager, miles below her world of romantic experiences? I'll show her, I thought.

"Our tongues touched this time," I said emphatically. Jade's eyebrows rose a bit. "Some boys are very sneaky about how they get to put their hands on you, but Charles Allen just went ahead and brought his hands up along my ribs and pressed his palms over my breasts."

Cathy lowered her head and stared at the floor.

"Wow," Star said. "Mr. Proper loses control." She raised an eyebrow as she looked at me.

"I don't let just any boy touch me," I said sharply, "so I pushed his hands away."

"What did he do then?" Jade questioned impatiently.

"He ignored it and kissed me on the neck. No one had ever kissed me like that on the neck before. The feeling scared me. It shot right through my body and I pulled back to my side of the sofa.

"He was so polite, he started to apologize, but I didn't want to hear that. I was confused. My heart felt like it was a kaleidoscope of emotions. I was afraid and yet I didn't want him to stop. I wanted to be kissed and held and needed.

" 'Stop being so damn polite,' " I ordered him.

Now he was the one who looked confused.

" 'I'm not being so damn polite,' he said. 'I just don't take advantage of people, especially when they're vulnerable.'

"That damn vocabulary of his, I thought. 'What's that supposed to mean?' I demanded.

" 'You're at a weak point because of what's happening with your parents,' he said, which just got me madder. He was a lot smarter than I ever imagined. He was manipulating me.

" 'I am not,' I fired back. 'I don't care what they do to themselves.'

"He smirked arrogantly. I felt like slapping him.

" 'The only reason you stopped is you're afraid,' I told him.

" 'What do you mean? You pushed me away,' he said.

"'You were just moving too fast. Girls do that when boys move too fast.'

Laughter rippled over his pretty-boy face.

"'What's so funny?' I demanded.

"'I was hardly moving very fast. You're just afraid, which is normal for a girl who is still a virgin,' he said.

"I was afraid, of course, but thanks to Doctor Marlowe, I now know I was afraid because I feared being like my mother, who, according to what my father said, found sex painful and unpleasant. I thought I would end up just like she did and drive away someone who had loved me," I recited. Doctor Marlowe nodded, pleased.

"So what did you do?" Star asked.

"'How do you know I'm still a virgin?' I fired back at him.

"He laughed that arrogant laugh and said, 'Oh, you're a virgin, all right. Pure as the driven snow.'

"'That's what you think,' I said. He laughed again and I said, 'Do you want to touch me?'"

"Is she telling the truth?" Star suddenly asked of Doctor Marlowe.

"You'll have to ask her and judge for yourself, Star. You'll all have to do that with each other."

Star curled her lip up and narrowed her eyes.

"So then what happened?" she queried like some cross-examiner out to prove perjury.

"He just sat there, a little shocked, I think. I really felt like shocking him, I suppose. So, I started to unbutton my blouse. He looked frozen and I guess I felt so powerful because of what I was doing to him that I continued."

Cathy lifted her head and looked at me with new interest in her eyes.

"My heart was pounding, but I reached back and unclipped my bra. I just sat there with it hanging loosely. His face got all red.

"'Well?' I asked him, 'Do you want to see and touch me or not?'"

"You were really playing with him," Star commented. "Like playing with a Yo-Yo or something," she added, nodding at Jade who rested her chin on her hand and stared at me, barely breathing.

"It felt like I was an actress in a play performing a role. He nodded and I took off my bra."

It was so quiet in the office, I could hear the water running through the pipes on the other side of the house.

"What did he do after you took off your bra?" Star asked breathlessly.

"What do you think?" I tossed back at her.

"You did it in his room the first time you were there with him!"

"No, not that time. A different time," I said, "but only once."

"Only once? Why?" Star asked.

For a long moment, I couldn't bring out the words. It was like swallowing a wad of gum and waiting for it to go down. They stared. Finally, I had enough air in my lungs to speak.

"Because I found out he was a bigger liar than all our parents put together," I told her.

I didn't know I was crying until the tear dripped off my chin.

Doctor Marlowe wanted me to pause here and take a break for a few minutes.

"Whether you want to or not," she said. "I need a bathroom break myself." She stood up.

The others were all staring at me, Cathy just as directly as Jade and Star.

I rose and followed Doctor Marlowe out of the office. The three of them sat quietly, watching us walk out, no one so much as taking a deep breath.

And that included me as well.

5

When I returned with Doctor Marlowe, I could see from the expressions on the other girls' faces that they had been talking about me. They had trouble looking directly at me, especially Cathy. I sat and waited for Doctor Marlowe, who put on her glasses to read something on her pad before turning back to us. She crooked her right pinky finger as if holding a thought around it and then smiled when she was finished reading.

"Do you want to continue, Misty?" she asked.

I glanced at the others. All three of them looked worried that I wouldn't.

"I don't care. Sure," I said and started. It was almost like having eaten something bad and needing to get it out of your system.

"A few days after I had gone with Charles Allen to his home, I brought him home with me after school so he could meet my mother and she could meet him. I had spoken about him a few times at dinner, and that was enough for her to start calling him my boyfriend.

" 'I should meet your boyfriend,' she insisted, putting on that official mother's face she hated because it made her look older. 'I should know what he's like since you're spending so much time with him and have even gone to his house and met his mother.'

"She whined the last part, sounding hurt that I had met his mother before he had met mine. Ever since the divorce, it was like my mother was on an Easter egg hunt for possible ways to make me feel guilty.

" 'First, he's not my boyfriend, Mother,' I told her. 'Second, I'm not spending all that much time with him. And, third, you never asked to meet any of my other friends and I've been to lots of their houses and met their parents, too.'

" 'That was different,' she replied. My mother always nods after she says something she wants you to agree with. It's like she's coaching your thoughts.

" 'Why?' I wanted to know. Of course she was disappointed I would question her. The corners of her mouth dropped.

" 'Because your father was still living here. For God's sake, Misty, surely you're old enough to realize that all the responsibility is mine now,' she moaned with a sigh to suggest the great weight that had been dumped on her fragile but perfect little shoulders.

"Of course, I knew she was being overly dramatic just because she wanted to see what sort of boy I was with. Nevertheless, I brought Charles Allen home and introduced him to her."

I turned to the girls.

"I should tell you that my mother is in the running for the title, World's Biggest Flirt. As soon as she saw that Charles Allen wasn't the son of Frankenstein, she went into her Scarlett O'Hara act. I nearly puked up lunch.

"Right off, however, she made a gross mistake. She started calling him Charlie. He grimaced in pain every time she did it, but he was too polite to say anything to her.

"Since I had told her Charles Allen's family was very wealthy, she just had to give him the grand tour of our home, pointing out the expensive paintings, our Baldwin piano, her Lalique collection, even furniture and rugs that she called imported and very pricey. I know she thought she was impressing him, but one look at his face would tell you he couldn't have been more bored.

"Then she embarrassed me to the point of tears.

" 'It's so hard being the mother of a teenage girl when you, yourself, keep being mistaken for her older sister,' she said with great flair, fluffing her hair and turning her shoulders. 'I keep up with all the music and read many of the same magazines Misty reads. We like the same shows on television, too, don't we, Misty?'

" 'I don't watch all that much television,' I muttered and she giggled like a silly teenager.

" 'Of course she does, Charlie.'

" 'His name is Charles Allen, Mother, not Charlie,' I corrected.

" 'Oh, fiddlesticks,' she cried, threading her arm through his to lead him out to our patio. She was practically leaning on him. 'That's what his parents call him,' she lectured. 'You don't like to be addressed so formally, do you, Charlie?'

" 'Actually,' Charles Allen said, 'I'm used to it, Mrs. Foster.'

" 'Oh pleeeeze,' she cried, grimacing as if she had just seen a dead rat, 'don't call me Mrs. Foster. That makes me sound so old. Call me Gloria. All of Misty's friends do,' she added, which was another lie in bright neon lights.

"He glanced back to me for help and I told my mother he had come over to help me study and we didn't have all that much time because he had to be home early. She looked like we had told her she had two days to live or something.

" 'Oh,' she said, reluctantly releasing his arm and stepping back. 'Of course. I know how important all that is. I just wanted to make Charlie feel at home,' she said.

"For one small second, I felt sorry for her. I actually thought she was suffering loneliness and I felt bad about cutting it all short like that, but Charles Allen was very grateful for my rescue.

"We went up to my room and I apologized for my mother's behavior. He fell back on my bed with his arms out and stared up at the ceiling for a moment.

" 'I hate to be fawned over like that,' he finally said. 'I have an aunt who always does that. As soon as she comes into the house, she always finds me and hugs me so tightly, I nearly suffocate. She wears this heavy perfume, too, the kind that you continue to smell for hours after she leaves a room. She loves messing my hair and keeping me trapped on her lap, wrapping her long, thin bony arms around me like some sort of octopus.'

"He sat up with a big smile on his face.

" 'What?' I asked.

" 'Whenever I complain about her now, my mother always reminds me that once when I was about three, I urinated on her, right through my clothes. It didn't stop her from scooping me up the next time, though. She's my mother's older sister, a spinster. She took care of my grandmother for years after my grandmother's stroke so we have to put up with all of my aunt's eccentricities, and believe me, there are plenty of them.'

"He paused and looked around my room, nodding as he gazed at the armoire, the vanity table, the computer, and my closets and mirrors, as well as my posters, wall of family photos and doll collection.

" 'Your room is just as I had imagined it would be,' he told me.

" 'What do you mean?' I asked. If he had said it's cute, I would have thrown him out the window right then and there."

"What did he say?" Jade asked.

"He said, 'It's cozy and warm.' Charles Allen knew all the buttons to push," I said with a tight smirk.

"You sound like you really hate him now," Star said.

I glanced at Doctor Marlowe. Her eyes softened.

"I don't hate him. Actually, I pity him. He's even more confused by life than . . . than I am," I replied.

"Anyway, it got pretty hot and heavy that afternoon. We came very close," I said quickly for Star's benefit. She looked disappointed that we only came close. "We just started kissing again and he asked me to do what I had done at his house and take off my blouse and bra. There was something exciting about doing all this in my own house with my mother right downstairs filing her nails or something."

I paused in describing the scene, recalling that afternoon in my own mind first: his eyes, my own thumping heart, the cloud that had turned my room mysterious and dark for a few moments, the way his tongue glided over his lower lip.

My reverie was too long for Star.

"If you're telling it, tell it," she said with a little smile.

I looked at her with an expression that clearly said, you better be just as honest about yourself as I am about myself. I had told Doctor Marlowe most of it before, so it wasn't hard to describe things in front of her now.

"We got into my bed and kissed for a while. I kept my eyes closed and held onto him as if I would drown if I didn't, and then he unbuttoned my jeans and put his hand in them. No one had ever touched me where he touched me. Then he really surprised me by taking down his own pants. He squirmed out of them like a snake. I thought that was funny, but after he had done it and I felt him between my thighs, I panicked and asked him to stop. He said he couldn't. He said it was too late and that was the way it was with boys.

" 'Don't you know about this stuff?' he asked and I didn't want to seem stupid, so I said I did. Of course, like all of you I suppose, I've had sex education. I knew what happens but it's different when it's happening to you and you're not just reading some textbook.

"Anyway, he said, 'So you know I can't just stop now and he got excited and made me wet. My heart was pounding so hard, I thought I would faint. I got up quickly and went into the bathroom. I couldn't get my heart to stop thumping. When I came out, he was dressed and sitting calmly at my computer, acting as if nothing at all had happened. After he was ready to get up and go, he apologized for not being properly prepared.

" 'Prepared?' I asked.

" 'You know,' he said, 'contraception. Next time we won't be like a couple of kids.'

"I nodded, wondering just how sophisticated did he think I was?

" 'I wasn't expecting us to have the opportunity,' he explained. Somehow, it didn't sound very romantic or exciting the way he put it.

"He said good-bye to my mother, who prolonged it with her announcement that she was considering changing her hair color and style. She had pictures of models on the table in the living room and wanted Charles Allen's opinions. He kept telling her she was fine the way she was, but she insisted he give her his opinion and finally, he chose a picture just to end it. Of course, she said it was exactly the one she had chosen herself.

"I walked him out to his car where I apologized for my mother again.

" 'That's all right,' he said. 'She's actually amusing.'

" 'Amusing?' I asked. I really didn't like that characterization of her, but he just smiled and started his engine. Then he leaned out the window to kiss me.

" 'You're the nicest girl I know,' he said. 'It's good to have your judgments confirmed,' he added.

"I knew it was supposed to be a compliment to me, but it sounded instead as if he was complimenting himself for being so good at choosing a girlfriend.

"When I went back inside, my mother astonished me by complimenting me on my choice, too. She said it was reassuring for her to see that I had a gentleman for a boyfriend. She ran on and on about it and how important it was to be very discriminating and particular about men, even in these little high school romances. Her divorce proved that, she said. Then she really surprised me by adding that she had decided to go on her first date since my father had left. The owner of one of the restaurants she frequented for lunch had learned of her divorce and had asked her out.

"I think then, more than at any other time, it really sunk in that my parents were two separate people forever."

I stopped and took a breath when I noticed Cathy was trembling so badly she looked like she was literally freezing. She was embracing herself hard. Her face was so white it looked like she had cut off the supply of blood. Jade and Star saw it too and we all looked at Doctor Marlowe, who shook her head slightly to tell us not to say anything. I knew she wanted me to just keep talking.

"As it turned out then," I continued, my eyes on Cathy, "that weekend both my mother and I had dates. She was going to dinner and I was going to an early movie and then to have pizza with Charles Allen.

"There we both were that Saturday afternoon, primping at our vanity tables. She'd come running in to get my opinion of her lipstick and I couldn't help asking her to help me choose how to wear my hair and what to do about my eyes, for as I've been told by Daddy many times, we have to give the devil her due. Mommy was an expert when it came to makeup and hairstyle. I wanted to look older, as sophisticated as Charles Allen apparently believed I was.

"I suppose it was a very funny scene, the two of us marching back and forth, checking ourselves in mirrors. She put her arm around me in front of her full-length mirror and chanted in a high-pitched, sugary voice, 'Mirror, mirror on the wall, who are the prettiest girls of all? Hear that,' she said laughing. 'It said you are, you are!'

"I imagine you all think that was very silly, but I couldn't help laughing with her and at least for a little while feeling like we were close.

"We both took bubble baths and I let her pour her skin treatments into mine. Of course, she didn't like what I was wearing. Despite her claim of being young in heart and mind, she just wasn't in favor of my clothes. I wore a tank top with a pair of jeans.

" 'Don't you want to wear one of your pretty dresses?' she asked.

" 'I'm just going to the movies and out for pizza, Mommy, not the prom.'

" 'You should always dress and look like you're going to the prom,' she said.

"I told her to give me a break and she stopped complaining and complimented me on everything else. I was leaving first, of course, so I got the final check about fifteen minutes before Charles Allen arrived.

" 'You look beautiful,' my mother said. 'Too bad your father isn't here to see this.'

"I hadn't heard from Daddy all week and I knew he was going to be away for the weekend. The plan was for me to stay with him on the following weekend. What I didn't know at the time was Daddy had already started dating, too. In fact," I said, swallowing down my throat lump, "I think he had started dating Ariel even before he and Mommy had decided to get a divorce. He had been cheating on my mother."

"How do you know that?" Star asked.

"The first time I saw them together, I felt they were just too comfortable with each other. They acted as if they had been living together a long time. It's just something you know," I concluded.

"Yes," she agreed. "It is."

I began to think we all had a lot more in common than we first thought. I guess Doctor Marlowe knew what she was doing after all.

"When Charles Allen came by to pick me up, I realized this was actually my first real date. I had gone to the movies with other girls and met boys and then we'd all gone for pizza and stuff.

"Daddy always used to tell me he would be there to greet the first boy who came to take me out. He liked to tease me about it and threaten that he was going to 'inspect that boy like a Marine drill instructor.' The boy would tremble in his shoes and he would know that 'if he didn't respect my little girl, he'd have hell to pay.'

"I used to dream of that scene. It was nice to think of your father as your great protector, suffering that delicious pain all fathers have to suffer when they see their little girls grown and ready to be dated. How many movies had I seen where the mother in the film reminds the father that 'She's not your little girl anymore. She's a young woman.'

"Daddy wasn't there, however. He was off with his new young woman and I was the last thing on his mind," I said. I felt my throat closing and the weight in my chest grow heavier and heavier. Everyone's eyes were on me, big eyes of pity. I hated it. I looked away, bit down on my lower lip until it hurt and then turned back almost angrily.

"Charles Allen was wearing a sports jacket and jeans and he looked more handsome than ever. My mother made sure to appear when he came to the door. I remember I thought she might as well be using a sledgehammer to beat in her comments.

" 'Oh, what a beautiful young couple you two make,' she cried. 'You look very handsome, Charlie. And just look at Misty. She's blooming like some magnificent flower. She reminds me so much of myself at her age. But that's what a daughter's supposed to do for a mother, right?

" 'You two have a great time,' she said waving her hand as if she was laying a blessing.

"I practically dragged Charles Allen out of the entryway and fled to his car.

" 'Quickly,' I told him, 'drive before she thinks of something else.'

"He laughed and we shot off and I felt as if I was beginning the rest of my life.

"Neither of us liked the movie. We left early and went for pizza. Charles Allen shocked me when the waitress brought our Cokes. He pulled a small metal flask from his inside jacket pocket and whispered that it was rum. He poured a little into my Coke and a lot into his own. I was really surprised. He had such prissy manners in public, I never would have dreamed he would do something like that in a restaurant.

"I wasn't that excited about rum. I mean, I've had it before at parties and pretended to like gin, even though I thought it tastes more like medicine, but the rum in the Coke wasn't bad. I didn't notice it having any effect on me.

"After we ate, he suggested we go to his house. He said the servants had the night off and we could listen to music and talk and not worry about anyone looking over our shoulders.

"It was still quite early so I agreed."

"I know what he wanted," Star said.

I turned to her.

"I really wasn't going there to do it," I said.

"Right," she said and rolled her eyes.

"I wasn't. I was going to tell him that, too. I wanted us to know each other more and care about each other more."

Star looked as skeptical as could be.

"When we arrived at his house, it was as quiet and as empty as he had said it would be. We went into the media room and he put on some music and then he went to his parents' bar and made us both another Coke spiked with rum.

"The sofa had a control panel built into the arm and he could dim the lights and raise and lower the volume of the music.

"'My father has some X-rated movies hidden. I know where they are. You want to watch one?'" he asked.

"'No,' I said quickly.

He didn't look disappointed. He nodded and smiled as if I had passed some sort of test.

"'Good. I knew you were a mature girl,' he said. I suppose that made me feel very happy and maybe I was a little less aware of what was happening. I drank the Coke and rum a little too quickly, too.

"Suddenly, Charles Allen put his hands on my hips and then brought them up and began to fondle me.

"I was very excited but frightened too as his hands explored under my clothes.

"'Maybe someone will come in,' I warned.

"'No,' he insisted. 'Everyone's out for the night. Relax,' he added, kissing me on the neck and cheek. 'You smell so good.'

"I had a whole speech ready, but the words got jumbled in my brain. It didn't take long for him to get my tank top off and my bra and then he showed me he was prepared.

"I did put up some resistance, started to talk him out of it, but he had a whole speech ready, too."

"Oh, I can't wait to hear what that was," Jade said.

"He said things like we shouldn't deny ourselves now. Our parents were off making themselves happy, so why shouldn't we? 'What do you think your mother's going to be doing tonight? And what do you think your father's doing? Same as mine, I'm sure,' he said."

"So you let him do it," Star concluded.

"It happened so fast. We were both naked and he started. I remember I was trembling so hard, he laughed, but I was terrified that it would be so painful. Of course, it was my first time, so there was pain and I concentrated on that so much, I didn't enjoy a moment and I don't think Charles Allen did either. It all happened quickly, more like something that had to be done and over with.

"He started to complain, blame everything on me. I didn't need someone to be nasty to me then. I needed some understanding. He made me feel so insignificant, talking about how inexperienced I was and how experienced he was. I challenged him, telling him I didn't know any girls he had been with, and I knew he had no love affair with any college girl."

"I bet I know where he claimed he got his experience," Star said.

"Where?" Jade asked her.

"The street," she replied and looked to me for confirmation. "Am I right, girl?"

I nodded.

"He went with prostitutes?" Jade asked. I nodded.

"He bragged about it."

"Ugh, how could you continue to go out with him?" Jade asked me.

"I didn't much longer," I said.

"How come?"

I closed and opened my eyes.

"After I got home that night, I wasn't feeling very good about myself. I felt . . . dirty. I took a bath. The house was empty, quiet. Mommy was still not home. I had no one to talk with. I just needed someone. I called Daddy. Of course, I wasn't going to tell him what I had done, but I just wanted to hear his voice. It wasn't terribly late, but all I got was his answering machine and I didn't leave a message.

"I cried a lot that night. I felt so lonely, never as lonely and afraid as I did then."

"What about your girlfriends?" Jade asked.

"I had drifted away from most of them and I didn't know anyone I thought was mature enough to talk about it all anyway. Mommy didn't come home until very late that night. I was asleep, but I woke for a moment when I heard her footsteps and heard her open my door to peek in at me. I didn't say anything. She closed the door and I fell back to sleep.

"In the morning I felt as if I had been wounded and a great scab had formed over me. I think if Charles Allen and I had gotten to really know and like each other and really fallen in love with each other, it would have been different, but I kept thinking about how he had made me drunk and I just felt as if I had been used like some prostitute. It's hard to hold onto self-respect when you let things like that happen to you."

I paused and smiled at Doctor Marlowe.

"A lot of this I've realized with Doctor Marlowe's help," I said. The others looked like they understood that.

"Mommy slept late that morning. I made myself breakfast and went out back to relax on the chaise by the pool. It was a beautiful day, warmer than usual. I knew Mommy wouldn't be getting up soon. Whenever she stayed out late, she had to sleep late to protect her youthful skin and keep her eyes from drooping.

"Bored, I got up and fetched our Sunday paper off the driveway and then went out back to look at the magazine section. As I was thumbing through the paper, I came upon the social pages and nearly missed it. I actually started to turn the page when the name Fitch struck me and I sat up and spread the paper out to read under the picture. I recognized Charles Allen's mother, of course.

"His father was with her. They had attended a charity affair and they were listed as one of the important couples. That's where they were the night before.

"I was very confused. Do rich divorced people still go to social affairs together? I wondered.

"There was a tiny trickle of ice water running down the sides of my stomach. I rose and went inside, dazed, afraid. I didn't know what to do, but an idea came to me and I called Charles Allen's home, only when the butler answered, I asked for Mr. Benjamin Harrison Jackson Fitch.

"The butler wanted to know who was calling and I said an old friend from college.

"When he said, 'Just a moment,' my heart did flip-flops. Moments later I heard Charles Allen's father say, 'Hello,' and I hung up.

"His parents weren't getting a divorce?" Jade asked astounded.

I shook my head.

"The bastard," Star said.

Cathy was nodding.

"Did you confront him with it?" Jade wanted to know.

"That day," I said.

"What did he say?"

"He claimed they had reconciled, but I pointed out that he had told me they were divorced just the night before and I repeated things he had said to me before we had made love."

"And?" Star pursued. She was leaning over, her hands clenched as if she was ready to jump up and follow me over to Charles Allen's house to beat his face into mush.

"He paused and said, 'What difference did it make now?'

" 'If you don't know, I feel sorrier for you than I do for myself,' I told him and hung up.

"I've never spoken with him again," I said and looked at Doctor Marlowe. Her eyes told me I could say what was in my heart so I did.

"But you know what," I told the others, "I don't hate him as much as I hate my parents."

"Why?" Star asked.

"Because they put her in that place," Jade said, her eyes small and sharp as she stared right through me. "They left her naked and alone and vulnerable, to use Charles Allen's word."

"Yes," Cathy said in a loud whisper. We all looked at her. "That's very true."

We all became very quiet, each of us looking behind our own eyes at the thoughts and pictures that played on our private screens.

"How do you all feel about continuing?" Doctor Marlowe asked. "We can take a short break, have a little lunch, go outside, walk around the house, get some air and put in another hour or so."

"Misty is the one who should decide," Jade said, her voice filled with compassion.

"Yeah," Star seconded. Cathy nodded.

"I'm all right," I said. I wasn't. I had a long way to go to be all right. Maybe I would never be all right.

But at least I was with people who would know why not.

6

The breezes were sweet with the newborn fragrances of spring. Now that we were outside after lunch, we all felt even worse about going back inside, where we had to revisit our private nightmares. Doctor Marlowe walked with her head down, her arms folded and her shoulders a little slumped. My mother would be very critical of her posture, I thought. The four of us remained a little behind her, none of us really walking together. Cat stayed at the end, walking the slowest, her eyes shifting cautiously from Jade to Star to me.

"My gardener tells me I'm going to have to tear out all those oleander bushes," Doctor Marlowe said pausing and nodding toward the rear of her property. "Some disease is running rampant through the lot of them. He wants me to plant something new now so it will all grow during the summer months."

"Can't he just cure them?" Star asked.

"He doesn't think so."

"Get another gardener," Jade said.

Doctor Marlowe laughed.

"No, he's very good. He's been with me for years and years. It's easier to replace the plants than to replace the gardener."

"Too bad we can't do the same with parents," I said. They all looked back at me. I shrugged. "They don't work so we just replace them with ones that do."

"None of us have any guarantees about anything in this life, Misty," Doctor Marlowe said. "We've just got to learn how to deal with it and go forward."

"It's always easier for someone else to say," Jade muttered. Star nodded.

"That's right," she said.

"I'm not someone else," Doctor Marlowe declared. "I'm not just your therapist," she continued. "My parents divorced when I was just a little younger than you. I think that's what gave me the idea to go into psychiatry . . . my own pain."

"Is that why you're not married?" Jade asked her.

"That's another story," she said. "Besides, I'm the therapist here, remember? I ask the questions. Let's keep walking around the house and go back in," she said.

Jade threw a conspiratorial smile at me and I threw one back.

"Come on, girl," Star said as she waited for Cathy to catch up. "You walk slower than my grandma."

Surprised that Star would pause, Cathy quickly caught up to her.

Everyone went to the bathroom again. I just wanted to rinse my face in cold water. We had to wait for Cathy, who took so long, we began to wonder if she had left.

"Sorry," Cathy said when she finally came in and took her seat.

"Let's let Misty continue and finish out the session. It's getting late and I'm sure you all have other things to do with such a nice day."

"I suppose what bothers me the most, what I think about a lot is what their divorce means about me. Before I visited Daddy in his new home, I met him for lunch one Saturday after he had moved out of the house. That was something we had never done before, had lunch together without my mother. He invited me since the plans he had made for me to visit him in his new apartment had to be canceled because of what he called an emergency business trip. Later, I found out he was going to San Francisco with his new girlfriend.

"But at the time, I was excited about meeting him at a fancy Beverly Hills restaurant. He sent a cab for me, which triggered one of my mother's familiar favorite chants about how he always manages to get someone else to fulfill his responsibilities.

" 'Why couldn't he pick you up himself? It's Saturday. He can't be meeting anyone for business. It's just inconvenient for him, that's all; so he sends a cab. Typical Jeffery Foster behavior,' she raved.

" 'How can you hate him so much now and have loved him before?' I asked her.

" 'That's what I keep asking myself,' she replied. She thought for a moment and then added, 'I was just deliberately blind. I refused to admit to his weaknesses and failings. I didn't want to face the fact that

I had made such a mistake. I don't know. I was just too young to get married," she concluded. "I was a hopeless romantic who believed when a man said you were the earth, moon and stars to him, he meant it.'

"Self-pity, like evening shadows, came to darken her eyes," I said, remembering.

" 'They put you on a throne until they marry you and live with you a while and then the throne turns to cardboard and all the jewels melt,' Mommy continued. 'Don't believe anything any man tells you, even if he wants to write it in his blood,' she warned me.

"None of that made sense to me and it didn't take long for her to forget it and look for another man to make her promises. All I kept thinking was if my parents' relationship was such a colossal mistake, what am I, the product of that relationship? How can I be right? I bet someone who was born as a result of a rape doesn't feel that much different from the way I feel," I said looking to the others for agreement.

"You know someone born out of a rape?" Star asked me.

"No."

"It's not quite the same thing," she said. Her eyes were cold with a wisdom beyond her age and mine, maybe even beyond Doctor Marlowe's.

"I understand what Misty means, though," Jade said. "I've had similar feelings." Cathy nodded to indicate she had had them too.

"I know my mother hated it when I asked her all these questions and forced her to dwell on the situation," I continued. "She wanted to treat the divorce as a chance to be young again and not as some great personal failure. She wanted to pretend she had been freed from some chains, released from some prison where she had been prevented from being as young and beautiful as she could be.

"If you can believe it because of what I've already told you about her," I said to the girls, "after the divorce she was even more concerned about her appearance than before. She polished her nails so often, the house seemed to reek of the smell of polish remover. She was always at the hairstylist's and she piled up style and glamour magazines to the ceiling, spending hours reading and studying them to be confident she was in fashion.

"She even spoke differently, trying to make her voice sound younger, and not just in front of Charles Allen. I couldn't help thinking that if she wanted to forget she was ever married to Daddy, if she wanted to be young and free again, what did she feel and think when she looked at me? All I could be was a reminder of the failure.

"I was really very interested in how my father saw me now, too, so when he asked me to meet him for lunch, I couldn't help but be excited.

"It was really the first private conversation Daddy and I'd had since he and my mother told me they were getting a divorce. He wasn't at the restaurant when I arrived and I began to worry when he was more than fifteen minutes late. The waiter kept asking me if I wanted to order and I didn't know what to do. I was considering calling my mother, which would set off a nuclear explosion in an already fractured family, so I tried to stay calm.

"Finally, he showed up, apologizing, claiming he was in traffic. He kissed me, which was something he hadn't done for a while, and sat.

"The first thing I noticed about him was how different he looked. He was letting his hair grow longer and he was dressed more informally than usual. He used to always wear a tie when he went out. He wasn't wearing a jacket and slacks either. He was wearing a sweat suit and sneakers. He explained he had come from the gym.

" 'This is a great place, one of my favorites,' he said gazing around. He held up the menu. 'Everything is very good here.'

" 'Did you come here with Mommy?' I asked him.

" 'With your mother? No, I don't think so,' he said. He thought for a moment and added, 'It's mostly where I meet people for business meetings.'

" 'I don't know what to order,' I said. 'Everything is so expensive.'

He laughed and said he would order for me, but he really wasn't sure what I liked and he had to keep asking.

" 'I guess I should know,' he admitted, 'but your mother always took care of the meals. So,' he said after we finally gave the waiter our order, 'how's your school work? Any improvement?'

" 'Not really,' I told him.

" 'Maybe I should look into getting you a tutor,' he thought aloud.

"Mommy was right, I realized, Daddy always looks for ways to slip out from under his responsibilities.

"When his food came, he talked about his work and his new apartment and for a while I felt as if we were really two people who didn't know each other all that well and were just getting acquainted. I could see that he was as nervous as I was, too.

"Divorce was like some devastating illness that wiped away more than memories; it turned a father and a daughter into strangers.

"Halfway through our meal, I paused and looked directly into his eyes and asked, 'Daddy, what happened? Why did you and Mommy break up after so many years together?'

"He looked very uncomfortable. He had taken me to lunch to do some small talk and then go off into his new life again, and here I was making him deal with our cold reality. Sort of what you try to do with us, Doctor Marlowe," I said and she smiled and nodded.

"Very good, Misty. It's true, girls," she continued, directing herself at the others. "Every one of you naturally practices some therapy."

"Maybe we'll all follow in your footsteps, Doctor Marlowe," Jade said. She had an underlying biting tone in her voice and I thought that despite her beauty and her style, she was in just as much pain if not more than I was.

"Worse things could happen," Doctor Marlowe countered.

"And have," Jade threw back.

She and Doctor Marlowe locked gazes for a moment and then Doctor Marlowe turned back to me.

" 'When you're young and in love, or at least think you're in love, sometimes you don't let yourself see the loved one's faults,' Daddy began.

" 'That's exactly what Mommy says,' I told him.

"His eyes became steely cold.

" 'Is that what she said? What were my faults?" he demanded to know, raising his voice, "I was always a very good provider, wasn't I? She never lacked for anything she wanted no matter how frivolous it was,' he whined.

"The way he was dressed, the way he was talking, all made me see him suddenly as much less mature. I felt all my respect for him, as well as for my mother, sliding out of my hands like a wet bar of soap.

" 'Maybe you were too busy and didn't pay enough attention to her,' I suggested.

" 'Is that what she said?' he demanded, sitting back.

" 'No. I just thought that might be a reason.'

"He stared at me as if he was readjusting his thoughts a moment and then looked calmer and went back to his food.

" 'No, that's not it,' he said. 'I never neglected her. If I was away too long, I called and called and always brought something nice back for her. Besides, if I wasn't out there busting my hump, she wouldn't have been able to spend so much money on the things she wanted.

" 'She's spoiled,' he offered as an explanation. 'I take the blame. I spoiled her. No, Misty, there's nothing to be said about me being neglectful. In fact, it's the exact opposite. I spent too much time and money on her and she took it all for granted. When I asked her to step back and reevaluate what she was doing, she accused me of being selfish and un-caring.'

" 'Then what could be so terrible, Daddy? Why did this happen?' I demanded.

"I didn't think he was going to answer. He sat there quietly for a long, long moment, debating about it in his own mind, I imagine. Then he looked at me with such a serious expression, it made my heart hiccup.

" 'Your mother and I haven't enjoyed each other for some time now. I don't want to put some kind of stain on your image of her. She is still your mother and she will always love you, I'm sure, but she's a disturbed woman. She has a serious psychological problem that rears its ugly head in our bed.'

"I'm sure I looked terribly confused.

" 'Technically, it's called functional dyspareunia,' he said.

"I could hardly breathe. It sounded so serious.

" 'What is that?' I asked him.

" 'Whenever we make love, made love, I should say, she suffered persistent genital pain. I finally forced her to see her gynecologist, but he said that there was nothing physically wrong with her. In other words, it's psychological and that's what it's called. I took the time to find out for myself what it's called and I told her. She refused to face that, refused to see a psychiatrist and things only got worse.

" 'Sex isn't and shouldn't be all there is in a marriage, but it's a big part of it, Misty. I think you're old enough to understand this.'

"I didn't know what to say. It felt so hot around me and I had such trouble breathing, I thought I might faint at the table and embarrass him.

" 'You all right?' he asked.

"I nodded and quickly took a drink of water to swallow down the lump of tension in my throat.

" 'Why is she like that?' I finally asked him. He shook his head, smirked and then looked angry again.

" 'I'm no psychiatrist,' he said, 'but my guess is she fell in love with someone else.'

" 'What? Who?' I quickly asked. Mommy had a lover all this time, I thought. Where was I?

" 'Herself,' he said. 'If there was ever a case of narcissism, she's got it. You ever wonder why our house has so many mirrors? There is hardly a wall, a corner, a space without a mirror on it or near it so she can check her face and hair and be sure she didn't age a day. She's obsessed with it. It's madness.

" 'Whenever I told her she needed professional help, she went into a rage.'

" 'You were unfaithful to her, Daddy,' I said. 'I even heard you admit it.'

"I really felt like jumping up and running out of the restaurant. It hurt to hear him say such nasty things about Mommy and it always hurt when she said nasty things about him. I usually end up defending the one who isn't present. Doctor Marlowe and I have spoken about this a lot. I feel I have to do it, but I hate doing it. I hate it!"

The others all wore faces of understanding. I took a deep breath. Once again I felt like a coiled fuse attached to a time bomb. Sooner or later, I would explode.

" 'Now you know why. A man has needs,' he said.

"He started to play with his food, move it around on the plate with his fork as he spoke.

" 'It isn't easy to be married to someone like that, Misty. Whatever compliment you give her is not good enough, and if you don't remember to say something about her appearance, you're immediately accused of not loving her anymore. I found myself defending myself constantly. It got so I hated to come home. Of course, I wanted to be there for you,' he said quickly, 'but it wasn't easy.'

" 'So you went looking for someone else?' I asked him.

" 'You want to know what I told my therapist?' he asked.

"I was afraid to hear it, but I nodded.

" 'I told him I was married but I was lonely. He said under the circumstances it was understandable.'

"He was very quiet for a long moment. Then he put his fork down with a clunk on the plate and said, 'Please, let's not talk about it anymore. Maybe now she'll go and get some professional help. Let's just talk about you.'

"What I thought was, how can we talk about me and not about you and Mommy, Daddy? Where am I in all this? But I didn't ask it or say it. For the remainder of the lunch, he made all sorts of promises about things he was going to do with me. It was funny how when he and Mommy were together, these promises were never made. Maybe if we had all done some of these things together, we would still be a family, I thought, and Mommy wouldn't have any psychological problems. I was floundering in the world of adult quicksand. It was better to step out quickly.

"He drove me home, but of course he wouldn't come into the house. I was glad of that because I didn't want him to see how much that had belonged or related to him Mommy had already sold or given away. We made a date for me to go to his apartment and spend the weekend in two weeks and he drove off. I couldn't help but wonder what he felt driving up to the house that had been his home for so many years and treating it like just another house.

"You know those magic slates you write on and then you pick up the plastic sheet and everything disappears?" I asked the others. They nodded. "That's what I thought Daddy's mind was like now.

"The moment I entered the house, my mother pounced. It was like she had been waiting behind the doorway to the living room, just listening for my return. There she was, her hands on her hips, her eyes wide and wild, her lips stretched thin into a sinister smile.

" 'Well?' she asked. 'How was your little lunch with your Daddy? Did he bother to show up?'

" 'He was late, but he was there,' I said.

" 'Late. Typical. Was he alone?' she followed quickly, 'or did he have the audacity to bring his girlfriend along?'

" 'He was alone.'

"I wanted to run away from her, charge up the stairs and slam the door of my room closed so hard it would never open again, but she practically leaped into my path.

" 'What did he say about me?' she demanded.

I felt like a tight wire being pulled by both of them, stretched so taut I expected to break any moment.

" 'Nothing,' I said. 'He just talked about his work and what things he hoped he and I would do together.'

"Mommy looked at me with her eyes narrowed into slits of suspicion.

" 'He's got you lying for him,' she accused.

"I was never a good liar, nothing like Charles Allen, for example, and no one knew that better than my mother, but I was really trying to avoid a bitter, ugly scene.

" 'No, he hasn't,' I cried.

"She smirked and nodded, disbelieving me, her eyes turning into dark pools of accusations. Brittle as thin glass, her laughter tinkled.

" 'Daughters always favor their fathers,' she claimed. 'All my friends tell me that. It's got something to do with sex.'

"I had no idea what she meant, but it sounded disgusting.

" 'I'm not taking his side!' I screamed. 'I'm not on anyone's side. You can both kill each other for all I care!'

"I ran up the stairs before she could respond, and I slammed my door and locked it shut. I just buried myself under my blanket and tried to block out the static. She wouldn't stop. She came to my door and put her mouth close to the door and went on and on.

" 'This is what results from your being with your father just for a few hours. Imagine what it's going to be like when you're there in his den of sin for a weekend. He's going to try to poison you against me. He said terrible things about me, I know. You don't have to tell them to me. I know what they must have been. He's blaming me for everything. He's like that. He pushes his mistakes onto someone else all the time. I didn't want you to know how much of a weakling your father was. It's not nice for a daughter to know that, but now you can see it for yourself.'

"She started to cry and moan about the terrible plight she was in.

" 'I gave the best years of my life to that man. Now, he dumps me. I'm like a peeled apple. It's so much easier for a man in a divorce. He can always find a pretty young mindless thing to share his bed, but a woman has to be careful and hope for a decent and responsible new man, and what are her chances of ever finding him in today's selfish world? Not very good, I can tell you. It's degrading to be in this position. I only hope something like this doesn't happen to you. Look what he's done to me!

" 'How can you want to protect him?' she moaned.

"I pressed my palms as hard as I could against my ears to shut out her voice, but she droned on and on until I started to scream again. I don't know how long I screamed, but my throat started to burn. When I stopped, I didn't hear her at the door anymore.

"I didn't come out for dinner that night and she complained for a while at the closed door, but finally gave up and walked away.

"In the morning, it was as always, like nothing bad had happened. She was all smiles and full of gossip about new skin creams her friends had found and a better shampoo for your hair . . . bubbles, our lives were bubbles that burst and disappeared, I thought.

"Two weekends later, Daddy fulfilled his promise and invited me to his new home. Mommy was already fully occupied with her new role as the abused wife who had risen up from the ashes to be a strong, independent woman. She was drawn to her friends who were also divorced women who had made their husband's faces targets at which to throw darts of scorn.

"She surprised me when she didn't say anything nasty about my upcoming weekend visit with Daddy. I wanted to see him, but I was very nervous about it, for he had told me on the phone that I would meet a friend of his and the implication was quite clear what that meant.

"His new girlfriend would be there, too. I almost didn't go.

" 'Why can't you spend a weekend with just me first?' I asked him.

"He had his Daddy explanation, of course. The quicker I became accustomed to the new situation, the better it would be for everyone, including me.

" 'I wouldn't do this if I didn't think you were mature enough to handle it, Misty,' he told me.

"Good old reverse psychology, right, Doctor Marlowe?" I asked.

She didn't reply.

"Doctor Marlowe doesn't make judgements for us," I reminded the others.

Jade's eyes sparkled with impish joy. Cathy looked nervous and afraid, and Star looked like she couldn't care less what Doctor Marlowe did or didn't do.

What a mess we were, I thought. Maybe instead of our parents, we were the ones who were really like Doctor Marlowe's sick oleanders out back. Our roots were diseased and our flowers were pale.

What garden would want us planted in it now? How could we get anyone to like us?

We didn't even like ourselves.

7

"Even though Daddy is right about Mommy being obsessed with her looks and appearance, I would never say she wasn't a very pretty woman. Sometimes I think, if my mother has so much trouble with men and looks the way she does, what can *I* expect? Will I always be involved with men like Charles Allen, men who see my weaknesses so easily and take advantage of me?

"That's what I really thought Daddy was doing with his new girl-friend Ariel. It didn't take a rocket scientist to see that having a young, pretty girlfriend made him feel better about himself and his failure at marriage.

"However, Doctor Marlowe complimented me on my analysis, didn't you, Doctor Marlowe?"

"You're all bright young women," she said making a point of look-ing at Cat. "None of you has any reason to feel ashamed or inadequate because of what's happened to your parents."

"Right, sure, we're all lucky," Star said looking away.

"Daddy picked me up this time, but Ariel wasn't in the car with him. She was waiting back at the apartment, supposedly preparing dinner for us. It turned out to be ordered-in Chinese, which I guess was her favorite recipe.

"I could see Daddy was very nervous about my meeting Ariel. He started by trying to put the pressure on me.

" 'Ariel's very nervous about meeting you,' he said. 'She knows no one can replace your mother, nor should anyone,' he added quickly. 'What I mean is you shouldn't be comparing her. They're two different people.'

" 'I'm not visiting Ariel,' I said. 'I'm visiting with you, Daddy,' I told him.

" 'I know. I know,' he said, 'but Ariel's sort of my companion right now and I just want everyone to get along.'

" 'Companion?' I nearly laughed. 'Is that what it's called?'

" 'Don't get rude, Misty,' he snapped back at me.

"Before my parents' divorce, whenever my father used to yell at me or give me an order or sound gruff, I would never think to challenge him. When I looked at him now, dressed down, living in an apartment with a much younger woman, I had trouble thinking of him the same way. I guess I didn't respect him as much. I was certainly not afraid of him. It was easy to see how hard he was trying to get me to be on his side. The one thing he dreaded was my asking him to take me home.

" 'Ariel made sure to buy all new bedding for you. She's worked hard at setting up the guest room to make you comfortable. She was the one who got the television put in because she said teenagers like having their own television sets in their rooms. Then she went to the department store and bought all this stuff for your bathroom: magnifying mirrors, hair dryers, curlers, shampoos and conditioners, all sorts of woman's stuff that I would never have thought to buy.

" 'She did it all on her own. I swear,' he said actually holding up his hand.

" 'She's young. I'll admit, but she's uncomplicated and she makes me feel good. I need that now, Misty. This isn't easy for me, no matter what you might think. I didn't set out expecting all this to happen.'

"Maybe he didn't, I thought, but it did happen and it wasn't easy for me either. Nevertheless, I kept my mouth shut about Ariel all the rest of the way.

"Daddy had a very nice apartment, bigger than I had anticipated and high enough up to have a great view of the west side and the ocean. There was a patio outside the living room that was big enough for two chaise lounges and a small table and chairs.

" 'We're here!' he cried when we entered, and Ariel came out of the kitchen.

"My first thought was Daddy had to be kidding. She didn't look all that much older than me. I can't deny she's pretty. She has honey-blond hair almost to her shoulder blades with that soft, slightly tanned creamy complexion so perfect she always looks like she has just come from a photo shoot. I hated her smile, a smile of such disarming sweetness you'd do anything just to see that smile come out like sunshine after the rain. It made it more difficult for me to harden my heart against her.

She wore a basic black V-necked sweater with a sexy turquoise lace skirt. She was braless, but her bosom was firm and her waist was as small as mine. There were just the tiniest freckles visible on her chest, just above the start of her deep cleavage.

" 'Hi,' she sang and hurried to extend her hand. 'I'm Ariel. It's so nice to finally meet you.'

"Finally? I thought. That's when it occurred to me they had been together longer than I had imagined. Panicky butterflies were on the wing again, battering my brain with doubts, buffeting my heart with indecision. Should I smile back at her? Should I be cold and unfriendly?

"Her soft blue eyes were filled with more anxiety and fear than mine were, I thought, and it occurred to me that she might be just as much an innocent victim as I was.

"I didn't want to think that. I wanted to think of her as being a gold digger or something, exploiting Daddy at his weakest moments, taking advantage of someone else's pain and loss, whispering terrible things about my mother in his ear, seducing him with compliments. I could see from the way she looked at him and spoke to him that she had put him on some pedestal.

" 'Hi,' I said without much warmth. It was neutral, as if I had lost the ability to feel one way or the other.

" 'Well,' Daddy said, 'she's here. Let's show her to her room.'

" 'Oh, yes,' Ariel seconded and stepped back as Daddy carried my small suitcase across the living room. There were two bedrooms, side by side. Mine was the second. The bathroom for me was in the hallway.

"I was surprised at how much trouble Ariel had gone to to decorate the room as closely to my own room at home. There were similar white cotton curtains, a bedspread the exact same shade of pink, and some posters of my favorite rock bands.

"I looked at Daddy, my eyes full of questions. He laughed.

" 'What I did,' he said, 'was give Ariel a picture of your room. I went over to the house and took it one afternoon while you were at school and Gloria was at her personal trainer's.'

" 'Gloria?' I muttered. Daddy had trouble talking about Mommy in front of Ariel.

" 'We just wanted you to feel at home,' he added. 'It was really Ariel's idea.'

"She smiled nervously. I didn't think that was true.

" 'It's fine,' I said. Ariel then went through this ridiculous tour of the room, actually showing me hangers and drawers and then leading me to the bathroom to catalogue all the things she had purchased with Daddy's money for me.

" 'Let me know if there's anything you're missing,' she concluded.

"I wanted to let her know. I wanted to tell her yes, there is one small thing I'm missing . . . a normal life. You know what that is, Ariel? It's having both your parents at home, there for you, planning things with you, giving you advice together, eating together, laughing together, talking about relatives and thinking about parties and birthdays and holidays, being there with you when you go off to college, maybe even accompanying you and saying good-bye and holding hands and looking at you with pride before they walked off together, my father's arm around my mother, the two of them feeling like they've accomplished something with their lives, dreaming of my wedding and my children. I'm missing albums, Ariel, filled with pictures of family, together on vacations, at graduations.

"Have any of that in your back pocket, Ariel?

"That's what I wanted to say, but I kept my lips glued shut and just shook my head and swallowed down my anger and disappointment.

" 'I hope you like what we ordered for dinner,' she went on. 'I made sure to get one of everything, just in case. There's a shrimp dish and a chicken dish and a vegetarian dish and a beef dish.'

"Daddy laughed behind us. He had been hovering over us like some anxious referee, ready to leap between us at merely the suggestion of something unpleasant.

" 'She tries to think of everything,' he said.

"Ariel smiled back at him. I hated that worship I saw in her eyes. It wasn't that I didn't want anyone to like Daddy so much. I just didn't want to witness someone loving him more than me or my mother, I suppose.

"That's what you kind of agreed that I thought, right, Doctor Marlowe?"

"Kinda," she said with her inscrutable smile.

"Dinner didn't go over too well. I didn't have much of an appetite, even though the food did smell good. The sides of my stomach felt stuck together like those dumb plastic bags in the supermarket. I could barely get a few bites into it. Ariel didn't seem to notice. She ate for the both of us. Mommy would curse her for being able to eat so much and keep her figure, I thought. It was funny how I couldn't help but consider Mommy's point of view about all this.

"I found out that Ariel was a secretary in one of the companies Daddy's company had bought. She was from Santa Barbara, had gone to a small business school and then had gotten placed by one of those temp agencies into a job that developed into a long-term position. She went on and on like someone who was terrified of even a moment of silence at the table. I learned she had an older brother who was trying to become an airline pilot. Her father worked as a mechanic for Delta and her mother was a dental hygienist.

" 'That's why Ariel has such perfect teeth,' Daddy pointed out.

"She did have teeth that belonged in a toothpaste commercial, perfectly straight, milk white.

"She giggled and gave him her hand. Daddy's eyes shifted guiltily toward me and then to her and she withdrew her hand quickly. I imagined he had told her to cool it while I was there. I saw it made her even more nervous and she was off and running again, talking about her favorite foods, colors, clothes, searching wildly for something in common with me.

"I sat like a lump.

" 'Well, what should I do with my two best girls tonight?' Daddy asked.

" 'Maybe we should go to a movie,' Ariel said.

" 'I'm tired, Daddy. You two go. I just want to curl up in bed and read a little and watch some television.'

" 'Really?' He sounded like he couldn't believe his good luck.

" 'Yes,' I said. I half-expected they would put up more of an argument, but they accepted my plan.

"Ariel didn't want my help in cleaning up.

" 'You go spend time with your father,' she said. 'That's what you're here to do.'

"Daddy and I sat in the living room. He talked about the apartment, some of the changes he wanted to make in the decor, and he credited Ariel with coming up with all the good ideas. I knew that was a lie, but lies were truly like flies to me now. I just batted them away or ignored them.

"Our conversation went back to a discussion of my school work. He asked me what I wanted to do, what I wanted to become, and I felt like I was sitting in the office with my guidance counselor.

" 'I don't know,' I said when Ariel joined us, her face full of forced interest, like it was suddenly the most important thing in the world to her to know what I wanted to do with my life. 'Maybe I'll go to business school and get a job through a temp agency and meet a nice man like you, Daddy,' I said.

"He sat there with this dead smile glued to his face as if I had just hit him on the side of the head with a rock. Ariel's hands fluttered about like two small, terrified birds, settling finally on top of each other and pressed between her beautifully shaped breasts.

" 'Well,' Daddy said, 'I guess maybe you are a little tired. It's emotionally exhausting, I know. We'll do something nice tomorrow, maybe go down to the yacht club and take a boat ride and then have a nice lunch. How's that sound? We haven't done that for a while, have we?'

" 'No,' I said. I thought a moment. 'Not for about two years, I think.'

"He forced a laugh.

" 'Then it's certainly time to do it,' he said standing.

Ariel practically leaped to her feet.

" 'Are you sure you don't want to go to a movie with us?' she asked.

" 'No thanks,' I said. The smile on my face was like a little mechanical movement made by thin wires attached to the corners of my mouth.

" 'We'll be back early,' Daddy promised. He went for his light jacket and Ariel went to the bathroom to fix her face and hair. They looked like two teenagers out on a date. I hated them for it, but I said nothing and they left.

"I remember it was so quiet in that apartment that I could hear my heart thumping. Natural curiosity took me on an exploration and I went into their bedroom and looked at Ariel's clothes. I even opened drawers and looked at her lingerie. I suppose I was searching for any trace of Mommy or myself in Daddy's life now. He didn't even have a picture of me.

"Finally, I did go to bed, watched a little television and fell asleep. I didn't hear them come home, but Daddy looked in on me and turned off the television set. That woke me but he didn't wait. I heard the door close softly and then I heard their voices through the wall. I heard Ariel's light giggles and his voice soft and low.

"They tried to make love as quietly as possible and I tried to ignore it, but I knew what was happening. Afterward, I lay there staring up at the dark ceiling wondering what Mommy was doing tonight.

"In my mind I saw her alone in her bed, confused. I guess it was only natural to feel sorrier for her at this moment. Daddy looked like he was reorganizing his life just the way he wanted it to be. He had his new romantic interest. I wondered if he was telling Ariel things he had told my mother when they were young and in love years ago. Did he use the same poetry, make the same sort of promises and vows? Maybe he even took her to the same places.

"I think the worst thing that's happened for me in my parents' divorce is my feeling that nothing Daddy says means anything anymore. His whole life was apparently a big lie. Maybe that's unfair considering what problems Mommy has, but I can't help it. It's supposed to be for better or worse, isn't it? Why should he keep any of his promises?

"I kept it all inside me. Ariel continued to be as nice to me as could be the next day. It wasn't a bad day. I enjoyed the boat. Daddy let me drive it while he and Ariel sat behind me and screamed at my abrupt turns, the water splashing over them. I began to think maybe I should just have fun and forget it all, forget trying to make sense out of it.

"I ate better at lunch and that night we went to the Third Street Promenade in Santa Monica where we walked and ate in a small Italian restaurant. Ariel and I went shopping in some of the fun stores and then we went to the music store and Daddy bought me three new CDs. He bought me another silly T-shirt, too, and a ring with my birthstone in it.

"Visiting with my divorced father was like having Christmas and my birthday all wrapped up in one trip. For now, at least, I could ask for the moon.

"It wasn't until the evening that I realized going boating had given me a tan. It was the first thing Mommy noticed when Daddy brought me back on Sunday.

" 'Look at you,' she cried. 'You're sunburned. Weren't you wearing any sunscreen?'

" 'I'm not sunburned, Mommy, just a bit tanned.'

" 'A bit. You should have known better, Misty, and he should have known better. I don't imagine his girlfriend would know any better. From what I hear, she's not much older than you.'

"Mommy was waiting for me to give her a report, of course, but I didn't offer any and that disappointed her. When she saw all the things Daddy had bought me, it was like salt on a wound. She was off again, complaining about the financial settlements.

"This is how it's always going to be, I thought, neither of them letting me enjoy myself as long as I was with the other. I was better off not being with either of them. That's what I began to think more and more and that's why I got into trouble," I said. I looked at Doctor Marlowe and added, "That's only one of the reasons." She was happier. I wasn't putting all the blame on my parents. I was taking some responsibility.

"My next visit with Daddy didn't happen when it was supposed to and that became sort of the rule and not the exception. Once again, he claimed business conflicts. Whenever he tried to reschedule dates, Mommy made him suffer. She had her attorney call his attorney and complain about the disruption it caused in her life.

"She wanted me to side with her so she talked about it incessantly at dinner or whenever I was available. She would come bursting into my room to tell me my father had called to say he couldn't make the next weekend. He was going to be in Chicago or Boston or someplace else.

" 'I have a life to resurrect too,' Mommy complained. 'I'm not going to go and change all my plans because his life is a mess.'

" 'I don't care,' I told her.

" 'Of course you don't care. Who can blame you for not caring? Look how selfish he is. The judge set down the rules and he's going to have to learn how to live by them whether he likes it or not,' she vowed.

"Not once did it ever occur to her that I was the one who was suffering with all this. When was it supposed to end? When does the thunder and lightning move on? Every time her phone rang at dinner, I anticipated trouble. She seemed to be on the phone with her attorney every single day. No matter how much they made, I thought, divorce attorneys couldn't really enjoy their work, especially if they had clients like my parents."

"You haven't heard anything until you've heard about mine," Jade piped up. Until then she had been sitting attentively, her legs pulled up under her, looking like she was almost enjoying my story.

"You poor rich girls," Star quipped. Jade threw her a look that would knock over a cow.

"I'm not rich," I said.

"You're a lot richer than me," she retorted. "And you," she directed at Jade, "You're probably richer than Doctor Marlowe."

"I resent being blamed for having money," Jade cried.

"Didn't you ever hear that money can't buy you happiness and love?" I asked Star.

She twisted up the corner of her mouth.

"No, but give me the chance to be disappointed," she said.

Doctor Marlowe laughed loudly this time. We all turned to her, Cathy looking more surprised than any of us.

"It's all right, girls," Doctor Marlowe said. "I'm glad you're not alike and that you don't all think the same way. You'll have more to offer each other that way," she pointed out.

Jade looked skeptical, but not as skeptical as Star.

"Just have the patience to give each other a chance," Doctor Marlowe pleaded.

Everyone relaxed again, their eyes back on me.

"I was barely hanging on in school, but the worse I did, the more they blamed each other and the more static there was at home," I said. "I started to get sloppy in other ways, too, my clothes, my hair, how I ate. I hated what I looked like. I hated everything about myself.

"The thin threads that had kept me tied to my old girlfriends snapped completely then. They wanted less and less to do with me so I started hanging with a different crowd. Finally, I got involved with a boy named Lloyd Kimble, who was about as different from Charles Allen as any boy could be.

"Lloyd's parents really were split up. He lived with his mother but she was out of the house so much, he was really on his own. He had nothing to do with his father. In fact, he hated him. He told me he had actually had a fist fight with him when his father tried to punish him the last time they were together. He wasn't bad looking even though his nose had been broken in a fight. He said the other boy hit him with a baseball bat. He had dark, brooding eyes and a narrow face with a nearly square jaw. He just looked tough and ready and hard. He seemed always angry and really hated all the kids I used to be friends with. He had been to family court, suspended from school, and put on probation. I kept thinking if my mother even knew I was talking to him, she would have a nervous breakdown. Maybe that was why I did it.

"Doctor Marlowe and I are still exploring that, aren't we?"

"Among other things," Dr. Marlowe said, nodding softly. "There's no single cause for the difficulties you all suffer."

"Maybe that's why you did what?" Star asked, her face full of impatience.

I looked at Doctor Marlowe and then I looked at her.

"Ran away with him," I said.

Star smiled.

"Ran away? You're here, aren't you?"

"That's why," I said.

8

"**I** didn't set out to be friends with Lloyd. Until the day he came over to me in the cafeteria, I don't think I had so much as looked at him twice.

"I was sitting alone, feeling sorry for myself and hating everything and everyone around me. I guess I had that bitter, unhappy look on my face. When Lloyd dropped his tray on the table and slid into the seat beside me, I was so deep in my well of dark thoughts, I didn't even hear him or see him. He deliberately knocked his shoulder against mine to get my attention, which caused me to spill the soup out of my spoon. I was ready to jab it into the face of whoever had done it.

" 'Sorry,' he said, 'but you was leaning over too far and takin' up two places.'

" 'I was not,' I protested. He shrugged.

" 'Then, maybe I was,' he said and laughed.

"I knew who he was, of course. Everyone knew who Lloyd Kimble was, the way you knew what a scorpion or a rattlesnake was. You didn't have to have any actual contact to know you should keep your distance.

" 'What happened?' he asked with a half-smile. 'Your friends dump you?'

He nodded in their direction.

" 'No,' I said sharply. I wasn't in the mood to be made fun of. 'No one dumped me.'

"Lloyd has this infuriating smile. He pulls his lips in and you can almost hear the laughter coming from his arrogant eyes, but at the same time there's something sexy about it. He's dangerous and I suppose that makes him exciting. He does what he wants to do when he wants to do it. He's impulsive and has no respect for rules or authority.

"Mr. Calder, the cafeteria monitor, was staring at me with such a look of disgust, like, how could I lower myself to permit Lloyd Kimble to sit next to me and talk to him? Suddenly, I felt as angry and as rebellious as I imagined Lloyd was. What right did Mr. Calder have to decide who my friends should and should not be? He was my English teacher but not my father or my older brother. At that moment I despised all the adults in the world for being bossy and hypocritical.

" 'A Beverly like you doesn't usually sit alone unless somethin's wrong, and I'm sure it ain't your breath,' Lloyd commented as he bit into his hamburger.

" 'What's a Beverly?' I asked.

"He stopped chewing a moment, smiled and then chewed on until he swallowed and gestured toward Darlene and my other girlfriends.

" 'A Beverly. You know. Girls from Beverly Hills, spoiled bitches.'

" 'I live in Beverly Hills, but I'm hardly a spoiled bitch,' I responded with more courage than I thought I had. His laugh made me angrier. 'I'm not!'

" 'Good for you,' he said. 'So why ain't you sittin' with them?'

" 'They're a bunch of phonies, if you must know,' I said.

" 'Oh, I know that,' he told me. 'What they do to ya, cut up your credit cards?'

" 'Very funny. They didn't do anything,' I said. 'They just . . . think they're better than me now.'

" 'Why now?' he followed and I turned and looked at him, wondering why he was suddenly so interested in me. 'You look like you could use a real friend,' he offered with that infuriating shrug and smile.

" 'You're going to lower yourself and be my friend?' I challenged. 'A Beverly?'

" 'I do what I want,' he said sternly. 'No one tells me who to be friends with.' "

He smiled softly again. Suddenly he didn't seem as dangerous to me as everyone I knew always said he was, and sitting this closely to him, I realized he was much better looking than I had thought, too. He had great dark eyes, eyes that sparkled wickedly. Maybe I was just in the mood for him. We talked some more and I discovered that he had a good sense of humor, especially about some of my friends. I laughed and he laughed and I told him about my parents and how my so-called friends had reacted. He knew more about me than I had expected. He knew I had gone out with Charles Allen and when I told him that was another big mistake of mine, his smile got even warmer.

"I could see that the longer I talked with him and remained sitting with him, the more my friends were chatting about me. I admit that at first I just wanted to shock everyone, but after I spent more time with Lloyd I actually really began to like him. He and I had more in common than I would have ever realized or cared to admit. He truly seemed to understand my feelings about my parents and then he said something I thought was very true."

"What?" Star asked. She was really into my story now.

"He said sometimes kids like us have to grow up faster and adults don't realize it or don't want to realize it so they keep treating us like kids, but we're already miles away. And not because we want to be. It's just what's happened.

"He also said you can't worry about whether it's fair or not. You just take it and do what you have to do and if adults don't like it, let them lump it."

"Brilliant," Jade said, puckering her mouth up like a drawstring purse.

"I thought it was," I fired back at her. "It's not fancy, like out of some book you and I might read, but it's still true, especially for me and I bet for you."

She looked thoughtful for a moment and then looked away.

"So what happened with him?" Star asked. Reluctantly, Jade turned back to hear.

"We started spending more and more time together, meeting between classes, at lunch, after school. He didn't have a car; he had a small motorcycle, which I found out had no insurance on it and had an expired registration. It didn't worry Lloyd.

" 'Don't sweat the small things,' he told me.

"He made me laugh a lot and I felt better being with him. I felt . . . free from everything. When I was with him, the static died.

"Mommy had gone on a few more dates with different men, but none of them were any good in her eyes. She turned bitter because my father was happier. She went to lunch and dinner with women who had similar feelings about men and they became what I call today, the MHA, Men Haters Anonymous. From what I read about AA, Alcoholics Anonymous conducts meetings that are not too different. These women have been at our house for coffee meetings and I've heard them clucking like angry hens. Each of them begins by telling how she was made a fool of by her husband or a recent boyfriend. She admits it was largely her own fault and they all sympathize. They take oaths not to get serious with any man again. They gloat over anyone who has taken advantage of a man or broken a man's heart.

"My mother brags to them about how she makes my father's life as miserable as she can, proudly using me like a sword over his head whenever possible. She told them all about the bills and how she wields her attorney's power over him and his attorney and the other women clapped and congratulated her, cheering as if she had won some major battle for women's rights.

"I told Lloyd about it and he said he never wanted to be a parent and he wouldn't get married unless the woman he was with felt the same way.

" 'Who wants to ruin someone else's life?' he said.

"I thought that was very sad, but I understood. He and I had been seeing each other on and off for a little more than two weeks by this time. Mostly we saw each other at school or met at the mall. I knew all my friends expected that he would be like some sex maniac, but he wasn't like that at all. He was actually shy, almost afraid to touch or kiss.

"When I told this to Darlene, who had been constantly after me to tell her something just so she could go gossiping, she said he was probably just using a technique on me, like some spider trying to tempt me into his web. I admit that put the idea in my head, but even when I agreed and went to his home with him one afternoon, he didn't try anything.

" 'You sure you want to permit a Beverly to see your room?' I asked him and he told me he was absolutely sure now that I wasn't any Beverly. Two weeks before I wouldn't have considered it much of a compliment, but it was the same as him telling me he trusted me, he respected me, he thought I was real.

"His apartment was small and his mother didn't keep it well. There were dishes left over from yesterday's meal, dust on the windowsills and furniture, bad stains in the rugs. Everything in it, the appliances, the furniture, the rugs and even the walls looked tired, worn. He explained that at the time his mother had a new boyfriend and was at his place a lot. I didn't realize that meant Lloyd was home alone for days sometimes, but I soon understood that was the case. That first day there, I actually cleaned a lot of it up, something I rarely if ever had done in my own home. Lloyd kept telling me I didn't have to.

" 'I know I don't,' I said, 'but I want to do it for you.'

"He looked at me differently and I saw he really cared for me.

" 'My mother will know I brought someone up here,' he said. 'She knows I don't do much house cleaning.'

" 'So let her know,' I told him. He liked that, too.

"One night when my mother was having the MHA over, I told her I was meeting Darlene at the mall and took a cab to Lloyd's apartment instead. He was very surprised to see me. What he liked the most was my just doing it, being impulsive like him. I was afraid I'd find him with some other girl or his mother would be home and she wouldn't approve, but he was alone.

"We played some music and talked for a while and suddenly, finally, I was in his arms, kissing him. It didn't take us long to get undressed and into his bed. I was very frightened, but not of him. I was afraid of myself, afraid that I suffered Mommy's problem, whatever that was, and Lloyd wouldn't like me anymore just like my father didn't like my mother. I really wanted to find out for myself.

"Lloyd was surprised to learn that I wasn't a virgin, but he wasn't upset about it. He took his time and was caring, far more gentle and romantic than Charles Allen with all his wealth and sophistication.

"We began slowly. I kept anticipating great pain, but instead, I began to feel great pleasure. I knew I was being reckless because he didn't use any protection, but I felt drunk on my feelings, rushing over erotic highways, and not caring if I crashed.

"I was so happy afterward. I felt like I had proven I could be normal and that the man I married wouldn't find me frigid and divorce me too.

"Lloyd and I grew closer, of course, but I was afraid to invite Lloyd to my house. I knew what my mother would think of him when she saw him and how she would react and make my life even more miserable at home. The following week Lloyd and I were plotting how to spend an entire night together at his house. On Wednesday, however, he was very depressed when I met him at school and he told me his mother was going to be home and her boyfriend was spending the weekend with her. I had been trying to find someone I could trust to pretend to have invited me over and now I didn't have any reason to.

"Then, my father called. I had forgotten I was scheduled to be with him at his place, but as was often the case, he had a reason why I had to skip the weekend. He was going to be away on business again.

"Only this time," I said smiling at Star, "I didn't tell my mother. She thought I would be with my father all weekend."

"Cool," Star said.

"Weren't you afraid she would find out?" Cat asked. She had been sitting so quietly, barely moving, acting like a little girl hearing a story read by her mother or teacher, terrified someone or something would interrupt.

"I didn't care. Maybe I wanted to get caught," I told her. She looked down quickly.

"So where were you two going to go, a motel?" Jade asked.

"No. Someplace better. Daddy had told me where he kept the spare key to the apartment hidden just in case I ever was to come over and he and Ariel weren't there yet. It was behind a cabinet in his parking space under the building.

"We went to the apartment. Lloyd was very impressed with the place. He got into Daddy's liquor cabinet and I made us something to eat. We pretended like it was really our apartment and we were married. We watched television and began to get passionate. It was my idea for us to use Daddy's bedroom instead of mine. It just seemed . . . more of a risk, I guess. We made love and then I remade the bed. Both of us took showers. I gave Lloyd one of Daddy's robes to wear and we returned to the living room and curled up on the sofa, watching television again. We both fell asleep.

"Some time after midnight Daddy and Ariel came home and found us there."

"You're kidding!" Star exclaimed.

"Wow!" Jade said.

Cat looked frightened for me.

"Daddy was furious, of course. He said some nasty things to Lloyd and I said some nastier things to him. Ariel made some small attempt to calm things down, but Daddy's fury turned on her and she retreated quickly. Lloyd got dressed and left and Daddy called Mommy, waking her up to tell her what was going on. Of course, he blamed her.

"I didn't get much sleep. The next morning Daddy brought me home. Mommy was waiting in the living room. He hadn't been in the house since he had taken the picture of my room and was surprised at some of the changes, but this wasn't the time to talk about that. He described what he had found when he and Ariel had returned to his apartment.

" 'You lied to me,' Mommy said shaking her head like it was something she could never believe.

" 'Everybody lies in this house,' I snapped back at her.

" 'You watch your mouth,' Daddy yelled.

" 'You lied to me,' I retorted. 'You said you weren't going to be home and that's why I couldn't spend the weekend with you.'

"He looked guilty, caught. He glanced at my mother and then turned back to me.

" 'My plans changed. That happens sometimes, Misty, but it doesn't give you the excuse to do what you did,' he said and then he returned to the familiar battleground with my mother. 'Do you realize what she's up to these days, Gloria?'

" 'She's got the perfect model of morality to follow,' my mother said, glaring at him. 'Look how you live. Look what she sees whenever she visits with you. What do you expect she'll turn into? What can I do?'

"They got into one of their worst battles and I went up to my room. At least for the moment, they were directing their venom at each other instead of me. After Daddy left, Mommy came up to see me and asked me what I had been doing and how long I had been doing it.

"She acted very hurt. I was making a fool out of her, hurting her, making things more difficult for her. Everything was her, her, her. Daddy had done the same thing earlier, telling me how my behavior was only going to make things more difficult for him, him, him.

"Of course, Mommy wanted to know who the boy was. Who were his parents? Where did they live? That seemed to matter more than anything. I refused to tell her anything about Lloyd and she ended it by grounding me for a month. I was to come directly home after school every day and spend all my weekends at home. She forbade me from having phone calls again, but this time she surprised me by calling the phone company and having my line disconnected.

"I don't think I ever felt more miserable. Lloyd blamed himself. He told me he should have known better and expected it. Later that week, about Wednesday, I think, Mommy found out who my boyfriend was. Clara Weincoup's mother had told her. When I got home, she was waiting for me and went into a new rage about my slumming.

"How could I go around with someone like that? Didn't I have respect for myself?

" 'Maybe my boyfriend isn't rich and his parents don't live in a big, expensive house, but at least I can enjoy being a woman,' I shouted back at her, and she turned all red.

"She chased after me demanding to know exactly what I had meant. She kept it up until finally, in a rage myself, I blurted out the things Daddy had told me at that first lunch when I asked him why they were getting divorced. She turned a shade paler than the dead leaves on Doctor Marlowe's oleander bushes out back. I thought she was going to faint. Her mouth opened and closed without a sound coming from it. I really got frightened. She had to take hold of the back of a chair to steady herself.

"Then, she just turned and walked out of the room. We never said anything more about it, but later I found out she had called her attorney who had called Daddy's attorney. There was a serious threat to go to the judge to end Daddy's visitation rights with me.

"Everything just seemed to be getting worse and worse. Early the following week, Lloyd got into a bad fight at school with another boy. When Mr. Levine tried to break it up, Lloyd hit him and he was expelled. I found out late that afternoon. Darlene couldn't wait to tell me.

" 'Your boyfriend is in big trouble,' she said and described what had happened at the gym. She and the others gloated. It seemed to prove they were right about me and Lloyd.

"But I said, 'Lloyd was right about you! You're all a bunch of Beverly's. Go to hell!' I screamed at them.

"I ran away from them and after school, I went to Lloyd's mother's apartment, but no one was there. I was very depressed and disappointed. My phone was still disconnected. How would he call me? I was hoping he would come to my house, but all that day he didn't. I tried calling him on my mother's phone when my mother wasn't watching, but there was no answer.

"I hated being in school the next day. I failed a math test. I hadn't even cracked open the book to study for it. The girls were talking about me constantly. I stayed in the bathroom the whole lunch period rather than sit in that cafeteria and be under their laughing eyes. I was inches away from cutting class and going to look for Lloyd. When the final bell rang, I shot out of the building and went to his apartment again. Again, I found no one there.

"My mother wasn't home when I got home. I sat in my room, brooding, when all of a sudden, I heard the sound of a motorcycle and looked out the window to see Lloyd pull into our driveway. He sat on his motorcycle and beeped the horn, and I ran out to him.

" 'Where have you been?' I cried throwing myself into his arms. 'I went to your apartment two days in a row.'

" 'Just been riding around,' he said, 'thinking. I stayed at a friend of mine's place in Encino and finally made a big decision,' he said.

" 'What decision?'

" 'I'm leaving California,' he told me and my heart fell.

" 'Leaving? Where are you going?' I asked.

" 'Anyplace away from here. I got a cousin in Seattle who owns a garage. I think I'll go up there and work for him awhile and just see how it goes.'

" 'What about your mother?'

" 'She practically threw me out of the house,' he said, 'when she found out I was bein' thrown out of school. She said I'm too much trouble for her. She can't handle me anymore. It's making her old and sick.'

" 'My mother says the same thing about me,' I moaned.

" 'So . . . maybe you should come with me,' he said and I thought, why not?

" 'Maybe I will,' I said.

"For a long moment, we just stared at each other and he could see in my eyes that I was really going to do it.

" 'Pack a really small bag,' he said without a beat. I hesitated one short moment and then ran into the house to stuff my backpack.

"That was the hardest part, deciding what I wanted to take with me. I mean there were some essential clothes to take and a pair of boots and a pair of shoes, but of all the things you own, of all the things you've been given, what would you choose if you could take only a very few things, and of course, nothing large or heavy?

"Suddenly nothing seemed as important as it had been. All the things my parents had given me were just things. There was one doll, my first real doll, the one I kept on the bed, a soft rag doll. I took that, but I didn't take any jewelry. I should have probably. We could have used the money if I sold it. I grabbed a toothbrush and a hairbrush and turned in circles trying to decide what else, what else mattered?

"Lloyd began to honk his horn. I scooped my leather jacket out of the closet, took one last look at my room, the room that had been my whole world for so much of my life. These walls held all my secrets, had seen all my tears and heard me whisper all my fears.

" 'Good-bye,' I whispered and ran down the stairs. I didn't even look back and I didn't leave my mother a note or anything.

"I stepped out, slipped on my backpack and hurried to get behind Lloyd on the motorcycle. He turned his head and smiled at me and we took off. My heart was thumping so hard and fast, I was afraid I might faint and fall into the street. I wrapped my arms around him and held on for dear life. It was mostly cloudy and very breezy that day. The wind whipped through my hair and blasted my face, but I didn't think about the weather or anything. I really thought I was free, free of all the static, free of all the hate and pain. I dreamed I wouldn't write or call my parents for years and then, when I did, they could do nothing but accept what had happened and where I was.

"It wasn't exactly comfortable sitting on the back of that small motorcycle for hours and hours. We rode through a short rain shower and it got cooler fast. Finally, we stopped at a roadside restaurant for dinner and counted up the money we had together. I had scooped up all I had in my dresser drawer, but it wasn't much.

"Lloyd thought it was warm enough for us to spend the first night at least sleeping off the road. It was still quite an adventure for me, so I didn't mind cuddling up in his arms under a small bridge. We talked ourselves to sleep, making all sorts of plans. Maybe I was a fool, but I fell asleep thinking it was all possible. He would get work; I would get work. We would be able to afford a small apartment and in time we would have enough to really live right. Finally, we were both free of all the phonies.

" 'There are no Beverlys where we're going,' Lloyd promised as we drifted into our private fantasies.

"It was colder than we had expected during the night. I kept waking and I couldn't get very comfortable. Both of us looked washed out the next morning. We found a small restaurant where I cleaned up and fixed my hair. We had a hot breakfast, which made us feel a lot better.

"By this time I imagined my mother was in some kind of a panic, enough of one to have called my father. But I also envisioned them blaming each other as usual and not really doing anything about it.

"Lloyd was worried about us not having enough money to make it to Seattle and get situated. As we started out that second day, our enthusiasm had softened and thinned somewhat. I fell asleep on and off with my head against him. He mumbled something about our need to sleep in a real bed that night. About two hours later, he pulled into the parking lot of a small convenience store and told me to wait on the motorcycle. I thought he was just going in to get us a snack, but when he came out, he was running. He hopped onto the cycle and we took off so fast, I nearly fell backwards. He sped up and I screamed at him, asking why he was going so fast. He didn't say anything. He just kept us going faster and faster. I was really frightened. A little more than a half hour later, I looked back and saw a police car closing on us.

" 'You better slow down and stop. I think he's after us,' I shouted to Lloyd, but he just went faster, trying to lose the police car by cutting off the highway at a turn. We nearly spilled and then he had to slow down because the road turned into nothing but a gravel path.

"I was surprised to hear the siren and see the police car still behind us. It caught up and pulled alongside. Lloyd finally had to slow down, cursing under his breath. When the policeman stepped out of his car, he had his gun drawn and I was so frightened, I started to cry.

"He made Lloyd get off the cycle and lay face down so he could put handcuffs on him and then he did the same to me. After that, he put us into the back of his car.

" 'You're arresting us just for speeding?' I cried at him.

" 'No ma'am,' he said, 'just for robbing that convenience store back there,' he said.

"Lloyd had his head down. I asked him if that was true and he nodded and admitted that he had pulled a knife on the frightened elderly lady behind the counter.

" 'I thought if we just had a little more money, we could make it all right,' he said. 'I'm sorry I got you into trouble,' he told me and I cried all the way to the police station, cried for both of us.

"I was permitted to make a phone call. That was the hardest decision: whom to call, Daddy or Mommy? I remember standing there with the receiver in my hand, staring at the numbers.

" 'You can't have all day,' the female officer nearby told me and I dialed Daddy. I was afraid Mommy would just get hysterical and forget to get me help. He wasn't at home, so I called his office. He listened and then spoke like someone on a telephone in his grave. He asked me to put one of the police officers on and I stepped away.

"All I wanted to do was die before I had to face my parents again."

Epilogue

"Lloyd told the police that I had no knowledge of the robbery and I did not know what he was doing when he stopped at the convenience store, but I had to go to court anyway. Daddy hired a lawyer for me. Lloyd had someone from the public defender's office. Because of his previous record, he was sent to a juvenile facility. I was put on probation but with the stipulation that I begin to see a therapist. It was what the school recommended too.

"For a while both my parents acted as if they had been given lobotomies by my actions. I never saw them so quiet. I think they were just terrified. I was expecting them to shout and blame each other as usual, but they sat next to each other in the courthouse and agreed with the attorney and with each other that neither had paid enough attention to me and that I was reacting to their breakup.

"Finally, I thought, finally, the static will stop.

"Of course, that truce didn't last long. They're both back to their old selves again, but for a short time at least, I felt relieved."

"Did you ever hear from Lloyd again?" Jade asked.

"I received a letter from him about a month later. The only reason I got it was I happened to be there when the mail arrived. I'm sure my mother would have torn it up if she had found it first. It was full of apologies. He said he was doing all right and at least there were no Beverlys where he was. I wrote back, but I had to do it secretly, of course. I told him to send his next letter care of Darlene Stratton, but I haven't heard from him since.

"Things are more or less back to normal at my house. My mother is on her tenth or eleventh new male acquaintance, as she calls them, but there are still frequent meetings of the MHA at our house. There seems to be more of them, too. They cackle so much and so loudly, I have to turn my music up to drown them out.

"For a while afterward, my father was a little better about keeping his dates with me. We had some nice weekends together, one trip up to Santa Barbara and one to San Diego. I even began to enjoy Ariel's company, too. She doesn't seem as worried about my behavior. I know a lot of people started to think of me as reckless and maybe even as dangerous as Lloyd. Who knows what I would do?

"Ariel's just . . . air molded into this soft, pretty person. Funny, but now I keep waiting for Daddy to hurt her and I feel sorry for her. He has started to voice little complaints about her, about the way she keeps the apartment, her inability to boil water, her vapid conversation.

"That's right, Daddy used Charles Allen's very word, 'vapid.'

"Maybe Mommy is right. Maybe all men are monsters, even daddies."

I glanced at Doctor Marlowe.

"I guess I still suffer from a great deal of anger, right, Doctor Marlowe?"

"It's a concern of mine," she admitted.

I smiled at the others.

"Recognizing your problem is the first step toward solving it," I recited.

Jade laughed and Star relaxed her lips with an impish gleam in her eyes. Cathy looked nervously at Doctor Marlowe.

"Well," Doctor Marlowe said, "this has been a good beginning. Wouldn't you all agree? Cathy?" she asked, spotlighting her.

Cathy looked at me and nodded.

"Yes," she said softly.

We heard a small rap on the door and looked up to see Emma.

"I don't mean to interrupt, Doctor Marlowe, but you told me to let you know when their rides arrived. Jade's chauffeur is here and Star's grandmother and Cathy's mother have arrived as well."

"I have to call my mother," I said.

"You can use the phone on my desk, Misty," Doctor Marlowe said. Everyone rose.

"Shall we say the same time tomorrow then?" Doctor Marlowe asked.

"Whose turn is it tomorrow?" Star asked.

"How about you?" Doctor Marlowe countered.

Star shrugged, gazing at me. I dialed my mother and punched four when the answering machine began. It forwarded the call to her cellular. When she said hello, I heard laughter around her.

"I'm ready. It's time. Where are you?" I asked.

"Oh, we were just finishing. I'll be right there, honey. How did it go?"

"Peachy keen," I said. "I'm cured."

She laughed nervously and repeated she was on her way.

The others waited for me and we started to walk out together.

"Misty, do you want to wait for your mother inside?" Dr. Marlowe asked.

"No, it's too nice out. I'm fine," I said.

"Okay. Bye," she said and we all stepped out.

We paused outside the door. I saw Cathy's mother studying us. She was a small woman who wore thick glasses and her dark brown hair cut very short. Jade's chauffeur looked bored and nearly asleep. Star's grandmother waved. Her modest older car with its dents and scrapes looked so out of place between the limousine and Cat's mother's late-model Taurus.

"That took a lot of guts today," Jade told me. "I hope we're all as honest and forthcoming," she added her eyes fixed on Star.

"Maybe all our stories aren't as interesting," Star said. "What about you?" she asked Cathy. "Are you going to be as honest and forthcoming?"

Cathy looked very frightened, shook her head, and hurried toward her mother and their car.

"See you tomorrow, Cat," I called.

She looked back, surprised at the use of a nickname, but a small smile on her lips.

"Cat?" Jade said and I explained why I called her that.

"Yes, that fits," she said.

"It doesn't matter. She's probably not even coming back," Star said.

"Well, it would help if you didn't try to scare the hell out of her," Jade muttered.

"Scare the hell out of her? How did I scare the hell out of her?"

"You just have that look," Jade said.

"What look is that?"

"Like you're going to eat her alive," Jade said.

Star looked angry for a moment and then smiled.

"Well, from now on, I'll try to be sweet and prissy like you Beverlys," she said and sauntered off.

I had to laugh.

"She's not funny," Jade said.

"Yes she is. And I don't think she's as bad as you make her out to be."

"Oh, really?" Jade demanded sounding annoyed that I had disagreed with her.

"And I wonder what her story will be like tomorrow."

Jade was quiet for a moment and then nodded.

"Yeah, I wonder," she said.

We watched Cathy and her mother drive off. Cathy had her head down and her mother was talking at her. She looked like she was lecturing her. Then Star and her grandmother drove past us. Star looked out and pulled her shoulders back, her head up, pretending to be a snob. Even Jade laughed.

She continued to stand there, waiting with me.

"Don't you have to go? Your chauffeur's been here awhile."

"He can wait. He gets paid enough," she said.

"My mother will be here any minute," I said. "It's all right."

She nodded, but still hesitated as though she didn't want the conversation to end. She held onto the moment as if it was a raft in a treacherous sea.

"Doctor Marlowe's okay, isn't she? I mean, she's not what you would expect a therapist to be," Jade said.

"I do like her, yes. Do you think she's helping you, then?"

"I suppose. Now, we're all supposed to help each other, right?" Jade asked.

"Right," I said smiling.

"See you tomorrow," she said, "when Star will be the star." She laughed at her own joke.

"I wouldn't mess with her," I called as Jade started toward her limousine. She looked back at me and smiled. She's really a very pretty girl, I thought. I bet my boyfriend stories were nothing compared to hers.

I watched her get in and the limousine start away. She waved and in moments, was gone like the others.

The sun was almost directly above the house now. It was warmer, but there was still a nice breeze. I wasn't as tired as I expected I might be after talking so much. In fact, I felt lighter, even more energetic. It was as if I had truly unloaded my dark baggage of trouble for a while.

Why was it so hard to be happy? I wondered. Was anyone ever happy? Even Doctor Marlowe?

Was Daddy happier now? Would Mommy ever be happy again?

What about me?

My mother would be here any moment and we would start for home. Across the city, we four girls went off in different directions, our lives like four comets in space, traveling through the dark.

For a short while, thanks to Doctor Marlowe, our paths would cross. We would share smiles and tears, laughter and heartbreak and we would hopefully learn that we were not as alone as we had thought.

Maybe that was enough.

Maybe we really could start again, holding hands, marching out this door, together, like renewed blossoms, welcoming the sun.

Maybe.

Star

Prologue

When my grandmother drove me to Doctor Marlowe's for my second group therapy session, I sat in the car for a few moments and thought, girl, just have her turn around and take you home. What good is it going to do you to tell your troubles to these three rich white girls, although I did think Cathy, or Cat as Misty called her, wasn't as well-to-do as Misty and Jade seem to be.

As we drove into Doctor Marlowe's driveway, I saw Jade's chauffeured limousine pull away, so I knew I wasn't the first to arrive. I couldn't help wondering if Cat was coming back. The whole time Misty talked yesterday, Cathy the cat looked like she was sitting on a cold, wet park bench, ready to leap off and scoot into a dark alley the first chance she got. She sighed and squirmed and looked at the ceiling and the floor, everywhere but at us or at Doctor Marlowe. I think if she could have crawled under her seat, she would have.

My story wasn't at all like Misty's. It wasn't about spoiled rich boys and big houses with ballrooms and such. I wasn't going to complain about all the meaningless toys and dolls and clothes I was given. What I was given probably wouldn't fill a corner in one of their rooms anyway. And I wasn't going to describe parents who couldn't see eye to eye about their egos. The last thing my momma worried about was her makeup, her complexion, and whether or not her hair and clothes were in style. I couldn't even begin to imagine Daddy going to fancy gyms and wearing expensive sweat suits. If Cathy the cat thought Misty's descriptions of what she called a hard life were hard to swallow, she'd surely choke to death in Doctor Marlowe's office once I began telling about my life.

The thing is, did I want to begin? What were these girls going to tell me about me and my troubles that I didn't already know myself, huh? What did Doctor Marlowe expect out of us? I couldn't tell Misty anything that would help her yesterday. She wouldn't be able to tell me anything that would help me today. And that Jade . . . I was sure she'd be sitting there with her nose pointed at the ceiling, refusing to lower herself to look my way. I bet she'd make me feel like she was doing me a favor just staying in the room while I talked.

I had tossed and turned and fretted about it quite a while last night, worried they might laugh at me or think my story was beneath them. I didn't want to go in there and have to look at their smiles of ridicule.

Granny looked at me, surprised at my hesitation.

"What do you plan on doing, Star, just sitting there in the car all morning? You know I got chores to run."

"Coming here is a waste of time, Granny." I looked at her. "It is!"

"Yeah, well the doctors and the judge don't think so and that's what counts here, Star, so you just better get on in there. I can't abide any more trouble. Not with this old heart ticking down like some tired old grandfather clock," she said.

Granny knew that was all she had to say to get me to do what she wanted. There was nothing I feared more for myself and my brother Rodney than her having another heart attack. She was the only one left in the world who cared about us and loved us, and she was the only one we cared to love.

I opened the car door and started to slide out.

"Okay," she sang to the front window, "I guess there's no sugar for me this morning."

I shook my head and leaned over to give her a kiss on her plump right cheek. Then she grabbed my hand as I turned away and held it so tightly it sent a shiver down the bone and into my spine. Her face was like one of her pieces of antique china, full of tiny cracks, still beautiful, but on the verge of shattering the moment it was tapped a bit too hard.

Granny and I had the same eyes, only hers were just a bit rounder and somehow still lit up with hope more often than mine. However, this morning her eyes were full of worry, making them look heavy, so heavy she looked like she wanted to just close them and lay her head back on that double down pillow she claimed was full of good dreams.

How I wished I had a pillow like that.

Granny had had so many troubles in her life, troubles she had buried so deeply in her mountain of memories, I never even knew about them. She didn't want me to know. If I asked her too many questions about her own youth and her own hardships, she would just shake her head and say, "You don't need to feed the hatred living in your heart anything extra, Star. Your momma and daddy done enough to provide it with a feast that's kept it too fat as it is."

"What is it, Granny?" I asked as she squeezed my hand.

"You give Doctor Marlowe a chance to help you, Star. Don't shut up all the doors and windows, child, like you done so many times before. You're too young to become someone's lost cause, hear? Your momma likes to wear them shoes, but you kick 'em off."

"Yes, Granny," I said smiling.

If I had inherited just a small piece of that steel spine of hers, I would surely make it through all the rain and wind on the road ahead of me, I thought, and there was plenty still to come.

She let go and I continued out of the car.

"And don't look down on those other girls just because their families got some money," she warned me.

I shook my head at her.

"What do you know about people with money, Granny? You haven't ever had any rich friends to complain about, have you?"

"Never mind your smart mouth, child. I don't have to have rich friends to know having lots of money doesn't mean you don't need any sympathy and a helping hand. Those other girls wouldn't be here otherwise, would they?" she pointed out.

She was a smart one, my Granny. I guess something could be said for the school of hardship, too. Granny could be the valedictorian of that school and graduate with honors, I thought, not that it was something anyone would want or be proud of, especially Granny.

"Okay, Mrs. Anthony," I said. Whenever I called her by her name, she knew I was teasing her.

"You hold your tongue in there, child, and be civil, hear?" she warned me firmly.

"Yes, Granny."

"I'll be back the same time as yesterday," she said and started away.

I watched her drive off, a little old lady, not more than five feet four inches tall with shoulders still capable of holding up the responsibilities my much younger mother couldn't tolerate. Granny still had plenty of grit and walked proudly with her head high.

Granny always kept her smoke-gray hair brushed back and tied neatly in a bun. She wore just a touch of lipstick, but no other makeup, ever. Her eyeglasses were really the only frilly thing she permitted in her life. They were fashioned like expensive designer glasses with dark frames. It gave her just enough of a touch of style to make her comfortable with her public appearances, and she loved it when her older men friends kidded her and called her Miss America.

She was once a very pretty woman. She didn't look her sixty-eight years, despite the tensions and disappointments in her life. Granny wasn't as much of a churchgoer as most of her friends, but she had a deep faith in the goodness of people and the promise of an everlasting paradise at the end of the difficult journey. In her mind there were always people worse off, and she put more of her strength and energy into feeling sorrier for them than she did for herself. There was nothing she taught me that was more important to her than to despise and avoid self-pity. She said it was like "shackles around your ankles, keeping you chained to disaster and defeat. Instead, you pick yourself up when you get set back some and move on until it's time to stop and put your trust in the Lord," she advised.

Maybe you had to be old to believe like that, I thought. I wasn't ready to simply accept disappointments and defeat and move on. I refused to bend and I let whatever winds that blew at me know it. I'd break before I'd bend. Granny told me that was just defeating myself, but I still had the need to scratch and claw, kick and punch and spit into the faces of those who made my life miserable.

It was supposed to rain all day in Los Angeles and the clouds were blowing in from the northwest and thickening rapidly as the hands of the wind molded them like clay. Doctor Marlowe's large Tudor house looked darker, the windows reflecting the gray skies. It was a very big house, the biggest house I had ever been in, and here in one of the wealthiest neighborhoods in Brentwood, too.

There was nothing to reveal that Doctor Marlowe's house was a place where she treated patients, or clients, as they liked to call us. I guess that was deliberate. Doctor Marlowe certainly didn't want us to feel like freaks or anything. She wanted us all to be relaxed like people just visiting, but I had no other reason to come to this part of the city where so many rich people lived, no other reason than supposedly getting my head put back on straight.

However, no matter what the courts and the schools and the other doctors had said, I still didn't believe in the value of coming here even though Doctor Marlowe used words as her medicines. She prescribed different ways of thinking about things, used questions the way other doctors used X-rays and always tried to turn your eyes around so you were looking into yourself instead of at her.

I admit that she made me think about everything twice at least, but it still hadn't made me feel any better about myself or the things that had happened to me and my brother. I wasn't going to walk out of this big house and her office one day and be picked up by loving new parents, was I? She wasn't going to wave a magic wand over my horrible history and make it dissolve into thin air like some bad dream. I'd still be what Misty called an orphan with parents.

It was a good description. My mommy and daddy weren't dead and buried, but they were dead to me even though there were no funerals. Instead of a procession to the cemetery, there had been a parade of lies and crippled promises limping along from the day I was born until today, until this moment, all of it parked outside, still following me everywhere, waiting to be told where to go.

Me too, I thought, I'm waiting to be told where to go. Doctor Marlowe wanted to take me to some second chance, some new start full of new hope. She wanted me to believe that the only thing holding me back was myself. She made it sound like I didn't long for a real family and a nice home and nice friends, and I had to be talked into it. Right.

It made me angry just thinking about how she wanted me to blame myself. She expected me to discover what was wrong with me and fix it rather than point to a drunken mother and a deserter and deadbeat for a father. I wasn't ready to excuse them or forget them and it would be a cold day in hell before I would ever forgive them. Granny was right about the hatred gnawing away at my heart, but for now, I didn't see any-place else for it to be.

Doctor Marlowe's maid Sophie opened the door for me and stepped back quickly as soon as she set her eyes on me. Maybe she thought I had something contagious. The doctor's sister Emma was nowhere in sight, which was fine with me. She was a big, heavy older woman who always looked at me as if she thought I might steal something from the house. I know I made her so nervous she couldn't wait to get out of my sight. I didn't want her there, anyway.

As it turned out, I was the last to arrive. They were all sitting where they had sat yesterday with Doctor Marlowe in her chair. She wore a navy blue dress and had her hair brushed down. I thought it made her look older. Maybe she thought she had to look that way with us. She was tall and lean with long arms and legs. Yesterday, we asked her why she wasn't married, but she wouldn't tell us. She claimed she was the doctor here. She'd do all the asking. It was on the tip of my tongue to say, "You're just hiding behind that like you say we hide behind stuff, too," but I promised Granny I would try not to let my mouth and tongue have a mind of their own.

Jade and Misty glanced at Cat and then at me with self-satisfied smiles on their faces because I had been wrong about her not showing up. After Misty had told her story, I predicted Cat would quit group therapy, but if anything, she looked a little better than she had yesterday. Her hair was neatly brushed. She wore some lipstick and she wore a light-blue cotton dress with loafers. Doctor Marlowe looked pleased about it too. Maybe we were all a good influence on Cat, I thought. At least someone might get something valuable out of this. It was just that I would have guessed Cathy would be the one least likely.

"Good morning, Star," Doctor Marlowe said with a warm smile on her face. Whether she meant it or not, she did make me feel like she was happy to see me.

"Morning."

I took my seat and looked at Misty, who seemed the most anxious of all for me to get started. What did she think I was going to do, I wondered, entertain her?

"It's getting so dark outside," Doctor Marlowe said and turned on another lamp. "We're in for a storm. So? How are you all today?" she asked.

Jade was the only one who really responded.

"Tired," she said with great effort. She was dressed as stylishly as she had been the day before. Today she wore dark blue silk pants with a sash, a ribbed cotton bodysuit and a cardigan sweater tied over her shoulders like some fancy college girl. It all made my red and white dress and scuffed loafers look like some hand-me-downs Granny had found at a thrift shop.

Misty was in jeans and sneakers and wore a T-shirt that said *Mommy went to Paris and all I got was this stupid T-shirt*.

"Still not sleeping well?" Doctor Marlowe asked Jade.

Jade had a way of turning her head so her chin always stayed high. I hated admitting she was pretty, but she was. Those green eyes made her special.

"Nothing's changed," she replied. "Why should I sleep any better?"

Doctor Marlowe nodded. Misty tucked the corner of her mouth into her cheek and Cat stared with admiration at Jade as if she had said the most important thing and was more important than Doctor Marlowe was.

"Anyone want anything before we start?" Doctor Marlowe asked.

"Got milk?" Misty asked with a silly grin. Jade laughed and Cathy the cat smiled. Misty was making fun of the television commercial of course. I couldn't help but snicker myself. At least Misty had some smiles and giggles to carry around as well as the tears and rage. I secretly hoped she had enough for all of us.

"Well, when we take a break, we'll have something," Doctor Marlowe said. She looked at me. "So, today is your day, Star," she said.

"I don't know how to begin," I said, folding my arms under my breasts the way Granny always did when she was setting to hunker down behind an attitude or thought.

"Begin any place you want," Doctor Marlowe said.

"Noplace comes to mind," I said sullenly.

"Do you remember the first time your mother and your father had a bad argument?" Misty asked. "I mean a really bad, all-out argument."

"Maybe she didn't have a father right from the beginning," Jade said in her most arrogant, haughty voice.

I spun on her.

"I had a father," I snapped. "My momma and daddy had a proper wedding and all, too. In a church!"

She shrugged.

"Mine too," she said. "You see all the good that's done me. Now look where I am."

I stared at her for a moment and then gazed at the other two. Each girl seemed to have the same desperate and lost look in her eyes.

It occurred to me that despite our differences, we all had a similar way to say, "Once upon a time."

I guess I could find mine, I thought.

1

"There's no beginning. I don't know as there was ever a time in my house when there wasn't trouble between my momma and daddy," I started. "I saw them be sweet to each other sometimes, but as my granny says, it was like waiting on rainbows after storms. Sometimes the rainbows came, but most of the time not. I think I got so I was surprised to hear them talk to each other without one or the other shouting before they were finished.

"I heard Misty say yesterday that sometimes people get divorced because of money problems. Well, that wasn't the only reason my parents broke up, but it sure didn't help any that my daddy didn't make good money and was out of work often. He was a painter and a carpenter mostly but did other types of work. He could be handy everywhere except around his own house. When he did work, he worked hard, long hours. I think he had a good reputation as far as that goes, but he didn't belong to any unions and he wasn't part of any company that guaranteed him regular work. So there were long periods when times were hard for us and my momma wasn't what you'd call an efficient housewife. I don't know if Daddy would even call her a housewife. He had other names for her and none of them were nice.

"My daddy's a good-looking man, a strapping six-feet four. Anyone would take one look at him and think he must have been a ballplayer in high school, but he always told me he was just too slow to be a good athlete. He said his problem was he thinks too long before he does something. He says he likes being precise and that helps him in all the work he's done as a painter and a carpenter.

"Momma's completely different. She doesn't think so much before she decides to do something. Most of the time, I don't believe she thinks at all. She just does what she wants when she wants. They got into lots of arguments because of that. Daddy said she had a brain that was like a house without any doors. Stuff just went in and out. She'd say she was bound to be on old age Social Security before he did anything worthwhile. Granny used to call them Oil and Water.

"They probably shouldn't have gotten married in the first place, but my momma was pregnant with me before they got married and the way Daddy talked sometimes, I thought he blamed her for all their hard times because of it. If she complained about anything, he would sure always be reminding her that she was the one who had gotten pregnant, as if men could also get pregnant, but had the good sense not to."

Misty laughed and Jade smiled. Cathy smiled too.

"That would be good. That would be fair," Misty said. "At least they would know what it's really like. I know my mother would like that. She'd love to see my father have morning sickness and labor pains."

"Men are babies," Jade declared as if she was standing on the top of some mountain. "If they were the ones who had to get pregnant, the human race would be listed as an endangered species."

We all laughed, including Doctor Marlowe. It made me feel easier about talking, but I still hesitated and looked at Doctor Marlowe for encouragement before I started to talk in great detail about Momma.

It wasn't just because I was ashamed of her, which I had every right to be. Momma had done so many things to make me want to stick my head in the sand. I used to hate to meet up with any friends of mine from school whenever I was with Momma. Not only was there no telling what she would say or do, she usually had bloodshot eyes and smelled like One-Eyed Bill's Bar and Grill down on the southeast corner from our apartment in West Los Angeles. There was a barstool in the place that practically had Momma's name on it. I heard that if she came in and there was someone sitting on it, he or she would just move off and look for another stool—or stand.

When I was just seven, Daddy used to send me to fetch her when he had come home and found she wasn't there making dinner for us. I hated going there, but even then I knew Daddy was sending me because if he had gone instead, they would have had an all-out fight that would turn physical. Daddy would even get into a fight with some other bar customer who felt he had to protect Momma or might even have been flirting with her and wanted to show off.

Sometimes it took so long for me to get her to leave and go home with me, I would start to cry. That usually made her mad because all the other barflies would make fun of her and tell her to go. There was nothing Momma hated more when she drank than anyone telling her what to do. It was like lighting a wick on a dynamite stick. She'd fume and fume and she'd get real nasty and explode into curses and maybe even throw something or swing at someone, especially Daddy, or me for that matter. When Rodney was a baby, I'd have to worry about him crawling around on the kitchen floor because there still might be pieces of plates she had smashed against the wall.

But my hesitation over telling things about her came from another place inside me. Despite what I always told Granny, I hated hating Momma. Mixed with all the bad memories were lots of good ones. There were many times when she had held me and had sung to me and had fixed my hair and kissed me. She used to call me her Precious and she used to dream big dreams for me. All those memories were planted in someplace special in my heart too, and I couldn't help feeling like I was betraying them when I told about all the bad things.

For now, though, that seemed to be what Doctor Marlowe wanted me to do. From the way she talked about it, holding the bad down was like trying to keep poison in your body.

"I can't remember exactly when my momma started drinking," I began, "but it was always a lot and it was always bad, especially for me and my brother Rodney."

They all lost their smiles and their eyes became hard and cold like the eyes of those who had seen terrible things happen and knew what I was going through in just talking about it, for there was no way to talk about it without reliving it. Remembering made me a five-year-old girl again, brought back all the demons, all the dark shadows that haunted my bedroom after something awful had happened between Momma and Daddy.

The monsters were a part of me now, dormant, lying around and waiting to be nudged by the sound of someone shouting, by the sight of some poor child playing in the gutter because his mother was neglecting him, by the wail of ambulance sirens or police sirens, or merely by the sounds of someone crying in the darkness, someone as alone and afraid as I had been and maybe forever would be.

"When I think back on it now, it seems to me that there was always a lot of drinking going on. Momma smelled from it so much, I used to think it was a kind of perfume she wore," I said.

Misty laughed.

"Of course, I wasn't very old when I thought that.

"Sometimes, she would just let me stand there by the door and pretend she didn't know who I was. I was afraid to call to her. I knew how mad that made her. Finally, she would look at Bill and say, 'My ball and chain is home from work,' and they would all cackle and tease her, and she would blame me.

" 'Why did he have to send you here?' she would snap at me.

" 'He wants you to come home and make us supper, Momma,' I would tell her and she would shake her head and mimic me.

"She'd stare at herself in the mirror behind the bar for a few moments and then finish her beer in a gulp and get up a little wobbly.

" 'What's for dinner, Aretha?' someone would shout.

" 'My heart,' she'd scream back and whoever was there would laugh and laugh. 'Go on,' Momma would tell me. 'Get outta here. You made enough trouble for me.'

"I'd wait for her on the sidewalk. Sometimes she'd come right out and sometimes, she'd start up again and I'd have to go back inside and then she'd come.

"Usually she wouldn't say much as we walked home, but when she did it was almost always about what a big mistake her whole life was.

" 'That man who calls himself your father promised me Easy Street,' she'd claim. 'He said we'd live in a nice house in a nice neighborhood and I'd have a yard for a garden like my momma has. Not some rat hole four-room dump that it doesn't even pay to clean. You wipe the dust off the table and it just floats back a few minutes later. I told him why bother with it when he complained about my housekeeping.'

"She'd stop and look at herself in a store window and maybe make a small effort to fix her hair and straighten her dress. It was funny how no matter what happened between her and Daddy, Momma always wanted to be pretty for him.

"Momma's about five feet six. No matter how much she drank, she didn't seem to lose her figure. She never grew those big hips many women her age got from eating and drinking the worst stuff. Daddy would say all the booze went to her head and soaked her brain instead. I always thought she was pretty and only looked ugly when she got real drunk. Her lower lip sags and her eyes droop. Daddy told her he couldn't stand looking at her when she was like that, and one time, when they had an all-out slam-bam, he put a pillowcase over her head and tied it at her neck so that she spun about and whipped her arms wildly, knocking things over, falling over a chair, and kicking like some wild animal."

Cat's mouth was wide open. Jade looked like she might throw up and Misty bit down on her lower lip and looked at Doctor Marlowe. It occurred to me that their parents probably only threw nasty words and threats at each other and probably mostly through their expensive attorneys. Most likely, they couldn't even imagine their mothers and fathers trying to do physical harm to each other. The stuff I was telling them and was about to tell them, they saw only in the movies or on television.

"That wasn't the worst thing," I said, "but my daddy was generally an easy-going man."

"Easy-going?" Jade asked snidely.

"I can't recall him ever lifting his hand to threaten me or my brother Rodney, but when my momma got real drunk so that she slobbered and cursed and called him all kinds of dirty names, he lost control of himself, that's all.

"Once, when I was still only about five, I remember him trying to scare her by smashing a plate on the floor. She went even wilder on him, however, and scooped out cups and saucers, glasses and bowls from the cabinet, sending them flying every which way and screaming 'You want to see something break, Kenny Fisher? I'll show you something break.'

"The only way he could stop her was to wrap his arms around her and hold her down. She tried kicking at him and even tried to get her head down low enough to bite his arm. She'd bitten him plenty of times before, but he's a strong man and he lifted her and carried her to their bedroom where he threw her on the bed and practically sat on her while she flared about, slapping at him, until she grew exhausted and passed out.

"When he came out of the bedroom, he had scratches on his neck and his arms that were still bleeding. I was too scared to move. In fact," I said glancing at Doctor Marlowe, "I think I peed in my pants."

The others were gaping at me as if I was something from out of space. You all asked for it, I thought, well, I'll give it to you.

"I had that problem for a long time after I was supposed to. Momma even took me to the doctor once and he told her it was all in my head. She got mad at him and called him stupid because it was all in my panties not in my head. He wanted me to go see a psychiatrist back then and Momma called him nuts and dragged me out of the office, screaming she wasn't going to pay no quack a penny. She vowed she'd cure me and her way was to force me to wear wet panties, even when Daddy complained about the stink."

"Ugh," Jade moaned. "That's disgusting. Can I get a glass of water or something, Doctor Marlowe?"

"Sure. How about the rest of you?" She smiled at Misty. "Want milk?"

"No thanks," she said quickly, looking like she was holding breakfast down. "I'll just have water, too."

"All right. Let me get a pitcher of ice water for now. It's so humid, isn't it?" Doctor Marlowe looked at me and I thought she looked pleased. I guess she wanted me to shake up our little group after all.

She rose. Cathy said she had to go to the bathroom and left with her. Jade and Misty turned to me.

"Do you see your mother much anymore?" Misty asked.

"No. I'll talk about all that when they return," I said. "Otherwise I'll just be repeating myself and these things aren't things I like to talk about, much less repeat."

She nodded. They were both quiet for a moment, but I could see Jade's mind working.

"It's not really my business," she said softly, "but under the circumstances, how can your grandmother afford Doctor Marlowe? I mean, I know what it's costing my parents," she added, looking to Misty, who nodded.

"The court told some agency to pay for it. I don't know all the details, but no one asks me or my granny for any money. If they did, I wouldn't come back. That's for sure. We got better places for Granny's money."

They both looked sorry for me.

"Don't worry about me," I told them sharply. "I'm not looking for anyone's pity or charity and I'd really rather not come here, but I got to."

They both nodded, trying not to look too sympathetic so I wouldn't get mad at them.

Cat returned first and avoided my eyes.

"You look nice today," Misty told her. "You oughta cut your bangs, though."

"You have split ends, too," Jade told her. "Where do you go to get your hair done?"

"My mother does my hair," Cat said.

"So, just tell her to trim it more," Misty said with a shrug.

She ain't so bad, I thought. At least she don't seem as stuck up.

Doctor Marlowe set the tray with a jug of ice water and glasses on the table.

"I've got a surprise for you all today," she said. "Since we started a little later this morning, I decided it would be nice if we had a real lunch break, so I'm having some pizzas brought in."

"Maybe I won't take that long," I suggested.

"Then Jade will get started," Doctor Marlowe quickly replied. Cat looked relieved knowing she didn't have to be next. When her turn came, she would definitely fail to show up, I thought.

Doctor Marlowe poured everyone a glass of water. Then she nodded at me to continue.

"When I was nearly nine years old, Momma got pregnant again," I said. "I thought she was never going to have another baby. She had kept from getting pregnant for a long time. I didn't know it until much later, but Momma had been pregnant before. She had lost a baby when I was only two, lost it in our bathtub."

The three of them froze in anticipation of me describing how. I thought about it for a few moments and decided not to. When I talked about the next pregnancy instead, they looked very relieved. It almost made me laugh out loud. I was beginning to enjoy the grimaces, looks of shock and disgust on their faces.

Doctor Marlowe could see that in my face, too. She gave me a look that told me so and I wiped the smug smile off my face quickly.

"For a little while after my momma became pregnant, things settled down in our house. Momma actually cut back on her drinking because the doctor told her she could hurt the baby. She did a better job of cleaning our house. She cooked again and Daddy got more work. We had a little money and did some nice things together, like taking trips to Magic Mountain and once to Knott's Berry Farm. We went to visit Daddy's cousin Leonard in San Diego, too, and went to the zoo.

"Momma was pretty big by this time. Sometimes, Rodney would kick in her stomach and she'd call me to put my hand on it and feel him. We didn't know it was a boy yet, but I got so I was excited someone was coming. I thought it would be fun to have a little baby in the house and to help look after him or her. Little did I know just how much looking after I would eventually have to do."

"A lot?" Misty asked.

I stared at her for a moment.

"Sometimes, I thought he thought I was his mother instead of his sister."

"Terrible," Jade said. "Putting that sort of responsibility on you when you were so young."

"Yeah, well, what you have to do, you do unless you got all kinds of servants to do it for you," I told her.

She looked away.

"When Momma was about in her seventh month, Daddy got laid off again and we had to watch every penny. Momma just hated that. It made her more wasteful just for spite. I guess it was her way of telling Daddy he'd better find new work soon. She wasn't going to deny herself anything, especially her cigarettes or occasional beer.

"One night soon after, while Daddy was trying to find some work, she went to One-Eyed Bill's. When he came home and found she was gone, he went into a rage and this time he didn't send me to go fetch her. After all, she was pregnant and she wasn't supposed to be drinking, so he went himself, nearly ripping the door off its hinges when he charged out of our apartment.

"At One-Eyed Bill's he hit a man who came between him and Momma and the police had to come. I'll never forget that," I said and looked down at the floor. The memory put ice around my heart for a moment.

"I was just sitting in the living room watching television and looking at the door every once in a while, terrified of what Momma was going to be like coming through it when I heard a knock and then saw a policewoman and a policeman. The policewoman was black.

"She knew my name and all and told me she had come to be sure I was all right. Daddy had told her I was here. She said I'd have to go with them for a while and I shook my head and started to cry. I even tried to run away from them, but they caught me and made me go with them to the police station. I remember thinking I'm being arrested for being Momma's daughter because she was so bad."

I looked up. The three girls were staring at me, none of them taking a breath.

"They kept me in a room and gave me hot chocolate and cookies while they waited to see what was going to happen to Daddy and Momma. She had torn up some of the bar, too, but One-Eyed Bill didn't press any charges and Daddy was released pending a court appearance. The other man didn't show up and they dropped all the charges against Daddy, but it was enough to put a little scare into Momma.

"She behaved herself for quite a while afterward and then Rodney was born in the bathroom."

"What did you say?" Jade immediately asked. Her head spun around at me so fast, I thought it might keep going around and around on her neck.

"Daddy wasn't home," I continued, ignoring her. "It was the middle of the afternoon. I had just come back from school. I was in the fifth grade by then. I came into the apartment and called for Momma like always, only she didn't call back. I looked for her in her bedroom and I saw she wasn't there. Then I heard her scream and I ran to the bathroom.

"She was on the floor and I could see the baby coming. The sight nailed my feet to the floor. She was yelling for me to go get help, to call nine-one-one. I started crying. I couldn't help it and she kept screaming and yelling at me. Finally, I went to the phone and called and told the operator my momma was having a baby on the bathroom floor. I gave her our address and hung up. Then I heard Rodney cry and when I looked back in the bathroom, Momma had him on her stomach, but there was blood and the afterbirth and . . ."

"Oh, my God, do we have to listen to this?" Jade cried with her mouth twisting into a grimace of disgust.

Cathy looked a shade whiter than milk. Misty sat with her eyes wide, her mouth dropped so that I could practically see what she had for breakfast.

"I don't want you to be upset, Jade, but you should know what Star's life is really like and when your turn comes, you shouldn't hold anything back for fear of upsetting the others either."

"Like I have something that gross to tell," Jade replied, swinging those green eyes toward the ceiling.

"What might not be as disagreeable to you, could be to Star."

"Oh please."

"Why don't you put your fingers in your ears?" I told her.

She looked like she was going to say something back, but held off.

"Just finish describing what happened, Star," Doctor Marlowe commanded.

"She asked me to fetch her a towel and I did and then I got some hot water for her and we waited. The paramedics came and finished off Rodney's birth, but they took them both to the hospital just the same. Granny came to be with me and finally Daddy showed up and saw Rodney and Momma. She was all right, but mad as hell at him for not being there. They had another argument in the hospital, Daddy defending himself for being out looking for a job and Momma screaming about how she almost died giving birth to his son.

"Right from the start, she made it sound like Rodney was only his and she was just delivering him. That way she blamed Daddy for all the work and all the problems, starting right then and there. The nurse had to ask them to stop yelling.

"Momma and Rodney stayed only that night. I went home with Granny and she brought me back the next day. It was one thing to see Rodney behind that window in the hospital, but quite another to see him in his little crib beside Momma and Daddy's bed. I thought the sight of him was a wonder. His head didn't look much bigger than one of my rubber balls and when he cried, he lifted his small, puffy arms and waved his tiny fists in the air like he was looking for someone or something to punch. I stood there for long periods of time watching him breathe and then wake up and scream, taking a breath and then throwing out this shrill little cry.

"The only thing that seemed to quiet him was Momma putting his mouth on her nipple."

"Oh, my God," Jade muttered, but both Cathy and Misty looked fascinated. "Are you going to describe breast-feeding in great detail?"

"Scare you?" I fired back at her.

"It doesn't scare me, but I'm not going to do it."

"My mother didn't do it," Misty said. "She had read where it could scar her breast and she could lose shape. What about your mother?" she asked Cathy.

Cat shook her head vigorously.

"I don't know," she said in a voice just above a whisper.

"You never asked?" Misty pursued.

"No," she said. She looked like she would get up and run out of the room if Misty didn't stop.

"It's a natural thing to be curious about," Misty muttered, not wanting to look bad for asking.

"It's not necessary to know," Jade insisted. "It's like hearing about someone's bowel movements."

"It is not!"

"I hope that's not next," Jade muttered without looking at me.

"I guess we know where her hang-ups are," Misty said.

"You don't know anything about me!" Jade cried. "What right do you have to judge me?"

"Girls," Doctor Marlowe said calmly, "this is not going to be productive if you don't show each other at least a minimum of respect. No one here has had it easy, but if you don't give each other a chance to be as open as possible, you won't help each other."

Jade didn't look convinced, but she relaxed in her seat and Misty looked sorry.

"From the way my granny talked about a new baby, I always thought we would become a happy family when Rodney was born, but Momma only complained about our lives more and more. Daddy got new work, but now he was never making enough money for us. When they argued and shouted at each other, I heard her blame him for Rodney all the time, claiming he was the one who wanted a son. She talked like she didn't want him and when I looked at my little brother, I couldn't imagine anyone, least of all his own momma, not wanting him.

"He was a colicky baby. Nothing seemed to help. He did cry a lot and Momma would rage about the apartment, complaining that the doctor didn't know nothing and she would go mad. She made Daddy get up with Rodney every night, no matter how early in the morning he had to go to work. When she saw I could help, really help, could hold Rodney safely, get him to drink his bottle and rock him to sleep, even if it was only for a little while, she started to keep me home from school more often. She did it so much, the school truant officer came by and when he saw I wasn't really sick, he threatened the school would take Momma to court and maybe take me away from her.

"I heard her mumble, 'Take them both.'

"Maybe she said it because she was frustrated and tired, but it hurt to hear it. It felt like it burned into my brain. I thought it might really happen, too. I had trouble sleeping and every time someone came to our door, my heart would race for fear it was someone to come take both Rodney and me away and put us in some institution.

"Granny came by often as she could, but she and Momma got into arguments about the way Momma kept the house and how she took care of Rodney. She knew Momma was starting to drink again, too.

"By this time, Momma was hiding booze all over the house. She was drinking vodka because it didn't smell as bad and she had it in shampoo bottles and even in a hot water bag she kept in the closet. For months and months, Daddy didn't discover it, but soon she became sloppy about hiding it and he would find a glass of orange juice or cranberry juice and taste it and know she had vodka in it.

"When he complained, she screamed about how hard her life was with two children to look after, one being a twenty-four-hour responsibility. Of course, she brought up money problems continually, and then he would accuse her of wasting what little we had on her booze habit. She claimed it was the only thing keeping her sane and he said if she was sane, then he didn't know what crazy meant anymore.

"I'd come home from school and find Rodney lying there in unchanged diapers. From the rashes and irritation on his legs and little behind, I knew he had been like that almost all day. Of course, that made him scream and cry more which sent Momma to the bottle more. She got so she could sleep right through him wailing away. I guess she was really more passed out than sleeping. I'd find her everywhere like that, even on the floor in her bedroom sometimes."

"She should have been locked up," Jade said.

I stared at her for a long moment and then I looked out the window at the drizzle that had begun. Maybe Jade was right, but it hurt to have someone else say it.

There were lots of worse things in life that could and maybe would happen to us, but hating your own mother had to be at the top of the list.

"She's right," I told Doctor Marlowe, "but I don't want her to be."

"I know," she said softly. "That's why you're all here: to find an alternative to hate."

"Why do we need to?" Misty asked with that little sarcastic turn in her lips.

"Because I think you all know by now, that you can't hate your parents without hating yourselves."

No one had to agree out loud. We could just look into each other's eyes and see that Doctor Marlowe was right.

2

"When Rodney began to crawl and then stand, things got worse because he was a curious baby from the start and he would get into places and things in a flash. One afternoon, I came home and found Momma had left him alone while she went out to get herself a couple of six-packs of beer. I guess he was asleep when she had left and she thought he'd be all right. I didn't know it, but she had left him alone many times before and once when she was with a girlfriend, Maggie Custer, they had left him in Maggie's car and a policeman had seen it and nearly arrested her.

"Anyway, this time Rodney woke up, crawled out of the cot-bed we now had for him and went looking for her. He wandered into the bathroom where Momma had left some of his rubber toys in the tub. There wasn't any water in the tub or he'd'a drowned for sure because he managed to fall into it when he tried to get to his toys. He hit his head on the faucet, I suppose. At first I thought Momma had taken him out with her because it was so quiet, but when I walked into the bathroom, I nearly jumped out of my skin. There he was lying on his back very still, his eyes wild and full of terror. I found out later that a head wound usually bleeds a lot, but at the time it turned my heart to stone. I saw all the blood around his head and I started screaming. I was familiar with calling nine-one-one by now. I told the operator my little brother had fallen and put a hole in his head. It didn't turn out to be that bad, but he did need ten stitches.

"The paramedics were there before Momma returned. She met one of her barfly friends who had talked her into just one drink at One-Eyed Bill's and she just forgot how much time went by, I imagine.

"The paramedics took him to the hospital emergency room where the doctor sewed up Rodney's wound. The paramedics wanted to know everything while a policeman went to fetch Momma. I had to tell them what had happened and they looked at each other angrily. When Momma arrived, she was fit to be tied that I had called them because they pulled her aside and gave her a what-for that spun her eyes. They threatened to tell the police and have someone from the Child Protection Service on her back if she let something like this happen again. They even told her she could go to jail for endangering the life of an infant.

"After we all got brought home, Momma started on me. Daddy came home right in the middle of it, saw Rodney and heard enough bits and pieces to realize what had occurred. I guess he knew about some of the other times, but he didn't get as wildly angry as I had expected he would.

"Instead, he got all quiet, this strange mood coming over him as if he was a clam or something and just closed up his shell. He looked at me and at Rodney and just sat with his eyes glazed while Momma went on and on like a worn CD, repeating her same complaints and trying to excuse herself.

" 'Who do they think they are telling me I'm not a good mother just because I stepped out for a moment? Huh? Who knew he'd get up and walk himself into the bathroom and fall into the tub, huh? I'm no fortune teller. I was coming right back. He was asleep. Who do they think they are reading me the riot act, huh?

" 'Why are you just sitting there staring into space like that, Kenny? What's this act supposed to be. You trying to make me feel bad? You know what it's like being stuck here with an infant all day? I'm talking to you. I'm looking at you and I'm talking to you.'

"Daddy said nothing. Still looking dazed, he just got up suddenly and walked out of the apartment. Momma stood there with her hands on her hips, her mouth wide and her eyes blazing. He closed the door softly behind him.

"She turned to me and said, 'Did you see that? Did you?'

"My heart was thumping like a parade drum. I couldn't speak or swallow.

" 'Of all the raw nerve . . . Well, good riddance to you too!' she screamed at the door. Then she opened it, stuck her head out in the hallway and screamed it again, but he was already out of the building.

"I saw my daddy only once after that."

"Saw him only once? What do you mean? Your father just left you and Rodney for good?" Jade asked, practically jumping out of her seat.

It was funny, but while I was telling them about it all, I really did forget they were there. Something like this had happened before, of course, but usually only with Doctor Marlowe. My memories would get so thick, they'd block out the present, where I was and what I was doing. I felt like I had fallen back and I was really there again. Momma's angry face was so vivid in my mind, those eyes bloodshot, her mouth twisted and her shoulders hoisted making her look like some kind of wild bird about to pounce.

Whenever she went into her ranting, my stomach would close like a fist and my breath would catch in my throat, making me feel as though I could choke on air. Retelling these bad times put me back into that state of mind and I wouldn't snap out of it until my lungs screamed. I'd blink a lot and realize where I was and I'd be grateful I wasn't back then.

That's how I felt now when Jade blurted her question at me. I looked at her for a few moments without realizing who she was and where I was. Her face got all twisted with confusion.

"Why doesn't she answer me, Doctor Marlowe? Why is she just staring at me like that?" I heard her ask.

"Star?" Doctor Marlowe said. "Star?"

That was my name, I thought. I heard her, but she sounded like she was at the other end of a long tunnel.

"Doctor Marlowe?" Misty said. "She looks spaced."

"She'll be all right, girls. Relax. Don't let her feel your panic. Star, honey?"

"Star, honey," Granny was calling. "You got to go to school, child, or they won't let you stay here with me. You know what that judge told us. Get up now, honey. C'mon, child. Wake up. Your eyes are open, Star. Wake up!"

I felt my body shake.

"Star, come on. You're not there; you're here," Doctor Marlowe said.

My face felt cool. She was dabbing me with a wet napkin.

"That's it. You'll be fine, Star. Come on. Stay with us."

She took my hand and squeezed it gently. My eyelids were fluttering like butterflies in a panic and then they slowed and I looked into Doctor Marlowe's eyes. They were moving over my face like two tiny searchlights. She smiled.

"There you are. You're fine," she said.

I looked at the others. They were all staring at me, each of them looking more shocked and afraid than the other.

"What is it?" I asked.

"Nothing. You drifted off a bit," Doctor Marlowe said. "It's no big deal. No problem. You're fine. Here, take some water," she said offering me my glass. I sipped some and took a deep breath.

"I forgot what I was saying," I said. My memories were jumbled like a can of alphabet soup.

Doctor Marlowe smiled and sat back.

"Well, you were telling us about the time your father got up and walked out of the house," she said. She made it sound as if it was just another part of the story, nothing terribly serious. Her voice had a calming effect.

I nodded.

"He didn't say good-bye to me or nothing," I muttered.

"That's right," Doctor Marlowe said as if she had been there with me.

I looked at her and realized in a way she had because I had told her about this before, many times before, and I always had trouble going on after that.

The others were still staring at me, their eyes so unmoving they could have been glass.

"Why're you all looking at me like that?" I snapped.

Jade smirked.

"She's fine," she said and sat back. "She can go on and on," she added.

"It's not that easy," Misty said. "Just because I did it yesterday, doesn't mean it was simple and it will be simple for you or for her or for Cat."

"Don't tell me how it's going to be for me," Jade fired back at her.

"I'm just trying to be . . ."

"What? Another Doctor Marlowe? One's enough," Jade quipped and turned away.

"Well. At least we're not boring each other," Doctor Marlowe said. Jade made some sound under her breath. Cat looked from one of us to the other, her eyes still full of terror.

"Try to go on, Star," Doctor Marlowe urged. "Tell them the rest of it," she urged as if it was more important for them to hear it than for me to get it out.

Jade turned her head slowly toward me to see what I was going to do. Almost for spite, I continued.

"I just saw him once after that time. I didn't speak to him. I was on my way home from school. It was just starting to rain and I saw him come out of our apartment building carrying some of his things and walking quickly toward his truck. I sped up and called to him. I know he heard me because I saw him slow down even though he didn't turn his head. He looked down at the sidewalk and then sped up again until he reached his truck.

"I was running by now, thinking maybe he didn't realize it was me calling to him, but I couldn't get to him before he started the truck and pulled away from the curb. With all my might, I shouted.

" 'Daddy! Daddy!' I stopped when my lungs were ready to burst, my ribs aching, and I watched the truck go down to the next corner, turn and disappear. The rain came down harder and harder so I had to go inside. You couldn't tell the difference between my tears and the raindrops streaking down my face."

"What happened to him? Where did he go?" Misty asked, her eyebrows knitted with concern.

"Momma heard stories that he was with another woman and he went north to San Francisco, but I never knew if the stories were just some gossip or what."

"Your father just picked up and deserted you and your brother? That's what you're telling us?" Jade asked, still sounding skeptical.

"He wasn't the first husband and Daddy to do that," I told her. I looked at them. "Your parents deserted you, too. They just did it more respectfully or, what word did you use yesterday, Misty, civilly? Something like that anyway," I said.

"Isn't that against the law?" Jade asked Doctor Marlowe. "What her father did?"

"Well, Star's father would be what we call a deadbeat dad and yes, what he's done is against the law," she replied. "There's even a federal law against that now."

"Did your mother have him arrested?" Jade followed.

"She went down to welfare and reported her situation so she could get some money, but it didn't get put at the top of anyone's list. It wasn't exactly what you would call a high priority," I said.

"Men are creeps," Jade muttered.

"My momma ain't exactly an angel," I told her. Her eyebrows lifted.

"What happened to her?"

"Why don't you give her a chance to tell it her own way?" Misty asked Jade.

"I'm sorry," she said. "It just makes me . . . mad."

I widened my eyes.

"It doesn't exactly put joy in my heart either," I said.

Jade's lips stretched into a tight smile. Damned if I didn't know whether I should hate her or like her.

"Momma didn't realize Daddy was gone for good that first night he walked out on us, of course. She made us some supper and sat drinking her beer all night and watching television. I put Rodney to bed. He was groggy and tired from his ordeal, but he was still in some pain. The paramedics had instructed us to give him some Tylenol, which I did. I sang a little to him and his eyes slowly closed.

"After he had fallen asleep, I went out and sat with Momma and watched television awhile, hoping Daddy would come home while I was still up, but he didn't. Finally, exhausted myself, I went to sleep.

"As soon as my eyes snapped open the next morning, I hopped out of bed and looked in on Momma and Daddy's bedroom, expecting to see his long, lanky body stretched over the comforter, his arm dangling over the side as usual. He usually ended up on the cover instead of under it.

"Momma had fallen asleep with her clothes still on and was spread-eagle, alone, breathing through her mouth and looking like she had been put into a trance. Rodney, who still slept next to them on his cot-bed, was sitting up, playing quietly with one of his toys. He looked happy when he saw me looking in on him.

"My heart felt like a Yo-Yo whose string had broken. All night it had gone up and down with every sound in the building that suggested Daddy's return. Now, it was clear he hadn't come back and I was sick with fear.

"I took Rodney into the living room and fixed him some breakfast. Momma woke up looking dazed and confused as usual after a night of drinking. She was surprised to see Daddy hadn't returned, too.

" 'Where'd Daddy go?' I asked her.

" 'How would I know? Who cares?' she said, but it bothered her when he didn't return the next day. She got on the phone and complained to Granny and then two days after that, she started to call some of Daddy's friends and I guess she found out he had left Los Angeles. That was when she went to welfare and cried about our situation.

"For a long time, I expected Daddy would come back, even after I saw him that last time and he hurried away from me. I never told Momma I had seen him. I knew it would just make her wild and angry and after a while, I began to wonder if I had really seen him or just imagined it out of hope. Whenever the phone rang, I hoped it was him calling, but it never was. Momma was so furious she would swear she wasn't going to take him back if he did show up, but I knew in my heart she would.

"Granny started to spend more time with us soon after all that. She lives in Venice Beach so it was a trip for her. When I would go to see her,

I'd have to ride the Big Blue Bus for nearly two hours to make the right connections and you know the buses don't run that often."

I glanced at them.

"Well, you girls probably don't know 'cause you probably never been on a Big Blue Bus in Los Angeles, have you?"

"I have," Cat blurted. She looked like she had confessed to a crime or something. "My mother didn't know I did, but I did," she added.

"How'd you like it?" I asked her.

"It was all right," she said. "Nobody bothered me."

"Why should they? Just because someone don't have enough money to have his or her own car don't mean they're rapists and serial killers, you know."

"I was just scared," she said. She said it with such honesty, I couldn't harden my heart against her for it.

"Yeah, well, I've been scared on the bus too," I admitted, "especially at night.

"But I often had to ride it then because I would have stayed at Granny's too long and I didn't want her to have to drive me home in the dark. Her eyes weren't so good back then and they are even worse now.

"I got so I ran to Granny every so often because I couldn't stand coming home from school and finding Momma drinking, Rodney still in his pajamas, and the house looking like ten slobs lived in it. Granny knew why I showed up at her house in the afternoon from time to time, but she didn't harp on it. She had tried and tried with Momma and finally just threw up her hands and declared, 'My Aretha's just one of those people who have to decide to help themselves because they won't let anyone else do it.

" 'Your momma will wake up facedown in the gutter one day and maybe then she'll decide to do something about herself,' Granny told me.

"She told it to me so often, I began to wish for it, wish I would come home and find Momma outside facedown in the street. I suppose it don't say much for you when all you can hope for is your momma hitting rock bottom sooner than later, but that's how it was and I'm not ashamed of praying for it.

"That's right," I said glaring at them before they could gasp or ask some stupid question, "I did pray for it. I went to sleep asking God to send my momma close to hell as soon as He had the opportunity.

"So yes, I did get so I hated her. At times it was like a rat of hatred was gnawing at my heart. I probably will always hate her," I declared firmly.

No one said a word. It was as if we were all in freeze-frame, not a movement, not even the sound of anyone breathing.

"Not having Daddy home even once in a while was like taking a leash off a dog as far as Momma was concerned. She didn't have to worry about him coming back from work and not finding her in the house. She didn't care what the house looked like either, since he wasn't there to criticize and complain. At first, it was like her way of getting even with him for leaving her. I could almost hear her say, 'He thought I was a no-good drunk slob before? Well, he should see me now.'

"I stayed home from school even more because after I saw to Rodney, it was often very late in the morning and I'd have missed the first two classes by the time I got there.

"Then Momma went and did the worst thing of all: she got herself a night job at One-Eyed Bill's waitressing and helping out in the kitchen.

"By then I was able to make dinner for Rodney and me, and I cleaned the house and did most all the chores. That's why I told you earlier that it got so my little brother didn't know who was his mother and who was his sister.

"Momma was supposed to always be home by one o'clock, but there were many nights when I know she didn't come home until three or four. She'd be so dead out of it in the morning, I could drop a frying pan next to her bed and she wouldn't as much as bat an eyelash. Lots of nights she was too drunk or tired to bother getting out of her clothes. She smelled so bad from beer and whiskey, the whole bedroom reeked like a One-Eyed Bill's. The stench would reach through the walls into my room. I'd have to open all the windows in the place."

"Ugh," Misty said holding her stomach. Jade swallowed hard and turned away for a moment, pressing the back of her hand against her mouth. I couldn't blame them.

"You get used to it," I muttered. "You'd never dream you would, but you do. There ain't much else you can do, but turn the other way most of the time."

"I understand," Cat said in a quivering small voice. She was holding her attention on me.

"You do? That's good, because I don't," I said. She just continued to stare, but I felt she was looking at her own memories now, not mine. After a moment she seemed to snap out of it and look down again.

"Granny came by often to help out and occasionally make us a real good dinner," I continued. "She and Momma had some big fights, but Momma would wail and claim she was doing the best she could, deserted by a husband and left with two kids to raise and support.

" 'Why do you think that man left you?' Granny would ask her and that would be the same as lighting that wick again. Momma would go wild, her arms and legs and even her head swinging so hard, I thought they might just fly off her body and bounce against the wall along with her screams.

" 'How can my own mother blame me for that rotten man? Why is it always my fault? He was the one who made all them promises, wasn't he? I did the best I could with the little money he brought us. Lots a times he brought us nothin' because he was out of work so much. It's no loss him bein' gone, no ma'am.'

"On and on she would go and I'd listen and wonder if she really believed the things she said. Maybe her eyes saw differently. Maybe she was just a step or two off-center and her world was running on a different track, you know. She always looked so satisfied with herself after one of those explosions of temper, like she had made important points and shut everyone up. That's when I began to understand what was meant when someone said 'You're only fooling yourself.' Momma really was fooling herself. She truly believed she was the victim and not us, not even me and Rodney. We were . . . just unfortunate enough to be born.

"Like I said, I guess no matter what your life is like, you can get used to it and just accept things as they are. Of course, I knew other girls my age didn't have this kind of life. Oh, they helped out with their little brothers and sisters, but their little brothers and sisters didn't become their children. They still thought about boys and parties and going to the movies and having fun. I couldn't think of anything without thinking about Rodney being a part of it. I didn't have a night off, so to speak," I said. "I was afraid of bringing anyone to my house. I didn't want my friends at school to know just how bad things were for me and for Rodney.

"Then," I said, taking a sip of water and thinking for a moment, "then I got so I could live through their stories. Their lives became my life. It was easier to pretend, to imagine my name was Lily Porter or Charlene Davis and in my mind go home to their houses and live with their families.

"You're all looking at me like I was crazy. Well, maybe I was for a while. Doctor Marlowe says I'm not crazy now."

"No one's crazy here, Star. It's an inappropriate word, a meaningless word," she said.

"Yeah, maybe, but I sure wasn't in my right mind. I did some things," I said. After a moment, I added, "Things I haven't even told you yet, Doctor Marlowe.

"Whenever I met someone who didn't know me, for example, I would give them a phony name, one of the names of the girls I envied and I would talk like I was Lily Porter or Charlene Davis, describing their homes and their families as if they really were mine.

"A couple of times, I went to Charlene Davis's house, walked right up to the door, pretending I was coming home. One time, I nearly got caught doing it. Her sister Lori came up behind me without me knowing and asked me what I was doing.

" 'I was just going to see if your sister was home,' I said. She looked at me sideways because she knew I knew her sister was on the cheerleading team and would be at practice. I made believe I forgot and walked away quickly. When Charlene asked me about it the next day, I said I was just in her neighborhood and had to kill some time. She didn't believe me. They all started looking at me as if I was funny.

"I couldn't help it. I wanted their lives so much I'd follow their mothers around a supermarket, pretending I was with them, buying food.

"You think I was pretty pathetic, don't you?" I asked Jade.

"No," she said. "Really," she added, when I looked skeptical. "I can understand not wanting to be who you are. I've felt like that lots of times."

"Me too," Misty said.

"Yes," Cat said. "Me too." She looked like she meant it more than any of us. How could her story be worse than mine? I wondered.

"There's more," I said, now willing to tell it all. "One time I hurt my ankle in gym class and the teacher sent me back to the locker room to get dressed. I noticed Charlene's locker was unlocked and I opened it and took her blouse."

"Why?" Jade asked with a grimace.

"To wear it later, when I was alone at home in my room. I pretended I was her and I lived in a nice house with a real mother and a father. Her daddy works for the city. He's some kind of traffic manager, makes good money, and her mother always looks stylish. They come to the basketball games and watch her cheer for the team. She's about my size, too, so the blouse fit real good."

"What happened when she found her blouse was missing?" Misty asked. "Did they accuse you?"

"No. The teacher made everyone open her locker and she looked in all of them."

"How come they didn't find it in yours? Where did you put it?"

"I didn't put it in my locker," I said. "I told you I wanted to take it home with me so I hid it under my skirt and no one dared look there. They just thought someone had come into the locker room and robbed it. Things like that had happened before. Charlene had to wear her gym uniform top for the rest of the day.

"About a month or so afterward, I brought it back and left it on the bench near her locker. Everyone thought it was weird. It was weird," I admitted.

"No it wasn't," Cat piped up. Everyone looked at her. She didn't hide her face this time.

"Why not?"

"I don't just want to be in someone else's clothes; I want to be in their bodies," she confessed.

Everyone was quiet. The air felt so heavy and even with the lights, a thick shadow seemed to hang over the ceiling and walls.

"Well," Doctor Marlowe said. "Why don't I go check on the pizza for us? It's getting close to that time."

She rose and looked at me.

"I guess you'll continue after lunch, right?"

I nodded and she left us. As soon as she had, Jade turned to me.

"I'm sorry I was nasty to you before," she said and then quickly added, "and I'm not trying to show you any pity so don't get mad at me."

"It's all right," I said. "About now, I could use some, I suppose."

"I suppose we all can," Misty said.

"As long as we don't depend on it," I said. "It's a little scarce outside this place. My granny says if you wait too long for pity, you'll miss the train to happiness."

They all smiled, even Cat. Everyone looked a lot more comfortable. It was like we were all trying each other on for size, making adjustments here and there and finding ways to make it work.

"Your granny sounds like a wise old lady," Jade said.

"She is. Well, I guess I am hungry," I said. "Least we'll get something out of this, lunch. I hope I didn't spoil anyone's appetite."

"Not mine!" Misty blurted and put her hand over her mouth.

And then we all laughed.

It felt good, like some of that sunshine after the storm Granny always expected.

3

Doctor Marlowe had a table set up for us in her closed-in back patio. There were large windows facing the pool and yard and a sliding door. It was still raining lightly, the drops zigzagging to outline odd shapes on the glass. Birds flitted from tree to tree, probably excited by the sight of worms that had come out of the dampened earth. The birds were about to enjoy a little feast too, I thought. When I caught sight of my reflection in the glass, I saw I had a smile on my face. It happened so rarely these days, it took me by surprise and I touched my cheek as if to be sure it was me.

I don't often look at birds, I thought. I know they are there where we live with Granny, but I just don't take the time to notice or care. Here, with such beautiful grounds, bushes, hedges, flowers and a small fountain, I felt different, almost as if I was out of the city. I imagined it wasn't as big a deal for the others. They looked like they took it all for granted . . . big houses, birds, trees, flowers and fountains.

"I see your gardener took out those oleanders," Jade said, remembering what Doctor Marlowe had told us the day before.

"Yes. I hated to see them go, but they were dying and had to be replaced."

"My mother doesn't know one flower or bush from the other on our property. She only knows they cost a lot," Misty muttered. "She deliberately got a new gardener recently who's more expensive." She smiled and added, "Because it's part of the agreement she has with Daddy that he has to maintain the property. That was one wham-bam of an argument—the new gardener," she told us gleefully. She had a mischievous looking little smile on her face.

Sophie brought out a jug of lemonade and the pizzas. It occurred to me that if we weren't brought here by our parents, courts and schools, the chances of the four of us sitting around a table and having lunch together were almost as small as Granny winning the lottery. Maybe we had passed each other in some mall or in the lobby of some movie theater, but I was sure we had never looked at each other and actually seen each other. Up until now we were as good as invisible to each other.

"I wasn't sure if everyone liked pizza," Doctor Marlowe said as she took a seat. "It's just a good bet."

"I eat everything," Misty said.

It was something I would have expected Cat to say. She was the one who looked like she could afford to shed some pounds. However, when she ate, she ate like a mouse, nibbling with hesitation like she thought she was going to be caught doing something illegal.

"Of course, my mother thinks that's terrible," Misty continued. "She has this list of foods she pinned on the wall in the kitchen. She calls it her *Ten Most Wanted No-Nos* because they will wreak havoc on your complexion and make you fat. Pizza is at the top of the list," she said, and bit into her piece with added pleasure.

"Momma gave my brother Rodney leftover pizza for breakfast sometimes," I said.

"You're kidding. For breakfast? Did she at least give him a daily vitamin?" Misty asked.

I looked at her as if she was crazy.

"You look pretty good. What's your brother's health like?" Jade asked.

Doctor Marlowe sat back and ate her piece quietly with a tight smile on her lips. It made me feel like we were all being taped for some psychological study she was doing.

"Granny calls him a beanpole. He's almost as tall as I am already. He looks like my daddy more than he does Momma. He's a good boy, shy and quiet, too quiet for his teachers. He's not doing so good in school."

"Well," Jade corrected.

"What?"

"He's not doing so well in school."

"Yes, Miss Perfect," I said. "He's not doing so well. Maybe, if you got the time, you can come over and tutor my brother."

Cat stopped chewing and looked from Jade to me, anticipating more nasty words.

"I'm sorry," Jade said. "It's a habit, correcting people. When I do it to my mother, she gets all flustered. And maybe I will," she added.

"Will what?" Misty asked.

"Tutor her brother. I've done it in school as part of the Big Sister program."

"Sure," I said. "Only, I won't hold my breath."

"People do help each other sometimes," Jade said, "no matter what you think."

"Right," I said. "Look how much we're already helping each other."

She smirked. Maybe we couldn't be friends after all, I thought. Maybe we were what Granny called Momma and Daddy: Oil and Water.

"I hope you girls will eat all this. I don't want to have it in the house. It's too tempting," Doctor Marlowe said. She looked at Cat, who was encouraged to take a real bite.

"Where's Emma today?" Misty asked. I wondered if, like me, she was imagining Emma eating it all. Doctor Marlowe's sister was twice her width.

"She's a little under the weather. She has bad sinus trouble, especially on days like this," Doctor Marlowe explained.

"How long have you and Emma lived in this house?" Jade asked her.

"I've been here all my life. My situation after my parents divorced was a little different from your situations. My sister and I lived with my father because my mother wanted it that way."

"Why?" Misty asked first.

Cat looked up with interest, probably just as eager as the rest of us to know more about the person who was supposed to bring us to all the important answers about ourselves.

"My mother was more into her career than into being a wife and a mother. I suppose that contributed to why they got a divorce in the first place, not that I'm suggesting for one moment she couldn't or shouldn't have had a career."

"So you lived here with your father?" Jade asked.

"Yes, and then Emma returned about twenty-two years ago after her divorce," she said.

"So actually you've lived in the same house all your life?" Misty asked.

"Yes."

"What did your daddy do?" I asked. Since everyone else was badgering her with questions and she wasn't refusing to answer, I thought I might ask something too.

"He was a corporate attorney and my mother taught Drama-speech at UCLA," she revealed. "I saw her often, more often after I had gone to college."

"Are they both dead?" I asked.

"My father is," she said. "My mother is at an adult residency now. She suffers from Alzheimer's disease. You all know what that is?"

"You forget everything," Misty said.

"What a good idea," Jade quipped. Everyone stopped eating and looked at her. She shrugged. "If we could forget everything and then start over like a blank cassette, I mean."

"You don't have to forget the past," Doctor Marlowe said softly. "What you've got to learn to do is handle it, live with it, put it in perspective, keep it from permitting you to have a future.

"After all, that's what we're here to do," she concluded.

No one responded. We continued eating instead, each of us hoping she was right. Misty and Jade got into a conversation about clothes and Misty admitted she had some very nice things to wear when she wanted to, but just felt more comfortable in jeans and T-shirts.

From the way the others acted when Doctor Marlowe offered to show us the rest of the house when we finished eating, I gathered they, like me, were brought only to the office before this. She took us to the living room first and explained some of the paintings her father had purchased in Europe years and years ago. She told us he favored the Impressionists and one of the paintings was an authentic Monet. I didn't know anything much about Art, but I saw that Jade was impressed.

One picture caught all our interests. It was a painting of a little girl, maybe seven or eight, standing by a pond and looking at her own reflection in the water.

"My father liked this one a great deal, too," Doctor Marlowe said, standing behind us. "He told me that to him it was as if the little girl realized for the first time that she was really beautiful."

"That's not supposed to be the first time she'd seen herself, is it?" I asked.

"I don't think so, no."

"Maybe nobody told her she was pretty and so she thought she wasn't," Misty said.

"And she didn't dare hope otherwise," Jade added.

"Maybe they told her she wasn't pretty and she knew they were liars," Cat interjected with more anger in her voice than we had heard before. Misty shifted her eyes to look at her. Jade kept staring at the picture, but nudged me. I looked at Cat. She had her teeth clenched and her eyes looked like they had a little candle behind them.

"Does the painting have a name?" Misty asked.

"It's called *Reflections in a Pond*," Doctor Marlowe said.

"That's it?"

"Sometimes, things are nothing more than what they are," Doctor Marlowe replied.

"If that were the case all the time, you'd be out of work," Jade quipped.

Doctor Marlowe laughed hard. She really roared. It brought smiles to all our faces. I felt so light and happy that I almost didn't want to go back to the office and tell the rest of my story. I knew what that was going to do to our merry mood.

But that's what we had come here to do and anyway, everyone expected it. We all went to the bathroom and then settled back in the office.

"I really appreciate how smoothly things are going here. Thank you, girls," Doctor Marlowe said after we were seated. Then she turned to me.

Here I go again, I thought. It was like getting on a roller coaster.

"I keep saying things got worse after this and worse after that," I began, "so you probably all think it was about as bad as it could be, but it wasn't. It got worse again when Momma got a boyfriend.

"I knew she was going out with different men from time to time, but she never brought anyone home with her before Aaron Marks. He was someone new to the neighborhood and One-Eyed Bill's, which is where they met, of course.

"I gotta say that I never thought Momma was faithful to Daddy when they were together anyway. Whenever Daddy went off on a job that took a few days, I had the feeling Momma was with someone. She'd never admit it to me, of course, but you hear things on the street, hear talk and whatnot and just pick up on it if you wanted to be smart enough.

"Momma'd be with me and meet some girlfriend from One-Eyed Bill's and they'd get to talking and laughing and I could read between the lines that Momma went off with someone, maybe even just to his car behind the bar or something. I was worried she'd get some disease or get pregnant with some other man's baby, but I was afraid to say anything.

"If I looked suspicious or surprised, she'd just say, 'You know Shirley was fooling. She doesn't mean half of what she says, Star. Don't you go saying anything to your Daddy or Granny, hear?'

"If I didn't answer she'd slap me on the arm or shoulder until I turned to her and cried, 'What?'

" 'When I'm talking to you, I expect you to say something. You understand what I told you?'

" 'Yes,' I'd cry.

" 'Well, you just don't make any trouble for me. I got enough trouble without you making any,' she'd say and mumble the rest of the way home.

"I know it sounds like we never had any mother-daughter talks like you all probably have had with your mothers, but we did. Not toward the end, of course, but before things got so bad so that I couldn't look at her, much less talk to her."

I paused and turned to Misty.

"I remember yesterday how you kept asking how two people who were supposedly in love could suddenly hate each other so much. What happened to all the nice things they said to each other and the nice things they did together? I thought about that too and one day, when Momma was sober enough and being nice to Rodney, I asked her something like that.

"I said, 'You loved Daddy once, didn't you, Momma?'

" 'So?' she said.

" 'I was just wondering why you stopped, is all,' I said. I didn't want to spoil her good mood, so I spoke softly and looked down quickly.

" 'Because he's not the man I fell in love with,' she said. 'He fooled me is what happened. When we were first going together, he used to tell me how different he was and how different things were going to be for us. We're not going to be like these poor, drifting folks around us. We're going to build a real home.

" 'He was going to have his own company and I'd be a lady in style. I'd have my own car and we'd have a nice house and on and on he'd go with that web he was spinning to trap me good. That's what he did. I gave myself to him expecting he'd live up to those promises. Every one of them turned out to be just a lot of hot air and when I asked him what happened to all those promises, he said he's doing the best he could, to be patient.

" ' "Be patient? I'm growing old being patient," I told him. Then he'd clam up the way he often did and pretend I wasn't in the room. He could be so infuriating. You know that. You've seen him like that.'

" 'Maybe he was trying,' I risked saying. She didn't get mad. She laughed.

" 'Yeah. Look around you at the palace he built. Men,' she said, 'are born liars. Don't believe a one.'

"She looked down at Rodney playing with his toy truck on the floor and shook her head.

" 'They're so sweet when they're little boys and then something happens to them. They let their thing take over and run their lives and ruin ours,' she said.

"I knew what she was saying, but I just didn't believe she was saying it. Momma and I never really had a heart to heart about sex and stuff. She just assumed I'd learn it like she did, from girlfriends. I guess when your hormones screamed, it was all supposed to just pop into your head and you'd know what to do and what not to do. Most girls didn't know what not," I said. "At least, most I knew."

"My mother didn't exactly offer me any sage advice," Jade said.

"Excuse me?"

"Womanly wisdom," she muttered with that corkscrew smirk of hers.

"Oh. We got taught stuff by the school nurse, of course. She even gave girls sanitary napkins. I remember when I first started getting cramps, I complained to Momma and she just handed me one and told me to wear it just in case.

" 'In case?' I asked her.

" 'Well, look at you,' Momma declared, 'you about to bust out, aren't you? Welcome to woman's misery.'

"That was about all she told me about it. I learned the rest from girlfriends and the nurse's pamphlets. Then one day when I was nearly thirteen it just happened. It was like an explosion inside me. I got this terrible cramp which about folded me over. I couldn't move without the pain. The nurse came down to the classroom to help me back to her office. I saw the other girls laughing behind my back and some of the boys, too, but I was suffering too much to care.

"She had me rest and called home. Momma answered and after the nurse told her about me, Momma said, 'Well, what am I supposed to do about it?'

"The nurse told her she should come for me, but she claimed she couldn't because Rodney was home sick, which I had a feeling was a big fat lie. She was probably with someone and drinking. When I was able to get up and about, I went home myself and discovered I was right.

"That was the first time I met Aaron Marks. The music was loud. They had been drinking gin. Momma was wearing only a slip. When

Momma saw I had entered, she stopped dancing with Aaron and wobbled for a moment and then laughed.

" 'This here's my daughter, Star. She started the monthlies today.' She lifted a glass full of gin and added, 'Let's toast to her happy days.'

"I didn't take much of a look at Aaron Marks that first time. I was so embarrassed, I just made a dash for my bedroom and slammed the door. I heard them laughing and drinking. When Rodney came home, they were in Momma's bedroom. I hurried out and brought him into my room and told him to just stay there. He cried because he had to go to the bathroom so I had to let him out and he heard Momma's laughter and went to her room. The sight of another man in bed with her just put the freeze in his face.

"Rodney ain't only shy. When he gets frightened or upset, he has a hard time talking and starts to stutter. It almost sounds like he's choking on a chicken bone. I grabbed his hand and pulled him back to my room. He sat staring with his eyes full of questions I couldn't even begin to answer for him.

" 'She's drinking again,' I told him. 'We have to wait here until it's over.'

"It was like hiding in a storm basement while a hurricane or tornado passed overhead. I tried to keep him occupied, but every time we heard a laugh or something bang against the wall or on the floor, we both froze and listened, our hearts pounding. I knew Rodney was afraid of the new man in her naked arms, but I didn't know anything more about Aaron Marks than Rodney did at the time.

"I prayed that it would all end soon, but it went on and on that whole afternoon, until Momma passed out and Aaron quietly left the apartment. I heard the front door open and close and then I inched out of my room, leaving Rodney behind. I looked in on Momma. She was naked, facedown on her bed, snoring away.

"Maybe all that made my first period worse. I don't know. I hear that stress and such can make trouble for you in that way."

I gazed at Doctor Marlowe, who nodded slightly.

"I had such bad cramps, I could barely move about the kitchen to make Rodney something for dinner. I finally gave up and just made him a peanut butter sandwich. He was still too scared to eat much anyway.

"He fell asleep on my bed that night and I let him stay even though I had a very bad night and had to get up and change and just walked about moaning and groaning. Some time very late, I heard Momma get up and bang into a chair in the kitchen. I heard her curse and run the water and then she went back to sleep and was still sleeping in the morning. She woke up as I helped Rodney get ready for another day of school.

"I felt like I had been punched and punched in the stomach. I ached right down the back of my legs and I was in a nasty mood myself, so when Momma stuck her head out to ask what was going on, I shouted back at her.

" 'What do you think is going on? It's morning and Rodney slept in my room all night because of your carrying on with that man,' I cried.

"She blinked as if she couldn't remember if she had or not and then she got mad at me for yelling at her and started screaming back.

" 'I ain't got rid of that man you called your daddy just to have you on my back,' she said. 'Don't you go lecturing to me, hear? You don't open your mouth.'

" 'Yeah, well you should learn to keep yours closed,' I snapped back and she looked like her eyes exploded in her head. She came charging across the kitchen to slap me, only I wasn't going to let her slap me anymore. I had been in enough pain all the previous afternoon and night anyway so I pushed a chair in her path and she fell right over it. It stunned her and she just lay there staring up at the ceiling.

"Rodney was in a terrible state. He wasn't just stuttering and frozen now. He was trembling so much that I heard his teeth click. I pushed him up and out of the apartment, taking his hand and walking him out of the building. I forgot everything: my books, my purse, everything, including the sanitary napkins, of course."

"Oh no," Misty groaned.

"Yeah," I said. "I had an accident after I brought him to his school."

"What did you do?" Cat asked. She was leaning toward me now, her hands clasped on her lap.

"I wanted to go to Granny's but I didn't have any money for the bus, so I had no choice. I had to make my way home. I practically snuck back into the apartment. Momma was back in bed with a cold rag over her forehead. She didn't hear me. I tiptoed around, got what I needed, changed, and then slipped out of the apartment. I was late to school and they sent me to the assistant principal, Mr. McDermott, who wanted to put me in detention because I had a record of tardiness that stretched from one side of his office to the other. That's what he told me.

"I told him I couldn't stay. I had to be home for my little brother. He said if I didn't, I'd be in bigger trouble and he told me that my mother would just have to take care of my little brother. That's when I guess I went a little nuts. That was the first time."

I paused. Even though I had eaten plenty at lunch, I suddenly had this terribly empty feeling in my stomach made worse by the sensation of a fistful of worms crawling around in there. I squirmed, took a breath and closed my eyes. I felt dizzy and had to lay back.

"Let's all give Star a couple of minutes," Doctor Marlowe said. "I meant to show you all my library," she added. "Star, take a little break," she added. "Lie down for a moment if you like."

I did and I heard them all leave.

"She'll be fine," I heard Doctor Marlowe tell them just outside of the office. Their footsteps died away.

Whenever I recalled Momma falling over that chair and hitting the floor, I remember the way Rodney's mouth opened wide, but nothing came out. Where did that scream go? I wondered. If you swallow back a scream, does it echo in your heart? There is something extra terrifying about seeing your mother or your father faint, fall, get hurt. They're your parents and in your mind, as silly as it may be, you think they are like Superman and Superwoman. Nothing happens to parents. Parents are there to take care of us. We get sick. We fall and scrape our knees. We burn ourselves and do silly and stupid things, but they are always there to comfort and look after us. We're too young and frightened to take care of them. Nothing happens to them.

Momma didn't have an iota of dignity when she flopped over that chair. She flailed about like a fish out of water for a few moments and groaned. As I hurried Rodney out, I looked back at her and saw her dazed expression. She didn't know why she was on the floor. It had surprised and frightened her more than it had hurt her.

The tears were streaming down Rodney's face so fast, I couldn't wipe them off. As soon as the ones on his cheeks were gone, they were followed by more until I held him tightly and promised him things would be all right.

"I'll go back and help her," I promised. "You just go to school and everything will be all right later. You'll see."

He stopped trembling and after we walked some more, he calmed down enough to at least go to school. But the memory of all that was too much for me to swallow. It came up and up like bad food and I had this rush of dizziness and the trembles.

It passed after a few calm moments and I felt my breathing get regular again. I sat up, drank some water and went to the window. The rain had stopped. Sunlight was slicing through the clouds, turning the drops into jewels on the leaves and on the grass. Everything glittered and looked fresh and clean.

It really wasn't much of a storm, I thought, but it was something, and now look how beautiful the world becomes.

Why can't that be the same for us?

Why can't Doctor Marlowe help us spread the dark clouds apart and let in some sunshine?

I heard them coming back and sucked in my breath, willing to try, willing to hope.

That was something, at least.

Wasn't it?

4

"How are you doing?" Doctor Marlowe asked as soon as they were all back in the office.

"I'm okay," I said.

"We can stop for today," she suggested.

I saw the looks of concern on the other girls' faces. They looked sincere, worried.

"I'm all right," I said more firmly. "I'd rather get it all out and finished than have to sleep on it and come back and do it again tomorrow."

Doctor Marlowe looked at the girls and they all took their seats. I remained standing, my arms folded under my breasts. I felt like one of those lawyers on television talking to a jury. Doctor Marlowe was the judge and the other girls were the jury, but who did I want to make look guilty? Just my parents or the whole world?

"Doctor Marlowe always says we should try to face our demons head on," I said.

Jade nodded. Misty's lips relaxed into a small smile and Cat stared intensely, making me think hard about every single word.

"I hate remembering that day, but I hate being afraid of the memory more. Anyway, after the assistant principal threatened me again, I just started screaming and pounding my own legs. It felt good, like I was unloading all this weight. I guess he'd never seen anything like it and went rushing out for the nurse. She came back with him. By that time, I was pulling on my hair and shaking my head so hard, I could feel my neck twisting to the point of snapping. The nurse put her arm around me and tried to hold me.

" 'Call for the paramedics!' she ordered and the assistant principal ran out again to do it. I did calm down, but I couldn't stop gasping. I had painful hiccups too. The paramedics came in and got me to lay down on the stretcher. They buckled me in and rolled me out of the office and put me in the ambulance.

"There were lots of kids watching from windows and from the doorway, but I didn't care.

"At the hospital emergency room, they lifted me onto a table in an examination room and left me there. A nurse looked in on me from time to time and kept telling me the doctor would come soon, but I think I was there for almost an hour before any doctor showed up. I kept dozing off and waking to the sounds in the hallway: people crying, orders being shouted, footsteps and stretchers being rolled.

"They called Momma but she didn't answer. She had gone out, I guess. That's what she told everyone later anyway. The nurse came in to ask me if I knew where she might be and I told her about One-Eyed Bill's.

"Finally, the doctor saw me. I was asleep when he came and he woke me up and told me I'd be fine and I didn't even need any medicines. I remember thinking he was very young, too young to be a real doctor.

" 'What I believe you experienced was an anxiety attack,' he said. 'You've got some heavy personal problems,' he added.

"He recommended I see the hospital psychologist. When Momma finally showed up, he told her the same thing and wrote out the name of the doctor.

"She was angry more than worried because it cost her two cab fares, one to come down to get me and then one to get me back home. From what I could tell, she couldn't remember what had happened that morning. She told the young doctor I'd be all right and I didn't need to see a psychologist and besides, there was no money for such things. We didn't have health insurance.

"So I went home with her and went to bed. She gave Rodney dinner and then I woke up because she was moving Rodney's cot-bed and things into my room. She pretended she was doing it for me, but I would soon learn she was doing it because she wanted to bring Aaron Marks home with her and Aaron didn't want a child in the same room.

"Momma then went off to work at One-Eyed Bill's as if nothing had happened. Rodney didn't understand why I had been in a hospital, but he was happy to be in my room, staying as close to me as he could. I was so tired from my period and the events, I couldn't keep my eyes open. I remember I helped him go to sleep and then I slept so deeply, I thought I dreamed hearing Momma come home, hearing her laughter and Aaron's voice. It was real late.

"I woke before Rodney did the next morning and I sat up thinking about my dreams, wondering how much was true and how much was imagined. A little afraid and a little curious, I slipped off the bed and walked barefoot to the door of Momma's bedroom. It was shut tight, but I opened it slowly and quietly and peeked in to find Aaron Marks beside her in the bed, the both of them naked, their arms twisted around each other like pipe cleaners.

"I closed the door and quickly retreated to my bedroom, still feeling too sick to have an appetite or to want to get up and dress.

"Rodney got himself up and all, but he didn't want to go to school. I had to force him. I wanted him out of the house so he wouldn't see Aaron there. I stayed in my room until I heard Aaron get up and go.

"The school nurse called and I told her I was fine and resting. Momma still hadn't gotten up. When I went out to the kitchen though, she shouted for me to make her some coffee and bring it to her.

" 'As long as you're home, you might as well be of some use,' she said.

"I made her the coffee and brought it to her. She groaned and sat up, keeping her eyes closed as if the lids had been turned to lead. After a sip, she fluttered them open. They were so bloodshot, I could barely make out the pupils.

" 'Your brother off to school?' she asked. Why didn't she think of that first? I thought.

" 'Yes. That man was here with you last night,' I said.

" 'So? Get used to it. I ain't becoming a nun just because your no-good-for-nothing of a father deserted me. Truth is, he wasn't much of a lover-man anyway.'

"I didn't want to hear any more of it so I went back to my room. She spent almost the whole morning sleeping and then she went to work earlier, probably to meet up with Aaron, I thought. As usual, I made Rodney supper and helped him with his schoolwork. By now we were almost by ourselves in the world anyway.

"When I returned to school the next day, the assistant principal didn't bother me. Most of the other kids had found out about my episode in his office and there was gossip, but after a while, they lost interest in it and for me it was just like a bad dream.

"This particular episode had all begun with my first period. That was my entrance to womanhood," I added. "For a while after, every time I got my period, I thought about all those events. Maybe remembering made it worse for me each time. Things certainly didn't get any easier around the house and Aaron was there more than I wanted him to be.

The more Momma did with him, the less she did for Rodney and me, not that she ever did all that much.

"There were times when we didn't have what to eat and I had to go look for her to get some money. She tried having a charge account at the Spanish grocery on the block, but when she failed to pay the bill on time twice, they stopped letting us charge things. Rodney was eating so much peanut butter, he could have made commercials for the company.

"He was outgrowing shoes and clothes, but Momma didn't seem to notice or care unless I pointed it out and then there was all the complaining about how much things cost and where was my good-for-nothing father who could make a kid but not care for him? If Momma was drunk, she could rant about this for hours. I'd hear her voice in my dreams. I used to think her shouting and hollering got stuck on the walls like glue and just played itself over and over until I was sleeping with my hands over my ears or my pillow over my head.

"It's raining pain, I would tell myself. Once, when Momma began one of her frequent tirades, I actually went to the closet, took out the umbrella and opened it, holding it between me and her. She went wild, screaming about all the bad luck I was bringing into the house.

" 'What about all you're bringing in?' I screamed back and she threw a frying pan at me. It would have hit me if I didn't have the umbrella and use it like a shield.

"Rodney started to cry so I scooped him up and went to my room, shutting the door. She kept yelling for a while and then settled down, but while she did, I held Rodney and petted his hair and kept him from crying. It got harder and harder for me to handle it all until one day, I did something that helped, something that really could stop the rain of pain."

"I'd like to hear about that," Jade said. "Nothing really helps me."

"Me too," Cat added softly, almost under her breath. "What stopped your pain?"

Misty just had that happy-go-lucky smile on her face as if she knew.

"I had a blanket when I was little that Daddy once jokingly called my magic carpet. It stuck in my head and when I saw the movie *Aladdin* and saw the magic carpet, it made a big impression on me."

"So you went flying off on your blanket?" Jade asked with disappointment darkening her eyes.

"I suppose I did," I said.

"What?" Misty said, her smile widening. She looked at Jade, who grimaced, shook her head and raised her eyes toward the ceiling.

"Go on and laugh, but it worked for me."

"What worked for you?" Jade demanded. "You're not making any sense."

"I took my blanket and put it on my bed and lay down on it, folded myself up so my knees almost touched my stomach. It felt better that way."

"Oh," Jade said as if she thought that was it: a way to ease the menstrual cramps.

"And then I left," I added.

"Left?"

"Yeah, I guess I left in my imagination, but it helped. I saw myself flying off, out the window and out the city. I went to every place I ever dreamed about or saw on television and wished I was.

"I floated over the ocean, over forests and other cities. I actually saw things as if I was up high, everything looking so small like toys. My imaginary trips took long too because when I returned to my bed, more than an hour passed sometimes and I always felt better.

"It got so I began to lay on my blanket whenever I was unhappy or Momma made me mad. I'd just wander off to my room, spread the blanket out on the bed and spread myself over it, folding my legs and closing my eyes. Then I was gone and I didn't hear anything, not Momma's stream of complaints or drunken laughter or shouts at Rodney. I was gone.

"When I came back, I felt refreshed, lighter. Rodney would tell me he had shaken me to tell me something and I didn't open my eyes. He said he shook me hard and finally, he gave up. Once, he did it and just sat on the floor waiting and when I opened my eyes, he said he had been watching my face and I had been smiling so much. He wanted to know why. I didn't want to tell him so I just said I had had a good dream."

"That's all it was anyway, right?" Jade asked, looking to Doctor Marlowe, "a dream? She didn't go anywhere."

Doctor Marlowe hesitated before responding and looked at me as if she was deciding whether or not to bust my bubble.

"It might have been more than just a dream," she said. "It might be a form of meditation. I meditate myself," she confessed.

"I really don't know what that is," Misty said. "I thought it was the same as dreaming."

"No. When you dream you are really still in a conscious state but the mind is being bombarded by different images you don't control. Dreams are more or less random. You can deliberately think of things, but there's no guarantee you'll dream about them after you've fallen asleep. Meditation is a higher form. In meditation, you deliberately set out to put your mind on another plane, another level. What Star was doing was concentrating so hard on her desire to leave her surroundings, she took herself to a higher plane and the result was it relaxed her. People meditate to avoid stress."

"Can we do that, too?" Jade asked.

"Yes. After we've all had an opportunity to talk, we'll discuss ways to relieve the tension and stress you're all experiencing and one of those techniques will involve some meditation. I'm not suggesting it's the cure-all, but it can help."

"I always did feel better," I emphasized. The others looked at me with envy. "Sometimes, I wished I never came back," I said.

Doctor Marlowe's face grew darker, her eyes more intensely on me.

"There's always that danger," she said. "We're here to make sure that doesn't happen." She looked at the others. "To any of you."

Maybe it was the way she said it or the way the others looked after she had said it, but suddenly it occurred to me how serious all this was, how we were all walking along the edge of different cliffs and how we could misstep and fall or deliberately fall into our own private oblivion. The atmosphere in Doctor Marlowe's office suddenly seemed heavier, all of us lost for a moment or two, thinking about our personal danger. I didn't know Jade's story or Cat's yet, but I looked from face to face and saw an identical terror in their eyes. I saw the concern in Doctor Marlowe's too and I remembered what Granny had said when she had dropped me off this morning.

"You're too young to become someone's lost cause, hear?"

I hear, Granny, I thought. I hear.

They were all waiting for me to continue. I took a breath and did so.

"I was listening closely to you yesterday, Misty, when you started talking about how you felt about your father's girlfriend and about going to his apartment when you knew she was there with him and what it was like for you," I said. "But at least you could choose to go or not.

"I was about fifteen by now. One afternoon when I came home from school with Rodney, we saw suitcases and a couple of boxes in Momma's room. She wasn't there. Rodney looked at me and I thought first, maybe it's Daddy. Maybe he's finally come back.

"Rodney couldn't remember him, but I could, of course. Lots of times I have come here and talked about how I felt about my daddy, so I guess I should talk a little more about him. I told you how I was always hoping that he would return and how I always hoped the phone was ringing because he was on the other end ready to tell Momma he was on his way.

"We all talked about hate here, maybe me more than anyone yet.

Maybe Jade and Cat are going to say a lot more when their turn comes, but my granny isn't wrong when she says hate is a two-edged sword. Yeah, you stick it in someone, but you're sticking it in yourself at the same time. That's what the minister said in church one Sunday when I went with Granny. She kept shifting her eyes at me as he preached about driving the hate out of your heart before it rots the good in you.

"Nothing made me hate my daddy more than his leaving us, and nothing made me want him more. When I was little and we had some good times, I remember him carrying me on his shoulders. I remember holding onto his hand, feeling how tight and strong a grip he had, and I remember never being afraid as long as he was with us.

"After he left and me and Momma and Rodney went anywhere, I couldn't help but feel this empty place beside us. Sometimes, I'd forget and think Daddy just walked away for a moment. He will be standing right next to me soon. Of course, he wouldn't, but that didn't stop me from glancing to the side and thinking about him.

"Momma's a tough little woman. I don't think too many people, including men, would want to tangle with her. She could be a wildcat, so it wasn't that I was physically afraid. I just felt . . . like we were less, if that makes any sense," I said.

Misty looked like she understood more than the other two. Jade turned her eyes from me and Cat stared at the floor.

"What I mean is it didn't help me just to have another man come into our house. It didn't make me feel better or safer. If anything, I think it went the other way.

"But that's what those boxes and suitcases meant: Aaron Marks was moving in to live with Momma. I could smell him in the room already.

" 'Whose is that?' Rodney wanted to know. 'Are we moving away, Star? Did Momma pack us up?'

" 'No Rodney. We aren't moving anywhere. We're stuck here.'

"About two hours later, the door opened. Momma and Aaron came in, both laughing. I was mashing up some potatoes for Rodney to have with his hamburger. Momma was dressed in her Sunday clothes and Aaron was in a suit with the tie loose. He was not quite as tall as my daddy and much wider in the hips with a little paunch. His head was rounder and his hair was thinner, showing a lot more forehead, which I thought made his eyes look larger. He had a nose with a bump in it because it had been broken a few times. He had tried to be a prizefighter when he was younger and ended up being one of those sparring partners that gets his head beat in regularly, which was what I thought accounted for his dull, dumb face and empty eyes.

"As you can tell, I was never fond of Aaron. I never could understand what Momma saw in him and when I said so once, she just laughed
and said, 'When you start being with a man, you'll understand what matters most about him.'

"I wasn't stupid. I understood she meant sex.

"Anyway, I stood there, gazing at the two of them, both wearing
these big fat grins that put little drops of ice down my back and around
my heart. I reached out and pulled Rodney closer to me and he held
onto my leg.

" 'Well, there she is, my little cook,' Momma cried. 'Or our little
cook.'

" 'What are you talking about, Momma? What's going on?'

"Aaron laughed and went to the cabinet below the sink where
Momma stored her vodka, gin and bourbon. He took out the bourbon
and said it was time for another celebration.

" 'Right you are about that,' Momma cried.

"I watched him pour them each half a glass of bourbon and then
toast and drink. Rodney didn't fully understand what booze was, but he
hated the smell and the taste and just knew that whenever Momma
drank some, she was usually unpleasant and often frightening, so he
clung tighter to me.

" 'Why are you celebrating, Momma?' I finally asked.

"The two of them looked at each other and laughed as if I had asked
the silliest question.

" 'Momma?'

" ' 'Cause Aaron and I just got married,' she said.

"Naturally, I grimaced and shook my head.

" 'You can't marry Aaron, Momma. You're already married,' I told
her.

"The smile flew off her face like a frightened sparrow and she
slammed her glass down on the counter so hard, it almost shattered.

" 'A man just walks out of here one day and never calls,' she said
pointing at the door, 'never comes back, never sends a note, and goes off
with another woman and I'm still supposed to be married to him? No
ma'am, I'm not.'

" 'Don't you have to go to a court, though?' I asked.

" 'Courts mean lawyers and lawyers are just crooks who hang out a
shingle off their doors,' she said. 'Aaron and I talked it over and I declared, officially declared that is,' she added pulling up her shoulders
and standing as straight as she could, 'that I ain't married to Kenny
Fisher no more. I declared it this afternoon and then we went over to

Preacher Longstreet down in South Central and he married us right and proper with a Bible and all. I even got a ring,' she bragged and stuck out her hand. It didn't look like much of a ring, but I didn't say so.

" 'Don't you have to get a license and stuff?' I asked.

" 'Will you stop with all those questions. Just say hello to your new daddy,' she ordered.

"I turned back to the potatoes.

" 'Star, you hear me? You show your new daddy respect, hear?'

" 'He's not my daddy,' I said.

" 'What? What did you say?'

"She started for me, but Aaron held her back.

" 'Hold on now, Aretha,' he said. 'We don't want any unpleasantries tonight on our wedding night. Our honeymoon,' he added and she stopped fighting him and smiled.

" 'You're right, Aaron.' She looked at me, her eyes shooting darts across the kitchen. 'We'll talk about this later. Aaron and I are going out for a celebration dinner. I just want to freshen up a bit,' she said and went to the bathroom.

"I continued to work on Rodney's dinner and he held onto me the whole time. It was difficult to breathe, not to be drowned by everything that was happening so fast.

" 'That boy looks like a sissy holding onto you like that,' Aaron said. A terrible anger washed over me. I felt the heat rise into my face.

"I turned and glared at him, gave him my coldest look and said, 'He'll grow up to be easily twice the man you are, not that it would be hard to do.'

"He stared at me for a moment and I saw rage start to build in his eyes, but suddenly he stopped it as if he knew he might lose control of himself if he didn't. He laughed, but it was one of those soft, unsure laughs, a laugh to cover up his own discomfort.

"I didn't stop glaring at him and he pointed his thick, crooked right forefinger at me.

" 'Your momma's right about you. You're too sassy. We'll deal with it later,' he said and went to the bedroom to start unpacking and moving in."

I paused and looked at the other girls. Each in her eyes showed she understood what a low moment that was for me and my little brother. I didn't even have to ask, but I did.

"How would you like that to happen to you?"

Doctor Marlowe's face brightened with interest and excitement as she looked at them and waited.

"They make decisions about our lives as if we were nothing more than ornaments on Christmas trees," Jade said, her eyes darkening as she fixed on her own thoughts.

"My daddy never even told me he was seeing someone else, much less look for my opinion about it," Misty said.

Cat remained quiet, but her eyes filled with a cold look of fear that made me wonder again how different her life had been and what troubles she had seen, troubles so bad they had stolen her voice and her smile.

"Yeah, well despite what Aaron and Momma threatened, Momma didn't say anything more about it to me that night. She and Aaron went to their celebration and came home very late. Their door was closed when I got up the next morning. Rodney and I had our breakfast and left without seeing them, which was fine with me.

"Aaron supposedly worked for a used-car dealer, but I always thought he did something else on the side, something illegal. After he moved in, there were lots of phone calls for him at all hours of the night, and he would always talk too low for me to hear.

"Right from the start, I was never comfortable with him in the house and especially uncomfortable when he was there without Momma. Most of the time, he was out or with Momma at One-Eyed Bill's, but when he wasn't, he made both me and Rodney nervous and Rodney would just retreat from the living room and stay in our bedroom. It wasn't a big apartment, probably not much bigger than this office, and we had only one bathroom for all of us to share.

"But I want to say right away that he never tried anything with me. I know that's the first thing everyone's supposed to think, but he didn't and he had his reasons, which he came out and told me once."

"I'd like to hear about that," Jade said.

"I thought you might."

"What's that supposed to mean?" she fired back.

We stared at each other for a moment and then she smiled and I just laughed and shook my head. Cat's eyes filled with confusion and she looked at Misty.

"Maybe after dealing with us you oughta rethink the use of the word *crazy,* Doctor Marlowe," she said.

Doctor Marlowe laughed.

"The only place I approve of its use is in the Patsy Cline song," she said.

"Who's Patsy Cline?" Misty asked and looked from me to Jade.

"She's a country singer, or was, right?" Jade asked Doctor Marlowe.

"Yes."

"Oh."

"There is other music besides hip-hop and rock, girls."

"I know who she is," Cat said. "My father listened to her music, but my mother threw all of his stuff out of the house after he was gone, just like Misty's mother did, except my mother even got rid of the bed-sheets, blankets and pillowcases he had used."

No one spoke. We could hear footsteps in the hallway, a door close and then the sound of a vacuum cleaner Sophie had started.

"So, are we going to hear more about Aaron Marks or not?" Jade asked impatiently.

"He's not that interesting to hear about," I said, "but yeah, I'll tell you more about Aaron.

"I'll tell you more about it all."

5

"Early one evening about two months later, I gave Rodney dinner and then decided to take a bath. I had my portable CD going with my earphones on and I didn't hear Aaron come home. He rushed into the apartment and moments later, he was in the bathroom."

"Didn't you lock the door?" Jade asked.

"The lock was broken some time ago and nobody bothered to fix it," I said.

I was about to continue when I looked up at her, and I noticed Cat was twisting her left hand so hard, I couldn't imagine it not hurting her. I studied her and noticed her legs begin to tremble. Her knees were practically knocking together.

I glanced at Doctor Marlowe, who was studying Cat even harder than I was. She leaned over and took Cathy's right hand to stop her from twisting her left. Cat's legs slowed their trembling.

"It's all right, Cathy," Doctor Marlowe nearly whispered. "We're listening to Star now."

Cathy looked up at her and a calm seemed to settle in those frantic eyes.

"Okay?" Doctor Marlowe asked.

Cat nodded. Doctor Marlowe smiled, patted her hand and sat back.

"Sorry," she said. I still hesitated. "Everyone's fine, Star. Go on."

"It's not that bad so nobody's got to go get worked up or nothing," I muttered.

"We'll be the judge of that," Jade said. "What you think is bad and what I think is bad might not be the same thing."

"Well, who says you're right?"

"Nobody says I'm right. It just might not be the same, that's all. You don't have to jump down my throat every time I open my mouth," she whined.

"Well, then don't say you'll be judging me. I don't need you to judge me."

"I didn't mean that literally. If you weren't so trigger-happy . . ."

"Girls," Doctor Marlowe warned before I could respond. She flashed a "no" at me.

I sat back, holding my eyes on Jade a moment longer. She turned away and crossed one leg over the other.

"I saw the bathroom door open and I screamed when Aaron came in. He acted as if I wasn't even there. He went to the sink, opened the cabinet and found his razor and shaving cream. Really feeling sick, I still managed to find a voice.

" 'Get out of here!' I cried pulling off the earphones. 'I'm taking a bath.'

" 'Got to shave fast,' he muttered, looking at his ugly face in the mirror. 'I have to meet your mother in ten minutes. We got tickets to the heavyweight exhibition fight, but we can't be late or we'll lose the seats and they're great seats.'

" 'I don't care. I'm taking a bath. Get out!' I screamed now, covering myself the best I could.

"He looked down at me.

" 'I won't be but a few minutes and I ain't interested in you so don't worry,' he said. 'I don't touch virgins,' he bragged."

"What?" Jade said, coming back to life and turning to me. "He said he won't touch virgins?"

"That's what he said. He started to shave and kept talking, telling me that virgins were too much trouble and he preferred a woman who was broken in like a good riding horse. He laughed at his own joke.

"Meanwhile, I nearly shriveled to nothing in the water, of course, but he didn't look at me. He was more interested in himself. He finished shaving and rushed out again.

"My heart was pounding and I was furious. After he put on his suit and tie, he came hurrying back just after I had gotten out of the tub. I had the towel wrapped around me, but before I could protest, he grabbed his hairbrush, swiped himself a few times, and then turned and asked me, had the nerve to ask me, how he looked.

" 'Like a moron!' I screamed at him.

"He stood there, chewing his lip for a moment, nodded and then walked out of the apartment. That night I fixed the lock, even though it wasn't strong enough to hold him back if he ever wanted to come in."

"Did you tell your mother what happened?" Misty asked.

"No. She didn't get home until very late and even if I got up to talk to her, she wouldn't have been in any sort of condition to listen or care.

"Besides, what was I going to complain about? She would only have defended him for having to hurry and she'd say I was lollygagging in the tub or something. She'd defend him no matter what. I sensed that from the start."

"I always thought most mothers would defend their children no matter what," Misty muttered.

Jade snorted and Cathy shook her head.

"Not no matter what," Cathy said in a voice just a shade above a whisper.

"Momma never wanted us and she never made a big secret of it," I said.

"What was your grandmother doing all this time you were living with that monster in your house?" Jade asked, not hiding her anger.

"She wouldn't have hesitated to come over and get me and Rodney if I told her all the grimy details," I said, "but I couldn't for a long time."

"Why not?" Misty asked.

"About a month before Aaron moved in with us, Granny had a heart attack," I said. It brought tears to my eyes just to mention it. "I didn't even know it had happened for two days afterward. Momma had kept it to herself. She probably knew I'd want to get down to the hospital right away and she didn't want to deal with it. She actually went to work the night they took Granny into the hospital. I found that out later, too.

"One of Granny's friends, Mary Wiggins, luckily had come to visit with her just minutes after Granny lost her breath and sat herself down on the floor in front of the sofa in her living room. That's the way Mary found her, clutching her breast, her eyes closed, gasping.

"She had the sense to call nine-one-one immediately and then tried to keep Granny calm. Granny was calm, even though she was struggling to breathe. I never saw anyone as calm about her own possible death as Granny. She has this abiding faith in the hereafter."

"What about you?" Misty asked. She looked at me like my answer really would matter to her.

"I always thought that if things were going to be good afterward, why couldn't they be good now? No one's looking after me in this world, why should I expect anyone will be in the next?" I told her. She nodded slowly, thinking. "We'll probably be on our own just as much," I added.

"My mother says this whole life is just a test," Cat offered.

"Yeah, well, I'd just as soon cheat and pass then," I said.

Jade laughed and Misty folded her face into a small smile, like someone half in and half out of a dream.

"Anyway, the way I found out about Granny was the hospital called for Momma while she was working. Granny wanted some things from her apartment and had asked the nurse to contact Momma. I felt real stupid not knowing she was in the hospital, stupid and angry.

"As soon as I hung up the phone, I searched through the dresser drawers in Momma's bedroom until I found where she hid some money. It was suppertime, but I grabbed Rodney's hand and dragged him out with me to the waiting taxicab that took us to the hospital. When we got there, I bought Rodney a candy bar to keep him satisfied while I went up to what they call the CCU and asked for Mrs. Patton. I thought they might not let me in, but when the nurse heard I was her granddaughter, she said it was okay. She said, 'It's about time someone came to visit her.'

"I started to cry and told her I had just learned my granny was there. My mother hadn't told me. The nurse softened her disapproving look and took me to Granny's bedside. She said Granny was doing very well, that the doctors decided there wasn't very much damage to her heart muscle, but she would have what they called angina pain from time to time. It was treatable, she said. I guess she was happy to finally have someone to talk to about Granny, someone who cared and would listen.

"Granny was surprised but happy to see me. I told her how Momma hadn't said a word and she just pressed her lips together and shook her head.

" 'It's okay. She probably didn't want you worrying,' Granny told me.

"She could forgive Judas," I said.

"Who?" Misty asked.

"Judas. You know, the one who betrayed Jesus."

"Oh."

"I guess you never went to Sunday school."

"Hardly," she said laughing. "The only prayers I ever heard in my house were, 'God, please don't let that be a gray hair.' "

Jade really laughed and Cat widened her eyes and stretched her mouth in glee.

"Anyway, I stayed with her as long as I could and then I took Rodney to the hospital cafeteria and bought him and me some sandwiches with some of the money I had found in Momma's dresser drawer. Then I did to her what she had done to me."

"What was that?" Jade asked quickly.

"I didn't tell her anything. I got a cab home and Rodney and I did some schoolwork, watched some television and went to bed. I heard Momma come home at night, but I didn't go out to talk to her. In the morning, she was sleeping when Rodney and I got up. I fixed his breakfast and after we both got ready for school, I left without telling her a thing about my hospital visit.

"She was home when we got back from school, but I never mentioned anything then either. I could tell she hadn't called the hospital because Granny would surely have said something about my visiting her.

"Momma didn't find out until the day after that when she finally checked on Granny, who I knew had been moved out of the CCU and into a room for a few more days of observation. I came home with Rodney and Momma was confused almost as much as she was upset. It was like she couldn't understand what had happened. Had she told me or hadn't she? I could see the uncertainty in her eyes.

" 'Why didn't you tell me you saw Granny in the hospital?' she demanded. 'You made me look like a fool.'

" 'You don't need me to do that. You do it yourself,' I said and she slapped me.

" 'Don't you talk back to me like that!' she screamed.

" 'Why didn't you tell me about Granny?' I wailed through my tears. 'The nurses thought nobody cared about her. You didn't even call to see how she was doing.'

" 'It's none of their damn business. Everybody sticks their nose in my life. I didn't tell you 'cause I knew you'd go off on me and carry on and make things harder.'

"She paused, thinking for a moment.

" 'How did you get there and back?' she asked. 'Where'd you get the money for carfare?'

"I didn't answer and she went stomping into her room and searched her drawer.

" 'You stole from me!' she screamed. 'You went and took my rainy day stash.'

" 'That wasn't there for a rainy day, Momma,' I said. 'It's been raining around here for some time and you never touch it until you want to buy yourself some vodka or whiskey,' I fired back at her.

"She gaped at me, raised her finger to point and then looked at Rodney, who was staring up at her with his eyes full of fear. It slowed her down and all she did was shake her head.

" 'You two kids are punishment for me, that's all. I'm being punished for having you.'

" 'What should we say, Momma? We don't drink and get into fights at One-Eyed Bill's. I don't bring a man home to be in my bed,' I said, the tears streaming down my cheeks, 'look how we're being punished.'

" 'You're a regular smarty pants,' she said nodding her head slowly. 'Okay, don't feel sorry for me, a woman with kids deserted. I only hope nothing like this happens to you someday. Then you'll be sorry for what you say to me,' she whined. 'I do my best with what little I have.'

"She sat herself down and sobbed. Rodney, who started trembling and crying himself, went to her when she held open her arms and she clung to him, crying over him, trying to make me feel like I was the bad one. In the end I did say I was sorry and she cried about how she wished she could do more for her old, sick mother, but she was just overwhelmed and I should be understanding.

"I didn't say anything more. A little less than a week later, Granny went home from the hospital. We went to visit her and she did seem okay. Most of the visit, Momma complained about her own problems anyway, so Granny wouldn't have had a chance to talk about herself much even if it was in her nature to do so, which it wasn't.

"I checked on her as much as I could, took the bus to see her whenever I had the chance, and then, as I told you, Aaron moved in and our lives were turned even more topsy-turvy for a while.

"Before Daddy had left, Momma at least did a little something for Rodney and me. There were times she did the cooking and she went shopping for stuff we needed. Sometimes, when she drank, she got all maudlin and sobbed, clinging to Rodney and acting as if she was sorry for us. That was about the only time she gave him any real affection.

"I was always more or less on my own, but at least she cared something about him.

"However, after she started with Aaron, she acted more and more like a woman without any responsibilities. Everything that had to be done for us was an effort. She wanted to be free to party and sleep late every morning.

"I got so I didn't care. As I said, I didn't have any social life of my own. I never went to a school party and rarely went to the movies. If I did, I'd have to take Rodney along with me because Momma was never there to watch him at night, especially on the weekend.

"Her conscience reared its weak head from time to time, but when it did, she moaned and groaned about how she had been cheated of her youth by a man who had made her pregnant with me. When Daddy was there, she'd try to make him feel guilty about it. He used to say, 'From the way you talk, Aretha, people might think I raped you.'

"And she would counter with, 'That's what it was. You didn't tie me down, but you tricked me, Kenny Fisher. You bedazzled me before I had enough sense to stop you.'

"He'd laugh at that. He'd look at me and laugh at her. Yesterday, Misty, you were talking about how your parents complained about each other to you. That's what mine did, too, only I was too young to understand most of it. Daddy would turn to me as he laughed and talk about Momma and then she would turn to me and do the same and I'd look from one to the other, not knowing whether I should smile, laugh or burst into tears. Yeah, I got so I wanted to put my hands over my ears like you, too.

"It got so I didn't have to, though. I'd stop hearing them even though they were shouting at me. I didn't see them either. I know because suddenly, I'd blink and discover they were both gone. Daddy had left the house and Momma was in the bedroom mumbling to the mirror.

"I didn't have my magic carpet then, but I guess I still left."

I reached for my glass of water and took a sip. How different all their faces were now, I thought. Jade didn't look as arrogant to me anymore. Misty had lost that cute smile and Cat, who looked everywhere but at me most of the time, stared with eyes that were full of sympathy and understanding.

"One day Aaron and Momma started talking about a vacation they wanted to take. They were planning on driving north to San Francisco where Aaron supposedly had some acquaintances who owed him a good time. The plan was to leave us with Granny. I didn't mind that. I was actually looking forward to it.

"But a few days later, Rodney was burning up with fever when I went to wake him in the morning. He was so hot, my fingers actually jumped back from his cheeks. I couldn't get him to really wake up. He groaned and his eyes were so glassy, I couldn't imagine him seeing anything.

"I shouted for Momma who immediately started complaining about being woken until I got her into the bedroom and she touched him herself. She looked real scared and that made me more afraid.

" 'We better get him over to the hospital emergency room,' she said and went back to wake Aaron. Both of them looked like they were the ones with fevers. Aaron practically had to have his eyelids pinned open. We wrapped Rodney in his blanket and Momma carried him out to Aaron's car.

"I'd been to the emergency room a few times before in my life besides that time with Rodney when he needed stitches. It was always crowded with people, each one looking sicker than the next. Everyone in the waiting lounge is coughing or sneezing, moaning and looking like they're moments away from dying, so even though Rodney was so bad, we couldn't get him any immediate attention. We sat there for nearly two hours. Aaron fell asleep in his chair and Momma got into one of her mean moods and bitched so much, she made the nurses furious at her.

"I thought Rodney would be the one to suffer for that. They wouldn't rush to help us now. I tried to tell her that. Granny always says you can get more with honey than you can with vinegar, but Momma was just so angry her life had been disrupted, she wanted to take it out on anyone she could.

"Finally, they called us in and the doctor began to examine Rodney. They had to run tests and we were there for nearly five more hours before the doctor came out to see Momma to tell her Rodney had an infection in his spinal cord.

" 'I think we're going to get to it in time with antibiotics to prevent a really serious situation, but he's a sick little boy for now,' he said.

" 'Well, why the hell you make us wait out here so long? I knew that boy was sick. I just knew it. Mommas know these things,' she lectured.

" 'There are many sick people here, Mrs. Fisher,' the doctor said calmly. 'We do the best we can.'

"Of course that wasn't good enough for her. She just repeated herself. Finally, he left us to get Rodney into treatment. He said Rodney would be there most of the week, which set her off on another stream of complaints. Now her vacation was ruined.

"I should tell you that once in a while, Momma would be in a good mood. After she had begun with Aaron, she seemed to have more smiles and she'd sing around the house the way she used to when I was a little girl. I got so I concluded Aaron was a good thing for her and therefore, for me and Rodney.

"But Rodney's getting sick just as she was about to have what she called her first 'real vacation,' turned the clock back and she was meaner and nastier than ever. She had already told One-Eyed Bill's she was taking off so she was home more and all she did was drink and complain.

"I was at the hospital visiting Rodney more than she was because two of the days that week, she had drunk herself into a coma.

"Rodney's illness seemed to seal up a decision working in the back of her head, that and the eviction notice we got."

"She wasn't paying her rent?" Jade asked. "But she was working, wasn't she?"

"Yeah, well I didn't know much about our bills. I remembered the phone being shut off twice and once we had no electric because she hadn't paid the bills, but she eventually got around to it and things were all right again.

"About three days after Rodney came home from the hospital, someone knocked on our door and I opened it to find a man in a suit asking for my mother. I told him she was at work and he smirked and said, 'If she's working, why doesn't she pay the rent?'

"I didn't have any answer for him. He handed me an envelope and said I should be sure she gets it. After he left, I opened it and read the warning that we were to be evicted in thirty days unless all the back rent was paid. In my heart I knew it would never be, but I had no idea what the solution cooking in Momma's brain was.

"When she came home, I gave her the notice. She read it and then crumbled it up and threw it in the garbage.

" 'What are we going to do about it, Momma?' I asked her.

" 'Nothing. Don't worry about it,' she said. She wouldn't say anything more about it.

"At the end of the week, she announced that she and Aaron had rescheduled their 'real vacation,' and she had made arrangements again with Granny.

" 'But how are we going to go to school?' I asked her. 'Granny lives too far away from where Rodney and I go to school.'

" 'You can miss some school so I can get a holiday,' she snapped back at me.

" 'The school's not going to like that,' I warned her, but she was about as worried about that as she was about our eviction notice.

"I was too tired to care anymore about school anyway. I was doing poorly in most of my subjects, failing math. The counselor had been calling me in at least twice a month, but even she seemed to give up on me. There are a lot of kids with problems in my school. After a while no one even noticed me. I bet they didn't even realize I was gone.

"Momma made me pack up most of Rodney's things and my own and then she and Aaron drove us to Granny's apartment. It's a smaller apartment than the one we were in, but it was on the ground floor and Granny had a small patch of ground behind it, almost a real backyard. Rodney and I would have to continue to share a bedroom, which was really Granny's sewing room that had a pull-out bed. Aaron had squeezed Rodney's cot-bed into his car trunk, so we at least had that.

"Momma went into this big act before she left, warning Rodney and me to behave while she was away. 'You're here to help Granny,' she said, and made that look like the main reason she had brought us.

" 'We'll call you in a day or so, Momma,' she told Granny and they left. She gave Rodney a quick peck on the cheek, but she just looked at me as if I was miles and miles away. There was something in her eyes that caused a flutter of panic in me. My heart skipped and my stomach felt as if it had filled with hot tears.

"Sometimes, I could look at Momma when she was unaware and I could catch a glimpse of who and what she had been when I was much younger. It was almost as if the face she wore now was really a mask and under it was the face of the Momma I had known and once loved like a Momma should be loved. Her eyes would twinkle and her lips would soften into a small smile. It warmed my heart and made me feel safe, if only for a little while.

"I saw that face glimmer for a moment as she stood in the doorway looking back at me. I wanted to run up to her and embrace her and get a real hug of love from her, but it passed and the mask came back strong.

" 'You take care of everyone,' she ordered.

" 'I always do,' I muttered, which she didn't like. She turned to Aaron and they left quickly.

"Momma didn't call the next day and most of the day after that. Then, just after we had eaten our dinner, the phone rang and it was finally her calling.

"I saw that Granny was doing more listening than speaking and keeping her eyes on me and Rodney as she did so.

" 'No,' she said. 'That so? You didn't tell me about that, Aretha. Of course I will,' she added.

"I was waiting nearby, wondering if Momma would ask to speak to me or to Rodney, but she didn't. Granny finally said good-bye and hung up.

" 'What's wrong now, Granny?' I asked.

" 'Your momma says you were all evicted from the apartment. You know about that?'

" 'Yeah, I do. I was home when the man brought the notice,' I said, 'and she told me not to worry about it.'

" 'Well, you lost your home,' Granny said.

"Rodney didn't understand it, but he knew it was bad so he just started to cry and I went to him and held him.

" 'What is she going to do about it, Granny?' I asked.

" 'She said she and Aaron are going to try to set up a home for you all in San Francisco. Aaron's been promised new work with some friends of his and she's looking for work too. Once they settle into a new place, they'll send for you,' Granny added.

"She might have even believed it when she told me then, but after a few days of not hearing from Momma, I could see the trust evaporating. Momma called once more the following week and gave basically the same story. When she didn't call at all the next week, Granny decided we should enroll in the closest schools and she saw that we did.

"Another week went by and another. Momma called once in a while with a different story. Then she called to say she and Aaron were thinking of trying their luck on the East Coast. Aaron had an uncle who owned a convenience store in Wilmington, Delaware and needed help. He supposedly said there was a lot of work Momma could get, too.

"Granny didn't believe her, but she looked at Rodney and me and I guess she thought what was happening was for the best. After she hung up that time, she and I talked about it and she said, 'Well, I guess I'll have to stay in this world a little longer than I had expected.'

" 'I guess you better, Granny,' I told her.

"So I became what Misty called yesterday a OWP, orphan with parents. Good riddance to them both, I say."

I paused, looked at the ceiling and then at Doctor Marlowe. I could see she was waiting for me to tell them, so I got up my courage and I did.

"My troubles," I admitted, "were just starting."

6

"As I said before, Granny wanted us to enroll in new schools and we did. I couldn't help being upset with all the changes in our lives. Rodney was bothered even more than I was, but rather than just clam up the way Daddy often did, he began to misbehave, deliberately breaking things in class, getting into fights and talking back to his new teachers. Twice the first month Granny had to go to school because of things he had done. He had grown up in a house with a mother who threw things when she was angry and didn't hesitate to use bad language in front of him, mostly because she had been drinking and didn't even realize what she was saying, so I guess he didn't have what you would call a good role model.

"Nevertheless, I tried being angry at him and bawling him out for the things he did, but when he turned his lost, lonely eyes on me, I stopped yelling and just hugged him. Finally, I got to him a little by telling him I was worried more about Granny's health than I was about him or me.

" 'Remember, she had one heart attack. She could have another and then where will we be? We'll be in some institution, that's where,' I told him.

"He seemed to understand that and calmed down enough so he didn't get into trouble, but his school-work didn't improve any.

"Neither did mine. The bad habits followed me, I guess. I didn't see how I could ever do anything for myself with studies, and when counselors asked me if I had any idea what I wanted to be or do, I just shook my head and stared out the window. The future was as cloudy as could be. It amazed me how anyone could look years and years beyond today and see what he or she would be doing. I just worried about tomorrow.

"I made some new friends quickly. Everyone's curious about a new student and asks questions and lots of kids were in situations like mine. I knew I was far from the only one who was living with her granny or granny and grandpa. One of the girls, Tina Carter, had a cousin in my previous school who had been a friend of mine so Tina and I became friendly and she told me stuff about many of the other kids, especially the boys to avoid because of their criminal records or gangs they were in.

"One boy she warned me about, Steve Gilmore, was interesting and attractive to me nevertheless. Tina said he was weird. He liked to be alone. He didn't have any real friends at the school and nobody knew much about him or saw him on weekends at the usual hangouts. The only one he seemed to spend any time with at school was a white boy, Matthew Langer, who had such severe learning disabilities he had been held back two grades. The fact that he would rather spend his time talking to Matthew than anybody else made him more interesting to me. It was sort of understood that Steve protected him too.

"Steve wasn't all that big and strong looking. He was just under six feet and only about one hundred and seventy pounds, but he had a wildness in his eyes that made other boys give him space. I guess it was because of the way he fixed his gaze on someone. People said they felt like he was burning into them. Someone had nicknamed him 'Laser Eyes' and the name stuck, but no one called him that to his face.

"There were all sorts of stories about him that were practically mythical."

"Like what?" Jade asked.

"He supposedly had killed someone in a fight when he was only nine years old, stole a car and got into an accident that resulted in the death of a young woman, stuff like that.

"However, from what I could tell, Steve wasn't in trouble much in school. He was an okay student, quiet and not disrespectful when his teachers approached him. I had one class with him, social studies. I would glance his way from time to time. He sat just behind me about two rows over, but he never seemed to look at me or take the slightest interest in me.

"I had begun to take better care of myself, fix my hair, wear some lipstick, polish my nails. Granny managed to get me some nicer clothes too. She did seamstress work for a department store sometimes and the manager got us some deep discounts.

"Granny told me I was pretty. I guessed she was saying that because she was my granny, but Tina told me she and her girlfriends had decided I was one of the prettiest girls in the school now. If that was so, I wondered why Steve Gilmore never gave me a first look, not to mention a second. I wasn't much interested in the other boys who had.

"What I would do occasionally in class was lean back on a slant so I could gaze at Steve without it looking too obvious. I guess another thing that attracted me to him was a look I saw occasionally in his eyes that suggested he was hurting in places I was hurting. He seemed to drift away, too.

"I know from the way you're all looking at me that it's hard to understand what I mean. Sometimes, I'd catch a glimpse of myself in a mirror and I'd do a double-take because there was this deep, dark shadow in my eyes that made them look like tiny tunnels running back to my most painful childhood memories. I'd be surprised at how much time went by with me looking down those tunnels. I guess we called them 'flashbacks,' right, Doctor Marlowe?"

She nodded.

"It would start with me thinking of myself as being five or six and wondering who was this looking at me in the mirror? Then I would just fall back through time. The whole experience leaves you with this heavy sadness, like a water-soaked blanket being tossed on your shoulders."

They all stared, no one speaking.

"I don't do a good job of explaining it," I added.

"Yes, you do," Jade said quickly.

I smiled at her and nodded.

"Anyway, when I looked at Steve one time like this, he turned slowly and looked at me for a moment. It was like we had said hello in a very private way and recognized we were from the same planet, Planet Pain."

Misty looked mesmerized, but her lips stretched slowly into a tiny smile.

"I live there too," she whispered.

I nodded at her, encouraged by how many similar notes we all heard.

"Something happened at that special moment I looked at Steve," I continued. "It was like he had opened his eyes or become conscious and finally noticed me. As it turned out, he wasn't weird so much as he was just very shy. It took another two days before he would utter a word in my direction. I was walking home after school, on my way to stop at Rodney's school and pick him up, when Steve came up behind me and passed me, but paused for a split second to say, 'Hi.' He kept walking, faster in fact, before I could respond. In seconds, he was gone around the corner, but it was enough to give my heart a tiny nudge and make me think about him all that night.

"The next day I became bold and when I saw him in the hallway just before social studies, I stepped up beside him and asked him if he had done the homework. We were supposed to describe four causes for World War One.

"He gave me those 'laser eyes' for a second as if he distrusted my intentions. Those remarkable eyes practically drank me in and swallowed me down before he relaxed.

" 'I only came up with three,' he replied.

" 'I only got down three causes, too,' I said.

"I told him mine and he told me his and between us we came up with five to use. When I got to my desk, I quickly scribbled it all down, looking over at him every few seconds to see him doing the same. He gave me a smile and I felt as if he had kissed me."

"Just a smile did that to you?" Cat asked. She had been so quiet and unmoving, I forgot about her for a while. As usual, she glanced from right to left in a small panic because her words had come out so fast.

"He had a really nice smile. His whole face would change, warm up and look more than just friendly. His eyes were laughing, full of sparkling light. He was . . ."

"Sexy?" Misty offered.

"No, not just that. It was full of understanding. That's it. I felt we spoke and thought alike. Granny has this expression 'birds of a feather.' She often looks at people in the street and says, 'Them two are birds of a feather.' People make fun of older people who have all these funny sayings and such, but some of them were dipped in a well of wisdom and make lots of sense. At least to me," I added.

"So?" Jade asked impatiently. "What happened after this great smile?"

"You can make fun all you want," I said, "but sometimes people say more with one look than they do with a thousand words."

"I'm not making fun. I just want to know what happened next," she insisted. She blew air through her lips and shook her head at me.

I glanced at Doctor Marlowe, who just wore that infuriating look of patience, waiting for one of us to throw a tantrum.

"After class Steve and I finally got into a conversation," I said, my voice taut and strained until I began remembering. "It continued into lunch and I sat with him and Matthew, who looked upset about it the whole time, practically eating nothing."

"He was jealous of the time you were taking with his only friend, huh?" Misty asked.

"I guess. I tried to be nice to him, but he looked angry no matter what. It took another few days of conversation before I found out that Steve's mother had been killed in a car accident about five years ago and he lived with his father and had no brothers or sisters, but I could tell from the way he spoke about his father that things were bad.

"Later, I would learn that it was his father who was driving the car and he was drunk. He was cited for DWI and actually charged with vehicular manslaughter, but he got probation, probably because of Steve losing his mother.

"We began to talk every chance we got at school. Sometimes, we ate lunch outside and really felt we had privacy because the other kids weren't staring at us and whispering. Eventually, I felt comfortable enough to tell him about my life, what had happened with my daddy and momma and such. He was less open about his life. If I asked him a question, he would look away, maybe eat some of his food, and then finally give me a short answer. I could tell pretty fast what he would talk about and what he wouldn't."

"What about Matthew all this time?" Cat asked.

"He followed us around sometimes and after a while, he was nicer to me.

"And then Steve asked me on a date. I guess it wasn't a date exactly, but it was the first time I had a boy ask to come by and get me to go someplace with him."

"He had his own car?" Jade asked skeptically.

"No. We were taking the Big Blue Bus," I said. "The poor people's limousine," I added dryly. She pursed those pretty lips and gazed at the ceiling.

"Where did you go?" Misty asked.

"To the Santa Monica pier. I asked Granny if I could go and then Rodney got all excited about it and I had to take him, too, but that was another thing I liked about Steve. He didn't mind Rodney being along. In fact, he felt better because he was coming along, I think. I think he was real nervous about being alone with me and jumped at the chance to be like a big brother more than a boyfriend.

"Of course, Rodney ate it up. I laughed to myself at the way he immediately looked up to Steve, hanging on his every word as if Steve was one of his television heroes or something. Then I thought to myself, Rodney never had a real father long enough to appreciate him and of course, he had no older brother, and Aaron was nothing to him. I was okay as his sister, but it wasn't the same thing for a little boy. No wonder he was so excited about the attention Steve gave him.

"They got this fun park on the pier. You all probably know about it."

They all nodded.

"Taking Rodney on the rides was fun for both of us. Steve insisted on paying for everything no matter how much I protested. He told me there was some money put aside in a trust for him from his mother's life insurance so he would have something with which to start when he got out of high school, and for now his father gave him a generous allowance because he was responsible for buying things they needed, food and such.

"We talked about what we'd do after we graduated. I still had no idea, but he thought he might enlist in the army. Because of his trust he was secure about his future, knowing he had something he could depend upon.

" 'My father can't get his hands on it, either,' he pointed out. 'My mother was smart enough to know my father wasn't going to provide all that well for us and she believed she'd be working her whole life too, just to make ends meet,' he said. 'She made sure I'd be all right.'

"His eyes always filled with tears when he talked about his momma, but he knew it was happening and snapped those lids like two rubber bands and brought that famous hard, cold look back into them.

"At the pier, he really seemed to be enjoying Rodney, laughing at the way Rodney's face filled with pure ecstasy at the prospect of going from one ride to the other, getting a hot dog and a cotton candy, playing machines in the arcade, trying to win cheap prizes that you'd be better off just going out and buying.

"I guess after a while I was jealous."

"Jealous?" Misty asked, jumping on what I had said. "Why should you be jealous of hot dogs, cotton candy and pinball machines?"

"It wasn't that. Steve seemed more excited about having fun with Rodney than being with me." I looked at Doctor Marlowe. She and I had discussed this and worked it out, I thought.

"Maybe he was just socially immature," Jade interjected. "You said he was shy."

"It wasn't that, either," I replied quickly. "He never got to be a little boy like Rodney was and have fun like this. He was having a, what did you call it again?" I asked Doctor Marlowe. "Vicarry . . . vi . . ."

"A vicarious experience," Doctor Marlowe said.

"Yeah, that. He was doing stuff through Rodney, being the little boy he wished he was."

"It amazes me how everyone's a psychoanalyst nowadays," Jade said smugly.

"Oh, and I suppose you don't do that?" Misty attacked. "You don't analyze everything?"

"He was probably just shy," Jade insisted. "Oh, what difference does it make what he was?"

"No difference to you, but a lot to her," Misty offered. Jade glanced at me and realized that might be so. Her expression changed.

"He ignored you the whole time?" she asked in a softer voice. "Some first date that turned out to be, I suppose. Boys can be so aggravating."

"I didn't say he ignored me. He was into doing things with Rodney more, that's all. I admit I was jealous and wished he paid more attention to me, but I saw how much fun Rodney was having and he hadn't had much fun in his life till then, so I wasn't about to complain.

"Afterward, Rodney sat on the beach and played in the sand while Steve and I took off our shoes and let the water run over our feet.

" 'Thanks for what you done for my brother today,' I told him.

"He nodded and looked out over the ocean and said he'd never been to the pier before. I was surprised to hear that.

" 'Me and my father never really went anywhere together, anywhere that was fun for me, that is. I've been to his friends' houses with him and such, but he never took me anywhere that was fun for me.'

"He said he could barely remember the places he went with his momma.

"Then he looked back at Rodney and said, 'I know what it's like for him growing up with a drunk for a parent.'

" 'Your daddy still drinks a lot?' I asked. I knew how hard it was to answer that question when someone put it to you, but I thought how could his father still drink after what had happened. Steve laughed.

" 'Still drinks a lot? You remember when you told me how as a little girl you thought the smell of whiskey on your momma was just her perfume?'

" 'Yes,' I said.

" 'Well, I grew up thinking whiskey came out of the kitchen faucet. I still wonder if it does,' he said. 'What difference does it make?' he added quickly. 'He'll die soon and put himself out of his misery.'

" 'You hate him?' I asked.

Of course, when he had told me about his mother and the accident, I just imagined he would blame his father forever.

But when he looked at me, those eyes were a mixture of hard, cold anger and some sorrow, too.

" 'I don't care about him enough to hate him,' he said. 'I don't even think about him much if I can help it.'

" 'But you live in the same house with him,' I said. 'You see each other every day, don't you?'

" 'We're more like two people renting some rooms together. I'm usually out of there before he gets up to go to work and I have my supper before he gets home most of the time.'

" 'You cook for yourself?'

" 'Yeah. The cook quit,' he said. He was quiet for a moment and then he added, 'He eats my food, too, when he wants to eat at home.'

" 'I'm impressed,' I said.

"He laughed. He had a nice laugh when he allowed it. It was like it was shut up in his heart and he opened the door just a little and let happiness breathe. Sadness can be more like a disease. It makes you sick anyway."

Without doubt the three of them understood that, I thought.

"Anyway, he turned to me and said, 'Why don't you come over for dinner tomorrow night? I make a great frozen pot pie.'

" 'Frozen? Some cook. I'm a cook, too,' I said. 'Not as good as Granny, but a lot better than my momma. I'll prepare the salad and Granny will let me bake an apple pie to bring.'

"His eyes looked like Rodney's when Rodney set them on the fun park.

" 'Really? You'll make an apple pie and come?'

" 'I don't say I'm gonna do something if I don't mean to do it,' I told him with my eyes fixed as hard and firm as his could be.

" 'Okay,' he said, smiling, 'Okay. It's a date,' he said.

"I laughed, but I was more than just happy about it. I was excited. Funny, how little things like that can give you so much hope," I muttered and reached for my water.

No one spoke. They all watched me drink.

"Granny got a saying for hope," I told them. "She says hope is what you cast out like a fish line and hook, hoping to pull in some happiness, but if you cast it too far or too often, the line snaps and you watch it all float away."

"What's all that supposed to mean?" Misty asked, scrunching up her nose.

"It means if you spend all your time dreaming and hoping, you'll be disappointed. You've got to work hard at being happy and not expect it'll just come floating along and bite your hook," I said.

Doctor Marlowe smiled.

"Maybe we should be sitting around with her grandmother," Jade offered dryly.

"It hasn't hurt Star," Doctor Marlowe said.

Jade pulled in the corner of her mouth. She looked like her eyes were tearing up.

Suddenly, I realized something about her. She has nobody, I thought. That's it. That's what makes her so mean and nasty sometimes.

Maybe she's not so rich after all.

7

"At first, Granny wasn't going to let me go to Steve's house for dinner.

" 'What do you mean you and this boy are going to make dinner for yourselves and you want to make a pie? Where's his momma? Why doesn't she cook?' she wanted to know.

"I explained what had happened to Steve's mother without telling her about his father and his drinking. I knew that would spook her, but she started to ask more and more questions about his father until I had to admit that I didn't know very much about him.

" 'You are going over to that man's house to eat his supper and you don't know anything about him? What if he doesn't want you there? I don't like this,' she said shaking her head.

" 'Granny, if there's any problem, I swear I'll just leave and come right back,' I promised.

" 'Why don't you bring this boy around here first?' she suggested. 'I'll cook him a meal.'

" 'He's too shy, Granny. He won't come.'

" 'He's too shy to come here, but not too shy to invite you there?' she asked, her eyes narrowing with worry and suspicion.

" 'He's living on his own, Granny. His daddy's not there much.'

" 'I don't like the sound of that, Star,' she said shaking her head.

" 'I won't get into trouble, Granny,' I told her. 'You don't think I'm a good girl? You don't think you can trust me?'

" ' 'Course I do,' she said, 'but sometimes things happen anyway.'

" 'I like him, Granny. He's a nice boy. He was good to Rodney and you know from what you heard Rodney say that Rodney likes him, too.'

" 'You want to take Rodney with you?' she asked. I couldn't tell if that would make her happier or more reluctant.

" 'No, Granny. I want to have some time to myself. Thanks to Momma, I never really did,' I said. 'I'm nearly sixteen,' I told her, 'and I haven't even been out on a real date.'

"I hated to sound like I was whining, but that was what I was doing. Granny gave it more thought and I guess she concluded I did deserve some freedom. We hadn't heard from Momma in a long time and there was little hope she would come back soon for me and Rodney. Together, Granny and I had a lot of responsibility now.

" 'Well, you call me if you have to leave and you be extra careful, Star. I don't have the strength to deal with some new big problem.'

" 'I know that better than you do, Granny. I keep telling you that you're doing too much, don't I? I tell you to leave the wash for me, but you do it all before I get home from school, and you hardly ever let me do any of the cooking, not to mention cleaning this place,' I reminded her.

"She looked at me and laughed.

" 'That's true enough,' she said. 'Okay. I'll help you make the pie,' she concluded and we set to doing it.

"Rodney was upset that he wasn't going along, but I promised him we would do something fun with him on the weekend and he settled for it.

"I don't think I was ever more excited about anything than I was about going to Steve Gilmore's house for dinner. I imagine it doesn't sound like much to you girls to go have frozen pot pies with a boy, but to me it was my Sweet Sixteen, a school prom, and a big fancy date all wrapped into one night."

"I would have thought it would be fun," Misty admitted with those big innocent eyes.

Jade looked away rather than comment and Cat looked like she agreed with Misty.

"So, after I brought Rodney home from school the next day, I packed up the salad and the pie and headed for the bus stop. I had to walk three blocks to Steve's neighborhood after I got off the bus and it wasn't the nicest section of the city. Some of the houses looked downright deserted. The streets were dirty and there were broken-down cars that looked like they had been left there for months.

"His house was small with just a patch of grass in the front. Some of the grass looked yellow and there were big dead spots. The front porch on the house leaned to one side like it had collapsed after an earthquake or the beams holding it up had just rotted: A front window had a crack in it and most of the siding was peeled and faded badly. The truth is when I first came upon it, I thought I might have the wrong address. I didn't think anyone lived in this one either.

"However, Steve must have been watching for me because the moment I turned into his short, chipped and broken cement sidewalk, he stepped out the front door.

" 'Welcome to my palace,' he said with a crooked smile, holding his arms out wide.

" 'How long have you lived here?' I asked trying not to sound too critical.

" 'Long as I can remember. It was my grandpa's house, my father's daddy. When he died, it was practically all he had to leave to him, I guess. Once it was nice. I know because I've seen some pictures.

" 'Well, come on inside. No sense in putting it off,' he added.

"You could tell two men lived there by themselves the moment you stepped through the door. The living room furniture needed a good dusting, the rugs were worn so thin in spots, you could see the wood floor beneath them. There were glasses and bottles on tables and the ashtrays were full of butts. On closer look I could see places where Steve's father had let a cigarette ash burn into the sofa or the easy chair. I knew his father must have done it because Steve didn't smoke and I also knew how careless Momma used to be when she drank and smoked.

"None of the windows had curtains, just shades, and the house itself had a musty, damp smell."

Jade grimaced as if she had stomach gas.

"The kitchen looked somewhat better, probably because Steve had done some last minute cleaning in anticipation of my arrival. They had a round, badly chipped wooden table and chairs in it, a microwave as well as a stove and a refrigerator that looked like it was threatening to drop dead. The motor made a small clang. The walls throughout the house needed a good whitewash, and in the kitchen, the linoleum floor was buckling in the corners and badly stained in many spots.

"There was little decoration on the walls, no flowers, no pictures, no knickknacks, no feminine touch anywhere. I had a glimpse of his father's room when he showed me the rest of the small house. There were clothes lying on the floor, over chairs and on the unmade bed. Steve's room was neat, but the furniture looked ready for the antique farm, if you know what I mean, dull finish, chipped and scratched, just like most of the pieces in the house. There was just an old, faded oval gray area rug beside his bed.

"Steve could see my reaction to his home. It's always hard for me to hide what I'm thinking. I've got a pair of eyes that might as well be magnifying glasses over my thoughts."

"You can say that again," Jade muttered.

I glared at her for a moment and then returned to telling them about Steve.

" 'When my mother was alive, this place looked decent at least,' he told me.

" 'I bet,' I said and he laughed at how I had said it. 'I mean you and your father aren't much at housekeeping.'

" 'He ain't much at anything,' Steve muttered. 'Hungry?' he asked.

" 'Sure,' I said and we went about preparing our dinner. He was excited about the pie. I told him my granny had made the crust. It was her specialty and no matter how much I tried, I couldn't get it as good. He liked hearing me talk about Granny, how she fidgeted over her home cooking, her stories about her own mother and father, and of course, her famous sayings.

"When I asked him about his grandparents, he could only remember his father's daddy. He had never seen his mother's parents; they had both died before he was five or six.

"I wondered why he didn't have any brothers or sisters and he said, 'Just luck.'

"I was going to laugh when I saw how serious he was about it.

" 'Can you imagine if there was another kid in this house, especially younger, like Rodney? You know what things have been like for him,' he said and we sat and talked a little more about life with an alcoholic for a parent. That's when I realized even more that we really were birds of a feather," I said and paused.

"Why?" Jade asked. She didn't want to give me a moment's rest, it seemed. Why was she so damn anxious to hear all my story? I had come this morning thinking they all wouldn't be interested in my poor girl's life, and they seemed more interested in me than in Misty and maybe themselves.

"Because of the feelings he had about it, the kind of things he thought.

" 'I used to feel like smashing things,' he told me. 'My father was drunk so much, I was sure he didn't care about me. Counselors and such always told me I couldn't do anything about his problem. He was sick. They wanted me to think of him as suffering some diseases, you know.

" 'I'm not religious,' he said, 'but I couldn't help wondering why God let this happen to me and especially to my momma. You ever think that?'

" 'Lots of times,' I told him. 'Granny used to tell me it's all just a test and we should feel sorry for those who are hurting us.'

" 'You believe that?' he asked quickly. I didn't want to say I did. I knew he didn't.

" 'Sometimes,' I admitted, 'but not often.'

"He laughed and talked about all the times he thought about running away.

" 'I almost did last year,' he said, 'but I talked to this counselor at school, Mr. VanVleet, and he said, "Just accept it, Steve. Accept it and move on with your own life. When your father's ready to help himself, he will, or if he won't, you can't make him."

" 'I thought that made sense so I tried doing what he suggested and I ignored my father as much as I could. If he wasn't home to eat, too bad. If he fell over and slept on the floor most of the night, tough, even if he threw up over himself. For a little while, it was like a truce or something in here. We didn't talk much and we didn't see each other much when he was sober.'

" 'Did it help any?' I asked.

" 'Some, I think. He drank less for a while and started to act like he cared about me, you know. He'd ask how's your schoolwork? What do you want to do with yourself after you finish school? Questions I guess other parents ask their kids all the time.

" 'And then . . .' He paused and looked like he wasn't going to go on.

" 'What?' I pushed.

" 'He got mixed up with a woman who drinks more than he does. I can't stand her. A lot of garbage comes out of her mouth and when he turns his back or leaves her alone with me, she . . .'

" 'She what?' I asked.

" 'Never mind,' he said. 'Luckily, most of the time he's at her place. That's probably where he's at tonight,' he told me.

"He was so full of rage, he made my anger look like a little drizzle. We were both quiet for a long moment, both trying to keep our blood calm.

" 'What does your father do for work now?' I asked him. He had told me his father once had a good job with the water department but got fired because he came in late too often and drunk once.

" 'He works at a garage. I think it's a chop shop, myself,' he added.

"I asked him what that was and he said a place where they bring stolen cars to tear off parts and sell them. Of course, that frightened me a little, but he shrugged and said, 'Like the man told me, ignore him.'

"In the fading, purplish light of the falling day, his glimmering eyes met with mine and we stared at each other for a long moment. Though I knew his heart had been shredded even worse than mine, I could sense his longing to put it together and fill it with some sort of love and he knew what I was thinking. Like I said," I added with a small smile, "two magnifying glasses on my thoughts.

" 'You're a really nice girl,' he said.

" 'Thank you,' I told him.

" 'I don't mean just nice,' he continued. 'I mean you're pretty in and out.'

"I smiled, not really knowing what he meant. He looked frustrated with his attempt to express himself.

" 'Granny's always telling me I'm pretty,' I said.

" 'She's right of course, but I mean more. There are lots of good-looking girls at our school, I guess, but they're just beautiful on the outside. Your beauty goes deep. Yours is where it really counts,' he said.

"I thanked him again. He felt awkward so we talked about dinner and set the table. Together with the salad and some fresh bread he had bought, our pot pies tasted pretty good. Afterward, we had the apple pie and he had some ice cream to put on it. We both had seconds.

" 'I bet you think I'm a pig,' I said. 'I don't usually eat like this.'

" 'I think when you feel happy, you have a bigger appetite,' he said. I agreed and I told him how I thought sadness was like a sickness. I couldn't believe how easy it was to talk with him now and how much I wanted to tell him. The more we talked, the closer I felt to him.

" 'When we got up to put the dishes in the sink, we stood really close to each other and we kissed. It was just a short kiss. I call it a test kiss. You throw your lips out there and see what happens."

"What happened?" Misty asked.

"We kissed again, longer, and then . . ."

"You forgot about the dishes," Jade said with a slow, know-it-all nod. Her eyes were bright and sharp and full of her own experiences.

"Exactly," I said.

Misty's smile widened into a small laugh. Cat looked like she was turning white from holding her breath so long.

A wry smile twisted Jade's lips.

"Thought so," she said with great self-satisfaction.

"Yeah, but what you think happened, didn't happen."

"Ever?" she challenged.

"That night," I said and she sat back, still quite pleased with herself. After a beat of silence, Misty asked, "Why didn't it?"

"His daddy came home," I said, "and things got very unpleasant very quickly."

Jade's eyebrows rose. Cathy bit down on her lower lip. Doctor Marlowe sipped some water and stared at me. I could almost hear her asking herself, "Would I go on?"

"Steve and I cleaned up the kitchen, neither of us saying very much. Every once in a while, we would look into each other's eyes and pause. My heart started a heavy, faster beat that grew louder and harder every time he and I grazed each other. It was like electricity was in the air.

"I know a lot of people, especially other girls my age, look at me and think I've been with a lot of boys, but I'd never had anything like a boyfriend before I met Steve. I had crushes on boys and some had crushes on me, but nothing had ever come of it.

"I read enough romance stories and stuff and had been around Momma enough to know about sex and such, but when it's you, really you, it's different."

"That's for sure," Misty said. Cat looked at her for a moment and then turned back quickly to me, anticipating.

"We just held hands first. It was like both our palms had magnets in them or something. My hand practically floated into his and next thing I knew, we were walking toward his room, neither of us saying a word.

"When we got there, he let go and flopped on his bed, on his back, looking up at the ceiling with his hands behind his head.

" 'I guess you know what it's like for me laying around in my room and hearing my father bang into things when he comes home from a night out there,' he said. 'I hear him cursing and ranting. Sometimes, I can hear him crying through the wall. That's how he comes down from a drunk.'

" 'He feels bad about what happened with your mother,' I said.

"Steve opened his eyes wider and looked at me.

" 'Yeah, I suppose,' he said. 'Maybe that's why he drinks more and more now, to forget. Only, I don't think it helps you forget. I think it makes it come back, only like some . . . some nightmare.'

" 'I suppose you're right,' I said.

"I sat beside him and he brought his hands around and took my right hand into his and just held it, studying my fingers as if they were something special. Then he looked up at me again, his eyes practically speaking to me, drawing me toward him. I didn't even realize I had leaned so far over we were close enough to kiss again until we did.

"Suddenly I was beside him on the bed and he was hovering over me, his face so serious it made my heart skip beats until he brought his lips to mine again and then, when he touched me and unbuttoned my blouse, my heart felt more like a wild, frantic animal in my chest, thundering hard against my ribs. I was scared but excited.

"It didn't take long to get half undressed. The whole time I kept thinking Granny might be mad. I told her I was a good girl and she shouldn't worry and now look what I'm doing. But some other voice inside me said I was still a good girl. This wasn't wrong. I wanted to be loved. I needed to be loved.

"And so did Steve. We were giving something precious to each other, something we had been denied too long, and I don't just mean sex," I added quickly, my eyes throwing warning darts at Jade, but she didn't look like she was about to ridicule me anyway. She looked sad and excited and full of sympathy, all at once.

"I loved his lips all over me. I would have given myself to him right then and there. I know it was foolish to be like that and not to think of protection. I was aware of all that, but now I understood firsthand why some girls forget or lose control. I remember I was the impatient one, pushing myself at him, helping him with my skirt zipper, struggling to get comfortable.

"He pulled back the blanket and I got under as he finished taking off his clothes. He was kissing me and caressing me and I was thinking I'm a woman now. I don't care what happens; I don't care.

"I felt him about to be in me when suddenly, we heard the door open, loud laughter and a chair or something get knocked over. Steve froze and then his face filled with fear. He pulled back.

" 'You better get dressed,' he said. 'That's him for sure.'

"I hurriedly did so. We heard a female voice, too.

" 'She's with him,' Steve said. 'It'll be worse,' he predicted.

"Now my heart was really pounding, but in a different way. It was more like a thump, a deep drum vibrating my bones. I had a cold chill up and down my spine. I wasn't quite finished dressing when the door crashed open and Steve's father stood there, wobbling and looking in at us.

"He was a big man, four or five inches taller than Steve and probably forty pounds heavier, with large facial features and a balding head. His eyes were a familiar bloodshot red and I thought to myself, all drunks look alike. He had that same slobbering lip, that same dazed, unsteady stance, that same stream of madness running through his brain like a polluted stream.

" 'Well now, lookie here,' he declared. 'The boy got himself some action.'

" 'Shut up,' Steve told him.

"His father laughed and then a small, buxom woman came up beside him looking drunker than he did, her hair down, her pearl white blouse open so that her bosom was visible almost to the nipples. She had dark freckles over her caramel cheeks. She was attractive enough that I was surprised she was with Steve's father. Steve had apparently gotten his good looks mainly from his mother.

"His girlfriend laughed.

" 'Well, let him be,' she said. 'He needs all the experience he can get.'

" 'That's for sure. It's about time he had a girlfriend. I was beginning to think he wasn't all right,' his father declared and swayed.

" 'Shut your foul mouth!' Steve shouted at him.

"His father seemed to swell, his shoulders rising and his neck thickening.

" 'Who are you talking to, boy?'

" 'C'mon, let 'em be,' his girlfriend said and tried to pull him away, but Steve's father hovered there, so wide he almost filled the doorway. She tugged to no avail and walked away.

"Steve turned his back on his father.

" 'Don't you have a smart mouth,' his father warned pointing a finger that looked as wide as my hand.

" 'Come on,' Steve told me. 'Let's go.'

"I was very frightened, but I walked toward the door with him. His father didn't move. He smiled instead and his eyes bounced from my terrified face down to my breasts, lingered for a moment and then went lower and lower to my feet before they traveled back upward, making me feel as if he could look right through my clothes.

" 'She's a nice one,' he said. 'What's she doing with you?'

"He laughed at his own stupid remark. Steve stepped between him and me and nudged him just enough to get him to step back so I could pass. I didn't see it, but his father slapped Steve on the back of his head. I heard it, but Steve didn't stop. He pushed me forward faster as his father began to rant.

" 'Who are you pushing, boy? You show me respect. I'm your father, hear? Who are you pushing?'

"We paused for a moment in the kitchen. His father's girlfriend was pouring herself some gin. She looked up at us.

" 'You're welcome to a nip,' she said, 'but not much more. I'm not saying you're too young. I just don't want to give it away.' She laughed.

" 'Keep it and drown in it,' Steve told her.

" 'What did you say to Debbie?' his father cried.

"Steve urged me on and we left the house quickly, Steve's father raging behind us, screaming, 'What did you say, boy? What did you say to Debbie?'

"We could hear her laughing. I was glad to shut the door on it all. We hurried down the sidewalk and into the street.

" 'I'll walk you to the bus stop and wait with you,' Steve said. 'Sorry about all that, but now you know what I live with.'

"I felt terrible for him, but I was also happy to be out of there and on my way home to Granny.

"At the bus stop, he sat with his head down, apologizing and swearing he was going to do something about it all.

" 'Don't get yourself into any trouble with him,' I advised. 'Soon enough you'll be on your own and you'll have your trust money and you can leave.'

" 'Not soon enough,' he said.

"Because the wait was long for the bus, we had time to calm down. I told him my granny had wanted him to come to our house for dinner.

" 'She really wants to meet you,' I said. 'Rodney's still talking about you all the time.'

"He laughed and promised he would come as soon as I asked Granny what night. I expected it would be on the weekend.

" 'Maybe the two of us can take Rodney someplace like the zoo or something and then come back for dinner,' I suggested.

"He said fine. The bus came. We kissed goodnight and I got on. He stood there on the sidewalk looking up at me until the bus started away, and then he turned and reluctantly walked back toward his house and what awaited him.

"Granny was right, I thought. I guess I could feel sorrier for someone else than I did for myself. I certainly felt that way for him that night."

I looked at the three others, their eyes unmoving, all looking like they were holding their breath under water.

"But I had no idea even then how bad it was all going to get for both of us."

8

"**I** waited for Steve at his locker the next morning until the last bell rang for homeroom. He never showed up for school all that day. Lunchtime, I called his house because I was worried about him, but the operator came on to say the phone had been disconnected.

" 'Why?' I screamed into the receiver.

"She cut me off and I fumed, frustrated. After school, I hurried Rodney home and shouted to Granny I had to go someplace and I would be back later. She called after me, but I practically ran out of the house. It started raining lightly, and I missed one bus connection and had to run in the drizzle nearly eight blocks to make another. It was almost five o'clock by the time I reached Steve's street. My hair was soaked and so were my clothes and sneakers.

"Nothing looked any different about the house from the way it had looked the day before, except now it was darker because of the overcast sky and no lights on inside. I knocked on the door and waited and then knocked again, louder. Finally, it opened and there stood Steve with a big bruise on his swollen right cheek. His eyes went from surprise to happiness to anger.

" 'What are you doing here?' he asked gruffly and turned away so I couldn't get a good view of his bruise.

" 'I was worried when you didn't show up at school. I tried to call you lunchtime, but the operator said your phone was disconnected.'

" 'It is. He didn't pay the bill again,' Steve said.

" 'My momma was always forgetting to do that too,' I said.

The rain started to get harder once more and the wind blew it in under the porch roof.

" 'Can I come inside?' I asked.

"He stepped back.

" 'Why are you keeping it so dark in here?' I asked immediately.

" 'I was in my room. I didn't even notice,' he said. He kept looking down at the floor.

" 'What happened, Steve? He hit you when you returned to the house yesterday, didn't he?' I asked him.

" 'I don't want to talk about it,' he said. 'You shouldn't have come.'

" 'Is he here?' I asked, thinking that was why he had said that.

" 'No, he's with Debbie. It's her birthday,' he told me. 'Just another excuse to get plastered.'

" 'I'm sorry, Steve,' I said. He turned to me.

" 'What are you sorry for?' he asked.

" 'Maybe I caused the trouble by coming here yesterday,' I said.

" 'Trouble was here long before you came,' he said. He finally smiled. 'I'd risk a lot more to have you here,' he added. 'Look at you,' he said finally taking a good look at me. 'You got drenched.'

" 'I know.' I was beginning to feel chilled as the dampness soaked through my clothes and to my skin.

" 'Come on,' he said, 'I'll get you some clean towels. You can use my mother's old hair dryer. It still works,' he added and I followed him to his room.

"He brought me some towels and watched me dry my hair and then I started to take off my clothes. I thought I might throw them into his clothes dryer for twenty minutes. He just stood there looking at me and I kept undressing until I was completely naked."

I heard Misty suck some air through her lips. Cat was looking down as if she couldn't look at me when I told them these things. Only Jade looked pleased, that small, pretty smile on her lips again.

"Yes," I said to her. "It happened." I paused and she looked disappointed, afraid I wasn't going to tell her how and why.

"His face just seemed to soften. It was like all the hardness and pain evaporated before my eyes and he looked almost like a little boy.

"My skin was still damp from the wet clothes, but I didn't dry myself. The excitement flowed through me and warmed my heart.

" 'You're so beautiful,' he said and he came to me and we kissed. He scooped me up and gently placed me on his bed as he stepped back and undressed. Once again, we were both under his blanket, embracing, kissing.

"He stopped and said, 'Last night, after it was all over, I fell asleep dreaming about you, imagining us right here. I hoped and even prayed it

might happen, and when I opened that door before and saw you standing there, you looked like a dream come true.'

" 'Even with my hair soaked? Didn't I look more like a drowned
rat?' I asked him.

" 'Hardly,' he said. 'Usually, I wouldn't have any faith in dreams and
prayers and hopes, but you made me believe when you came here yesterday,' he said, as if it had been an earth-shattering decision for me to
do so. 'I guess I expected you'd be here, somehow, someway again.'

"To prove it he reached under the pillow and produced a condom.
Of course, I had seen them and of course, I knew what it was for, but it
frightened me for a moment and he saw that in my face.

" 'We don't have to go further if you don't want to,' he said."

"What did you say?" Misty blurted, impatient with the small pause.
I couldn't help it. My heart was pounding, just telling them.

"I didn't say anything," I told her. "I just kissed him and that was
enough of an answer. It wasn't as painful for me as it was for you and
that wasn't because I wasn't a virgin or anything," I added quickly. "It's
not the same for everyone.

"Afterward, we fell asleep in each other's arms. We slept like that for
nearly an hour and a half. I woke first and then he did and we greeted
each other with smiles and kisses until I realized what time it was and
how angry and upset Granny could be. I couldn't call her because his
phone was disconnected.

" 'I gotta go, get to a phone and go home,' I told him. I had forgotten to dry my clothes. He gave me one of his pullovers and a pair of his
jeans, which were way too big, of course, but I rolled up the legs and tied
a belt around the waist. I used the hair dryer on my sneakers and put on
a pair of his sweat socks. I know I looked a sight, but I didn't care. I was
actually happy I was wearing his clothes. I put mine into a paper bag and
then he walked with me to the bus stop. We found a pay phone on the
way, but vandals had stuffed gum into the slots.

" 'I'll just go home,' I told him. 'You going to come to school tomorrow?' I asked.

" 'Yeah,' he said. 'I'll meet you at the locker in the morning.'

"The bus came moments after we arrived and I was on it, waving
good-bye. He looked so happy and my heart was so full and hopeful. All
the terrible things in my past seemed to dwindle next to his smile. Love
is really more powerful than hate, I thought.

"I didn't know. I didn't know," I said and paused.

I was crying and my throat felt so tight, I couldn't swallow.

"Easy," Doctor Marlowe said. "You're doing really well, Star. It took a long time to get you to this place. Don't give up."

I nodded, took a deep breath and looked at the girls. They all wore looks of deep fear. Misty and Jade had actually moved closer to each other and Cat embraced herself so tightly, anyone would think she would come apart if she didn't.

"Of course, Granny was very upset when I got home. She had given Rodney dinner and cleaned up, but it was like her to leave a plate out for me and keep some of her stew warming.

" 'Where've you been, child?' she asked from her rocker. 'I've been sick with worry. How come you're dressed like that? Where's your clothes?'

" 'They're in this bag, Granny,' I said holding it up. 'I got caught in a rainstorm and soaked to the skin.'

" 'Whose clothes are these?' she asked, her eyes more like two tight slits of darkness.

" 'They're Steve's,' I said and then I tried to explain it all quickly. 'I'm sorry, Granny, but I had to rush out like that and I couldn't call you. Steve's father didn't pay their phone bill and their phone was disconnected. I knew something was wrong with him when he didn't come to school today.'

"I told her about Steve's bruise and I told her I had spent time with him to help him. No," I added quickly, anticipating Jade's question, "I didn't tell her what we did or too much detail.

" 'That don't sound good, Star. You best not go to that house no more. You promise me that,' Granny demanded.

"I shook my head.

" 'I can't promise you that, Granny. I love Steve,' I said.

"She made a face, twisting her mouth like strips of clay and folding her brow like folding a fan and shook her head.

" 'Lord, you can't be in love with no boy that fast and you're too young for such talk. Now don't go making the same mistakes your momma made and end up on the same dead-end road, child. You promise me you won't go to that house no more, hear?'

"I shook my head. 'No,' I cried back at her. 'I'll never make such a promise.'

"I ran to my room and just stood there staring at myself in the mirror. Then I started to cry. She came to my door.

" 'You eat anything?' she asked.

" 'No.'

" 'Well come on then. Have some of the stew.'

" 'I'm not hungry,' I said.

" 'You don't eat something hot after getting soaked, you're going to get sick. Have some stew,' she insisted. 'Get out of those clothes and come on out here now, Star.'

"I didn't want to aggravate her anymore so I did what she wanted. Rodney sat at the table while I ate and told me about a new game he played in physical education class. I only heard bits and pieces. My thoughts kept returning to Steve and our time and the way he looked when I waved to him from the bus. It was like a picture that had been printed forever and ever on my brain.

"Granny didn't talk any more about it. She went into the living room to watch her television shows. Rodney sat at her side and I went to my room and just thought about Steve, fantasizing about our lives together, how when he was old enough to get his trust, we would go off and get married and love each other better than any two people. I'd be a good mother and he would be a good father because we both knew what it meant to have terrible parents.

"Before I went to sleep that night, Granny came to my doorway to ask if I was feeling okay.

" 'Yes,' I said. 'I'm sorry. I didn't mean to worry you, but I had to go,' I told her.

"She stared at me for a long moment and then said, 'I hope you're still a good girl, Star. The easiest thing to lose in this world is your own self-respect and that's the hardest thing to get back, too. Just look at your momma.'

"I didn't want to keep being compared to Momma. I hated the thought, so I just turned my back and pretended to go to sleep. I didn't for a long time. Granny's face and words haunted me even though I didn't feel like I should think of myself as being a bad girl. I really and truly loved Steve. I couldn't imagine loving anyone else more and I thought if this isn't love, if I'm too young to be in love, then I'll never be in love.

"Granny was fine the next morning. Rodney and I left for school. I was never so excited to go. I was at the lockers early and loitered, trying to act as if I had to straighten mine out. It grew later and later. The first bell for homeroom rang and Steve wasn't there again. I waited anyway and was late to homeroom. My teacher was upset and bawled me out, but I couldn't hear a word he was saying. I kept anticipating Steve's arrival.

"I can see in your faces that you know what I'm going to say next," I told the others. "He never came to school."

"Oh no," Misty said.

"Yes," I said. "He and his daddy got into it even worse than before. I don't know why. I never really found out details, but I always thought it was because of me."

"How come you never knew? Didn't Steve tell you?" Misty asked.

"He couldn't," Jade answered for me. Her eyes nearly stabbed me with their penetrating glare. "Right?"

"That's right," I said. "He couldn't."

"Why not?" Misty asked.

"His daddy beat him badly. He fought back and his daddy hit him so hard, he knocked him into a coma."

With my eyes closed, I said it all as fast as I could. It was like swallowing cod liver oil or something. You wanted to get it over fast.

No one spoke or asked anything. They waited for me to open my eyes and take a breath. I looked at Doctor Marlowe. It was always hard to go past this point. Sometimes I could; sometimes I couldn't.

"That whole day in school, I kept hoping he would show up late. I knew he would if he could because he would anticipate what I was going through, but he didn't come. The day ended and he never appeared. I was like a zombie in class, hardly hearing anything. In math I didn't even hear the teacher call on me and I got bawled out for that, but I didn't much care.

"I was afraid to go to his house again right after school, afraid of what Granny would say and how angry she would be, but I didn't know what to do. I couldn't call. The phone was still disconnected.

"I told her Steve hadn't come to school. She lectured me about how it was between him and his father and I shouldn't get too deeply involved, but I was deeply involved. It was too late to think of not being there. I couldn't eat. I did the best I could to please her and I helped her with the dishes and then I moped about, hoping that somehow he would get to a phone and call me. Why doesn't he call? I kept wondering.

"I was tempted to run out again so many times that night, but I held onto the hope that he would be in school the next day and the mystery would be over. Maybe he was still just too embarrassed to show up with that bruise and egg-shaped swelling on his cheek.

"Of course, I couldn't get around the fact that he would have called me or gotten some message to me about it somehow. Something was wrong. I knew it in my heart. I felt it in my stomach.

"The next day I waited at the locker and he didn't show up, but instead of going to homeroom, I went to the office and asked to speak to the guidance counselor, Mr. VanVleet, who had once given Steve advice about his father, advice he respected.

" 'What can I do for you, Star?' he asked. 'You're going to be late for homeroom again, you know.'

" 'I know, but I've got to talk to you,' I said desperately enough for him to agree. He told his secretary to inform my homeroom teacher I was with him.

" 'Okay,' he said taking his seat behind his desk. 'What's so important this morning?'

" 'I'm worried about Steve Gilmore,' I said and I told him how we had planned to meet at the lockers yesterday and then how I waited today. I told him quickly why I was worried. He didn't interrupt, but when I was finished, he looked down at his desk and then shook his head and looked up at me.

" 'I'm sorry to tell you that there was domestic violence in that house night before last. The police arrested Steve's father after some woman made a nine-one-one call and the paramedics found Steve unconscious. He's in St. Mary's hospital and he's in a coma,' he told me.

"Things get kind of gray for me at this point," I said. I looked at Doctor Marlowe.

"I guess this is about where we are, where we've been," I said, looking at her. She nodded.

"I can remember the pain. It was like when you get a paper cut and it stings so bad, only this cut was right through my heart. I felt all the blood leaking out. My head was suddenly very light and my legs felt wobbly, but I didn't faint. I remember that I nodded and left the office.

"When I stepped into the hallway, I remember I looked down toward my homeroom, but I found myself outside the school. I ran a lot. Eventually, I got on the right bus. Don't ask me how I knew where I was going at that point. I guess something takes over inside you, some second-self that works you like a robot.

"The next thing I remember I was standing in front of the hospital. I didn't think at all about being in trouble for running out of the school or about what it was going to do to Granny. I guess what I thought was if I could just speak to Steve, maybe hold his hand, he would be all right again and our future together could still happen.

"That's what gave me the strength to go into the hospital and ask for him at the information desk. They said he was in something called intensive care and only immediate family could visit. I said that was fine. I was his sister. No one challenged me so I followed directions and went to the elevator.

"When I opened the door to intensive care, I was greeted immediately by a nurse. Once again, I said I was Steve's sister. She looked like she didn't believe me, but something in my eyes must have told her that if she didn't show me to him, I would be trouble.

" 'He's still not responding,' was all she would say. She brought me to his bed and told me I could stay about ten minutes.

"His head was bandaged and there was another big bruise on his face, just on the left side of his jaw. His eyes were closed so tight the lids looked glued shut. They had all sorts of stuff flowing into his arm.

"I worked my fingers around his anyway and I began to talk to him.

" 'I'm here, Steve,' I said. 'It's me, Star. I knew something was wrong when you didn't show up. I knew you wouldn't let me down. Please get better, Steve. Please,' I pleaded.

"They said I was crying very hard and that was why the nurse came over and made me leave. The way it worked was I could return in an hour, actually every hour on the hour for ten minutes or so. Some nurses let me stay longer than others. I talked to him more the second and third times. One time I just held his hand.

"No one else came to see him of course. His daddy was still in jail and probably wouldn't have come. Debbie certainly wouldn't come.

"I didn't eat any lunch and I never thought about Rodney until it was too late. I found out later that he waited for me and then gave up and found his way to Granny's all right. He was crying when he arrived and Granny went frantic and called the police. By then the school had called anyway and I guess Mr. VanVleet came up with the thought that I had gone to the hospital to see about Steve.

"Late in the afternoon, before the police came to the hospital to look for me, something happened in Steve's head. Some kind of a blood clot. I don't know all the fancy medical details but his heart stopped and they went into an emergency procedure just as I walked in again. I saw them all around his bed working on him. No one seemed to notice I was standing there. I saw and heard them give up.

"I only have very sketchy memories after that: a policeman talking to me, walking toward the front entrance of the hospital, running, being in the street, being in some alley someplace, wandering through a lot full of garbage and broken-down cars, some old man smiling at me, his mouth toothless, grimy hair on his face and chin, standing by a heavily-traveled street and then . . ."

I looked at Doctor Marlowe.

"Then they said I tried to kill myself by walking out on the street and just standing in the way of traffic. Car horns were blaring all around me, people were shouting, one car hit its brakes too fast and another crashed into the rear of it. Glass was shattering. There was so much noise, I put my hands over my ears and pressed them so hard, they actually carried me off the street and put me into the back of the police car with my hands still pushing on my head.

"I ended up in a hospital, too. Suddenly, I blinked and found myself looking up at a strange doctor who smiled at me and told me to try to stay calm. I went in and out of sleep. Granny told me I was there nearly two days before I was alert enough to know where I was and who she was.

"Naturally, I was very frightened. Later, I found out about all the trouble I had caused, especially the car accidents. Someone had gotten hurt. Granny was so upset, I was afraid she would have another heart attack, but I felt so weak and tired, I just slept a lot.

"They put me in psychological therapy in the hospital and then I was released and Granny had to bring me to court where a judge put me on some kind of probation connected with seeing Doctor Marlowe.

"That's how I got here. Remember, we were kind of answering that question?"

The others all nodded simultaneously as if their heads were somehow connected by wires.

I sat back.

"Just recently, I found out where Steve is buried, but I haven't been able to go to the grave. Granny isn't too happy about the idea. She's afraid it might cause me to do something stupid like step out on a busy highway again. Doctor Marlowe is supposed to help me deal with all that, right, Doctor Marlowe?" I asked, not hiding my fury.

"I'll try my best, but you have to be the one who ultimately helps yourself, Star. You all have to make that commitment, to want to do it," she said.

"That's convenient," Jade said. "If we get cured, you're a hero. If we don't, it's our fault for not caring enough about ourselves."

"Would you rather I pretended to have all the answers and some miracle in my back pocket?" Doctor Marlowe asked her. Jade just stared. "I would have thought all of you were tired of hearing false promises."

"What am I supposed to do, forget what happened?" I fired back.

"We all thought Jade was saying something stupid at lunch when she wished we all had Alzheimer's disease like your mother," Misty said. "Maybe that wasn't so stupid. Maybe all this is stupid."

"I hate my memories," Cat suddenly added. "I don't want you to make me remember them," she said to Doctor Marlowe with more anger and aggression than any of us had seen in her so far.

For a moment I felt like we were all ganging up on Doctor Marlowe. If she felt it, she didn't mind it. She looked like she almost welcomed it. "You're all going to do this," she said slowly, "look for people to resent, targets for your anger. Your anger's justifiable, understandable, but if you let it run your lives, it will ruin them. What I want is for all of you to first admit to your anger, deal with what's caused it, and then use it, make it work for you. In short, free you from it."

"Right," Jade said and looked away.

"Did you want to tell us any more today, Star?" Doctor Marlowe asked.

"I don't think so," I said.

"What about your mother?" Misty asked, suddenly remembering her.

"Oh yes, Momma. She called while I was in therapy at the hospital. She was in North Carolina and now she was with Aaron's cousin instead of Aaron. Granny told her what had happened and she was disgusted and told Granny that she couldn't handle a problem like me just yet. She had intended to send for me and Rodney, if you can believe that, but once she heard about the trouble, she thought it would be better if we stayed where we were until she was better established.

"What were you saying about promises, Doctor Marlowe?"

"Exactly, Star. You know which to take seriously and which not to at least," she said.

"That's not hard, Doctor Marlowe. Any promises my Momma makes I throw in the garbage. Anybody else, I just don't believe."

Misty laughed.

Cat nodded and Jade looked up at the ceiling, took a deep breath and announced she was sufficiently depressed for the day.

"I hope you'll get more from this than that," Doctor Marlowe said.

Jade looked at me.

"I did," she admitted. "I'm sorry. I didn't mean to belittle your story."

"I'm not worried about it," I said.

"I know you're not," Jade fired back.

We stared at each other for a moment and then Doctor Marlowe stood up and we all followed her out.

"All right, girls. Thank you again. Jade, tomorrow?"

"I wouldn't want to miss it for anything," Jade said dryly. "The chance to be another Star."

She looked at me and laughed and I laughed too. Sometimes, it just felt better to laugh.

We stepped out.

Misty's mother had a cab for her this time.

"Daddy's got another bill to pay," she announced.

Jade's limousine was right behind it. Across from it Cat's mother waited and watched us like some bird, not looking directly, but nevertheless we could see she was aware of every step we took.

Granny pulled up last.

"What's your grandmother's name?" Jade asked. "You've only referred to her as Granny."

"Betty," I said. "Betty Anthony."

Jade sauntered over to the car as she walked toward her limousine.

"Hello, Mrs. Anthony," she said. "I'm Jade."

Granny smiled and said hello.

"Hi," Misty said hurrying toward the taxicab. "I'm Misty."

"Hi," Granny called back with a laugh.

Cat moved slowly toward her mother's car and paused to nod at Granny.

"I'm Cathy," she said but lowered her head and moved quickly away before Granny could respond.

I got into the car.

"That girl's plenty shy," she said referring to Cathy.

"Yes," I said. We watched her mother pull away first. She looked upset.

"Well," Granny said. "They seem like nice girls for spoiled rich girls."

"They're not all spoiled. Well, maybe they are. I don't know," I said. "Maybe it's not bad to be spoiled," I muttered.

"You all right, child?"

"Yes, Granny."

I looked back as we drove out. What a funny caravan we made, I thought.

"So you did fine?" Granny asked.

"I don't know, Granny. I did what Doctor Marlowe wanted me to do."

"Well, that's good, isn't it, child?"

"I don't know," I insisted.

Granny looked disappointed. I was tired of disappointing her.

"Yes," I said. "It's very good. Granny?"

"What is it, Star?"

"Tomorrow, after breakfast, would you take me to the cemetery where Steve is buried?"

She looked at me, her eyes filling quickly with fear.

"It'll be all right, Granny. I promise. I just want to say good-bye, Granny. I never said good-bye. And it's time."

Granny nodded.

"Okay," she said. "If you think it's time, then it's time."

"Thank you, Granny. Granny?"

"Yes, child."

"I love you."

She smiled.

"And I love you, child."

It can't all be bad then, I thought.

Can it?

Jade

Prologue

Even though I had been in Dr. Marlowe's office many times, for some reason I couldn't recall the miniature grandfather clock in the center of the bottom wall shelf to the left of her desk. It was encased in dark cherry wood and had a face of Roman numerals. It didn't bong or clang. It played no music on the hour, but the small pendulum swung back and forth with a determined little effort that caught my eye and held me mesmerized for a few moments while everyone waited for me to begin.

The beat of my heart seemed synchronized with the movement of the miniature clock's pendulum, and I thought, why can't we think of our hearts as being little clocks inside us, keeping our time. Even before we are born, our parents' magical hands of love wind them up. Maybe the lengths of our lives are in direct proportion to how much our parents wanted us. Maybe some behavioral scientist should do a study of unwanted children to see how long they live and compare their lives with the lives of children from perfect little families. None of us in this room would probably be happy with those results.

I could feel the other girls' eyes on me and just knew what each of them must be thinking. What was I doing here? I looked like I came from one of those perfect little families. How horrible could my story be? Why did I need the services of a psychiatrist?

I could understand why they would have these questions. No matter what had happened between my mother and father and to me afterward, I always held myself together, poised, with a regal air of confidence. I guess I get that from my mother, although my father is far from being an insecure person. It's just that my mother will never let anyone know she is at a disadvantage. Even if she loses an argument, she does it in such a way that the winner isn't sure he or she has won. Her eyes don't fill with surrender. Her shoulders never sag; she never lowers her head in defeat.

Mother gets angry, but Mother doesn't lose control. Control is in fact the essence of who she is. My father wants me to believe that it is exactly her obsession with being in control that has led them to what he calls their marital apocalypse.

I suppose he's right in his characterization of it. It is the end of one world, a world I was innocent enough to believe would go on until their clocks ran out. I used to think they were so much in love, that when one's pendulum stopped, the other's would soon follow.

Of course, I told myself that wouldn't be until many, many years into the future when even I was entering old age. Our world was so protected, I believed I lived in a grand bubble that kept out fatal illness, serious accidents, crime and unhappiness. I went from a luxurious Beverly Hills home to plush limousines to private schools with sparkling clean hallways and new desks. I came out of one womb to be placed safely into another, never to be too cold or too hot.

In the world in which I grew up, being uncomfortable was intolerable, a betrayal of promises. Shoes had to fit perfectly, socks had to be soft, no clothes could chafe our skin. Our meals had to be properly cooked and sufficiently warm, our bath water just the right temperature. Our beds smelled fresh or were deliciously scented. We fell asleep on clouds of silk and refused to admit nightmares into our houses of dreams. If one slipped under my door when I was a little girl, my father or mother was there instantly at the sound of my cry to step on it as they would some wicked little insect that dared show itself on our imported Italian marble floors.

I didn't think of myself as being exceptionally lucky or even fortunate. I was born into a life of luxury and it was there for me to discover and very quickly to expect. I had no deep philosophical explanation as to why I had so much and people I saw outside my limousine windows had so much less. Some great power had decided it would be this way and this was the way it was. That's all.

Of course, as I grew older and my mother talked about the things she had accomplished in her life and my father did the same, I understood that they had earned or won what we had and we therefore deserved it.

"Never be ashamed for having more than someone else," my mother once told me. More often than not when she made these pronouncements, she sounded like a lecturer. "Those with less are not ashamed of wanting more and especially wanting what you have. Envy always gives birth to resentment. Be careful to whom you give your trust. More than likely they have eyes greener than yours behind their dark glasses and artificial smiles," she warned.

How wise I thought she was. How wise I thought they both were.

Now here I sat after that magic bubble had burst and people who were really little more than strangers to me wanted me to give them my trust. The four of us were participating in what our therapist called group therapy, telling about ourselves, our most intimate selves in the hopes that we would somehow help each other understand and accept all that had happened to us. The more truthful we were about our intimate selves, the better the chances for success. That did take a great deal of trust.

From the way Dr. Marlowe talked, winning our trust was more important to her than the money she received for trying to help us to readjust.

I love that term, readjust. It makes it seem as if we are all some broken mechanical thing that our psychiatrist will repair with a turn of a screw here, a bolt replaced there, and lots of new oil and grease squeezed into places that grind and squeak.

When I looked at these other girls for the first time, I realized that no one was happy to be here. Not one of us had come here willingly. Oh, I don't mean we were dragged here kicking and screaming, although Star made it sound as if it was almost that way for her. It's for sure we would each like to be someplace else. Cathy, whom we nicknamed Cat, hadn't even told her story yet, but one look at her face and I knew she dreaded being here the most. Maybe she dreaded being anywhere. Misty looked the least uncomfortable, but still stirred and fidgeted about like someone sitting on an ant hill, her eyes shifting nervously from one of us to the other.

Yesterday, Star talked about times in her life when it felt like it was raining pain. Even though she came from a much different world, I knew what she meant. Our worlds were very different, but similar clouds had come rolling in and we were under an identical downpour of anger and hate drenching us in our parents' madness. I guess we were all just people who had been caught in the same flood and had been pulled onto the same raft, now tossing and turning, all of us looking desperately for an end to the storm.

However, now that I was here and it was my turn to talk about my life, I felt like I had been shoved into the center of this circle of eyes and ears. For two days I had been on the outside looking in, listening first to Misty and then to Star. I was able to maintain distance between myself and the others and to stay aloof like my mother, maybe I had inherited her desire for control. Today was my day and suddenly, I felt naked, conscious of every blemish, like some specimen under glass in our science class lab. Tears are more private than smiles, I thought. Why should I share any of them with these girls?

Look at them: Misty sitting there with her silly little grin and her tee shirt proclaiming *Boycott Child Labor, End Teenage Pregnancy*; Star, a black girl who was ready to jump down my throat every time I opened my mouth; and Cathy, a mousy-faced girl, who looked terrified enough to swallow her own tongue every time she blurted a comment and we turned to her. These three were to be my new confidants, my adopted sisters of misfortune? Hardly.

I wondered about this session all night, and then when the limousine brought me to Dr. Marlowe's house this morning, I sat there gazing at the front door and asked myself what was I doing here? The question still lingered. I'm not telling these people intimate things about myself just because they come from broken families, too. They're worse than strangers. They're so far from my world, they're foreigners. They'll just think I'm some spoiled brat.

"I can't do this," I declared and shook my head after a long moment of silence and expectation. "It's stupid."

"Oh, I see. It wasn't stupid for me, yesterday," Star said, turning those ebony eyes of hers into tiny hot coals, "but it's stupid for you today."

"I don't think it was stupid for me either," Misty said, wide-eyed. "I don't!" she emphasized when I gave her a look that said, "Spare me."

Cat kept her eyes down. I felt like crawling on the floor, turning over on my back and looking up at her and asking, "Do you think it's all right to talk about your pain? And when you do, do we have to all lie down on the floor like this and look up at you?"

"You sat here and listened and made your comments about my life with no trouble yesterday," Star muttered.

"This isn't supposed to be show me yours and I'll show you mine. I didn't say I was going to do this for sure. I don't owe you anything just because you did it," I declared.

"I didn't say you did. You think I'm dying to hear your story?"

"Good, so I won't tell you anything," I said and practically turned my back on her.

"Very often," Dr. Marlowe said softly after a heavy moment of silence, "we use anger as a way of avoiding unpleasant things. Actually, anger only prolongs the unpleasantness and that only makes it harder for us."

"Us?" I fired at her.

"I'm human therefore I'm not perfect, so I say we, us. I understand these things from my own experiences, which helps me help you," she said. "Don't forget, I've been in the center, too. I know it's difficult and painful, but it helps."

"I don't see how just talking about myself is going to help me." I looked at Misty. "Do you feel any better about yourself since you talked?"

She shrugged.

"I don't know if I feel any better. It felt like I unloaded some weight, though. Yeah," she said tilting her head in thought, "maybe I do feel better. What about you, Star?"

Star turned away.

"She doesn't care about what you feel or don't feel. She's just trying to run away," she said, jerking her head back toward me.

"Excuse me?" I said. "Run away? From what?"

"This is a process," Dr. Marlowe interjected, raising her voice a little. "A process that must be built on trust. I've said this before. You've got to try, Jade. Surely you've heard some things during these past two days that have helped you look at your own situation a little better. If anything, at least you know you're not alone."

"Oh no?" I said. "Not alone?" I stared at Misty for a moment. "I liked one thing you said during your session. I liked your classifying us as orphans with parents. Believe me, Dr. Marlowe," I said, turning back to her, "We're alone."

"The OWP! Let's get some tee shirts made up!" Misty exclaimed with a bounce that made her look like she was sitting on springs.

"Yeah, it could be a whole new club," Star said dryly. She looked at me. "Or a new street gang with a Beverly as our leader."

"A Beverly?"

I shook my head. This is impossible. I shouldn't have agreed to take part in it.

"Just forget this," I muttered.

"You see, it's hard to begin, right?" Misty asked.

"It's because my situation is a lot different from yours," I declared.

"Sure," she said with a smirk that twisted her little nose. "You're special. We're not."

"Look. You told about your father leaving you and your mother and moving in with a girlfriend, right?"

"So?"

I looked at Star.

"And you told about parents that have deserted you and now you and your brother live with your grandmother, right?"

"Like she said, so?"

"So my situation is a lot different. My parents fought over me like cats in heat and they're still fighting over me. Neither will ever give the other the satisfaction. You don't know what that's like. I feel . . . I'm being pulled apart, poked to death with questions from lawyers, psychologists and judges!"

I didn't mean to scream it, but it came out that way, and tears bubbled in my eyes, too, as my throat closed with the effort to keep them back. Who wanted to cry in front of them?

Star turned to look at me. Cat lifted her eyes slowly as if they were heavy steel balls and Misty nodded, her eyes brightening. They all looked suddenly interested.

I took a deep breath. How could I make them understand? I wasn't being a snob. I spoke again, slowly, my eyes on the floor, probably looking at the same tile Cat stared at most of the time.

"When I first learned about my parents getting a divorce, I didn't think much about myself and with whom I'd be living. I just assumed fathers left and you stayed with your mother. I was almost sixteen when this all began and suddenly I became a prize to win in a contest. The contest was going to be held in a courtroom and my mother and father were going to try to prove to a judge that the other was unfit to have custody of me." I looked up at Star. "Do you have any idea what that's like?"

"No," she said quietly. "I don't. You're right. My parents both ran away from having custody and responsibility, but that doesn't mean I don't want to know what it's like to have parents who want you," she added.

The sincerity in her eyes took me by surprise. I felt the blood that had risen into my neck and cheeks recede, and my heart slowed as I sat back. I glanced at Dr. Marlowe, who had raised her eyebrows.

When I first began seeing Dr. Marlowe, I wanted to hate her. I wanted her to fail from the get-go. I don't know why. Maybe I didn't want to admit that I needed her. Maybe I still didn't, but I couldn't get myself to dislike her. She always seemed so relaxed. She didn't force me to do or say anything. She waited until the gates opened a little more in my mind and I let memories and feelings flow out. She was like that now.

I still felt twisted and stretched like a rubber band, but the butterflies in my stomach seemed to settle. Maybe I could do this. Maybe I should, I thought. Sometimes, when you hear yourself say things, you confirm your own feelings, and it was true, I didn't have anybody else to talk to these days except my face in the mirror.

I looked out the window. It was a much nicer day than yesterday. We didn't even have our usual marine layer flowing in from the ocean this summer morning. When I woke, the sky was already clear and bright. Now, as I sat staring into the soft blue sky, I could see birds flittering from branch to branch on the trees outside Dr. Marlowe's Brentwood house. A squirrel hurried down the trunk, paused, looked our way and scurried into a bush. I wished I could do the same.

Our house and grounds were bigger than Dr. Marlowe's, but we were only a few miles down Sunset Boulevard in one of the most expensive sections of Beverly Hills, a gated community of custom homes owned by some of the richest people in the country, maybe even the world. Our neighbors were ambassadors and business moguls, even Arab royalty owned homes there. It was one of the most desirable places to live. My parents had bought and built there knowing it would be. No wonder I grew up feeling like I was living in a protective bubble.

However, it wasn't difficult to be comfortable with our surroundings here. Dr. Marlowe was good at making me feel like I was just visiting with her. I didn't feel I was in treatment of any kind, although I knew that's exactly what this was. I supposed . . . no, I hoped, somewhere deep down that it was more, that I was with someone who cared about me for other than professional reasons.

Dr. Marlowe had told us she and her sister were children of divorce. They had ended up living with their father. Even though her experiences were different, there had to be some similarities, something that helped her to sympathize. She was right about that. It helped me to talk to her.

Maybe telling us a little about herself was just her way of getting the trust she was after. Maybe it was all part of the technique. Maybe I didn't care.

Maybe I did.

"I'm like everyone here," I admitted. "I don't want to hate my parents."

"Good," Dr. Marlowe encouraged. I could hear and sense the others relax. "That's a good start, Jade." Her eyes were full of expectation.

"Once they were in love," I said. "They had to have been in love. I saw all the pictures. They held hands and took walks on beaches. They smiled up at the camera while they sat at dinner tables. They had pictures of each other smiling and waving from horses, from cars and from boats. They were kissing under the Eiffel Tower in Paris, in a gondola in

Venice, and even on a Ferris wheel in some amusement park. No two people could be more in love, I used to think.

"Now, I think, no two people could hate each other more."

I paused, feeling my face harden again with frustration and confusion.

"And I'm supposed to care about living with one more than the other."

"Do you?" Misty asked.

"No," I answered honestly. "Most of the time, I don't want to live with either of them."

"Whose fault is that?" Dr. Marlowe threw out at me. She had asked me this before and I had turned away. Now, I looked at the others. They all seemed so interested in my answer, even Cat stared intently at me.

I looked from one to the other, at their desperate eyes searching my face.

"I don't know!" I screamed back at them all.

"Me neither," Misty said.

Star just shook her head. She didn't have the answer either.

I looked at Cat. The terror was back in her eyes.

"That's what we're here to find out, then," Dr. Marlowe said. "You've all come so far. Why not take a few more big steps to see where it leads? Isn't that worth the effort, Jade?"

I turned away, tears burning under my lids.

"Jade?"

"Yes," I said finally.

I looked up at her through my tears.

"Okay," I said. "I'll try."

And I stepped out of that precious bubble again where the rain was cold and the sun was hot and people willingly and often told each other lies.

1

"As long as I can remember, both my parents always worked even though we never needed money. My mother has told me and reminded me even more often lately that for six months after I was born, she remained home to raise and nurture me. She always makes it sound like those six months were the ultimate sacrifice in her life. She says my father would never even think of taking a leave of absence to care for me even though he is essentially self-employed and doesn't have to answer to anyone but himself. That, she tells me, is a big difference between them and why I shouldn't even consider living with him.

"Now she tells me that new studies in women's magazines argue that the mother doesn't have to be at home during her child's formative years as much as was previously thought.

"Have you read that, too, Dr. Marlowe?" I asked.

"I've read similar arguments and data, but I haven't come to any definitive conclusions myself," she replied. "There are good arguments and data on the other side, too."

"Yes, well, I think she's been telling me that because Daddy says I would have had less emotional problems if my mother would have given me more tender loving care. I know for a fact that's part of my father's motion for custody."

I turned to the girls who looked lost. I hadn't heard Cat's story yet, but I knew neither Star nor Misty were really thrown into the lion's den of divorce courts. They were in for a real education listening to me.

"My father and his attorney claim my mother was insensitive to my needs. He says she was too self-centered and that was why they only had me. As soon as he realized what a poor mother she was going to be, he decided not to have any more children."

Star grunted.

"In my case and especially Rodney's, we were lucky our momma didn't spend more time on our formative years," she said. "Otherwise, we might never have formed at all."

Dr. Marlowe surprised us with a small laugh.

I continued.

"Of course, my mother says she decided not to have any more children because she knew what a poor father my father was and would continue to be. She said he couldn't blame his failings as a parent on her career. She claims it doesn't interfere with her responsibilities toward me."

"So your mother still works?" Misty asked.

"Are you kidding? Of course."

"What does your mother do?" Misty asked.

"She's a sales manager for a big cosmetics company—if you want, I could probably get your mother some real discounts," I said, remembering how she described her mother's obsession with her looks.

"My mother never worries about discounts," she replied. "The more she spends, the more she can complain about the alimony being too little to provide her with the lifestyle she was accustomed to before the divorce," Misty declared with a dramatic air that brought a smile to my face.

"You probably don't realize it, but that's an important legal consideration," I told her.

"What is?"

"The wife and the child or children enjoying the lifestyle they enjoyed before the divorce. It's one of the things the judge will consider to determine support payments should my mother win custody. My mother wants to be considered fully independent, but her attorney wants her to sue for some alimony so my father still bears his burden of expenses for her well-being as well as mine."

I paused and looked at them.

"Are you all sufficiently fascinated yet? Does this compare to your favorite soap opera?"

Misty held her smile in check.

"What's your father do?" Star asked.

"My father is an architect. He's actually a very successful one who designed some of the buildings in Los Angeles and one of the big malls now being built. He has designed buildings outside of California, too, and even did one in Canada. My mother and her attorney have tried to make a big thing of his travel to point out that he would be away too much to provide proper parental care and supervision, especially for a young teenage girl.

"Daddy says my mother's grueling schedule is worse than his and she, too, often travels on behalf of her company, so she would be away too much to provide proper care and supervision. They have subpoenaed each other's travel receipts, business diaries and credit card records to support their arguments in court."

I thought for a moment and looked at Dr. Marlowe.

"I've been wondering what will happen if the judge believes they are both right. That would leave me with parents who are both incapable of being proper parents, right, Dr. Marlowe?"

"That situation has occurred, of course, but I doubt it will in your case, Jade."

"Really. That's a relief," I said. "Otherwise, I might have had to move in with Star and her granny."

"Like you could stand one day without maids and chauffeurs and such," Star shot back.

Misty laughed and Cat smiled.

"Maybe you're right," I said, "but I can tell you this . . . I'm not giving anything up to make their lives easier for them. They raised me to expect a luxurious life and that's what they have to provide. Enjoy the lifestyle to which I have been accustomed, remember?"

Everyone stopped smiling. I sat back.

"You all know I'm a Beverly. Star called me that just a few minutes ago," I said, looking at Misty who had told us about her boyfriend classifying spoiled rich girls as Beverlys because they came from Beverly Hills. "I'm not ashamed of being rich. I don't think of myself as being spoiled. I think of myself as being . . . protected."

"Against what?" Star asked. "Certainly not unhappiness."

"There are degrees of unhappiness and different things that make you unhappy. I don't have to worry about buying anything or going anywhere I want."

"Big deal," Star said.

"It is to me and no matter how you act here, I know it is to you too," I said recalling my mother's advice about people who had less.

"You don't know anything," Star fired back.

"Oh, and you do?"

She folded her arms and sat up straighter, putting herself in a defensive posture.

"Do you have a big house?" she asked me.

"Bigger than this in fact," I answered, looking around the office, which was admittedly quite large. It had a desk and bookcases on one end and the sofas, chairs and tables on the other with large windows facing the back yard. "My father designed our house, of course. It's not a Tudor like this one. He thought there were just too many Tudors in Los Angeles.

"We have what's called a two-story Neoclassical. It has a full-height, semicircular entry porch with Ionic columns. It has two side porches and all the windows are rectangular with double-hung sashes, nine panes to each sash. It's very unique and always gets a lot of attention. Cars actually slow down when they come up to it and people gape even though there are many other magnificent homes in the community.

"What is this house, Dr. Marlowe, four thousand square feet?" I asked her.

"Something like that," she said.

"Mine is closer to eight. Does that give you an idea?" I asked Star.

"So you have a big house. Do you have your own car?" Star questioned.

"I will have this year. I haven't decided what I want yet. My mother suggested I ask for a Jag convertible after my father had suggested a Ford Taurus. Now my father is thinking maybe a Mustang. They're both dangling carrots. Until I do decide, I have a limousine available whenever I need to go anywhere."

"Great. Glad you explained all that," Star quipped. "So you have transportation. I'll bet you also have lots of clothes."

"My walk-in is almost a third as long as this office and full of the latest trends." I glanced at Misty. "I know from what you told me you have nice things, but the difference is I wear mine. This gray sleeveless sheath I'm wearing today is a Donna Karan," I pointed out.

"I don't have anything that expensive," Misty said. "My mother does."

"You poor thing," Star said. She turned back to me. "And you have a maid and gardeners and a cook to go with your expensive wardrobe, I bet," she said.

"Yes, I do as a matter-of-fact. The current maid's name is Rosina Tores. She's about twenty-five and from Venezuela, and my cook's name is Mrs. Caron. She's from France and was once a cordon bleu cook for a famous restaurant."

"Our maid is our cook," Misty said. "You have a separate cook? Wow."

"So you have a big home and cars and a maid and a fancy cook and

I still say, big deal," Star declared. "Stop paying the maid and the cook and limousine driver and you'll see how fast they stop caring about you," she added. "And when you go home, you just have more room for your loneliness in your great big house. With all your money, you can't buy what I have."

"What's that, poverty?"

"No, a granny who gives me love and not because she's hired to do it," she said with glee. She looked like a little girl sticking a pin into someone else's beautiful balloon.

I looked at Dr. Marlowe. Her eyes were fixed so hard on me, I felt my face grow warm.

"I have grandparents," I said.

"You do?" Misty asked, the expression on her face looking as though she anticipated all sorts of warm stories about family gatherings and holidays. I hated to disappoint her almost more than I hated disappointing myself. Wait until they heard about my last Christmas, I thought.

"Yes, they just live far away. My father's parents live back East. He has two brothers and a sister and they are all married and have children, too. My mother's parents live in Boca Raton, Florida. They're retired. My mother has one brother who works on Wall Street. He's not married."

"What do your grandparents say about the divorce?" Misty asked.

"Not much, at least to me. My father's parents have told him to work out his problems and my mother's have told her they are too old to deal with these kinds of crises now. They want to be left to their golf and bridge games."

"Do they ask you to visit them?" Star wanted to know.

"They have, but not lately," I confessed. "They all probably think I'm a big mess and they can't deal with it. I don't like visiting with them anyway," I added. "There's nothing for me to do and they all complain too much about their aches and pains and digestion.

"Besides," I realized aloud, "if I decided to visit my father's parents, my mother would want me to visit hers and spend equal time."

"They'd fight over that?" Misty asked, astounded.

"They fight over postage stamps. My house is like a war zone these days. Sometimes, I feel like I'm risking my life just walking between them."

"You mean, they both still live there in the house together?" Cat asked astonished.

I had almost forgotten about her because she was so quiet. I certainly didn't expect she was following my every word so closely.

"Yes, they do. Of course, they don't share the same bedroom anymore, but they are both at home when they're here in Los Angeles."

"Why?" Misty asked, grimacing. "I mean, if they are in the middle of a bad divorce and all, why would they want to still be living together?"

"My mother let it slip that at first my father wanted to move out, but his lawyer explained to him that in general, if one parent has moved out of the home without the child by the time the trial has started, it will be more difficult for that parent to win custody of the child. She says that's the only reason he's still with us."

"Wow," Misty said. "Your father must really love you if he is willing to stay in an emotional fire zone just because of that."

"Her mother could move out, but didn't. Don't forget that," Star reminded her.

"They're not doing it for me," I said through clenched teeth. I didn't realize I was pressing my teeth together, something I'd caught myself doing more and more lately.

"Who are they doing it for?" Cat asked.

"Themselves. I told you. I'm a prize, a trophy, a way of one getting it over on the other. Don't you listen?"

She shook her head.

They all still looked confused about all these legal maneuvers that occurred in a custody battle. I gazed at Dr. Marlowe, who wore a small smile on her lips.

I sighed deeply, lifting and dropping my shoulders.

"I guess in a sense this legal war and my status as a trophy is my story," I said and truly began.

"My parents didn't have me until almost six years after they had gotten married. I always had a suspicion that I was a mistake. My mother forgot to take her birth control pills or I was one of the small percentage of pregnancies that can't be prevented. I like to think they had some wild passionate time and threw all caution to the wind, that the both of them, normally well-adjusted, perfect and organized people, were impulsive and made love when either least expected it. And, as a result: *moi*."

I held out my arms. Misty laughed. Star let her lips soften into something of a smile. Cat just continued to stare wide-eyed, as if it was incredible to even think of such a fantasy.

"When I was about nine, I used to sit on the floor in the living room and look through their vacation albums and actually envision love scenes. As I told you, they went to so many romantic places. To me they seemed to have lived in a movie. I could even hear the music."

Misty lowered her chin to her hand and stared at me, a dreamy haze in her eyes as I continued.

"There they were in the gondola in Venice listening to the music and the singing and then afterward, rushing up to their hotel room, laughing, my mother throwing herself into my father's arms, and as the moonlight poured through the window and someone sang in the street below, they made me."

"Right," Star said. "It probably happened in the backseat of some car."

"Maybe for you," I snapped at her. "My father and mother would never . . ."

"Why are you lying to yourself? Don't enough people lie to you as it is?" she asked, angrily.

I stared at her and then looked at Dr. Marlowe, who raised her eyebrows, which was something I noticed she always did when she thought a valuable thought had been dangled before me, or any of us, for that matter.

"I'm not lying to myself. It might have been that way once. Both of you talked about your parents loving each other once and doing and saying nice things. Why couldn't it have been the same for mine?" I asked, my voice sounding almost like I was pleading.

Star looked away. In my heart I knew that she wanted to dream the same sort of fantasies, but was afraid of them after what she had been through. I guess I didn't blame her. Maybe she was right.

"My mother got pregnant," I said dryly, "and she was about to be promoted at work. That I know for a fact because I've heard it too many times for anyone to have made it up. So that's why I think I was probably an accident."

"Why didn't they just have an abortion?" Star asked.

"Sometimes, I think they did," I said.

It was like I was looking in three separate mirrors and saw my face in each of theirs. How many times recently had each of them felt the same way, a burden, unwanted?

"They wanted me and didn't want me. Their lives were less complicated without me and yet, I guess, grandparents, friends, society, kept them thinking about having children, starting a family. My mother was thirty-two and hovering over her shoulder, she says, like the good and bad angels, was this biological clock, the hands pointing at her like two thick forefingers, warning her time was running out.

"Anyway, once she discovered she was pregnant, they had the first of their many, what should I call them?" I wondered aloud looking at Dr. Marlowe. "Post-nuptial agreements?"

"What's that?" Star asked quickly.

"Lots of people today sign pre-nuptial agreements before they get married. Some do it to protect their personal assets or to guarantee things they don't want to change won't change just because they get married." I paused and laughed.

"As you see, thanks to my parents, I'm practically a paralegal.

"Anyway, my parents didn't have a pre-nuptial, but after they got married, they agreed certain things would always continue.

"Namely, my mother could pursue her career and my father would do what he could to ensure that happened. Nature, and shall we say unprotected sex, had thrown a new ingredient into their lives, a fetus they would name Jade. I threatened their wonderful status quo so they had to reassure each other, understand?" I asked Star. She didn't look like she understood. "Do you?"

"I feel like I'm a nail and you're a hammer. I'm not stupid," she quipped.

"Well, I just want you to appreciate my situation."

"Appreciate?"

Frustrated, I looked at Dr. Marlowe. Couldn't she see how much more difficult this was for me? These girls were so . . . unsophisticated.

"You were telling them about the post-nuptial," she said firmly, insisting I keep trying. I sighed and continued.

"Yes, the post-nuptial. So they sat down and wrote out what they expected of each other if I were to be permitted to be born," I said.

"What are you telling us?" Star asked, her eyebrows rising like question marks. "If they disagreed about it, they wouldn't have had you?"

"Let me assure you," I replied, "I have little doubt, especially after the last six months or so."

Star shook her head.

"I swear," she said, "Granny's right. Rich folks are not just different. They are another species."

"I don't know that it's just money that makes people different," Misty offered. She looked at Cat, who bit down on her lower lip so hard, I was afraid she would draw blood. "Jade already told us her mother didn't have to work, and both her parents having careers made for big problems, right?" Misty asked Dr. Marlowe.

"I think these are questions Jade will have to answer."

"I agree. Money doesn't make you more selfish necessarily," I said. "Yesterday, you told us just how selfish your parents were," I told Star.

"Yeah, but just writing it all down like that," she said, grimacing. "And if they disagreed, they'd stop you from being born . . . that's cold."

"What did they write down?" Misty asked. "Did they ever tell you?"

"Of course. They both throw it back in each other's faces all the time. First, they agreed that my mother would stay home for only six months and then my father would pay for the nanny afterward out of his money."

"What do you mean, out of his money?" Star asked.

"They always kept track of what each other made. They have always had separate bank accounts and they agree on what they are both responsible for like the mortgage, real estate taxes, utility bills. She has her car and he has his and they keep the expenses for each car separate. Food is shared, of course, as it's a basic maintenance expense."

Star was looking at me with her mouth open as if I really was from another planet.

"They do that to maintain their self-integrity. My mother's not such a radical feminist, but she believes it's important for her to keep her identity and if she turns all her money over to her husband, she loses that identity, and my father certainly wouldn't turn all of his money over to her."

"So does she call herself Mrs. Lester?" Star queried with a twist in her lips.

"She uses her maiden name for her professional name, Maureen Mathews." I thought for a moment. "Often, when they sent out invitations for things, they did write Mr. Michael Lester and Ms. Maureen Mathews."

"My mother's gone back to her maiden name now," Misty said. She turned to Cat. "What about your mother?"

"Yes," she said.

"Your parents sound like they were divorced before they got married," Star muttered.

I almost laughed. It was something I had thought myself.

"Let's just say they were together but divided. Equally," I added.

"What else went into the agreement?" Misty wondered.

"After my mother returned to work, my father was to share full responsibilities for my care. If I needed to be brought to the doctor and my mother was at work, he would have to leave work. The following time, she would. The same was true for school events, dentist visits, dermatologist visits, optometrist visits, orthodontist . . ."

"We get the point," Star said.

"They actually kept track?" Misty asked.

I nodded.

"I grew up believing everyone had a large calendar on the wall in their kitchens with their father's first initial in some squares and their mother's in others. When I visited friends and didn't see their calendars, I asked and they either laughed or looked at me funny. Some admitted their parents kept small diaries for scheduled appointments, but few talked about it like I did.

"I guess that's when I began to feel a little different from some of my friends. Actually, what happened is I started to feel guilty about it all," I said.

"Why?" Cat asked and as usual looked down almost immediately.

"Because I knew my mother would rather be someplace else or my father had to shift some important meeting because he's forced to be doing things with me instead. Whenever they could when I was older, they just hired a limousine to cart me around but for quite a long time, one or the other had to be with me and there are places and meetings that require a parent to be present."

"All your expenses, they shared, right?" Misty asked.

"Almost all. There were times when my mother didn't agree about something my father had bought me or vice versa and the way they settled it was the other didn't have to contribute."

"They were always like this and you thought they were in love?" Star asked with a smirk.

"Yes, I did. I don't think they were like this from the very start. As I said, I think they were romantic and then they just became . . ."

"What?"

I looked at Dr. Marlowe. There was no doubt she was very interested in my answer. It had taken me a long time to find it, many hours of watching my parents argue and gradually become more comfortable as strangers than lovers.

"Threatened," I said.

Star looked at Misty, who shrugged.

"Can you explain what you mean, Jade?" Dr. Marlowe asked so softly, I almost didn't hear her question.

"I guess they each realized how much of themselves they would have to surrender to make the marriage work, and when I came along, the price went up. My mother was always afraid she would become less and less if she had children, and my father was always afraid he would get weaker and weaker as my mother demanded more of him."

"Is she right about all this?" Star asked Dr. Marlowe. "Does she know what she's talking about?"

"Maybe," Dr. Marlowe said.

"Don't you ever say yes or no?" Star snapped at her.

Doctor Marlowe just looked calmly at her. "Yes," she said finally, holding her expression for a moment and then we all laughed. It felt good, like we were all able to stop pulling on a rope.

From the way Star looked at me, I knew she had another delicious question rolling around in her brain.

"What about this?" she asked, motioning around the room.

"This?"

"Coming here to see the therapist. Who pays for that?"

"Oh, they both do that," I said. "Although there's no question my father thinks it's my mother's fault and my mother thinks it's my father's."

"So how did they agree on it?" Misty asked.

"The judge made them agree," I said.

"The judge made them?"

"I'm practically a ward of the state at the moment," I said. "You didn't have all that much to do with your parents' divorce, did you?"

She shook her head.

"You do?" she asked.

"Are you kidding? I have two new best friends," I told her.

"Who?" Star asked.

"My parents' lawyers," I said and I laughed.

None of the others joined me.

They were all just staring at me. Why weren't they laughing too? I wondered.

Until I felt the first tear slide down my cheek.

2

"Sometimes I wish my parents had sued each other for divorce immediately after I was born," I said after I regained control of myself. "That way I wouldn't have to live through all this. Everything would have been decided down to the last Egyptian vase or Persian rug before I even had a chance to understand that most kids have two parents living at home, parents who are not on opposite sides of a seesaw trying to outweigh each other in importance.

"What you don't have, you don't miss, I suspect. At the beginning of all this, things were not all that different from the way they are now. I used to think of myself as the golden latchkey child who returned to an empty house in which there was still a maid, a cook, and around it, a small army of grounds people cutting and pruning to keep our home looking like something special in the gated community. My parents were rarely home when I got home from school. Most of the time though, my mother would get home before my father. One day I think she decided that getting home ahead of him made it look like her job was less important, so she started to stay later and later in order to arrive home after my father.

"Then there was the division of labor. My mother discussed the menu with the cook. My father was in charge of the grounds maintenance employees. They had a business manager to help with the bills and keep the separate accounts, and everything they bought for the house they evaluated together and both had to agree to buy or it had to be bought with separate money."

"That doesn't sound like a family. It sounds like a business," Star muttered.

"You're probably right. They saw it more like a partnership with each of them holding equal shares. Maybe my family can go on the stock market, Dr. Marlowe," I said. "Lester Incorporated. Only, who'd want to invest in it since the partners don't?" I added.

She gave me that blank therapist's face, that look that made me turn to myself for the answers.

"Yes, that's what's happened," I said to Star. "You've hit it right on the head—their relationship was more like a business than a marriage. And now the company's gone bankrupt."

"You've still got plenty of money," Star said with that now familiar twist in her lips that assured me I would find no sympathy on this subject.

"Oh, yes, plenty of money. The company's just out of that other stuff families need. You know, what's it called, Dr. Marlowe? Love?" I nodded before she could respond. "That's it. Love. We ran out of love and there just wasn't any to be had so we had to close the company doors.

"Now, the partners are fighting over the assets and I just happened to be another asset. Each of them wants to be sure he gets his fair share, you see. Well, maybe each would like to get more than his fair share. That way, he or she can claim some kind of victory. That way they won't feel so bad about the years they've invested in this business.

"And so my dear sisters, or OWP's as Misty has called us, I find myself in court where the most personal details about my life are openly displayed, renamed as exhibits and spread out on tables for lawyers, sociologists and therapists to gawk at. Do you have any idea what it's like to have to answer personal questions in the judge's office with a court stenographer taking down your every word and the judge peering at you with fish eyes?" I asked them, raising my voice.

Misty shook her head. Star stared and Cat bit her lower lip and nodded. Maybe she did know. We'd soon find out, I thought.

"I knew things were getting worse and worse before the beginning of the divorce, but I guess I either wouldn't face the possibility of their getting a divorce or I thought they wouldn't do it because of the waste of time and money. They would just continue to live through periods of war and truces until one or the other got tired of it and compromised.

"One thing about them, they didn't stop caring about public appearances, right up to the day my father's lawyer served my mother with a copy of the petition for divorce. They would get dressed up, my father in one of his stylish tuxedos and my mother in a designer gown and her diamonds, and even tell each other how nice they looked. Then they would leave, maybe not arm in arm, but together enough to give the appearance things were fine. All they had to do was tell each other how important an event was to her or his careers and they would cooperate, as if it was part of the rules of war that you didn't harm the other's professional life.

"It's weird. They still compliment each other when they speak to other people. I've heard my mother, just as recently as yesterday, brag about my father's talents and the buildings he's designed, and my father has told people how good a businesswoman my mother is. I guess they want to reassure themselves and others that they had every reason to be fooled. Anyone would have wanted my mother for a wife or my father for a husband. Talk about being civilized about hating each other," I said, shaking my head. "They smile as they shoot at each other with legal bullets."

"Your father's lawyer served your mother papers?" Cat asked. "Where?"

"What difference does that make?" Star asked, but I thought that was a good question because the event of actually receiving such documents is traumatic. I began to wonder more about Cat's story and what had happened between her parents.

"Actually, he just mailed them to her," I said. "She received them at home and found them while she was sifting through the pile of mail with her name on it. Her professional name," I added.

"What did she do?" Star asked.

"Nothing special that night. You'd never know anything was wrong. Remember what I told you about my mother's ability to maintain the fortress of her pride? She might lose, but she's never defeated.

"They were both at dinner. I remember that meal; I remember almost every detail of that, what should I call it, that Last Supper, even though we still ate together afterward. We might even eat together tonight, but that was the last dinner where they pretended they cared enough about each other and me to keep the marriage on track.

"I remember we had chicken Kiev with wild rice. Mother had chosen the wine, a French Chardonnay. For dessert there was a deep dish apple cobbler with vanilla ice cream."

"You make it sound like a restaurant," Star said.

"It's as good as any I've been to and I've been to quite a few in New York, here and London," I said.

"You've been to London?" Misty asked.

"Of course. We were supposed to go to Paris this year. Mother claims we still will, but just she and I of course, and my father says he will take me on a business trip and has upped the bid to Paris and Madrid.

Mother is now considering Venice, Madrid and Paris. It's all on hold, dependent upon the outcome of the divorce, final financial arrangements, custody, etc.," I said.

They were all giving me that look again, those wide eyes of amazement.

"Back to the Last Supper," I continued. "As I said, you'd never have known anything was wrong. My father talked about his new design project and my mother boasted that she was having lunch with the president of her company the next day. They argued a little about politics. My father is more conservative, but sometimes I think my mother disagrees with his political views just to disagree, know what I mean?"

"Yes," Misty said.

"No," Star said.

Cat shook her head.

"My parents never talked about politics," she said.

"At the Last Supper, my father complained about some work the gardeners had done on the hedges and threatened to look for a new company to take care of the property and my mother announced the need to get new patio lounges. With those kinds of topics for discussion, how was I to suspect anything? There I was eating away, living in my own private bubble as usual, my head full of plans for the next day.

"Then dessert was served and my mother, in a tone as casual as though she were still speaking about patio furniture, said that she had received papers from Arnold Klugman, whom I knew from previous discussions about other legal matters to be my parents' attorney.

"Without a beat my father said, 'Good.'

"My mother said, 'I'll have Sheldon Fishman call him in the morning.'

" 'You're using Sheldon Fishman?' my father asked with mild interest.

" 'Judith Milner used him and was quite satisfied,' she replied.

"He nodded and returned to his dessert. When Mrs. Caron looked in on us, he complimented her on the meal and she thanked him. I went upstairs afterward to begin studying for an English exam, still not having an inkling of what was going on. I never took much interest in their legal concerns before. Why should I now? I thought."

"When did you learn what was really happening between them?" Misty asked.

"Two days later it was my mother's turn to pick me up after band rehearsal. My father had flown to Denver for a meeting and wouldn't be back until the next day. My girlfriends' mothers had picked us up all week and it was now my family's turn. The carpool arrangements made it difficult to just send a taxi and the limousine would have been overkill.

"I remember Mother was very irritable about it and constantly on the car phone, barking orders at her staff. We dropped the others off and then she pulled into our driveway, still talking on the phone. When I got out, she called for me to wait.

"She finished her conversation and got out of the car, folding her arms under her breasts and looking down as she paced around the driveway, her heels clicking like quarters falling on the black tile. I couldn't imagine what was going on. It looked like it was going to start raining any moment and I was anxious to get into the house. I wanted to call one of my girlfriends about a boy named Jeremy Brian who I thought liked me. That's how oblivious I was to the war about to begin raging around me.

" 'You know your father and I are not getting along, Jade,' my mother finally said, tossing her hair back as if the strands were annoying flies buzzing at her ear.

"So? I thought. I hadn't really noticed all that much of an escalation in their arguments, but maybe that was because I was no longer paying much attention.

" 'It's gotten worse,' she said. 'He's got his fixed ideas and his stubborn streak and I can't deal with it anymore. We've both gone to see our lawyers to do something about it.'

"My heart did flip-flops as I realized that was what they had been discussing two nights ago at dinner.

" 'What's that mean?' I asked.

" 'I want you to know, we're going to begin formal divorce procedures,' she said and looked up at me quickly. 'A no-fault, incompatibility,' she added. Before I could respond, her car phone rang and she had to pick it up and talk.

"I didn't wait around. I went inside and ran to my room where I sat on my bed staring at the wall, wondering how anything like this could happen to me. What had happened to all the perfection? Where was my protective bubble? I was thinking about the embarrassment, of course, but I felt very frightened, too, like a bird that's been flying and flying and suddenly realizes all her feathers are gone and any moment she's going to drop to earth, hard.

"My mother came into the house but just called up to me to tell me she would talk to me more later; she had to return to work for a big meeting. She said, 'Don't worry. It will be all right. I'll take care of you.'

"She'll take care of me? I nearly broke out in hysterical laughter, but instead I sat there and cried.

"Of course, I thought the real reason they were divorcing was either my mother or my father had fallen in love with someone else and one or the other had found out. I envisioned it to be someone with whom they worked. I almost wish that was the reason now. At least I might be able to understand that better than incompatibility. How could two people who had been married as long as they had and were as smart and talented as they were not realize until now that they didn't like each other? It made no sense. It still doesn't."

"That's what I thought about my parents, too," Misty said.

"I never thought that about mine," Star added.

Cat just looked from them to me and remained her silent self.

"When my father returned from Denver the next day, he was furious that she had told me about it all without him being present.

"I was already home from school. My mother was at work and my father came directly from his office. He knocked on my door. I was still feeling dazed and numb and had just flopped on my bed and was lying there, staring up at the ceiling.

" 'Hi,' he said. 'How are you doing?'

" 'Peachy keen,' I told him.

"I wasn't any angrier at him than I was at her. I was furious at both of them for failing. You know," I said, pausing in my tale, "that's something I've been wanting to throw up at them for some time now. Parents have so many expectations for us, demands, requirements, whatever. We have to behave and do well in school and be sure to make them proud of us and never embarrass them. We have to be decent and respectful and respectable, but why is it that they can go and destroy the family and drag us through all this to satisfy themselves?

"What about that, Dr. Marlowe?"

"It's a fair question to put to them," she said.

Star laughed.

"My momma and daddy would just feel awful if I asked them," she said. "First, I'd have to find them and get Momma while she was sober enough to understand."

"I thought of that question, too," Misty said. "I just haven't asked it."

I looked at Cat and she looked away quickly. What was her story?

"My father didn't even seem to recognize my anger. He had his own to express first," I said, getting back to my story.

" 'We were supposed to do this together,' he said, 'but it's just like her to do what she did. Just in character for her to take control. Don't you worry. It's been duly noted,' he assured me. He was already keeping a legal diary for his lawyer to use in court."

I sighed, crossed my legs and sat back.

"So from the very beginning, the divorce was to be bitter and I was the battleground. Suddenly, I, who had been nothing but an inconvenience, became important, but believe me, I wasn't flattered. On occasion, I've told both my parents they shouldn't love me so much. They both looked confused, but I think deep down in their hearts, they knew what I meant, they knew what they'd buried.

"Dinner that evening was under a cloud, but neither of them would give the other the satisfaction of knowing he or she was terribly upset. They ate like there was no tomorrow just to demonstrate that nothing had damaged their appetites. Neither noticed I hardly ate at all.

"Their conversation was limited to the most essential things and there was a new formal tone to both of their voices, but before the dinner ended, both directed themselves to me, asking me questions about school, about the band, about an upcoming dance I was sure they had forgotten until now. One would ask a question and the other would try to top it by asking for more detail.

"Suddenly, they were both trying to impress me with their concern and interest in my life and my affairs. I should have realized then that they were going to fight over custody, but as I said, I just assumed that if they really went through with the divorce, my mother and I would remain at the house and my father would live someplace else.

"The friends I had in school whose parents had divorced all lived with their mothers and had regular visits with their fathers, and like you guys, none of them talked much about the actual divorce proceedings. They were far more protected from the unpleasant parts than I would be.

"What was supposed to happen next was the lawyers were to get together and work things out. They did work out almost everything else but me and that affected all the other compromises. When it came to the question of custody, the war began. I think that took my mother by surprise, which my father enjoyed. I didn't know about that aspect yet. I just heard bits and pieces about their financial issues, the battle over what assets were joint and what were separate. Since my mother wasn't claiming any physical or emotional abuse, my father was permitted to remain in the house. At least they didn't have to work out any kind of visitation schedule for the time being.

"But a regular trial would have to take place for the judge to decide who should get custody of me. I realized pretty quickly that my opinions, my answers to the judge's questions, would all play a big role and that was why my parents were suddenly . . ."

"What?" Misty asked.

I stared at her for a moment as the words played in my head, waiting for the right one. It seemed so obvious.

"Parents," I replied.

"Huh?"

"She means a momma and daddy and not two business partners," Star explained.

"Exactly," I said, smiling. I looked at Dr. Marlowe. She seemed very pleased.

"That should have made you happy," Misty said.

Once again I glanced at Dr. Marlowe because I knew she would be interested in my reply.

"It does and it doesn't," I said. "I mean I like the attention and all, but I hate feeling that I'm getting it only so that they can each feel that they're outdoing the other. It's like having something nice that's also bad, like, like eating your favorite ice cream but it's so cold, it hurts your teeth."

They all looked confused.

"I guess I'm not making any sense," I said, sitting back. "That's why I didn't even want to start this."

"You're making sense," Misty said. She looked at Star.

"Yeah, you're making sense," Star agreed.

Cat nodded.

"A lot of sense," she said in a voice just a shade above a whisper, "even though it's confusing."

"Huh?"

"That's why we're here, to find a way to live with it," Cat continued and for the first time in three days, all of us looked at her as someone who could bring something to this beside shyness, fear and silence.

Before anyone could speak however, we heard the rattle of glasses and heavy footsteps in the hallway outside the office door.

"Lemonade!" Dr. Marlowe's sister Emma cried and came walking in, carrying a silver tray on which she had a jug of freshly made lemonade and four glasses with a plate of cookies.

"I hope I'm not too early, Dr. Marlowe," Emma said, looking afraid she had interrupted. We all thought it was amusing that she called her sister Dr. Marlowe. Misty suggested she might be a client of her own sister, but I thought that was some sort of a conflict of interest or something.

"No, you're right on schedule, Emma. Thank you."

Emma's plump cheeks rose as her lips formed a rosebud smile. She placed the tray on the table and stepped back.

"Everyone looks so bright and cheery today. It is a pretty day. I hope you'll give them time to enjoy some of it, Doctor. Young girls need sunshine," she recited as if it was some ancient truth.

"I will, Emma. Thank you."

She nodded, flashed another smile at us and left. I think all of us were wondering for a moment if that might be the way we would be years from now. How deep were Emma's wounds in comparison to ours and what happens if you can't mend, really and truly mend?

Will we always be this angry and afraid of forever failing at relationships and therefore always be terrified of being forever lonely? You didn't have to be a psychiatrist to see that loneliness was Emma's problem. It was like some disease affecting her smile, her laugh, her very movement.

"Help yourselves, girls," Dr. Marlowe said and we did. "I'll be right back. I have to check on lunch," she said and left.

Dr. Marlowe is very smart giving us these breaks, I thought. It's too exhausting otherwise.

"Where do you live?" I asked Cat as I reached for a cookie and lemonade.

"Pacific Palisades," she replied. She nibbled on her cookie.

"Where do you go to school?"

"I go to a parochial school," she said. She brushed back her hair.

"I see you cut your hair," I told her and she nodded.

"I did it myself."

"It's an improvement," I said, "but you should try to get your mother to take you over to Patty's on Rodeo."

She stared at me as if I spoke a foreign language.

"That's Rodeo as in Rodeo Drive," I said. "You know if you have a good stylist work on it, your face won't look as chubby."

"Maybe she doesn't think she looks chubby. Maybe she's happy with how she looks," Star said.

"I'm just trying to be helpful."

"Sometimes people can be too helpful."

"That's ridiculous. No one can be too helpful," I said.

"People who are always sticking their noses into other people's business are too helpful," she countered.

"I don't agree. I'm not sticking my nose into anyone's business. I'm giving her the benefit of my experience and my knowledge."

"Maybe she doesn't want it. You ever think of that?"

"Of course she wants it. Don't you, Cathy?" I asked her, practically pleading for her to agree.

She looked like she would cry.

"Don't you see that you're doing the same thing to her that your parents are doing to you?" Misty asked.

"What?"

"Trying to get her to take sides," she said.

I stared at her for a moment and then sat back. Star glared at me, and Cathy quietly ate her cookie, her eyes fixed on her lemonade.

Actually, Misty wasn't wrong. There had been something in my voice that reminded me of how my parents spoke to me now, that pleading to get me to agree with one or the other.

"She's right. I'm sorry," I said. "I was really trying to be helpful. I guess I should learn when to keep my mouth shut."

"Amen," Star said.

"You're not perfect," I charged.

"I'm not? Why bless my soul. I thought considering my wonderful home life and upbringing, I was a thing to behold," she said.

Misty laughed.

So did I.

Just as Dr. Marlowe returned.

"Well, I'm glad everyone's getting along so well," she said, and that made us all laugh, even Cat.

3

"Once my parents decided to do battle over custody, the beautifully carved figures on the civilized chess board of divorce changed to tiny knives they tried to stick into each other," I said. "In other words, things got nastier and nastier until today they rarely speak directly to each other. Civility hangs by a thin thread. What will become of me?" I declared in the voice of a Southern belle, like Scarlett O'Hara in *Gone With the Wind*. Misty laughed.

"Sometimes, if I'm in the same room with the both of them, my mother will say, 'Jade, please tell your father we're having trouble with the garbage disposal,' and my father will respond gruffly with, 'Tell her I already know about it and I'm taking care of it.' "

"So you really don't tell either of them what the other said, right?" Misty asked.

"Right. I'm like a filter through which the words they direct toward each other now have to go. I don't think I've ever had to actually repeat anything. As long as the words are directed toward me, it's all right."

"I couldn't stand that for very long," Star said. "I know it's miserable when they're spitting hate at each other, but I don't like being in the middle."

"Me neither. One day last week when they were having a conversation through me, I put my hands over my ears and I started to scream 'Leave me alone! Stop filling me up with all this garbage!'

"I thought I might tear the hair right out of my head. I know I was so red in the face I felt like I had a fever, but instead of worrying about what I was going through, they just began attacking each other.

" 'Look what you're doing to her,' my father accused.

" 'Me? It's you. You're the one who's putting us all through this ridiculous legal charade. Do you really think for one moment any judge in his right mind is going to grant you custody?'

" 'If he's in his right mind, that's all he can do,' my father responded.

"I turned and ran out of the room. I could hear them shouting at each other for a few more minutes. It was like the winding down of a storm, the slow rolling of thunder farther and farther toward the horizon until there was nothing but the drip, drip, drip of my own tears."

"I don't know how they continue to live in the same house," Misty said, shaking her head.

"Where does your father sleep now?" Star asked.

"In one of the guest rooms. That was something else that caused problems. He asked me to help move his clothing into the guest room. I didn't want to see that happening, but I didn't think it was any big deal for me to help him. Of course, as I did, he complained about my mother more and more and then she came home and saw me helping him and went ballistic.

" 'How can you help that man? Are you taking his side in this?' she screamed at me.

" 'I'm just carrying in some clothes and personal things for him,' I told her.

"That night, perhaps feeling threatened, she suddenly decided she and I had to go out to dinner. It was the first of the poisonings," I said.

"Poisonings?" Cat asked, jumping on my word, but then she looked guiltily at Star and Misty as if she had taken their assigned lines or something.

"I don't think she means she and her mother actually poisoned her father's food or anything," Misty said. Before I could respond she thought for a moment, the doubt shading her eyes, and asked, "Right?"

"Right," I said, "although I often wonder if that could be far behind. No, the kind of poisoning I mean is one planting unpleasant things about the other in my head. They're both treating my head like a garden of hate these days.

"Anyway, I couldn't remember a time before when my mother wanted to just be with me, to take me to lunch or to dinner and have a real mother-daughter conversation. Oh, I went shopping with her lots of times and we ended up having lunch at the mall or something, but most of the time, one of her girlfriends was with us or she talked about herself and her career. There wasn't anything really mother-daughter about it.

"It was funny, but when she asked me to go to dinner with her that first night, I felt bad for my father. I knew, of course, that it was a deliberate effort to exclude him, but all I could do is imagine him home alone at that big dining room table looking at all the empty chairs while Mrs. Caron served one of her gourmet meals.

"My mother made reservations for us in one of the more expensive Beverly Hills restaurants. She told me to get dressed up because we were going to an elegant place.

" 'I was after your father to take me to this restaurant for months before we started the divorce proceedings,' she explained as soon as we left the house.

" 'Why didn't he take you?' I asked.

" 'Why? You'd have to ask him and I'm sure he'll come up with some lame excuse like I was the one who was too busy or something.'

"She turned to me and smiled.

" 'You look very pretty,' she said. 'I'm glad you're wearing your hair that way, and I'm happy I bought that Vivienne Tam. It complements your figure.'

"I didn't know what to say. My mother didn't spend all that much time talking about style of clothes and hair with me very much before this. The truth was I picked out most of my clothes when I went shopping with my friends. When I went shopping with my mother she didn't give me enough time to try things on. She always wanted to get it over with quickly. She dresses stylishly herself, but she doesn't hide the fact that she thinks shopping is a waste of time. She did help me with my make-up because that was her area of expertise, being a sales manager for the cosmetics company, but she always spoke to me as if I was some client or customer in a department store.

" 'Of course,' my mother said still harping on my dress, 'your father didn't want me to buy that even though you wanted it so much. He thought it was way too expensive for a girl your age.'

" 'I don't remember that,' I said.

" 'Oh, yes. It's true. I had to pay for it myself out of my own money. I'll show you the canceled check if you like,' she told me. 'Don't be surprised,' she continued. 'Most of the nice things you have, you have because of me. I'm not the penny pincher in this family. He inherited that . . . that frugal way from his parents. You know what it's like to get a nickel out of Grandfather and Grandmother Lester. Look at the things they buy you for your birthdays. Most grandparents would have set aside some trust money for their granddaughter in a good interest-bearing account by now,' she said.

" 'But they have other grandchildren,' I said.

" 'So? They're not any more generous with your cousins. What are they going to do, take it with them and spend it in the grave? You know what they gave us for a wedding present? A five-hundred-dollar savings bond. That's right,' she said laughing, 'a savings bond. I think it's still in the safety deposit box. I get half of that and don't worry, I'll be sure I get it. If he so much as takes out one nickel from that safety deposit box . . . ,' she muttered, her lips nearly whitening in rage. She suddenly turned back to me with a smile.

" 'Oh, but I don't want you to worry about money, Jade. We're not going to end up like so many poor women and children,' she assured me. 'The fact is I have a better lawyer than he has. I should know. Arnold was my lawyer once. He doesn't have as much courtroom experience as my attorney. The fact is, I was surprised your father didn't look for a more experienced divorce attorney, a specialist like I have to get what I want and protect what you have.'

" 'I don't think Daddy wants to see me have less,' I made the mistake of saying.

"Her eyes looked like they were going to explode in her head. My mother is a very attractive woman. Her hair is just a little darker than mine and she wears it with a little sweep over her forehead like those actresses from the forties, the Veronica Lake look. She has blue-green eyes. They're more green when she gets angry. I know she's beautiful because every time I've gone places with her, I've noticed the way men turn their heads and even women look up at her with that *Why can't that be me?* expression on their faces.

"She doesn't do anything special to keep her figure either. Once a week she might go to the fitness center, but she claims hard work, being constantly on the go, and watching her diet is all she needs to do.

"She's about an inch shorter than I am. If she was two or three inches taller, I bet she could have been a model, not that she would have wanted to be," I quickly added.

"Why not?" Star asked.

"She thinks they're just meat on the hoof, that men treat them with less respect, regardless of how much they get paid. And they have a short professional life. If you're a career woman in business, your looks don't determine how long you'll be working or how fast you will be promoted."

"Don't believe it," Star muttered.

"Don't believe what?"

"That looks don't matter. They always matter."

I glanced at Cat. She kept her eyes down the whole time Star and I argued.

"If you have skills and talent, you will get to where you want to go, to where you deserve to go," I told Star.

"Men are always going to promote women who are prettier first," she insisted.

"What would you know about it? You've never had a job or been in the business world."

"I know what men want," she said dryly.

"Oh please." I looked at Misty, who just shrugged. From what she had told us, I knew her mother had never done a day's work. She wouldn't know either, I realized.

"You watch too many soap operas," I snapped.

"Soap operas?" Star laughed. "Half the time the television doesn't work or if it does, Rodney's glued to it, watching cartoons. We only have one set in our house," she pointed out. "I bet you have five."

I thought for a moment. We had seven, but I didn't say so.

"My mother," I continued deciding to ignore Star's interruption, "is not one of those women who look prettier or more radiant when they get angry. She looks . . . scary, at least to me.

" 'Believe me,' she cried, 'your father is not concerned about your getting less or more. He has his own agenda in this divorce and you and I are not at the top of the list. Why do you think he's fighting so hard to win custody? Because he wants to be responsible for you, to be burdened by your needs? Hardly. It's a negotiations ploy, that's what it is.'

" 'What's that mean?' I asked.

"She was quiet for a moment, nodding to herself and smiling before turning to me.

" 'He thinks I'm not as smart as he is. Most men make that mistake, but I've been in plenty of negotiations with men and I know how the opponent thinks and maneuvers,' she said.

"I hated the idea of her referring to my father as the opponent, but I could see that's what he was to her now, nothing more.

" 'He thinks if he carries this ridiculous motion for custody to court and we actually have a trial date scheduled, I'll give in to his financial demands and take less.'

" 'I thought the money part was all just about settled,' I said.

" 'It would have been if there wasn't this wrinkle,' she replied. That's what I was now, a wrinkle.

" 'I don't understand,' I said.

" 'He makes more money than I do. I want my share of that as well,' she explained. 'I'm entitled to it and there are other assets that he thinks are only his. Then, there's the house. Eventually, it all will be worked out, but until then, he's playing this new game.'

" 'What am I, a checker on a checker board?' I asked.

" 'Exactly,' she said. 'I'm glad you understand. I knew you would. We've got to be more like sisters now than mother and daughter, sisters fighting the same cause, hating men who are selfish and who will belittle us,' she told me.

"But in my mind, I saw her treating me like a checker on that board as well. I just didn't say it then. I was afraid her anger might drive us off the road if I did.

"As soon as we arrived at the restaurant, my mother became the mother I knew most of my life. She claimed she had brought me there to have a heart-to-heart, but she spent most of her time talking to people she knew in the business world. In between she had to explain who all these people were and why it was so important to touch base with them, as she put it.

"When would she touch base with me? I wondered."

"Why didn't you ask her instead of wonder?" Star questioned.

"I don't know. You're right, of course. I should have confronted her then and there, but I didn't. I ate; I listened and I found myself drifting away, like some shadow of myself, becoming more and more invisible. That's what this divorce does to me, it makes me invisible, no matter what they say about how important I am.

"Every once in a while, my mother would return to the subject of our family crisis and rant about my father as if she just remembered she was in the middle of this legal action to end their marriage. She drank more than I had ever seen her drink. Usually, one martini was enough for my mother, but she was lit up like a movie marquee, advertising her anger, her determination and her pride, so she drank another and then nearly half of a third.

"Her eyes looked droopy to me by the time they served dessert. Suddenly, she was so weird. She was just staring at me and she reached across the table and took my hand.

" 'Jade,' she said, her eyes tearing up, 'we've got to stick together on this. You don't know half of what I've been through these past few years. Your father is so different from the man I married. He's obsessed with himself, with his work. Nothing matters more, not you, not me, nothing,' she said.

"She pulled herself up, took a deep breath and said, 'My attorney is going to want to speak with you very soon. I want you to be cooperative and answer all his questions as fully as you can and keep in mind the things I've told you tonight.'

" 'What sort of questions?' I wanted to know.

" 'Questions about our life, your life. They won't be hard questions. Just answer them and remember, Jade, in the end I'll always be here for you.'

"I was afraid to ride home with her. I thought we might be stopped and she would be arrested for DWI, but somehow we made it home. In the hallway, she hugged me once. It was something she hadn't done for a really long time.

"It made me cry and made my stomach ache. I didn't want her to be so sad, but I didn't want to hate my father either. I had a lot of trouble falling asleep that night.

"Despite how much she had drunk at dinner, my mother was up as early as usual the following morning. In fact, she left before I went down for breakfast. She had some meeting in San Francisco and had to fly up there for the day.

"I didn't feel like getting up and going to school. My head felt so heavy and I was exhausted from tossing about, swimming from one nightmare island to another. I decided I would stay home and just rest.

"There was a knock on my door and my father peered in.

" 'Still in bed?' he asked. He was dressed in his jacket and tie, looking as spruced up as ever.

"My father is more than just handsome. He's . . . distinguished, like a United States senator or an ambassador. He's about six feet two and has just a touch of gray at his temples which, along with his perennial tan, brings out the soft aqua blue in his eyes.

"I've always looked up to my father, thought of him as someone special, like a celebrity. He's been in the newspapers a lot, and magazines have featured his buildings and put his picture in the articles.

"He has always seemed strong and successful to me. It was one thing to see him angry and firm with my mother, but another to see him sad and weak with me.

"He came into my room and sat on my bed, lowering his head like a flag in defeat and folding his arms on his legs as he wove his fingers through each other. He stared down at the floor for a long moment.

" 'I'm sorry you have to go through all this,' he began. 'I don't want you to dislike your mother and I especially don't want you to dislike me. I know she's probably been working on you, trying to get you to take sides.'

"He looked up at me quickly to see if he was right and I had to look away which was the same as admitting it was true.

" 'I know she's doing that and it's cruel and wrong of her. She's not herself these days. She's intent on getting her way and that's all that matters to her.'

" 'Why?' I asked.

"He studied me for a moment and nodded as if he had decided I was old enough or smart enough to understand.

" 'For some reason,' he said, 'defeating me makes her feel more like a woman of substance, it strengthens her self-image. I can't tell you why she feels that way. I haven't done much to frustrate her ambitions, have I? She wanted a full-time executive position with her firm. I said fine. Go ahead. I won't stand in your way. I'll pay for nannies and servants and do whatever is necessary to let you pursue your professional goals.

" 'But it wasn't enough for her. She wanted more. She wanted to dominate. You know how the Mathewses are,' he continued, now talking about her parents. 'Her father and mother's pictures are right beside *snob* in the dictionary. I never told you how badly I was treated by them when we were courting. I was just starting out and of course, no one could predict whether I would be successful or not. And my family didn't have a high enough social standing for them, either. To this day they still think your mother has married below her station in society.

" 'She can't help herself. She's inherited too much of that,' he added.

"He reached for my hand and looked me in the eyes and said, 'I don't want you to become a Mathews snob, Jade. You have a lot more than most girls do, but it's no reason for you to look down on anyone and lose out on real friendships. Just think,' he said dropping some of the poison seeds into the garden, 'does your mother have any real friends, any close friends? Anyone she knows and pals around with these days is just as snobby or even snobbier than she is.

" 'I just know that if I move out and leave you behind, you'll be worse off. I'm not going to permit it to happen,' he assured me.

" 'Soon my attorney will ask to meet with you. You've met Arnold before on social occasions, so you know you don't have to be afraid of him or his questions,' my father said.

"Here I go again, I thought.

" 'What sort of questions?' I asked.

" 'Simple questions about your life. Just answer everything honestly,' he said and rose smiling. 'It will be easy and all this unpleasantness will be cleared up.'

" 'All this unpleasantness?' Was that all it was to him, just some un-pleasantness? To me it was utter disaster.

" 'I know you can't be enjoying it,' he said. He started out. 'Say,' he said from the doorway, turning back to me, 'why don't you pop over to my office this afternoon after school. I'd like to show you the model of my last project. You'd probably enjoy seeing it. It's a four-hundred-mil-lion-dollar project. You'll be proud of your dad when you see what's in-volved,' he said.

"I couldn't remember the last time my father had invited me to his office. In fact, I think I had been there less than a half a dozen times. He has beautiful offices on the twenty-first floor of a building on Wilshire Boulevard. The view from his office is spectacular. You can see the ocean and on clear days, Catalina Island.

" 'I'm not going to school today,' I said just before he closed the door behind him. 'I have a bad headache.'

" 'Oh?' he said, looking at me with concern. 'How long has this been going on?'

" 'About three months,' I replied, pinpointing the date of the Last Supper.

"He studied me and then nodded.

" 'That's why I want to put an end to this stupidity as quickly as I can. Your mother puts up a big front, but she'll be happier being totally free,' he added. 'It's what she wants. Unfortunately, it's who she is,' he added and left, leaving me feeling as if he had taken all the oxygen out of my room along with him.

"Later, I was sorry I stayed home from school. There is nothing more dreary than an empty house filled with the echoes of people fight-ing and hissing at each other like a pair of snakes. The walls, the shad-ows in every corner, the bong of the grandfather clock, the long whistle of a tea kettle, every sight and every sound seemed hollow. I felt like I was on the set of a movie. Nothing was real to me anymore. All the pic-tures of them together that still hung on walls or were in frames on ta-bles were illusions. Even the family photos looked phony.

"All these smiles, I thought, were false. Suddenly my parents' faces resembled balloons that had lost air, whereas I felt I was floating away, drifting into the wind, belonging nowhere anymore, like you three," I said, looking from Cat to Misty to Star, "an orphan with parents."

I took a deep breath and held my head back to keep the tears from slipping down my face. Cat cleared her throat. Everyone was looking at me, waiting.

"So," I continued, smiling, "now it really began. Two days later, my mother picked me up at school and brought me to her attorney's office.

" 'You didn't tell your father about this, did you?' she asked me as soon as I got into the car.

" 'No,' I said, but I hadn't told her about him planning to schedule a meeting between me and Arnold Klugman, his attorney, either.

" 'Good,' she said. 'Not that we have to hide anything. It's just better this way.'

"Better for whom? I thought. Certainly not for me. I was literally trembling as if I were in Aspen in February without a jacket or boots."

"Where?" Star asked.

"Aspen. It's a place where a lot of rich and famous people go skiing," Misty said.

"Well, excuse me. I haven't even seen snow up close much less slid down a hill on stupid sticks," she muttered.

"Have you ever read the fable of the Fox and the Grapes?" I asked her.

"No, why?"

"You might appreciate it. This fox is trying desperately to get his mouth on these grapes on the vine only they're too high and he can't get to them so he turns around and says, 'They're probably sour anyway.' "

She glared at me.

"Your father might be right about that snob thing," she said.

"I'm not a snob, but I'm not ashamed of what I have and who I am," I said.

"What was it like at the lawyer's?" Misty asked quickly to stop any more bickering.

"It was horrible," I said. "Her attorney has these really plush offices in Beverly Hills. I took a look around at the three secretaries, the rich oak paneling, the expensive paintings and rugs and thought the divorce business must be pretty good. Everyone treated my mother as if she was the most important client they had. She loves all that stroking. I guess she should have been born into royalty. What a waste of regal posture and dignity.

"Her attorney, Mr. Fishman, was a tall, lean man with beady dark eyes and heavy eyebrows. He had a smile that reminded me of ice because it slid on and off his face so easily. After my mother introduced us, he asked me to take the seat in front of his large, dark cherry wood desk and then after my mother sat, he sat and rubbed his palms together before clapping his hands once like some magician who was going to lift a black velvet cloth to reveal the missing diamond or the end to this marital madness that was destroying us all.

" 'Well, Jade,' he began, 'you know your mother has hired me to help her get through this very difficult situation. Divorce is never pleasant, and your mother wants to make every effort to see that you come through this unscathed.'

"He looked at my mother to see if she approved of the way he had begun and she smiled.

" 'Jade is a very bright and mature young lady,' my mother told him. 'She'll do what has to be done and do it well.'

" 'I'm sure she will,' he said with that chilly smile.

"I kept thinking I'm sure he doesn't really care. I said nothing. I stared at him and waited.

" 'What I want to do today is make you aware of what is going to happen and what you will be asked to do,' he said. 'The judge is going to have a psychologist evaluate your family situation to produce a custodial assessment. We have learned today that Dr. Thelma Morton will perform the evaluation. I am familiar with her. She is a very competent and fair-minded person and I think you will like her. Besides her testimony, there will be testimony from some of your mother's friends and someone from your school.'

" 'Who?' I demanded.

"He looked at his folder for a moment.

" 'Your guidance counselor, a Miss Bickerstaff,' he said.

" 'Why her?' I asked. I didn't particularly like her. I thought she was cold and officious and I had always suspected that she didn't really like being around young people.

" 'She and I have met on two occasions for parent-teacher conferences,' my mother explained. 'Your father couldn't be there either time even though they were both very important meetings, remember?'

"Neither she nor my father had been to the last meeting, the one where colleges were being discussed, I thought.

" 'So we have your school officials, family and friends, and Dr. Morton,' Mr. Fishman catalogued. 'They will be the witnesses in the courtroom. The judge relies on their testimony a great deal, and of course, on what you will say to him.

" 'I can tell you right now,' he said, 'because of your age, he'll most assuredly ask you which of your parents you preferred to have custody and why. Most likely,' he added, seeing the look on my face, 'this will occur in camera, which means privately, usually with a court reporter present. It's rare for a child, even a teenager, to testify at trial,' he said flashing that cold grin at me.

" 'You can't be pressured,' my mother commented, obviously referring to the fact that my father would not be present during the interview with the judge.

"Is she for real? I thought. What is all this if not pressure?"

"I'm glad I didn't have to do that," Misty said.

"I'm not. If a judge had asked me, I would have told him I didn't want either one of my parents to have custody," Star said.

Cat's eyes flashed in silent agreement.

" 'Do you understand everything so far?' Mr. Fishman asked me.

"I shrugged. It wasn't calculus. What was there to understand? I knew what he wanted me to do and I didn't like it.

" 'In all my custody cases, and I have had a number, actually more than ever recently,' he added, nodding at my mother, 'I like to meet like this in a casual way with the child or children,' he explained, sitting back and pressing his long fingers into a cathedral.

"Casual? I thought looking around at his impressive office, the walls covered in books and plaques with framed degrees. Hardly casual.

" 'What I'd really appreciate hearing are your concerns,' he said.

"I simply stared at him coldly. He looked to my mother.

" 'Maybe you'd feel more comfortable speaking if it were just you and I,' he said, swinging his eyes conspiratorially to my mother and then back to me.

" 'Actually, I'd feel less comfortable,' I told him. That icy smile returned, stiffer, colder.

" 'I appreciate how difficult this is for you,' he said. 'Let me assure you it's not our intention to drive your father completely out of your life. Your mother has no opposition to reasonable visitations, trips, vacations.

" 'What we want to do,' he continued, 'is maintain as much normalcy in your life as possible under these trying circumstances. You're comfortable in your home, comfortable with your world as it is right now, correct?'

" 'Hardly,' I told him.

" 'I don't mean the confrontational atmosphere. I'd like you to stop for a moment and try to separate yourself from that and ask yourself how can you best keep the good things about your life, your world? Just think about that, okay? And when you are asked questions by others, think how your answers will support that, okay?'

"I looked at my mother.

" 'I'm not losing the house,' she said firmly. 'No matter what he and Arnold say.'

" 'You won't,' Mr. Fishman assured her.

"She looked at me as if that was the point. If she keeps the house, then won't I want her to have custody so I could stay in my room? As if my room, my things were all that mattered, I thought.

" 'Let me give you an idea of what sort of questions you might be asked,' Mr. Fishman continued. 'Think hard. Who seems to be around more when you need advice? With whom would you rather share your most intimate thoughts, your problems? Who understands you more? Who's been there for you more?

" 'You don't have all that much longer to go before you're an independent person, Jade. Think about what would be best for you in finishing out your dependence on your parents. Most importantly, don't think of this as if you're choosing one over the other. No one's asking you to love your father less or your mother more. You might just help make a decision that's better for them, too.

" 'You don't want to end up being a burden to your father,' he interjected. 'He's a very busy and creative man. He needs his mind free of worry.'

"I felt like two snakes had come alive in my stomach, the snakes that had replaced my parents in the house, and they were slithering over each other and under each other until they had tied their bodies tightly around one another and formed a painfully poisonous knot in my stomach, a knot so tight neither could unravel it. Instead, they panicked and pulled and tugged on each other, tearing each other apart and it was all happening inside me.

"Mr. Fishman must have seen something of this in my face. He very astutely looked at my mother and then smiled and said, 'Fine. This is a good start. We'll talk again.'

"He and my mother stood up, but my legs felt like they had turned to rubber. I actually wobbled.

"Mr. Fishman came around the desk and took my arm.

" 'Are you all right?' he asked me. His voice sounded far away, down at the bottom of a well, echoing.

" 'I feel a little nauseated,' I said. The bubbles were building in my stomach.

"They took me out to the bathroom quickly. I went into the stall and threw up in the toilet while my mother ran the sink to cover up the sound of my heaving and kept asking if I was all right.

"Finally, I came out.

" 'I'll take you to the doctor,' she said. 'You probably caught a bug.'

" 'I'll be all right,' I told her. 'I just want to go home and lie down.'

" 'Damn him to hell for doing this,' she muttered. 'Damn him.'

"I kept my eyes closed most of the time in the car and wished I could shut my ears as she rambled on about what my father was doing to us. I couldn't wait to get upstairs and into my room. I got undressed and into bed quickly and when she looked in on me later, I kept my eyes closed and pretended to be asleep.

"Mrs. Caron came up with a bowl of chicken soup. I ate a little, and the nausea subsided and a headache took its place. I began to wonder if my mother had been right and I had caught a bug. Maybe I should have gone to the doctor.

"Later, when my father came home and learned I had missed dinner and was in bed, he stopped by.

"He wanted to know what was wrong and I told him I had stomach trouble and a headache.

" 'Why didn't she take you to a doctor? Did she have some meeting that she had to go to instead?' he demanded. My headache got worse. 'Just come knocking on my door tonight if you don't feel any better, Jade. I'll call Harry Weinstein and he'll see you no matter what time it is. She was probably worried she'd have to spend time in a waiting room.'

" 'No,' I said. 'I didn't want to go.'

" 'When you're sick, you don't know what's best for you. That's what parents are for,' he declared.

"Where was he when I had the measles? I wondered. He was in Toronto at an architects' convention. And where was he when I had the flu so bad I lost nearly ten pounds? He was in Boston building an office complex. My mother was in Atlanta at a major corporate meeting.

"Lots of times, I thought, I had to be the one who knew what was best for me, sick or not.

"You were right before, Star," I said. "I want to run away. That night it was all I could think about.

"And later, I did."

"You did?" Misty asked. I remembered she had tried to do that, too.

"What happened?" Cat asked.

I stared at her for a moment. I was almost ashamed to tell them.

I gathered up my courage and told them the truth. "No one no-ticed."

4

"It took me a while to decide I was really going to run away. First, I didn't know where I would go. I would never want to go to any of my relatives. I never got along with my cousins on my father's side, and I had no relationship whatsoever with my uncles and aunts. My grandparents would just send me back, special delivery, in fact," I said.

Misty laughed.

"Whether or not I ran off wasn't going to be determined by having enough money. After the filing of divorce papers, my parents fell over themselves to set up a checking account for me, supposedly so I could learn how to be independent. There was also some psychological mumbo-jumbo about giving me a sense of security at a critical time in my emotional and psychological development," I added with a side glance at Dr. Marlowe.

"Years ago, they had decided that there might be occasions when I would need money and they would both be away on business. It had happened a few times. So they set up an arrangement at their bank to be sure I could get up to five hundred dollars out of their accounts anytime I needed it. I never did, but the opportunity was always there.

"Now, they both contributed a thousand dollars to a checking account of my own, and, in almost a ceremonial manner, presented me with the checkbook and ATM card after dinner one night. Dinners had become like wakes, with their marriage lying in a casket right beside the dining room table. At this point it was rare to hear either of them say, 'We agree,' on anything, but my father reached into his inside jacket pocket after dessert had been served, cleared his throat, glanced at my mother and began as if he were the master of ceremonies on a dais at a banquet. I imagined him tapping his spoon against the glass to get my mother's and my attention.

" 'Jade,' he said, 'your mother and I have decided that you are old enough now to have control of your own finances. You have to learn how to manage money. Someday you'll have a great deal of it. Hopefully, most of it will come from your own efforts and not only from what you inherit,' he added with a smile.

"My mother just pressed her lips together and stared down at the table, making little circles in the tablecloth with her forefingers.

" 'Anyway, recognizing this need, your mother and I have agreed to open this account for you. You have only to go to the bank at your convenience and finish this signature card to be able to write checks and use the ATM card. It's an interest-bearing account. We both thought that would be economically wise since we don't anticipate you'll be writing very many checks. Anyway,' he said, 'without any more talk, here's your checkbook and your ATM card.'

"He rose and brought it to me. I looked at the checkbook, saw the two thousand dollar balance and looked up at him and then my mother, surprised at the amount. Everything I needed was paid for: clothes, food, transportation. On what would I spend my two thousand dollars? New CD's, magazines?"

"I would have loved to have had that problem," Star grumbled.

" 'We each put in a thousand dollars,' my mother wanted me to know and then she added, 'but since he makes more than I do, proportionately, I've obviously put in more than my share.'

" 'Now that's not a fair statement,' my father countered. 'You never asked that I contribute any more than you—proportionately or otherwise.'

" 'It's just common sense, Michael. With all your business sense, you should know that without anyone having to point it out to you.'

"My father's stiff, regal posture softened as if he had been punched in the stomach.

" 'Do you want me to put in more?' he asked.

" 'Do what you think is right, Michael,' she said, shifting her eyes toward me with that conspiratorial look. I knew she wanted me to remember all the things she had said about my father's family and their tendency to be frugal.

"My father looked very uncomfortable, as if he had been trapped. It was like every sentence, every move each of them made was a well-thought-out strategy to make the other look bad in my eyes. I felt as if they were already in court, jousting with lances dipped in venom.

" 'Why didn't you bring this up before you had me present her with the checkbook and card, Maureen?'

" 'Why should I have to?' she threw back.

"He glanced at me. I could see he was absolutely raging inside. I could see his face turning more and more crimson as if there were a fire under his cheeks.

" 'I'll have the accountant work out what is proportionately accurate and add whatever has to be added immediately,' my father promised me.

" 'I don't care,' I said. 'I don't want anyone's money,' I added. I wanted to say more. I wanted to say I want my life to go back to what it was. I want you to act like you love each other again and stop all this bickering. I want the war to end. I had all that on the tip of my tongue, but I felt my throat close up and a lump like a small lead ball settle on my heart. I was glad that dinner was over. 'I've got homework to do,' I said. 'May I be excused?'

" 'Of course,' my mother said.

"I rose and started away. My father called to me.

" 'You might as well hold on to all of this until it's proportionately corrected,' he said as snidely as he could. He held out the checkbook and ATM card and I snatched it out of his hand and practically ran up to my room.

"When I got there, I threw the checkbook across the room. I retrieved it before I went to sleep and when I decided to run off, it came in handy. By then, my father had added an additional seven hundred and fifty dollars and I had gone to the bank and registered the signature card."

Star whistled.

"That's a lot of pocket money, girl."

I thought for a moment, sipped some lemonade, and then sat back. The miniature grandfather clock ticked. For a moment the numbers looked blurry to me. You really get to hate time when the world around you is crumbling, I thought. You just want the days to go by and you want to sleep and forget. Clocks and watches just remind you of upcoming dates with lawyers, judges, and therapists. You long for a world without clocks, a world in which, when you have a happy moment, you can stop the hands on the clock's face from moving and just remain forever and ever imprisoned in that good time.

Dr. Marlowe cleared her throat to remind me I wasn't alone and they were waiting. I sat up again.

"My father," I said, "was a great deal more subtle when it came to my meeting with his attorney. Instead of bringing me to his office for an interview similar to the one I had had with my mother's attorney, he told me he was taking me to lunch the following Saturday.

"My father and my mother belonged to an exclusive country club and often played golf on Saturdays. The entry fee to become a member was very high and that became a contested asset, of course. I thought the whole thing was getting so stupid that it wouldn't surprise me to hear them argue over how many golf balls each owned.

"Anyway, my mother went to play golf with one of her girlfriends and my father took me to lunch at a nice restaurant in Santa Monica where you could sit by a window and look out at the ocean. It wasn't until we were almost there that he informed me his attorney would be joining us.

" 'I just thought this would be a more relaxed setting,' he explained, 'and easier for all of us, not that you should feel uncomfortable with Arnold.'

"Here, I was thinking that at least something good was coming out of all this madness: my father was spending some quality time with me and instead it was another deception. I was sure I could count on the fingers of one hand all the times before when he and I were together alone, doing something that was pure fun.

"I felt this great disappointment, this huge letdown that resembled a kite just falling out of the wind and drifting to earth.

"However, I didn't say anything. There were enough complaints circling my head like moths all day and night. I didn't need to add any.

"We valet parked and went into the restaurant. Arnold was already there waiting at the booth.

" 'My goodness,' he exclaimed as we approached the table, 'look at how tall and beautiful she's become, Michael. I almost didn't recognize her. Hi, Jade.'

" 'Hello,' I said without much feeling and slid into the booth. I looked out at the ocean wistfully, wishing I was outside on that beach, just watching the waves roll in with the wind blowing through my hair. Actually, I was glad we had come here because I could drift off so easily during the dreary conversation.

"Arnold began almost in the same way Mr. Fishman had. He told me how hard he was going to work to make this whole unfortunate event as easy for me as possible. He knew about the custodial assessment, but he put a great deal more emphasis on it than Mr. Fishman had, or I should say, a great deal more pressure on me.

" 'The things you tell this Dr. Morton will have a great impact on the judge,' he said. 'Custodial decisions are usually based on what the judge comes to believe will be in your best interest, not in your mother's or even your father's. The way you describe your relationship with your dad is obviously going to be very important,' he emphasized.

"Arnold's smile was quite different from Mr. Fishman's. Fishman's had been so slick and cold, I could discount it, see through the insincerity instantly. Arnold was harder to read. He had a warmer-looking smile that almost made me think he had my best interests in mind. Almost, but not quite. I soon found out he was just as slimy and self-serving as Mr. Fishman. I suppose they were just two different sides of the same counterfeit coin. It didn't matter which side was up after you flipped it. I was in a phony world of lies.

" 'We don't want you to deal unfairly with your mother,' Arnold continued. 'I know your mother almost as well as I know your father, and I wouldn't want to do anything that wasn't right in regards to her, but what you need to do real soon is think about all the things your father does for you—things we would call day-to-day stuff, like getting you to important places, making sure you get the things you need, being there to talk, stuff like that. You're at the age when a father like yours can be very, very important,' he added with that deceivingly warm smile. 'Especially when you're considering colleges and traveling. Your father's been to an Ivy League school,' he reminded me. 'Your mother hasn't. As I recall, she went to some business school for a year, right Michael?'

" 'The Templeton School of Business. They don't even award an associate's degree,' my father said. I was shocked by the cruelty in his voice—I had never heard him belittle my mother's education like that.

" 'Precisely my point,' Mr. Klugman said. 'Your father's real college experience is what you need to rely on now. You've talked about possible colleges to attend, haven't you?' he asked.

" 'No,' I said.

"Our food had been served but Arnold refused to let me eat in peace.

" 'No?'

" 'No,' I said. 'I had a meeting with my guidance counselor, but both my mother and father were out of town that day even though the meeting had been scheduled a week in advance. The day of the meeting, my mother got called on a company emergency and my father had a very serious problem with one of his big projects. I forget where,' I said dryly. 'My guidance counselor wouldn't cancel on such short notice. I had to have the meeting without my parents.'

"Mr. Klugman turned to my father.

" 'But we went over what you discussed with your guidance counselor. We talked at dinner that night, remember?' my father said.

"I shrugged. To be honest, I couldn't remember if we had or not.

" 'I guess,' I said.

" 'See, that's the sort of thing I want you to try to recall,' Mr. Klugman jumped on. 'You know, it might not be a bad idea to write some of it down. If you have any questions about any of it, ask your dad.'

" 'You make it sound like a final exam or something,' I said.

" 'Oh, it is,' he said. 'It's just like a final exam and much more important.'

"He, too, talked about the other witnesses who would be called and he asked me questions about them.

"I ate fast, more out of nervousness than from hunger. Afterward, I didn't throw up like I had at my mother's attorney's office, but my food felt like it had all gotten stuck in my throat. I wished I hadn't eaten anything. It actually hurt when I tried to swallow.

"When we started out of the restaurant, I looked longingly at the beach and my father stopped and looked too.

" 'Do you want to take a walk on the beach?' he offered.

"Here he was dressed in a jacket and tie and wearing his expensive Bally shoes. How could we walk on the beach? I wondered.

" 'Yes,' I said and he led me onto the boardwalk.

" 'I'm really sorry about all this,' he began. 'Believe me when I tell you it was the furthest thing from my imagination.'

" 'The divorce or the custody battle?' I asked.

" 'Both,' he replied, 'but I have to admit, your mother surprised me with her decision to go to court about this. I never anticipated which one of us had primary custody was so important to her. I know the house is important, but her freedom to do what she wants to do is clearly what matters the most. At least, that's what I had assumed. Of course, there are other things involved here, more complicated things.'

"I knew what he was saying, but I didn't respond. The hardest thing about all this is to have to deal with each of them when they try to get me to take sides. Why couldn't we just walk on the beach and talk about other things? What about what Mr. Klugman had brought up at lunch: my college future? Neither of my parents had come right out and asked me what I wanted to do with my life. They were both too caught up in what they were doing with their own lives.

" 'I'm not going to lose the house,' he continued. 'My soul is in that house. I created it. It was born right here,' he said pointing to his temple. 'I can claim it as intellectual, artistic property, you know. Arnold is investigating that argument.'

"Here they both were vowing to me that neither would lose the house as if the house was more important than me.

" 'Don't worry,' he assured me. 'Your mother will have something quite upscale as an alternative. She knows that. She's just fighting that battle for spite. You know how much she hates anything that has to do with the house. Can you just imagine her being responsible for maintaining it?'

"He laughed. I kept my eyes down and walked with my arms crossed under my breasts. The ocean breeze felt so cool and refreshing. As we drew closer, I stopped and took off my shoes to walk in the sand. He hesitated, laughed and took off his shoes and socks. He rolled up his pants and joined me as we walked toward the water.

" 'This is fun. I haven't done this in years,' he said.

" 'Maybe that's why there are all these problems,' I muttered.

" 'Oh, is that what she's telling you these days?' he asked, pouncing.

"Jade, I told myself, just keep your mouth shut. They're both like dynamite sticks with short wicks. Practically every word I said could be a potential spark.

" 'No,' I said. 'You two used to have so much fun together. I just thought that was important.'

" 'It is!' he cried. 'But that old adage is true. It takes two to tango. I could make a list as long as my arm of places, events, things I wanted to do for pure enjoyment that she no longer had the time to do or cared to do,' he explained, which was exactly her complaint about him.

" 'It's all right; it's all right,' he quickly added. 'If that's who she is, if that's who she wants to be, fine. I wish her well, but I need to have a more relaxed relationship. I'm a creative person. I need to avoid stress,' he insisted.

"I stood on the beach and let the tide kiss my toes. He did the same, but rambled on about how things had changed and why he didn't want this to happen and why he hoped she would become reasonable.

"After a while the sound of the sea drowned him out and I closed my eyes and imagined myself on a sailboat, gliding along in the wind, the spray on my face.

" 'We should head back,' I heard him say. 'Jade?'

" 'What? Oh. Yes,' I said and followed him up the beach to a faucet where we could rinse the sand off our feet. He gave me his handkerchief to use as a towel.

"As I wiped my feet, I sensed him standing off to the side gazing at me, and when I looked at him, I saw this boyish grin on his face. I raised my eyebrows.

" 'What?' I asked with a smile of my own.

" 'Nothing. I was just looking at you and thinking how pretty you are. You look a lot like your mother when she was younger, you know. She's an attractive woman, although,' he said with a small smirk, 'that's never been enough for her. It isn't even a viable compliment. She's ready to claw any man who tells her she's pretty. You're not like that. I know you're not. You're going to be all right, Jade. This will all come to an end and you'll be like a cat and land on your feet, don't worry about that.'

" 'What about you, Daddy?' I asked him.

" 'I'll be fine. *We'll* be fine,' he insisted. He wouldn't consider his future without including me, at least, for now.

"What happens later when either he or my mother win the custody battle? I wondered. Would they both still include me in their lives with such passion?

"I guess what I mean to say is I stopped trusting both of them, trusting what they told me and what they promised."

I gazed at Dr. Marlowe. She nodded softly.

"What I've learned," I continued, "is that once they broke their vows to each other, they lost their credibility with me."

Star was looking at me strangely, as if for the first time she truly understood me. Misty nodded in agreement with me and Cat looked like she was poised to jump up and run from the room. I wondered why what I'd just said had affected her so strongly.

"They lied to each other. Why should I believe them? Ever," I emphasized. "Don't you all feel like that, feel you've been betrayed?"

"I do," Misty agreed.

Cat glanced at Dr. Marlowe and just nodded.

Star smiled softly. "My granny tells me we come into this world without a single guarantee and leave the same way. It's all promises, girl. Take your pick and play your chance."

"Well, I wasn't about to bet on either of them," I said. "I think the therapist making the evaluation has come to that conclusion, too.

"One day soon after I met with Daddy and his attorney, I came home from school and found this woman, Dr. Morton, waiting for me in the living room. Rosina had given her a cold soft drink and she sat with her little clipboard on the settee. As I crossed the hallway, I heard the doctor call my name.

"I paused and looked in at her, curious of course. Dr. Morton is a very short woman, probably an inch shorter than Misty, with very curly, dark brown steel-wool hair, and big almond shaped eyes, beautiful eyes.

"She has a very sincere warm smile. Even if you don't want to be co-operative, you are eventually, and that's because you can see she enjoys her work and sees herself as doing something very critical, almost as critical as heart surgery. She always concentrates on every answer I give her and she looks like she turns all the words around like some diamond cutter, studying, thinking, scrutinizing each syllable. It can almost drive you nuts!" I burst out.

Dr. Marlowe laughed.

"She has a wonderful reputation. Dr. Morton is highly respected," she said.

"I wouldn't want her job," Misty offered.

"It's like King Solomon in the Bible cutting that baby in two," Star said.

"Cutting a baby? I don't remember that," Misty said, "not that I've read much of the Bible."

"He didn't cut it. He said he would when the two women claimed to be the mother. And the one who was the mother told him not to do it. Told him to give the baby to the other woman," Star explained.

"She gave up her child?"

"She'd rather see that happen than the baby dead. That's not so hard to understand."

"My parents would rather see me cut in half," I muttered. Misty spun around to look at me. "I can't help it," I said. "That's how I feel. Stop looking at me like that. I'm not the bad one here."

My stomach tightened again.

"Talk about dynamite sticks," Star said, looking up at me. "No one's accusing you of anything."

"Yeah, maybe not now, but soon, one of my parents will, the one who loses," I said.

"No, they won't," Star said. "Your daddy will just accuse your mother of all that poison you mentioned before, or your mother will do the same to him."

"Maybe," I said, "but I couldn't help being nervous when I answered Dr. Morton's questions, no matter how harmless she made them sound.

"At first she asked me to talk about myself, my daily routine, my interests, my school work. That moved to what life was like in my house, how often I spent time with my parents, how often I was just with my father or my mother and if I enjoyed spending time with each of my parents. She wanted to know how I felt about either of them not spending more time with me, how interested I was in each of their lives, too. I think she was surprised at how little I know about their work. I wasn't even sure what my mother did at her job, and I couldn't explain what my father was working on at the moment.

"Dr. Morton had a way of keeping her attention on me while she jotted notes. I tried to figure out what was important to her and what wasn't, but everything seemed important. Finally, she asked if she could see my room. I took her upstairs and she walked around, looking at my things. Then she started to ask me questions about dolls, clothes, pictures. Who gave me what? How did I feel about it? What was precious to me? Why? Every time she asked me something and I answered, I couldn't help wondering does that help my father or my mother more?

"Then she set up some 'what if' situations for me and asked for my comments," I said.

"What if's?" Misty asked.

"What if your father won custody but your mother won the house, would you mind moving out with him and living with him someplace else? What if you had to leave the school you were in? What if your mother moved out and wanted you to live in a different part of the city? Would I miss my friends?

"Then she asked how I would feel if the court awarded custody to my father and how would I feel if it awarded custody to my mother?

"She was surprised when I said I didn't care.

" 'Do you say that because you don't want to hurt one or the other?' she asked.

"I thought about it for a moment and said, 'No, I said it because I feel like I'm not living with them now so who I live with afterward won't make much difference.'

"I remember she just stared at me and then jotted something on her clipboard and told me she might be back when my parents were there, too. I told her to call well in advance. 'I don't even know when they'll be here together,' I said.

"I was deeply in it now, deeply in the quicksand their marriage had become, and I hated it more than ever. Because of Rosina, my parents found out that Dr. Morton had been there and each of them found a way to be alone with me to question me about her and the things she wanted to know. Both were surprised I hadn't mentioned her visit myself, and I could see they each took that to mean I might have spoken against them.

" 'What did she want to know about us?' they both asked, but what each really meant was, 'What did she want to know about me and what did you tell her?'

" 'She asked me not to talk about the questions she asked me,' I told them, 'not that she asked that much or I said much. She had a lot of questions about the house,' I added. Of course, I made that up.

"I know neither was happy with my replies. I felt as if I was living in a spy school or something, each of them peeping around corners now, listening with one ear to my phone conversations, checking my mail, searching for clues as to what I have said and what I would say.

"It got so I didn't want to go home anymore. I dreaded the evenings and especially the dinners if they were both at the table. I could see the way they analyzed my every comment and soon I hardly said a word, or if they asked questions, I kept my answers to one or two words.

"The funeral atmosphere that I had felt in the house before thickened like fog. I could feel the crisis building, the tension stretching until something was bound to snap.

"The only way to escape the awful tension and avoid dealing with either one of them was to lock myself in my room and disappear into the world beyond my computer screen. I'd used my computer mainly for schoolwork but soon I discovered chat rooms where there were people talking about movie stars or bands I liked."

"Chat rooms?" Star asked.

"You don't have a computer?" I thought *everyone* had a computer these days.

"Hardly," she said. "We're lucky we have a microwave."

Misty laughed and even Cat smiled.

"You go on-line and you can talk to people all over the country, all over the world, for that matter."

"Talk?"

"Well, you don't actually talk. You write and they write back instantly and you carry on conversations, sometimes with a dozen people at once. Some of my friends are really into it.

"One night, I noticed a private chat room and just sat back and read the dialogues. Most people make up names to use, but sometimes you can tell a little about them from the names they choose, like Metal Man is probably into heavy rock music, understand?"

"I guess," Star said.

"Anyway, I was reading the conversation and I realized someone named Loneboy had parents who were in a bitter divorce, too. I asked him how old he was and he said seventeen. He said he had a younger brother who was taking the divorce a lot harder than he was. In fact, his little brother was already in therapy because he was acting out, much like you said your brother Rodney was doing, Star, breaking things, getting into fights with other children at school, stuff like that.

"Anyway, Loneboy and I exchanged some information and soon afterward, we skipped the chat room and E-mailed each other directly instead. He told me he lived in San Francisco. The more he told me about himself, the more I told him about myself."

"Why didn't you just call him on the phone?" Star asked.

"I don't know. He didn't suggest it and neither did I. I think he was afraid of hearing my voice or maybe me hearing his. He hadn't told me his name yet. I mean his real name."

"Just Loneboy?" Misty said. "All this time?"

"Yes. I have to admit it was just easier this way. You don't confront the other person as directly. You feel . . . safer," I said looking at Dr. Marlowe.

"I told him most of what I've been telling you. His home situation was a lot stormier, more like Star's in a way. His mother found out his father was seeing another woman and they got into a bad fight in front of the younger brother who saw his father strike his mother. The police were involved. It went from a domestic abuse case to a divorce. Loneboy liked his father but turned on him when he cheated on his mother and they had words. Later, he and his father had a calm conversation and Loneboy said he didn't hate him as much. He understood a little more about his father and why he had cheated on his mother.

"Still, he was unhappy about what was happening to his younger brother and he blamed his father mostly for that because his mother eventually deserted them."

"Why did she desert her own kids?" Misty asked.

"Maybe she just used the marriage problems as an excuse to run off and do what she always wanted to do anyway," Star suggested.

"That's what Loneboy believed, I think, although his father didn't avoid blame. He said he just felt trapped in the bad marriage and didn't know what to do."

"Didn't you ever find out his real name?" Misty asked.

"Finally, he told me his name was Craig Bennet. He gave me his address too and described his home as one that had been in his father's family for a long time."

"And he already knew your name?" Star asked.

"Yes. I didn't know much about chat rooms when I first started going to them so I just used my real name. After a while, Craig started to give me advice about how to deal with my problems at home. Some of it made sense to me, like advising me to get more involved in the things

I liked. He said the best thing for me to do at this point was to be self-centered, too, to stop worrying about my parents and their feelings and to care only about my own. Just because they messed up their lives, he said, it didn't mean I had to mess up mine.

" 'Survival,' he said, 'that's what you should think about and how you won't let them ruin your life with their petty problems.'

"He wasn't all seriousness though; he knew lots of good jokes and our Internet relationship grew stronger and stronger until I had the courage to scan my picture and E-mail it to him. I waited nervously to get his response. It came in one word."

"What?" Misty asked.

"Wow!"

Misty laughed.

"I asked him to send me his picture and he did. He wasn't bad-looking, kind of sensitive-looking, in fact. I didn't send back 'Wow,' but I told him I thought he was a good-looking guy and he shouldn't worry about finding someone.

"He said he already had. Me.

"I began to feel good about myself again, not that I didn't have lots of boys wanting to go out on dates with me, but none of them really wanted to hear about my problems. Craig seemed so much more mature than the boys at school and what I thought I needed at this point in my life more than anything was a mature, good friend, someone who could understand what I was going through. I was really lucky to find someone who was in a situation similar in many ways to my own."

"Yeah, wonderful," Star said. She looked like she was getting bored.

"I'm just trying to explain why I did it," I said.

"Did what?" Star asked.

"Decided that when I ran away, I would run to him. I don't know what I was thinking. I guess I got so desperate for good news and good feelings and thoughts, I let my fantasies explode.

"I envisioned being with someone who understood my every feeling and I wanted to shut the door on my life at home, not answer a single question more, not deal with lawyers or judges, and especially not listen to one of my parents downgrade the other with the hope I would agree.

"One night after the custodial assessment had begun and statements were being taken from my guidance counselor, some teachers and family friends, my parents had a particularly bad argument. They each accused the other of backstabbing sabotage with the intention of making the other look like an irresponsible parent. Their attorneys had been sniffing around Dr. Morton's assessment to date and apparently she wasn't very complimentary about either of them.

" 'You're trying to get my own daughter to hate me,' my father accused.

" 'That's exactly what you hope to do,' my mother responded. 'Fill her head with lies about me.'

"I slammed my door shut and turned up my music to drown out their voices.

"Later, they each took turns coming to my room to complain about the other. I ignored their complaints and reminded each that it was the week of the Honor Society inductions with a ceremony on Thursday night. I was still a member, somehow keeping my grades up, and there was a reception. Everyone's parents would be there. However, my father had to leave for Texas and my mother had already booked herself in Atlanta for a cosmetics convention. Neither had remembered the affair, but what I understood was when my father knew my mother wasn't going to be there and she knew he wasn't, they were both comfortable with not being there. Know what I mean?"

"Neither would look good to Dr. Morton because they both had deserted you," Cat said.

"That's right."

"But what about you?" Misty asked.

"Yes, what about me?"

They waited.

I smiled.

"I decided I wasn't going to attend either. I had another obligation too."

"What obligation?" Star asked.

"My obligation to run away," I said. "And that was just what I did."

5

"It's probably a good time to break for lunch," Dr. Marlowe said.

"I'd rather hear Jade's story," Misty whined.

"Speak for yourself, girl. My stomach's rumbling and her story will still be here when we get back," Star told her.

"Jade could use the rest, I'm sure," Dr. Marlowe said.

I wasn't hungry, but it was a good idea to stop for a while. When I rose, I felt as if I had been running, not sitting. Riding a roller coaster of emotions, even only in memory, was exhausting.

On a table on the closed-in patio, Emma had set up a buffet of cold cuts, cheeses, some salad, bread and rolls. There was a variety of cookies, too.

"I changed my mind," Misty said when she set eyes on it all, "I'm glad we stopped for lunch."

Star grunted, but Cat actually broke out in a wide smile. I say broke out because for her a smile was something smothered beneath shyness and fear most of the time I had been with her. Whenever she did smile, I felt as if it had escaped from under the weight of sadness that usually soaked her face like ink in a blotter.

"Just dig in, girls," Dr. Marlowe said.

We filled our dishes and sat at the table, Dr. Marlowe joining us last. Emma rushed in and out, replenishing meats and cheeses as if she had three times the number of people for lunch than were actually here.

"Thank you, Emma," Dr. Marlowe called to her as she hurried back to the kitchen.

"Why doesn't Emma eat with us?" Misty asked.

"Maybe she's afraid she'll catch something," Star said.

"What could she catch, a bad attitude?" I said. Star looked at me for a moment and then shook her head and bit into her sandwich.

"Emma has always been very shy," Dr. Marlowe offered. "And she likes to think the best of people, look harder for the good in everyone."

"That's why she's the way she is," Star muttered.

"What do you mean? You don't know how she is," I said. She smirked as if I had said something stupid. "Well, do you?"

"She's living here with her sister like some maid. What has she got for herself? I'm not blind and I don't look at the world through . . . what did you call them?" she asked Dr. Marlowe. "Rosy-colored glasses?"

"Rose-colored. That's what Emma wears," Dr. Marlowe said, nodding with a smile. "She's not as unhappy as you might imagine, Star. She's comfortable, safe and she's home. She knows I'll do whatever I can for her and she would do the same for me. The way the world seems sometimes, that's a lot."

"Amen to that," Star said, yet I could still see skepticism lurking in her eyes.

After having heard Star's story, I couldn't fault her for doubting Emma's happiness. I just hoped like Dr. Marlowe that we could have a positive effect on each other.

"Do you counsel her too?" Star asked the question we'd all wondered about.

"Not formally, but we talk a lot. You'd be surprised at how much she helps me."

"Were you close when you were younger?" Misty asked.

"Not as much as I would have liked us to be, no," Dr. Marlowe said. "And Emma got married early."

"How early?" Star asked.

"She was just nineteen," Dr. Marlowe said. By now it was possible for me to read her a little and know when something displeased her. I could hear it in her voice and in the way her eyes shifted quickly as if she hoped to change the subject.

"You didn't think she should get married?" I asked, turning the tables on Dr. Marlowe. Let her sit in the hot seat for a while.

"My father was a very strong man, strong-willed. He thought it would be the best thing for her," she said.

"You mean, he arranged it?" Misty asked with those innocent, wide eyes.

"Let's just say he exerted strong influences on everyone concerned," she replied.

"Everybody thinks they know what's best for everyone else," Star chimed in, but looking pointedly at me. "Giving advice at the drop of a moan. There are Dear Abby's preaching on every street corner nowadays."

Dr. Marlowe laughed.

"I'm afraid Star's right about that."

"Maybe people think if they fill their heads with someone else's business, they don't have to worry about their own," Star said.

"You might have something there," Dr. Marlowe told her. "That's an astute comment, Star."

Star took a bite of her sandwich and glittered with glee at the compliment. I couldn't help but laugh.

"What's so funny?"

"Us," I said. "Even thinking for one moment that we have anything to offer anyone else."

"Don't be so hard on yourself, Jade," Dr. Marlowe said. "You'd be surprised how difficulties in life often make you more of an expert than you think. It's why I wanted you all together."

"Maybe she should borrow Emma's glasses," Star said.

Cat laughed so loudly we all turned to her and she blushed.

"You think she's right?" I asked her sharply.

To my surprise she didn't back down. Her eyes looked directly into my own and then she said, "I hope so."

Misty smothered a giggle. Dr. Marlowe's eyes lit like Christmas lights and Star went to the table for seconds.

We'll see how smug and funny they are when they hear the rest of my story, I thought.

And then I asked myself why didn't I want them to be happy?

Was it because misery loves company?

I'd rather be happy and alone.

When we returned to Dr. Marlowe's office I felt like I was coming back to the stage after an intermission, as if I were in a school play. I had been in two plays, one in junior high and one when I was a sophomore and then I stopped trying out even though my drama teacher kept asking me to audition. Maybe I thought if the spotlight hit me, really concentrated on me, everyone in the audience would know I had been turned into a shadow.

Taking a deep breath, I began again.

"I had dinner by myself the night of the Honor Society induction. Mrs. Caron, feeling sorry for me, made my favorite meal: veal cordon bleu."

"What's that?" Star asked, grimacing. "Blue veal?"

"No," I said. "It's veal rolled and stuffed with ham and cheese. It's French."

"Pardon my ignorance," she said. "I'll take my grandmother's fried chicken. That's American."

I raised my eyes toward the ceiling.

"May I continue?" I asked.

"By all means," Star said.

"Thank you. I felt bad for Mrs. Caron, but I really had no appetite. She asked if I was sick and I apologized and told her to save the leftovers for me. She rarely did. My mother has this thing about leftovers. Every week we would throw away enough to feed a family like ours for another week. My father complains a lot about that, but my mother accuses him of wanting to take risks with our health just to save a dollar and he backs down.

"I rose from the table and wandered through the empty house. I could swear the echoes of a hundred recent arguments were bouncing from wall to wall in practically every room. I imagined the house itself taking on a dreariness, the colors fading, the windows clouding as if the storm of my parents' divorce was raining gloom and doom over furniture, pictures, and decorations. Cold hate was dripping down the walls in the house I once thought was my perfect little world.

"It made me laugh to think about that and I guess I laughed so hard and loud, it brought Mrs. Caron and Rosina out of the kitchen to see what was happening.

" 'Are you all right?' Mrs. Caron asked.

" 'What? Oh, yes,' I said. 'I'm fine. I was just laughing at the rain.'

" 'Rain?' She looked at Rosina and they both looked at me with concern. 'It's not raining, Jade.'

" 'No? I guess that's just tears then. The house is crying. Yes, that's it, Mrs. Caron, the house is sobbing. Don't you hear it? Listen,' I said and tilted my head.

"They stared at me with questions in their eyes. I smiled and told them not to worry. My father had designed the house so it could withstand months and months of weeping.

"Then I turned and pounded up the stairway, holding my hands over my ears, and shut myself up in my room. For a while I just sat on the bed and stared at myself in the vanity mirror. I tried to go through the motions of preparing for the Honor Society reception, but after I put on my dress and looked at myself, I just burst into tears.

"It's catching, I told myself. The house is infecting me. I've got to get out of here before it's too late, I told myself. I rushed around my room and threw some clothes together into a small backpack. Then I called for a taxi. First, I had the driver take me to the bank where I withdrew five hundred dollars from the ATM. Then I had him take me to the airport. I bought a ticket to San Francisco on the next flight. I remember looking at my watch during the flight and thinking I would have been sitting on the stage at this moment, gazing out at the audience of parents and friends, looking vainly for my own. I closed my eyes and fell asleep.

"When I arrived in San Francisco, I took a cab to Craig's home. I had no idea what I would say or do when I got there. I just wanted to talk to him, to spend time with him.

"He lived on Richland Avenue near Holly Park. I had been to San Francisco before, but I'd never been to his neighborhood. Craig's house looked as old as he had described it. It was a three-story Italianate with a low-pitched roof. The bottom floor had bay windows and the stucco exterior had faded into a brownish-yellow.

"It was just after nine when I arrived. Most of the windows were dark with just a dull glow in one of the first-floor windows. No one's home, I thought, but went up to the door and rang nevertheless. It took so long for anyone to answer that I had already started back down the short stairway.

" 'Yes?' I heard and turned to see a tall, lean man with thin, graying light brown hair, some of the strands so long, they drooped over his eyes and hung down over his ears. It was hard to make out the details of his face because the light was so dim behind him.

" 'I'm looking for Craig Bennet,' I said nervously.

"He simply stood there, gazing out at me as if I hadn't spoken. For a moment, I wondered if I had only imagined asking for Craig. I repeated Craig's name just in case.

" 'Who are you?' the man asked in return. I told him and again, he just stood there staring.

" 'Oh,' he finally said. 'Craig mentioned you to me. You're the computer girl.'

" 'Yes,' I said, smiling at the label. 'I'm the computer girl.'

"The way I was feeling, I might as well have been something created in a computer.

" 'Well, what are you doing here?' he asked.

" 'I came to San Francisco and I thought it would be nice for us to finally meet face to face,' I said.

" 'Oh sure. That is nice. Come on in,' he said.

" 'Is Craig at home?' I asked, hesitating. My legs were smarter than my brain. They held back on their own.

"No, not at the moment. He's gone on some errands for us, but he'll be home very soon,' he said.

"He stepped back and waited, holding the door open for me.

" 'Come on in. He won't be long,' he promised.

"I walked up the steps and entered the house. It was so dark and musty. There was a lot of wood trim along the entryway and on my right was a grandfather clock that wasn't working.

" 'I was just reading,' he said. 'You kids don't do enough of that these days, not since you discovered computers. Come into the living room. Can I get you something to drink?'

" 'No thank you,' I said, following him. The living room was small and cluttered with antique furniture."

"How did you know so much about all that?" Star asked skeptically. It was as though she thought I was making up the whole thing. As if I would make up something like this.

"My father," I said. "Some of it rubbed off whether I wanted it to or not.

"Getting back to what I was saying," I added, "he had one lamp on by a threadbare Chippendale wing chair." I said it with deliberate exactness to annoy her now.

" 'Well, have a seat,' he offered, indicating the settee across from him. 'You look like you just arrived in town.'

" 'I did,' I said.

" 'Who you visiting with?'

" 'No one,' I made the mistake of saying. 'I mean, it's a spur of the moment trip.'

"He smiled and sat. Under the lights I could see the resemblances between him and Craig from the picture Craig had attached to his E-mail. His eyes were as deeply set and his nose the same nearly perfectly straight shape, just a trifle too long, but adding character. His mouth had similarly full masculine lips and he had the same soft curve from his cheekbone to his jaw.

" 'Craig's quite taken with you,' he said. 'He talks about you a lot.'

" 'Does he? We did sort of hit it off and I thought it would be great to finally meet.'

"There was a strange smell—more than just a musty odor now. It smelled more like incense or something. I guess I twitched my nose and he saw it and laughed.

" 'We just finished dinner a little while ago. I'm not the best cook. I burned the potatoes. We were about to have coffee when we discovered we didn't have any. We're both failing pretty bad at domestic chores,' he explained. There was a little lisp in his speech and from the way his mouth dipped on the right side when he spoke, I wondered if he hadn't suffered a stroke or something. Now that I looked at him more closely, I could see how thin he was and how his right shoulder slanted a bit lower than his left.

" 'Where's Sonny?' I asked, referring to Craig's younger brother.

" 'Oh, he went along with him. You can't keep those two apart. Nothing Sonny likes more than spending time with Craig. He looks up to him like Craig's a superhero, and Craig loves and protects him. They've come together like this,' he said, holding his hand up in a tightly closed fist. 'Since she left us, all three of us are like this.'

" 'That's nice,' I said smiling. It did sound nice, although from some of the things Craig had said in his E-mails, I didn't think life was as rosy as Mr. Bennet portrayed.

" 'He told you about this house?' he asked.

" 'Yes,' I said.

" 'You can appreciate it since your father's an architect, I bet. It was something in its day.'

" 'Craig really has told you a lot about me, I see,' I said. 'You know my father is an architect.'

" 'Oh, yes. We don't keep much from each other anymore. That's because we're all like one,' he said, holding up that bony fist again. 'She didn't destroy us when she ran off. She made us stronger. In some ways I'm glad she went. She was never happy being tied down. She had the wanderlust. We got married too early. It was as if I had tamed a wild horse or something. Babies were lead weights around her neck. She and I stopped making love after Sonny was born; she was afraid of having another child. You know what happens to a marriage once the romance goes out of it?'

" 'Yes,' I said and thought it was a strange conversation for him to have with a total stranger, but I imagined that in his mind, because of my E-mail correspondence with Craig, he didn't think of me as a complete stranger.

" 'Craig told you a little about the divorce, right?' he asked. 'I know you told him all about your parents' situation.'

" 'Yes.' I said.

"Actually, I was getting a little upset at how much Craig had told his father. None of my friends would have shared so much with their parents. Had Craig gone so far as to print out my letters? I wondered.

"As if he could read my thoughts, Mr. Bennet added, 'Craig often read your letters at dinner to us. I'm sorry for your troubles at home.

Your parents sound like . . . dummies,' he suggested. 'Why can't they see what they're doing to you? It pains Craig to read some of that stuff. He gets so angry, he can't eat. He wants to know why adults are so cruel to their own children.

" 'Then he starts talking about his own mother and asking me more questions so he can tell you about her, I think. I hate talking about her. I try to forget her. I even got so I can't recall her face anymore. You can push things out of your mind if you want to, you know. You just think of something else every time the bad things come up. You say, no, no to it. Get out, out!' he practically screamed.

" 'I used to sit in front of a mirror and stare into my own eyes and just dare a memory to come into my head. You should try it sometime. It helps, believe me,' he said.

"I smiled at him and gazed around curiously. The room looked like it needed more than just a good dusting. I saw cobwebs in the corners and layers of dust on the marble mantel. When I gazed down at the floor around his chair, I saw what looked like caked old food and I could have sworn I caught sight of a rat slipping behind the armoire."

"Ugh," Misty cried. "Why didn't you just leave?"

"I still wanted to see Craig.

" 'You're as pretty as your picture,' Mr. Bennet said. 'Craig's going to be happy you came. I know what,' he said, slapping his hands together, 'why don't I show you his room and his computer while you wait?'

" 'He might not like that,' I said.

" 'Sure he will. Don't you want to see it? That's where your friendship began. It's like . . . like something historic for you two. Right?'

" 'Yes, but . . .'

" 'Well, then don't be shy. Not with Craig. Not after all you two have shared. Why, he's told you more about us than he's told relatives and best friends, and I bet you've done the same. I can see from the look on your face that you have. That's nice. That's something unusual these days . . . trust. You're the nicest thing to come into his life since . . . since before,' he said, and I could tell he was doing what he described: keeping the bad memories out.

" 'I bet you'd like to see this old house anyway,' he added, standing up. 'He told you how long it's been in the family, right?'

" 'Yes,' I said. 'I know the style. My father built a house like this for a client in Beverly Hills two years ago.'

" 'This house was built in 1870,' he began proudly as he headed for the door. He paused, waiting. Once again, my smarter legs hesitated, but

I forced myself up and followed him out. 'Of course, a lot was done to it since, but not so much over the past forty years or so.

" 'Craig's room is on the third floor with the best view,' he said, leading me up the rickety stairway after he flipped a switch that lit up a small, naked bulb overhead.

"We wound around and up. The second-floor landing was narrow and smaller than I had anticipated and the third floor was really more like an attic. There was just one bedroom and an adjoining small bathroom. He turned on the light and I saw the computer on the desk to the left. It was on, the monitor glowing. In the center of the room was a four-poster bed, and to the right of that, a dresser and a closet. The bed was neatly made, almost as tightly tucked as a military bunk.

"There was little on the walls, some pictures of Craig and Sonny but when they were considerably younger, a picture of a jet plane and a poster of an old Star Trek movie. It gave me a strange feeling, like I was moving back through time rather than looking in on what was someone's present bedroom.

" 'Here,' Mr. Bennet said, 'look at this.' He was at the computer table. 'Your most recent letter.' He held it up and I walked in and looked at it. It was my most recent E-mail. 'Just take a gander at that view from that window,' he suggested, moving away from the computer. 'You'll see why Craig would rather stay up here than any other part of this house. We've still got one of the best views in the neighborhood. Go on,' he urged.

"I walked to the window and looked out. The casing was so caked with dust, it was obvious that the window hadn't been opened for a long time, maybe even years. The view was nice, especially because it was night and there were so many lights.

" 'Very nice,' I said, turning. He was at the door, smiling.

" 'Good. I'm glad you like it. Enjoy,' he said and stepped out into the hall. 'I'll tell Craig you're up here when he comes home.'

" 'What?' I gasped as he closed the door. 'Wait,' I cried. I moved toward it but stopped when I heard the lock click. It was one of those skeleton key door locks that you could shut from the outside. The click was like a bullet whizzing by my head. What was going on? I wondered.

"I ran to the door and pulled on the handle, shocked now that he had locked me in.

" 'Mr. Bennet!' I cried. 'What are you doing? Why did you lock the door? Let me out. Please.'

"I could hear his footsteps as he descended the stairway and then all was silent and the glow of the computer played shadows on the opposite wall. I pounded on the door and screamed and pounded and then listened, but I heard nothing. I put my ear against the door, pounded and waited and listened and then I heard some music start below, light, big band music.

"I returned to the window, thinking I might be able to open it and shout down to someone on the street, but the casing really was as good as welded shut. For a few moments I toyed with the idea of smashing the window."

"That's what I would have done," Star said.

"Me too," Misty agreed.

Cat had her head down, her arms embracing herself. She looked like she was trembling. That's what I was like in that room, I thought.

"I thought about it, but to be honest, I was afraid of what he might do to me if I broke his window."

"You were worrying about his window?" Star asked, incredulous.

"Not his window. She was worried about what he'd do to *her*," Misty piped up. "Obviously, the man was deranged to have locked her in. You don't just challenge such people."

"What are you, an expert?" Star fired back at her.

Misty shrugged.

"She's right," I said, "and besides, I was hoping that Craig would be back any moment like Mr. Bennet had said and would come up and rescue me," I added before they could continue their argument.

"Sure. A crazy man locks you in a room and you decide to wait around. That makes a lot of sense," Star muttered and shook her head.

"While I waited, I explored the room," I continued. "I opened the dresser drawers. They were all empty. I looked in the closet and saw only half a dozen naked hangers. In the corner on the floor was some sort of rodent nest."

"Oh my God," Misty moaned. "You mean, rats?"

"Ugh," Star said.

"Anyway," I said, "I closed the door and went to the computer. There were some notes scribbled on a pad beside it. They looked like E-mail addresses. Mine was included.

"I tried the door again, pulling on it, pounding and then I sat on the bed, trying to think what I should do next. Where was Craig? Was he even coming home? I wondered. Moments later, I heard footsteps on the stairway. They sounded like someone running up and I assumed it was Craig, angry about what his father had done. I heard him stop just outside the door. I waited and listened, but all I heard was the music from below. Then I saw the door knob turning, but the door didn't open.

" 'Craig?' I called. 'Is that you?'

" 'Yes,' I heard after a long moment of silence. His voice was higher pitched than I had imagined it would be. 'I'm sorry about this. He's not well. The son has become the father in this house.'

" 'Can you open the door?' I asked calmly. This was something he had never mentioned in his letters to me, you see.

" 'I thought he left the key in the lock,' he said. 'I have to go back down and get it from him. I'll be right back,' he said.

"I heard his footsteps on the stairs descending quickly. What a mess I put myself in, I thought and tried to remain calm and keep my heart from thumping like a bongo drum. For a minute or two, all I heard was the music. Then, I heard loud voices, clearly voices in argument. I thought I even heard something smash against the wall, then more arguing and then silence. Even the music stopped. I waited by the door, listening hard for footsteps on the stairs.

"They came, but very slowly, heavy. At one point they paused and I called out. They started again and finally they reached the third-story landing. I stepped back from the door and waited.

"I heard the key in the lock. My heart wasn't thumping anymore. It was more like an oil drill pounding deeper and deeper until it vibrated down my spine. The back of my neck was perspiring so much, strands of my hair were soaked.

"The door opened slowly and Mr. Bennet was standing there. My heart sunk. What had he done to Craig? What would he do to me?

" 'I'm sorry,' he said in that high-pitched voice. 'My father is not the same since she left. There's no telling what he'll do sometimes. I didn't write about it in my E-mail because I never thought you'd come here like this, but I'm glad you did,' he added.

"I just stared, my eyes probably close to popping."

"How weird," Misty said in a loud whisper. She had her hands pressed to the base of her throat. Cat was biting down on her lower lip and even Star looked absolutely terrified. Dr. Marlowe sat watching them, her eyes moving slowly from one to the other and then back to me.

" 'You're not Craig,' I managed to say.

"He laughed.

" 'Oh, that was an old picture I sent. It's me, in the flesh, your old computer sidekick, Loneboy.'

"I shook my head, tried to swallow and then took a deep breath so I could speak.

" 'I made a mistake,' I said. I tried to smile, tried not to show my absolute terror. 'I have to go.'

" 'Oh, but you just arrived as I understand it. Don't go just yet. We have a lot to talk about. You want something to eat, drink?'

" 'No thank you,' I said, edging toward the door. However, he kept himself smack in front of it, blocking it.

" 'Go sit on my bed. It's comfortable,' he urged, nodding toward the bed. 'Go on.'

" 'I'd rather we went downstairs. The living room was nice,' I said.

" 'Naw. He won't let us talk. He'll butt in and Sonny will want us to pay him attention. We're better off staying up here. Go on. Sit,' he ordered.

"I shook my head.

" 'I really have to go,' I said.

" 'Oh, you can't leave now,' he pleaded. 'You're the first girl I've had up here, ever. I've dreamed of it, but you're the first. C'mon. Sit,' he repeated, moving toward me.

"I jumped back, holding my backpack up in front of me like a shield now.

"He smiled.

" 'Oh, you brought stuff. That means you're staying for a while. Good,' he said.

" 'No,' I cried. 'I've got people waiting for me. They're expecting me and will come looking for me.'

"His smile faded. It seemed to sink into his face.

" 'I thought you came to San Francisco to see me,' he said.

" 'I did, but I can't stay. I'm late,' I said, edging around, hoping to squeeze by him.

" 'You want to leave me, too,' he suddenly declared, as though he had come to some realization and it filled his eyes with anger. 'Just like her, you want to leave. You tell me you love me and you care and then you leave. That's cruel. That's selfish. Why don't you care about me? Was all that stuff you wrote just garbage? Why don't you mean what you say?'

" 'I do,' I said quickly. 'That's why I showed up. You were the first person I thought about when I decided to come here,' I added.

"His smile returned.

" 'I'm glad.'

" 'But I have to meet some people, relatives.'

" 'You never mentioned having any relatives here,' he said suspiciously.

" 'I know. I had forgotten about them. They called and invited me and I came, but I told them I had to stop by and say hello to you first,' I added. I was thinking as fast as I could, heaving words and thoughts at him in the hope that he would be satisfied and step aside.

"He didn't move.

" 'I'll be back tomorrow,' I promised. 'We'll spend the whole day together.'

" 'No, you won't,' he said, shaking his head. 'That's what she said before she left us. She said, I'm just going away for a little while. Don't be sad. I'll be back soon. I believed her and I waited. Every night, I sat by the window and looked out at the street and waited, but she didn't return. She just said she would.'

" 'But I will,' I insisted. 'I'm not her. I'm Jade, remember?'

"He didn't look like he was listening to me anymore. His eyes were glassy and he seemed to be gazing through me at his memories now. He seemed frozen, almost catatonic, so I started toward the door, inching along. Then, I lunged for it and he reached around and seized my hair, tugging me back with such force, I fell to the floor.

"I screamed and screamed and he just stood there looking down at me as if I was some curious new creature. He wasn't bothered or afraid or even angry. He was just looking at me until my throat ached and I stopped, covering my face as I began to sob.

"He reached down slowly and first took my backpack out of my hands. He tossed it out the door. Then, he surprised me by seizing the backs of both of my feet and pulling my shoes off. He tossed them out the door, too."

"Why?" Misty asked, grimacing.

"He didn't want her to leave," Cat said. It was as if her voice came out of nowhere, as if she was a ghost that had come to life.

Everyone turned to her and she looked down and then back up at me.

"Then what did he do?" Star asked.

"I don't know if I want to hear it," Misty moaned.

"I pushed myself back on the floor and he continued to hover over me.

" 'Go ahead and sit on the bed,' he said calmly. 'It's comfortable.'

"He took another step toward me and I did as he asked.

" 'Now isn't that better than the floor?' he asked.

" 'If you don't let me leave, you're going to be in big trouble,' I told him.

" 'If you leave, you won't come back,' he said. 'You'll run out on us, on me and Sonny. It's not our fault what he did to you. Why do you want to run out on us?'

" 'You're confused,' I said. 'Please, let me go.'

"My stomach felt so hollow. My whole body was shaking. I wanted to fight him, but I was terrified that I would be too weak and he might hurt me very badly.

"He reached back and closed the door behind him. Then he smiled at me.

" 'I'm glad you came back,' he said. 'We have so much to talk about, so much to catch up on.'

"He started toward me and I shook my head, hoping I could make it all disappear. He put his hand on my head and stroked my hair and then held my head in his hands and leaned over to kiss the top of my head."

"You should have kicked him where he'd remember it forever," Star said.

"I thought about it for a second. My heart was racing. I could barely breathe. When he put his hands on my shoulders, I tried to push his arms away and I did try to kick up, but he pressed harder and harder. I was surprised at how strong his fingers were. They seemed to cut through my jacket, through my blouse and into my skin.

"Maybe he cut off the blood to my head. I don't know, but one moment I was trying to struggle and looking up at him and the next . . ."

"What?" Misty asked, gasping. She had reached across the sofa to Cat and found her hand. Cat let her hold on, or maybe Cat was holding on to her.

"I passed out," I said.

"And when I woke up, I was on my back on the bed, naked."

6

All the girls looked sick to their stomachs. Misty's face was pale, Star's mouth gaped open and Cat had to be excused to go to the bathroom.

"Let me check on her," Dr. Marlowe said, rising. "Everybody take a deep breath. Maybe step outside and get some air, if you want," she added.

We watched her go, nobody moving.

"Do you want to go outside?" Star asked me. I nodded.

We rose and went to the patio door, stepping into the afternoon sun. It felt good on my face, almost like a mother's kiss should feel when she wants to reassure you.

"You sure don't look like a girl who had all that happen to her," Star said warmly. "Granny's always saying don't judge a book by its cover. Turn a few pages first and look it over and then she always adds, 'Remember, he without sin cast the first stone.' She's always telling me stuff like that. She's trying to make up for all the Sunday school and church I missed, I guess."

An awkward silence fell between us. Misty still looked shaken by my story and my own mind was back in that room in San Francisco.

"What's with that Cat girl? Do you think she'll talk tomorrow?" Star asked, finally breaking the tension.

"After what she's heard from us, she's probably going to be on her way out of the country," Misty said.

We all laughed. I saw Star staring at me.

"What?"

"Nothing," she said.

I smiled at her.

"It's all right. We're all going to be all right," I said.

"Another pair of rose-colored glasses working away," she declared.

Misty and I laughed and then we heard Dr. Marlowe returning with Cat. I looked through the patio door and watched Cat sit and Dr. Marlowe leaning over her, offering some comforting words.

"Maybe I'm not doing her any good," I thought aloud.

"Dr. Marlowe wouldn't let you talk if she thought that, would she?" Misty asked. "I mean, she knew most of what you're telling us, right?"

"Most," I said. "But not all," I admitted. "More seems to come back to me than usually does when I'm alone with her, but there's still a lot left to tell."

"I guess that's why she wanted us to do this," Star said. "The same was true for me."

"Me too," Misty said.

I nodded.

Dr. Marlowe took her seat and looked out at us.

"Time to go back," I said. I took a deep breath as if I was going under water. "Let's get it over with."

We returned to the office and our seats.

"How are you doing, Jade?" Dr. Marlowe asked.

"I'm all right."

"We could stop and let you continue tomorrow."

"No, I don't want to sleep on any of it," I said and she nodded, smiling in understanding.

I turned to the girls.

"He didn't rape me," I said quickly. "When I was unconscious, I dreamed of someone's lips on my cheek, in my hair, then lightly over my eyelids and finally on my lips, but nothing more had happened. Star was right. Everything he did, he did mostly to keep me from leaving. In his madness he figured that if I didn't have clothes, I wouldn't try to escape."

Cat looked like I had taken a weight off her shoulders, as if what had happened to me could have happened to her.

"When you realized what he had done, did you break the window?" Misty asked.

"I couldn't reach it," I said.

"What? Why not?" Misty followed. Star nodded like she already knew.

"He had tied my left ankle to the bed and my right wrist. He used the computer cables—I guess he didn't want me to be able to call for help over the Internet. If only I'd thought of that sooner. Turn and twist as much as I could, I was unable to reach the knots and the movement cut through my skin. My ankle actually started to bleed."

"Oh no," Misty cried. "What happened next?"

"I lay there as quietly as I could, trying to keep from passing out again. I was terrified of what he might do next.

"It seemed like hours before he returned. He entered the room, smiling. He was carrying a children's book in his hand.

" 'Oh, you're still awake,' he said. 'I bet you've been having those nightmares again. Don't worry. I'll help you fall asleep.'

" 'Please,' I pleaded. 'Cut me loose. It's hurting me.'

" 'No, no,' he assured me. 'Nothing will hurt you now. You're safe, forever and ever with me.'

"The sound of that put the greatest terror in me. It occurred to me that my parents would never be able to discover where I had gone. They might, with the help of the police, find out I had bought a plane ticket to San Francisco, but I had never told them about Craig and our E-mail relationship. It might take months, maybe years before a smart detective might look in my computer for leads.

"I started to cry. I couldn't help it. He smiled as if that was good and pulled the computer chair beside the bed. Then he wiped the tears from my cheeks and actually tasted them."

"What?" Star asked. "Did you say, tasted?"

"Yes. He nodded and smiled and said, 'I love the salty taste of your tears. I know sometimes you cry just to make me happy.'

"He looked so contented. I forced myself to stop crying. Then he sat back, opened the book and began reading a story meant for a preschooler. He read it to me as if I were only three or four years old, exaggerating everything, raising and lowering his voice, acting happy and then sad when it was appropriate. I didn't utter a sound. When he finished, he closed the book and then leaned over and kissed my cheek.

" 'Time to sleep,' he said.

" 'Please,' I begged, 'let me go.'

" 'I'll stay with you until you fall asleep,' he promised and then, he lowered his head to my stomach and rested it there.

" 'I hear you gurgling,' he said and laughed. 'Go to sleep stomach. Go to sleep kidneys and liver, spleen and gall bladder. You, too, heart. C'mon now,' he said, touching me. I cringed, but he didn't do any more. I could feel his hot breath on my skin. I was as still as I could be and soon his breathing was so regular, I was sure he was asleep."

"On your stomach?" Misty asked.

"Yes. Now I was afraid to move too fast or hard, afraid to wake him.

All I could do was close my eyes and try to do what he had said he did all the time, drive out the bad thoughts. I thought about my house, my bedroom, my comfortable bed and I pretended I was home, pretended I had never run away. Exhausted from all the fear and the struggle, I did fall asleep.

"I woke sometime in the middle of the night. I was still tied down, of course, but I managed to turn my body in very slow moves, enduring the pain until I was able to touch the cable with my free hand. I traced it down and worked on tugging it away from my skin. It took hours and hours to gain a quarter of an inch of space, but that was not yet enough.

"It was exhausting, too. I fell asleep again and then I was awakened by the sound of the key in the door. It was morning, but very early because it looked like the sun had just risen. He entered the room, carrying a tray of breakfast: a glass of orange juice, some toast, a bowl of cornflakes with bananas and a flowery weed.

" 'I picked this for you this morning,' he said. 'Isn't it pretty?'

"I was still very afraid, but also very angry now.

" 'You've got to eat your breakfast,' he said. 'It's the most important meal of the day.'

" 'How can I eat? I can't even sit up,' I said.

"He looked at my tied ankle, thought for a moment and then put the tray on the chair. He untied my ankle.

" 'You can eat with one hand,' he said. Even in his madness, he had some logic. He wasn't stupid.

"At this point, I thought it was best to play along so I nodded, pulled my legs up and let him put the tray on my lap.

" 'That's freshly squeezed orange juice,' he said. 'Nothing but the best for you. Go on, drink it.' "

"It could have been poison," Misty said.

"I thought of that, but I didn't know what else to do but sip it. It tasted good. Then I smiled and said, 'Please, I have to go to the bathroom.'

" 'That's all right,' he said. He went out to the bathroom and returned with a bedpan."

"You mean like in a hospital?" Misty asked.

"Exactly. I shook my head and said, 'Please, I want to go into the bathroom.'

" 'Oh no,' he said, 'you can't get out of bed yet. You're not well enough.' He slipped the bedpan under me. Then he sat watching as if I was some kind of a toy."

"I feel like I'm going to puke," Misty said.

"What do you think she felt like?" Star shot at her.

Cat just stared ahead, waiting.

"I couldn't help it. I had to pee. He left with the bedpan. I can't tell you how weak and sick I felt.

" 'Finish your breakfast,' he said from the doorway. 'I'll be back a little later. I have a few chores. I'm going to make us a great dinner tonight, and I promise,' he said smiling, 'I won't burn anything.'

"Then he closed the door, locked it and descended. I waited for a while before putting the tray on the chair. With more room now because my foot was free, I worked harder and harder on the cable around my other wrist. I got myself enough space to turn my body and step off the bed. Then I saw where the cable was tied to the bed and was able to get it untied. It seemed to take hours and I kept stopping to listen for him. Sure enough, I heard him returning so I fixed the cable loosely and then I got back onto the bed. I dumped the cereal behind the bed and shoved the toast under the pillow just as he worked the key in the lock.

"It must have grown very cloudy and overcast because the room was so dark now and when I gazed out, it looked like it was going to storm. It made me feel even more frightened and cold.

" 'Well, well,' he said, 'you ate everything. Good.' He took the tray off the bed and then he pulled my ankle back down so he could retie it.

" 'Look what I brought you,' he said and gave me another children's book. 'I'll be back later to read it to you, but you can look at all the pictures now.'

"He gazed down at me happily. 'It's so good to have you back,' he said. 'So good.' He touched my forehead and then he turned and left, locking the door again.

"I waited for the silence and then I rose and undid the cable that held my wrist. It took longer to free my ankle, but finally, I was able to move about the room freely."

"But you were still locked in," Misty reminded me and everyone else.

"Exactly.

"Again, I didn't just break the window and scream. What if I was unable to attract anyone's attention? I was afraid he'd hear me and come back to the room in a rage. For a few minutes, I just looked frantically about the room, searching for some idea, some means of escape and then I got down and looked under the bed. You can imagine the balls of dust, but I saw a bedspring was broken and I worked it loose.

"Then I straightened it out as best I could and went to the keyhole. It took forever. I nearly gave up a few times, but finally I heard the lock click. I tried the knob and the door opened. I returned to the bed and pulled off the sheet to wrap around me before returning to the doorway.

"I stood there, trembling, afraid to step out for fear he would be waiting in the small hallway. Cautiously, I peered around and saw there was no one. I also spotted my backpack and my shoes against the wall.

"As quickly as I could, I pulled out a pair of panties, jeans and a blouse. I put on socks and my shoes. I don't think I ever dressed as fast.

"Now that I was dressed and considering my escape, I was even more afraid. Just gazing down that dimly lit stairway put a finger of ice on the back of my neck, a finger that traced down my spine and made me shudder.

"I began to descend. The first step groaned, so loudly I thought, there was no way he wouldn't hear and there wasn't any other way out of the house from this level as far as I could see."

"No fire escape?" Star asked.

"Maybe there was, but I didn't think of it. I kept going down the stairs, each step creaking louder than the one before it, and no matter how slowly I went and how nimbly I stepped, the stairway croaked like some giant frog. It was as if the house was being loyal to its owner and was trying to warn him about my escape. Even the railing rattled. I debated whether I should just charge down the stairs as fast as I could or continue to sneak along. I decided to risk taking my time.

"When I reached the second floor, I paused and listened. He could easily be in any of the rooms, I thought. I heard nothing now, not even the music I had heard the night before. The whole house continued to creak and moan as the wind outside stirred up and whirled about it.

"Just above me the dim light flickered. The rain had started and I could hear the pitter-patter of drops on the roof and against the windows. Shadows along the vaguely lit walls seemed to tremble like ghosts suffering a sympathetic chill. My imagination was like some caged animal, flailing about and coming up with so many crazy and frightening thoughts and images. I had the kind of rippling sensation on the back of my neck you get when you feel someone is watching you. I searched every shadow, every doorway, looking for eyes. Was someone else in this house?

"My heart thumped. I couldn't swallow and it felt like a heavy weight on my chest, but I went on. I don't know where I found the strength to continue moving forward, but I did.

"When I reached the bottom floor, I stopped, caught my breath and listened. It was so quiet, I considered that he might have gone out again. Practically tiptoeing now, I started for the front door and paused when I heard what sounded like a little boy whimpering.

"It continued for a few more moments and then stopped. I realized it was coming from the living room, dead ahead of me and between me and the front door. I could barely keep myself from releasing a sob or a cry of fear. I felt like I was squeezing the breath back into my lungs. I know I was fighting hysteria, pushing my fears down long enough to get strength to go forward.

"As I reached the living room door, I peered through and saw him in his chair. He had my clothes crushed in his arms and against his body like he was embracing a child and he was asleep, his head thrown back and his mouth quivering with nightmare sobs.

"I stepped up to the door and tried to open it as quietly as I could, only it was locked the same way my room upstairs had been locked, with an old-fashioned skeleton key. My heart sank.

"I turned and headed back into the house, hoping that he hadn't locked a rear or side door. All the lights were off and the storm made it so dark inside, I was terrified of knocking into something and waking him. I practically glided down the hallway to the kitchen where I saw another door, but it was locked as well."

"You should have brought that bedspring down with you and used it again," Misty said.

"Yeah, I thought of that, but going upstairs to get it was not an option in my mind."

"Wouldn't have been in mine either," Star said.

"I looked over the countertop carefully, hoping maybe I would find a key, but there wasn't any. Finally I found a window that would open and I raised it a jerky inch at a time. It went about six inches before it got so stuck I couldn't move it. I groaned and strained until I was exhausted. I just wanted to sit down and cry. A throbbing pain in my head stabbed sharply. What had I gotten myself into?"

"How were you supposed to know a weirdo was writing you those E-mails?" Star asked quickly. I smiled at how she didn't want me to blame myself, but I knew it was my own doing. I should have been more careful and not thrown myself into a stranger's world.

"I tried another window and it was worse. How did he ever get fresh air? I wondered. This house was like a dungeon in which all the terrible memories were being held prisoner inside that sick man, I thought."

"So what did you do?" Misty asked. "How did you finally get out?"

"I didn't want to wander around the house looking for a window that would open. I was sure I would knock something over or do something to call his attention to me, so I took a chance and returned to the front door. He was still asleep in the living room.

"I looked around, saw that the space between the wall and the grandfather clock was wide enough to hide me, and then I pounded on the front door and hurriedly hid behind the grandfather clock. I waited and waited, my heart ticking as loud as that clock once ticked, I imagine. He didn't come. After a good minute, I tiptoed over to the door and looked in on him. He had turned, but hadn't awakened, so I returned to the front door and pounded harder and longer. I hit it so hard, I thought the house shook. Desperation gave me the needed strength. Then I hurried behind the grandfather clock again and this time, I heard him stumble around and come out mumbling.

" 'Who's there?' he called. He listened and then he went to the door and listened. 'Little bastards,' he muttered, I guess thinking some neighborhood kids were playing a joke on him. Maybe they had done that before. He did what I hoped he would. He took the key from his pocket and unlocked the door. It was my intention to just rush out, knock past him and lunge out of the house, screaming for help, but he paused and turned to look toward the stairway. I could see he was thinking hard. He closed the door and started for the stairs, only he hadn't locked the door again. My plan had worked.

"I waited until he started up and had time to make the first turn before I stepped out, opened the door and flew down that small stairway to the street. When I got there, I ran and ran, not knowing where I was heading, ignoring the sheets of rain that were whipping at me. I just wanted to get as far away as I could. I ran until I was out of breath and a stitch in my side made me stop. I stood against a fence, holding my side and catching my breath. I was literally soaked, my hair drenched, the water running down my face, but I didn't care. I was so happy, I didn't feel anything else.

"Then I walked down to the far corner, crossed the street and walked until I spotted a restaurant. I went inside to the bathroom and dried myself as best I could. Then I called for a taxi to take me back to the airport. When I got there, I had to wait another hour for a flight back to Los Angeles.

"I nearly fell asleep and missed it. I did fall asleep when I got on the plane. I remember thinking, so much for my running away from home to see someone who could sympathize with me.

"There wasn't any place I could run to, I thought. That's all I had learned on this trip."

"That wasn't all," Star said.

"No, I guess not." I looked at Dr. Marlowe. "I guess I learned a lot about trust.

"Anyway, it was quite late in the day by the time I arrived at my house. Of course, my parents were still away and there was no one checking up on me. Occasionally, Mrs. Caron would look in on me or ask how I was when they were both away, but that was the extent of it. I entered the house very quietly. There was no one waiting around to greet me. When I checked my answering machine, I found a message from my girlfriend Sophie. She wanted to know why I hadn't attended the Honor Society induction ceremony and reception. She told me it was the nicest one."

"People always do that, even your supposed best friends. They tell you something was great when you miss it," Star muttered.

I laughed. It was as if she had known Sophie as long as I had.

"There were no other messages. Apparently neither of my parents had called. You can imagine how exhausted I was. I practically passed out before my head hit the pillow. I slept right through breakfast the following day. I vaguely heard Mrs. Caron outside my door asking if I was feeling all right. It took my missing two breakfasts before she would bother inquiring. I couldn't blame her. I was never one to appreciate her concern and she had decided early on that she would do her work and not poke her nose into our lives.

"I shouted that I was fine and thanked her for asking. She went away without asking any other questions.

"About an hour later, I showered, dressed, had a bagel and some coffee and went to school. I was in quite a daze most of the day. All the rest of the day, people asked why I hadn't attended the Honor Society function and I just used a stomachache as an excuse.

"My mother was the first to return home late in the afternoon. She flew by my room, saw I was sprawled on my bed, and came back.

" 'Hi,' she said. 'I'm having a maddening time. Felix lost the orders for the entire Longs Drugs account. Can you imagine? His computer crashed. You can't imagine what's going on, and all this while I was away.

" 'Oh, how was the Honor Society function?' she asked without pausing for a breath.

"I just stared at her. If I hadn't been lucky, I might be dead up in a room in a strange house in San Francisco, I thought, and my mother had no idea, not in her wildest imaginings, what I had been through. Orders for lipstick and make-up products were temporarily missing and her world was in turmoil. For a moment I wished I was a tube of mascara."

Misty laughed and Star and Cat smiled.

" 'I didn't go,' I told her.

" 'Oh. Why not?'

" 'I wasn't feeling well,' I said. I wanted to blurt, I ran away from home two days ago, used some of my special funds designed to make me independent and confident, and searched for a soul mate who didn't exist. Instead, Mom, some crazed man tried to keep me prisoner. He even took off my clothes after I passed out. He did a lot of other horrible things to me.

"In my mind I imagined her hearing this and saying, 'Oh. That's too bad. Well, how long do you think it will take for Felix to fix his computer?' "

No one laughed at my attempt at sick humor. I guess it wasn't really funny.

" 'Are you all right now?' my mother asked. 'Do you need to see a doctor?'

" 'No,' I said. I meant I'm not all right, but she took it to mean I didn't have to see a doctor.

" 'Well, just take it easy. I know you're probably nervous about your appointment with the judge at the end of the month, but it will be fine. That stupid Felix,' she added. 'He's such a . . . what would you say, dork?'

"She waited to see if I appreciated her attempt to speak the lingo. I just stared and she smiled and shook her head and hurried away.

"My father arrived just before dinner. Mother was in the office barking orders at Felix. My father put down his leather case that contained his drawings and listened to her shouting for a moment.

" 'The world of beautiful people appears to be in a crisis,' he declared and laughed.

"There was a time when he would feel sorry for her, sympathize and even offer some suggestions. How far apart they've grown in a few short months, I thought.

" 'And how's my favorite scholar? Did you knock them dead at the induction, make a speech or something?' he wondered.

" 'I didn't go,' I told him. 'I wasn't feeling well.'

" 'Oh, too bad. What was wrong?'

" 'Stomachache,' I said, and he nodded.

" 'Woman stuff?'

"Whenever I had a stomachache or a headache, that was a convenient explanation for him. It was his excuse for not really worrying.

" 'Right,' I said, thinking, why bother?

"He refreshed himself quickly and came to dinner just after my mother finished her phone calls and we began the charade of another family dinner with storm clouds looming above."

"I think I was better off having my father move out," Misty said.

"You're right about that," Star seconded.

"I guess I would agree with both of you now," I said. "Their conversation was clipped, short and shaded with nasty innuendos. Neither really cared to know about the other's day. I suppose neither of them wanted to appear weak by asking a nice question. Before the dinner ended, they managed to get in another argument about me.

" 'She didn't go to the Honor Society induction,' my mother declared just before coffee and dessert.

" 'I heard,' my father said.

" 'I'm sure she was upset about having neither of us attending and that gave her a nervous stomach,' my mother said.

" 'Whose fault is that?' my father countered.

"It was as though I wasn't even there while they argued. Can you understand why I felt I was becoming more and more invisible, a shadow of myself?" I asked the girls. They all nodded.

"My mother wiped her mouth with her napkin and reached into her purse which she had brought to the table and placed on the floor beside her chair. When she had done that, I wondered about it, but I didn't ask. All the while she had anticipated this argument and was preparing for it, I discovered, and so did my father.

"She plucked her appointment book out of her purse and flipped through the pages.

" 'It's very clear that it was your turn to escort Jade to one of her school functions,' she said. 'If you want to check the calendar, it's right here. I went to the P.T.A. function two weeks ago while you were embroiled in a creative meeting in Pasadena. I have it written down. Care to look?' she said, holding out the book.

"My father glanced at me and then turned back to her, furious.

" 'You never mentioned the schedule before the two of us planned our appointments,' he said through his clenched teeth. That's probably where I get doing that. It's one of his precious gifts to me: clenched teeth during anger.

" 'I didn't think I would have to remind you of an obligation to your own daughter,' she returned sharply.

" 'It seems to me you missed something last month,' he said, but weakly because he wasn't nearly as prepared as she was. My mother has always been a lot better than my father at organizational details. He's more creative, abstract, lost in his images and visions. She's more precise, a manager. He was outgunned.

" 'You never mentioned it and I don't recall it, but this is clearly an example of your lack of responsibility when it comes to Jade's needs,' she said, flipping her appointment book closed and dropping it like a dagger back into her purse.

" 'Are you going to run right to the phone and tell your attorney?' he snapped.

" 'It will be properly noted,' she said as Mrs. Caron entered with the coffee and carrot cake.

" 'You just let this happen,' my father continued. Usually, they waited for Mrs. Caron to leave before having any words between them, but he was like a balloon about to burst, his face flushed and his eyes wide and angry. 'It's nothing more than entrapment, plain and simple and disgusting.'

" 'The bottom line is she didn't go to an important school function,' my mother insisted. Her calmness made him angrier. He flustered about a moment and then turned to me.

" 'I'm sorry, Jade, if you didn't go because of me, that is,' he said, hoping I would deny it.

" 'Of course she didn't go because of you,' my mother pounded.

" 'Let her speak for herself. That's something you never let the child do anymore, have her own mind.'

" 'That's ridiculous. I never . . .'

" 'STOP!' I screamed, my hands over my ears. 'I didn't go because I ran away. I flew to San Francisco and I was almost kidnapped and raped and killed and neither of you know a damn thing about it.'

"They both sat there, staring, their mouths open.

" 'What?' my father said. He looked at my mother and she shook her head, her face bright with shock.

" 'I HATE THIS! I HATE THIS!' I shouted, and ran out of the dining room, up the stairs and into my room, slamming the door shut and locking it behind me.

"About ten minutes later, they both came upstairs and stood outside my door together asking me to let them in and explain what I had said. I didn't answer them. My mother went down to question Mrs. Caron, but she knew nothing, of course, except that I had been gone. She couldn't tell how long. I never tell her when I leave, where I'm going or how long I'll be there. How could she be expected to know?

"My father continued to plead with me to tell him what had happened. Finally, they both retreated to their own affairs.

"Later, when I was calm and they asked me again, I told them some of it. Of course, they only blamed each other and threatened to use it against each other in court. My father pushed for more details so he could contact the police, but I didn't want to be part of any of that. Just the thought of seeing Mr. Bennet again sent electric chills through my heart. My parents gave up on it, and around me at least, pretended it had never happened.

"After a while it even diminished in my own mind, probably because as Dr. Marlowe has told me, I am using defense mechanisms to keep from reliving the events. I guess I ruined all that today, huh, Doc?"

"No," she said softly. "Sometimes, the best way to kill your demons is to let them out and expose them to sunlight."

"Like vampires, right, Dr. Marlowe?" Misty said.

Dr. Marlowe laughed.

"Yes, Misty, like vampires."

"What about the crazy man?" Star wanted to know. "Did he ever call you or anything afterward?"

I nodded.

"I couldn't help it," I explained. "In a bizarre way I was drawn back to my computer and sure enough, there was an E-mail from him waiting in my mailbox. Only it was from Craig, not Mr. Bennet, of course."

"What did he say?" Cat asked.

"He apologized for his father's behavior, claiming his father was under a lot of stress these days because he had lost his job and there were financial problems as well as a mountain of emotional ones. He said his little brother Sonny had gotten worse, too, and now he was becoming so withdrawn, he would barely talk to him. The school was recommending psychiatric care and he might have to be institutionalized. I think that was probably what had really happened to him."

"You didn't write back, did you?" Star asked.

"No. I changed my screen name and lost him forever in cyberspace," I said. "Which," I added, "is where I wish I could lose myself these days."

Everyone was absorbed in her own thoughts for a long moment. I took a drink of water and gazed at the clock. When I had first come here in the morning, I thought, I never imagined I would have lasted this long, or have had so much to tell.

"I guess I would have to say the events did sink into my parents' hearts after a while. I know the horrible events changed me and made me withdraw from a lot of things."

I smiled at Dr. Marlowe.

"That's part of why I was sent here," I said. She nodded.

"My grades started to reflect my lack of interest. I dropped out of one extracurricular activity after another. I lost contact with most of my friends. I hated answering questions about my home life and my parents' divorce and how I felt about it. Your life can turn into a soap opera pretty quickly at my school," I said.

Star grunted and nodded. Misty smiled knowingly at Cat who smiled back. She was coming out of her shell more and more, I thought. I guess Dr. Marlowe was right about all this.

"One afternoon when I returned home from school, I was surprised to find my mother already home. She had changed into a pair of jeans and a light blue blouse, put on sneakers and tied her hair with a bright yellow bandanna. She looked younger, younger than I could recall her looking for a long time.

" 'C'mon,' she said as I entered the house and she came out from the kitchen. 'I found this great crystal shop in Santa Monica and I want to get some things for the house. It'll be fun.'

"I was so taken aback, I just stood there with my mouth open, looking stupid. She laughed and urged me to change and come down in five minutes.

"I did and we headed for the beach town. All the way she didn't mention one thing about her job. She said she had been working too hard and been stupid to ignore some of the fun things in life. It was time to reap the benefits of all this hard work, she claimed.

"We had a nice afternoon shopping. She bought me a beautiful crystal to wear around my neck and then we went to a great bakery and picked up some delicious bread and a dozen cookies.

" 'Time to splurge,' she cried. 'Let's not worry about calories tonight.'

"That struck me as funny because she never did and often criticized me for worrying.

"She laughed too, and then she suddenly pulled over on Pacific Coast Highway before heading back to the house so we could look at the ocean. It looked so peaceful with sailboats gliding over glass, their sails floating against the light blue sky.

" 'It's so beautiful here. I often forget and take it for granted,' she said and then she turned to me with as serious and as concerned an expression as I had ever seen.

" 'I don't want you to think I'm totally oblivious to all you've suffered, Jade,' she said. 'And I'm not going to deny my own share of blame. What happened to you recently frightened the hell out of me. I tried to keep from thinking about it, but I couldn't. I'm so lucky you're all right,' she said with tears in her eyes. She fanned her face to stop herself from crying. 'I wouldn't have blamed your father. I would have blamed myself.'

"Then she sucked back her tears and promised things were going to change.

" 'We've got to become more like sisters,' she said. 'I promise I'll set aside more time to be with you. Let's make Saturday lunches our special time together, okay?'

"Of course I agreed, even though in the back of my mind, I could hear my father demanding Sunday lunches for himself or every other Saturday. It was the way things had been.

"But I don't think we ever get tired of hearing our parents' promises, no matter how many times they break them. It's like buying another lottery ticket after you've lost and lost and lost. You just can't help hoping and fantasizing.

"The following day, my father surprised me by showing up at school at the end of the day to drive me home.

" 'I realized I was nearby,' he claimed, 'and thought it would be nice. How was your day?'

" 'Okay,' I said. It hadn't been. I had failed an important math test and dropped my average so low, it was clear I was going to be kicked out of the Honor Society at the end of the year, but I didn't tell him that.

" 'I know you don't want to talk about your episode in San Francisco anymore, and to tell you the truth, I don't either,' he said with a smile. 'It gives me nightmares, too. It should never have happened and I should never have gone away before the Honor Society induction. I'm sorry,' he said.

"My parents' apologies were like cold raindrops. I hated them and fled from them. I said nothing. I just turned away and gazed out the window.

" 'What it told me was I'm really missing the boat here. I should be enjoying your adolescent years along with you more. I want to be part of what you do and what you enjoy. I've decided to cut back on my workload just for that purpose,' he added. 'Please don't hesitate to ask me to go to anything or be part of anything anymore. Forget schedules. I'll find the time. I'll change dates and meetings.

" 'We should just do more fun things together,' he added. 'Okay?'

"I turned back to him.

" 'Okay,' I said, but now I was so suspicious of both of them, I practically held my breath and kept myself from asking any questions.

"He decided it would be fun to stop to have an old-fashioned ice-cream soda and he knew a place that still made them that way. We drove to the soda shop and he talked about his high school days and told me things he had never told me before about overcoming his own shyness with girls, his first real girlfriend, and his disastrous prom date with someone named Berle Lownstein whose orthodontia retainer fell out while dancing. I couldn't stop laughing at some of it. No matter what his reasons for spending time with me, I thought, I was having a good time. It was fun.

"Suddenly, they were really competing for my attention, my time and filling my days with suggestions of fun things to do. Of course, I hated turning one down because of something the other had already planned, but they didn't argue or fight about it as I expected they would. They seemed to have stepped back to let me have breathing room. I began to suspect they had secretly agreed that they would conduct themselves this way and let the best man win.

"And then it occurred to me one night, that all this had begun after the judge who held the power of granting custody had made the date for my appointment in his office, in camera.

"And I went to sleep full of a new fear. I tossed and turned, shrinking into a tighter and tighter ball.

"What if all their expressions of love and all their fun and warmth was contrived again?

"What if I was still a pawn, a piece on a checker board, an asset, a trophy?

"What if all this was just another battle in their grand war?"

7

"**M**y appointment with the judge was on the following Thursday, at ten in the morning. The limo was taking me there and I had to go by myself so that neither of my parents could influence me. Dr. Morton asked me if I would like her to accompany me and I told her no. I should have said yes.

"I remember how alone I felt in that big backseat. I never really felt so alone in the limo before. It was raining hard. The drops pelted the roof and I thought God must have been angry. They sounded like His bullets. It was so dark and dreary and our travel was funeral procession slow.

"When we arrived at the courthouse, Judge Norton Resnick's assistant Marla greeted me after we pulled to the curb. I had spoken to her on the telephone the day before. She was a tall, slim woman with short blond hair and beautiful blue eyes, the sort of eyes that always accompany a warm smile which radiates through someone's face. Her warmth helped me relax a little, but being in the courthouse where my parents and their attorneys would do battle over possessions, the house and especially me, turned my nerves into thin piano wires on the verge of breaking. As we passed through the metal detectors, my heart skipped. Suddenly, after all these months of talk, talk, talk, everything seemed to be happening so fast. In moments I was being led down a wide corridor with polished marble floors. Voices echoed. Well-dressed men and women passed by us either laughing or arguing. I couldn't help but feel intimidated, out of place and very frightened. My heart was no longer skipping beats. Now it was hammering against my chest.

" 'Right this way, Jade,' Marla said, opening an office door with the judge's name on the front. We entered a small outer office. Marla asked me to wait for a moment and then went through the next door, closing it softly.

"I was afraid to sit, afraid that when it was time to stand again, my legs wouldn't support me. Fortunately, it was only a few seconds later that she emerged and told me to step into the office.

"It was smaller than I had anticipated. Judge Resnick sat behind a sizeable light mahogany desk with large, thick volumes piled on both his right and left and long yellow legal pads in front of him. There were plaques and pictures all over the walls and especially right behind him and beside the American flag. The governor's picture was prominent.

"The judge had two windows that looked out on the street, but rain-drops zigzagged like tears, blurring the view.

"Judge Resnick looked to be about fifty, maybe fifty-five, with curly black hair and dark round eyes. He had a thick nose and soft, almost Santa Claus cheeks, each with a light circle of pink at the crest. In his robes he appeared even bigger and heavier than I imagined he was, al-though when he stood, I saw he was very wide in the waist.

"There was a captain's chair set up directly in front of his desk. On the right, seated at a small table, was the court stenographer. He was a short, thin man with light brown hair, thick glasses, light brown eyes and what I thought was a mouth much too small for his oval face. He barely looked up at me and sat poised, making me even more nervous.

" 'Good morning, Jade,' the judge said with a smile that stretched his thick lips until they were nearly pale. He offered me his stubby fin-gered hand and I took it for a quick handshake. He nodded at the chair. 'Please, sit,' he said. He nodded at Marla and she quickly turned and left the office.

"I glanced at the stenographer who lifted his hands over the keys of his machine as if he were about to begin a magnificent piano concerto. The judge sat back and pressed his fingertips together. His eyebrows knitted together as he studied me and formed his first impressions.

" 'Let's relax for a few moments,' he began. 'This is Mr. Worth,' he said looking at the court stenographer. Mr. Worth nodded and barely grinned, much less smiled. He didn't seem to ease up a bit, his shoulders and neck remaining stiff. He even looked somewhat impatient.

"The judge cleared his throat.

" 'I don't want you to be nervous about this. I want you to speak freely. I understand from your teachers' reports, your school records, and your counselor that you are a very intelligent young lady. You're not that far away from being on your own, making your own decisions and taking responsibility for your own actions. From what I have seen, you should do very well.' His voice was smooth, easy, relaxed, but I was still on pins and needles.

" 'What we're going to do is have a relatively short conversation about all this so that I can best assess your feelings. I want you to know from the start that for me, you are the most important person in this matter. Your needs must be addressed before anyone else's. I hope you'll be as honest as possible,' he added, 'so I can do the best job for you.'

" 'My grades have slipped recently,' I said. I might as well be as honest as possible right away, I thought.

" 'A huh. And why is that?' he asked, his gaze fixed intently on me.

" 'I guess it's safe to conclude I've been somewhat distracted,' I replied rather dryly. He didn't want to laugh, but I saw a twinkle in his eyes.

" 'Yes, I imagine you have been, and that's part of what I'd like to learn. What's life been like for you these past few months?'

"I looked away, looked through the wet windows and the haze and the rain. What's life been like? Now there's a question, I thought.

" 'Difficult,' I said. He'd have to press and pry to get me to say much more. You see, right from the start, I was terrified of my answers, terrified of my words," I explained to the others.

"Why?" Misty asked.

"I was afraid I would give an answer that would make him decide in either my mother's favor or my father's and it would be solely my fault. No matter what my complaints have been about them, I didn't want either to hate me, and I didn't want to hurt either.

"Judge Resnick wasn't a bad judge. He must have had lots of experience with cases like mine because he practically read my thoughts, anticipating my fear.

" 'I want you to know,' he said, 'that your comments are very important, but there is testimony from other important people and facts you might not even know yourself. I have other things to consider here.

" 'You're old enough for me to cut right to the heart of this, Jade. Do you have any preference or reason to have preference for one of your parents to have full legal custody of you?'

"How do you answer that if you don't hate one or the other? I wondered. Would a judge ask a parent which child he or she prefers?

"Could I erase all the happy moments I had experienced with either of my parents? Did I have to concentrate on the times I was angry at one or the other so I could harden my heart against my father or against my mother? I wished I could be cut in half or cloned so each would have what he or she wanted.

" 'Do you feel closer in any way with either?' he pursued. 'Or, let me put it this way, do you think one or the other will be more important to you at this stage of your life? I've had girls your age who thought they would need more time with their mothers,' he added, raising those thick eyebrows in anticipation.

" 'I'd like more time with both of them,' I said. He nodded, his eyes encouraging. He just wants me to talk, I thought, to talk and talk and talk.

"So I began. I talked about my parents and their precious careers. I talked about the many times neither had been there for me. I guess I talked about my own loneliness. I laughed at his reference to my soon-to-be-independence. 'Sometimes,' I told him, 'I feel like I've brought myself up. Independence will be no novelty for me.'

"He listened quietly. I got so into it, I stopped noticing the stenographer's fingers taking down my every word with lightning speed. The judge's eyes gradually turned darker. He even looked angry at times.

" 'It's not fair that I'm even here,' I concluded. 'I shouldn't have to do this. It's their problem.'

"When I was finished, he just sat quietly for a moment. His face had become so somber, he looked like a different person. He leaned forward, studied a paper on his desk and then looked up at me and asked, 'What if you lived with neither for the next year? Would that be so upsetting?'

" 'With whom would I live? Where would I live?'

"He began by suggesting one of my grandparents and I laughed aloud then. His eyebrows bounced up and I explained my relationships with my grandparents and how rarely I had spent any time with either my father's or my mother's parents. When he asked about my other relatives, I had the same reply.

"From the way he looked, I imagined I wasn't making it any easier for him. How simple it would be if I would say, 'Oh yes, Judge. I need my mother more now. We have female issues to discuss and my father won't be able to help,' but I had other issues looming before me, and how easy it would be to say I need my father more for them.

"I know what we can do, your honor, I thought, instead of cutting the child in half, cut the parents in half and paste a half of one to a half of the other and give me a new kind of parent, part Daddy, part Mommy, only be sure to cut away the parts full of hate, okay?

"Thinking about that made me laugh and he smiled and asked what struck me funny?

"I decided to tell him and I did. He didn't laugh. He nodded with sadness in his eyes. I glanced at the stenographer whose bland face finally showed some surprise and interest.

"The judge asked me more questions about my daily routine, my ambitions. He talked about my parents' input into any of it, searching, I was sure, for evidence of one being more concerned than the other. I soon began to feel like a witness being cross-examined by a relentless prosecutor.

"Finally, I told him about my parents' recent expressions of repentance and their new promises about all the time each was going to spend with me and how much fun we would have. He seemed interested until I said, 'But in my house promises are lies tied up with pretty ribbons. Every week our maid vacuums them up and dumps them in the incinerator.'

"I followed that with another nervous little laugh. He asked me if I would like something to drink and I said hemlock. He didn't think that was funny at all."

"What's hemlock?" Star asked.

"Poison. Socrates drank it," I said. Star glanced at Dr. Marlowe and then turned back to me.

"I was tired of all this. The dreariness of the rainy day had moved into my body. I really just wanted to sleep.

" 'So,' Judge Resnick concluded, 'if I turn over legal custody to one or the other of your parents, you won't be that upset about it? Is that a fair assessment?'

" 'Frankly, your honor,' I said, 'I don't give a damn.'

"That's from *Gone With the Wind*, and actually, it was appropriate. *Gone With the Wind* took place during the Civil War and that's what was going on in my house.

"Once again, however, the judge didn't laugh. He scowled, made a note and sat back, very pensive.

" 'Okay,' he said, coming to some conclusion, 'I guess that will be all for now. You've been helpful. I do hope everything works out for you, Jade. You have shown evidence of strength and accomplishment and although I don't want to belittle the significance of all this, I think you're going to rise above it and become a fine young lady.'

"Was he a judge or a fortune teller or was that one and the same? I wanted to ask, but I didn't. I kept silent. Marla was called back in to escort me out to the limousine. I glanced at the stenographer before I left.

He looked like he had been bored out of his mind. I guessed it wasn't as exciting as a murder or something.

" 'Judge Resnick is one of the best judges when it comes to these matters,' Marla assured me on the way out. 'He's fair and very wise and he takes a great deal of time and does a lot of research before rendering any decisions.'

" 'Fine,' I told her at the limousine. 'I'll recommend him to all my friends.'

"It wasn't nice to be sarcastic to her, but I was very tired of all of it and she just happened to be a part of it. I did thank her before I got into the car.

" 'Home James,' I said. I've always wanted to say that. The driver glanced at me in the rearview mirror. He was a different driver from the one I had previously had.

" 'My name's not James,' he muttered.

"The rain had slowed to a slight drizzle, but the traffic was just as heavy as before. It was a nauseating ride for me. I closed my eyes to keep my stomach from churning. I hadn't eaten much for breakfast and I was glad of that now.

"I was happy neither of my parents would be home yet. I knew they would each have questions in their eyes and look for some hint as to what I had told the judge.

"Just the thought of that began to weigh heavier and heavier on my mind. I dreaded seeing them at dinner. I dreaded ever seeing them. What was the judge going to do with my testimony? Whose heart had I broken? Why didn't they think about my heart?

"The rain started to come down harder again. It was practically impossible to see out of the windows. The driver grumbled about it, but we continued on. When we reached the house, I just opened the door before he came around and ran inside and shook the water out of my hair.

"It was quiet and dark because Rosina had not turned on the lights in some of the rooms. Mrs. Caron was most likely in the kitchen working on the evening's gourmet meal. No matter what happened here, we would always eat well, I thought, and started up the stairs.

"My body throbbed all over. I didn't realize until that moment just how tense I had been in the judge's office. The back of my neck especially ached. I felt as though I had been in a car accident and now I was experiencing the trauma. This whole thing was like a big crash anyway.

"The urge to just lie down and sleep got stronger and stronger. I undressed and crawled into bed, but whenever I closed my eyes, Judge Resnick's big face appeared and I relived his questions, his expression, his penetrating eyes. Then I began to imagine my mother's disappointed face and my father's. Tossing and turning through these persistent nightmares, I finally sat up, feeling like I could scream and pull the hair out of my head. For a while I just stared at the wall and then I rose, slipped into my robe and went to my mother's room.

"I found her sleeping pills in the nightstand next to her bed and brought them back to my room."

Before I continued, I glanced at Dr. Marlowe and then I glanced at the girls. They all looked like they were holding their breath. I was tempted to smile and say, "That's all," but they all knew it wasn't right and besides, I wanted to tell them. I wanted to get it out, spit it from my body as fast as I would spit out sour milk.

"I thought if I took two pills, I'd be able to get some sleep, and then I thought, if I took three, I'd sleep right through dinner and not have to face them; if I took four, I'd sleep right through the night; if I took five, I'd sleep through breakfast.

"All those thoughts ran through my mind and I guess I started laughing and taking another and another until most of the pills in the bottle were in my stomach. Then I lay back, stared up at the ceiling and waited. My eyelids grew heavier and heavier and finally slammed shut like a steel door.

"It was as if the sleeping pills took me back in time, making me younger and younger until I was just a little girl again, years and years before my parents became the people they were now.

"They were still in love and we were still a family. I saw us doing things together, going to Disney World, going to the beach, going to restaurants. I sat on my father's shoulders when we walked and felt him bouncing me along. I heard my parents' laughter curling around me like a warm, protective cocoon.

"There were lots of kisses then. How safe I felt. Those were the days of my big bubble. It felt so good to return. It was as if all that had happened since was just a nightmare, a long, bad dream. I was waking up and I was calling for them. I could see myself, my mouth opening and closing, but I couldn't hear my voice. Somehow, they must have heard.

"They both came to my room and stood by my bed. They held me tightly and they rained down love and promises. I was drenched in happiness. And then I heard the screams.

" 'Get the paramedics!' Mommy was screaming.

"Why? I wondered. Was there emergency care for nightmares?

"I could hear and sense all the rushing about. Somewhere off to the right, I heard the sound of a siren. And then I heard this heavy, loud drum. It was coming closer and closer and getting louder and louder before I realized it was my own heart.

"Finally, I heard the grating noise of metal screeching as the heavy steel door was being lifted. First, a tiny shaft of light slipped in at the bottom and then the light grew larger and brighter until the door was nearly completely opened.

"As soon as it was, the light diminished and I was able to make out silhouettes behind it. The darkness gradually lifted from their faces and I saw it was my parents looking at me. My mother's mouth was opening and yet I didn't hear her voice. Soon, it became a muffled, far-off sound that slowly got louder and clearer until I understood she was calling my name.

"My father stepped up beside her and did the same. I just stared at them.

"How did they get so much older so fast? I wondered.

"Where am I? I wondered.

"The room was unfamiliar. What happened to my room? Where were all my things? Where was my big bubble?

"I wanted to sleep, but they wouldn't let me. They shook me and called to me until I kept my eyes open.

" 'Where am I, Mommy?' I asked.

"I saw tears on her cheeks. My mother never cried. What was going on? I wondered. I looked at my father. His eyes were glassy, too.

" 'You're in the hospital, Jade, but you're going to be all right,' she said.

" 'That's right, baby,' my father said. 'You're going to be all right.'

" 'Good,' I said. 'Are we going to the beach today?'

" 'Yes,' my father said, laughing, 'we're going to the beach today.'

"My mother smiled through her tears and brushed my hair off my forehead.

"A doctor stepped up beside them and said something too low for me to hear. They nodded and then each kissed me. That's what made me think I was still five years old, I guess. I wanted to hold on to that as long as I could," I added, glancing at Dr. Marlowe again. She nodded.

"My parents turned and walked out of the room and I thought, I could almost swear, they were holding hands. Maybe it was what I hoped I saw," I concluded sadly.

I stared at the floor. After a sigh that was so deep I could feel it in my bones, I looked up.

"It wasn't long afterward that I came to see Dr. Marlowe."

I took a deep breath and looked out the window. No one spoke. We could hear water running through a pipe somewhere off to our right in the house.

"What happened with the judge and all?" Star asked finally.

"It's not completely over," I replied, "but it looks like my parents are going to compromise and agree to joint custody. My father is talking about building himself a new house. He's getting more and more excited about it. He's brought me the plans and showed me where my room would be and he's asked me to make suggestions.

"My mother is talking about a leave of absence from her job, but I'm not holding my breath. Yesterday, she said the company management was thinking about giving her a significant raise to keep her from leaving, even for a hiatus.

"Things are different in the house. I'll say that. They both seem to tiptoe around me lately and they never argue or even discuss problems when I'm around. In fact, it's just the opposite. They're overly polite to each other. Their war is coming to an end," I said.

"Everyone talks about rebuilding, mending, putting it all behind us. There's a new reality and we've got to learn how to adjust to it," I said, repeating some of the platitudes I had been told.

"I feel like my whole life to this point was written in chalk and a few lawyers, sociologists, yes, even therapists, have come along and helped erase it and start writing new words. Sometimes, I think I should change my name and really go through a rebirth."

"You've got a pretty name," Misty said softly.

I smiled at her. She reached out to touch my hand and hold it for a moment.

"Well," Dr. Marlowe said, "I don't know about you guys, but I think I'm ready to call it a day. You heard Emma before. She practically ordered me to be sure you all enjoyed the nice weather."

I nodded. All the girls were staring at me now. Then Misty smiled and Star quickly followed. Cat joined them and I laughed.

"I guess I talked a lot more than I expected. Sorry."

"No, no, it was fine," Star said.

"Yeah, I'm glad you told us as much as you wanted," Misty said. Cat nodded.

"Me too," she said in a voice just above a whisper.

We all stood up and Dr. Marlowe led us out of the office and to the front door. My limousine and driver were there already, as was Star's grandmother and Cat's mother. Misty had to call for a cab and we all offered to wait with her.

"No, you don't have to," she said. "It won't be long. I'm used to waiting for cabs these days."

"I bet," Star said and then looked at Cat. "You coming back here tomorrow?"

She looked at each of us, her eyes fearful.

"Yes," she said.

"You'd better," Star said, "or we'll be coming to your house."

"Stop scaring her," Misty ordered. "She'll come. You want to come back, right, Cat?"

Cathy smiled at being called Cat and nodded. She looked toward her mother and lost her smile quickly.

"It's hard," I told her, "but it does help. You'll see." I squeezed her hand.

"Okay, bye," she said in a small voice, and walked to her mother's car. We watched her get in and then drive off. Her mother didn't look our way.

"Granny's scowling at me," Star said. "I better get a move on."

"I guess that's Rodney gaping at us from the backseat," I said.

"That's him," she said with a laugh.

"He looks cute," Misty said.

"Don't let him fool you. Cute only lasts a few minutes every day," she said, and Misty and I laughed. "See you tomorrow, girlfriends," she added and walked quickly to her grandmother's car. "What are you gaping at them like that for?" we heard her yell at Rodney. "They're just girls. Get your head in," she ordered and got into the car.

She smiled and waved to us as they pulled away.

Misty walked with me to the limousine. The driver got out to open the door.

"It is a pretty day. What are you going to do with the rest of it?" she asked.

"I don't know. I have some magazines to read. I guess I'll just lounge by the pool and work on my tan or paint my fingernails. What about you?"

She shrugged.

"Nothing," she said.

"Give me your phone number," I said. "I'll call you later."

"Really?" She gave it to me and I got into the limousine and rolled down the window.

"I guess what happens, what hurts the most," I said, "is you lose faith. You think, if they can fall out of love, the two people you love the most, the two people you idolized and believed in the most, then how can anything beautiful happen between you and someone? Understand?"

"Yes," she said. "Exactly."

I reached out and she took my hand for a moment.

"Maybe, we're better than them," she offered. "Maybe the best of them is in us and we're even better."

"Maybe," I said.

She let go and stepped back as the limousine started. Her hand had felt like the string on a balloon. As I rode off, the balloon rose in my imagination. Our four faces were on it and we were drifting into the wind.

Drifting toward something better.

Maybe.

Cat

Prologue

I woke with a terrible chill. I was shivering even before I opened my eyes. Cringing in bed, I drew my legs up tightly until my knees were against my stomach and I buried my face in the blanket, actually biting down on the soft, down comforter until I could taste the linen. No matter how warm my room was, I had to sleep with a blanket. I had to wrap myself securely or I couldn't sleep. Sometimes, during the night, I would toss it off, but by morning, it was spun around me again as if some invisible spider was trapping me in its web. I could feel the sticky threads on my fingers and feet, and struggle as much as I'd like, I was unable to tear myself free.

Exhausted, I lay there, waiting as the spider drew closer and closer until it was over me and I looked up into its face and saw that it was Daddy.

1

Because my daddy went to work so early, my mother was always the one left with the responsibility of waking me, if I didn't rise and shine on my own for school. She would usually wake me up by making extra noise outside my bedroom door. She rarely knocked and she almost never opened the door. I could probably count on the fingers of one hand how many times my mother had been in my bedroom while I was in it too, especially during the last five years.

Instead, she would wait for me to leave for school, and then she would enter like a hotel maid after the guests had gone and clean and arrange the room to her liking. I was never neat enough to please her, and when I was younger, if I dared to leave an undergarment on a chair or on the top of the dresser, she would complain vehemently and look like the wicked witch in *The Wizard of Oz*.

"Your things are very private and not for the eyes of others," she would scowl, and put her hands on me and shake me. "Do you understand, Cathy? Do you?"

I would nod quickly, but what others? I would wonder. My mother didn't like any of my father's friends or business associates and she had no friends of her own. She prized her solitude. No one came to our house for dinner very often, if at all, and certainly no one visited my room or came upstairs, and even if they had, they wouldn't see anything because Mother insisted I keep my door shut at all times. She taught me that from the moment I was able to do it myself.

Nevertheless, she would be absolutely furious now if I didn't put my soaps and lotions back in the bathroom cabinet, and once, when I had left a pair of my panties on the desk chair, she cut them up and spread the pieces over my pillow to make her point.

This morning she was especially loud. I heard her put down the pail on the floor roughly, practically slamming it. She was cleaning earlier than usual. The mop hit my door, swept the hardwood floor in the hallway and then hit my door again. I looked at the small clock housed in clear Danish crystal on my night table. The clock was a birthday present from my grandmother, my mother's mother, given only weeks before she had passed away from lung cancer. She was a heavy smoker. My grandfather was twelve years older than she was and died two years later from a heart attack. Like me, my mother had been an only child. Not long ago I found out I wasn't supposed to be, but that's another story, maybe even one that's more horrible than what's happened to me recently. Whatever, one thing was certain: we didn't have much family. Our Thanksgiving turkeys were always small. Mother didn't like leftovers. Daddy muttered that she threw away enough food to feed another family, but he never muttered loud enough for Mother to hear.

Part of the reason for our small Thanksgivings and Christmas holidays was because my father's parents had nothing to do with him or with us; his sister Agatha and his younger brother Nigel never came to see us either. My father had told me that none of his family members liked anyone else in the family and it was best for all of them to just avoid each other. It would be years before I would find out why. It was like finding pieces to a puzzle and putting them together to create an explanation for confusion.

When my mother hit the door with the mop again, I knew it was time to rise, but I was stalling. Today was my day at Doctor Marlowe's group therapy session. The other three girls, Misty, Star and Jade, had told their stories and now they wanted to hear mine. I knew they were afraid I wouldn't show up and to them it would be something of a betrayal. They had each been honest to the point of pain and I had listened and heard their most intimate stories. I knew they believed they had earned the right to hear mine, and I wasn't going to disagree with that, but at this very moment, I wasn't sure if I could actually gather enough courage to tell them my tale.

Mother wasn't very insistent about it. She had been told by other doctors and counselors that it was very important for me to be in therapy, but my mother didn't trust doctors. She was forty-six years old and from what I understood, she had not been to a doctor for more than thirty years. She didn't have to go to a doctor to give birth to me. I had been adopted. I didn't learn that until . . . until afterward, but it made sense. It was practically the only thing that did.

My chills finally stopped and I sat up slowly. I had a dark maple dresser with an oval mirror almost directly across from my bed so when I rose in the morning, the first thing I saw was myself. It was always a surprise to see that I had not changed during the night, that my face was still formed the same way (too round and full of baby fat), my eyes were still hazel and my hair was still a dull dark brown. In dreams I had oozed off my bones and dripped into the floor. Only a skeleton remained. I guess that signified my desire to completely disappear. At least that was what Doctor Marlowe suggested at an earlier session.

I slept in a rather heavy cotton nightgown, even during the summer. Mother wouldn't permit me to own anything flimsy and certainly not anything sheer. Daddy tried to buy me some more feminine nighties and even gave me one for a birthday present once, but my mother accidentally ruined it in the washing machine. I cried about it.

"Why," she would ask, "does a woman, especially a young girl or an unmarried woman, have to look attractive to go to sleep? It's not a social event. Pretty things aren't important for that; practical things are, and spending money on frilly, silly garments for sleep is a waste.

"It's also bad for sleep," she insisted, "to stir yourself up with narcissistic thoughts. You shouldn't dwell on your appearance just before you lay down to rest. It fills your head with nasty things," she assured me.

If my daddy heard her say these things, he would laugh and shake his head, but one look from her would send him fleeing to the safety and the silence of his books and newspapers, many of which she didn't approve.

When I was a little girl, I would sit and watch her look through magazines and shake her head and take a black magic marker to advertisements she thought were too suggestive or sexy. She was the stern censor, perusing all print materials, checking television programs, and even going through my schoolbooks to be sure nothing provocative was in them. She once cut illustrations out of my science text. Many times she phoned the school and had angry conversations with my teachers. She wrote letters to the administrators. I was always embarrassed about it, but I never dared say so.

Yawning and stretching as if I were sliding into my body, I finally slipped my feet into my fur-lined leather slippers and went into the bathroom to take a shower. I know I was moving much slower than usual. A part of me didn't want to leave the room, but that was one of the reasons I had been seeing Doctor Marlowe in the first place: my desire to withdraw and become even more of an introvert than I was before . . . before it all happened or, to be more accurate, before it was all revealed. When you can lie to yourself, you can hide behind a mask and go out into the world. You don't feel as naked nor as exposed.

I wasn't sure what I would wear today. Since it was my day in the center of the circle, I thought I should look better dressed, although Misty certainly didn't dress up for her day or any day thereafter. Still, I thought I might feel a little better about myself if I did. Unfortunately, my favorite dress was too tight around my shoulders and my chest. The only reason my mother hadn't cut it up for rags was she hadn't seen me in it for some time. What I chose instead was a one-piece, dark-brown cotton dress with an empire waist. It was the newest dress I had and looked the best on me even though my mother deliberately had bought it a size too big. Sometimes I think if she could cut a hole in a sheet and drape it over me, she'd be the happiest. I know why and there's nothing I can do about it except have an operation to reduce the size of my breasts, which she finds a constant embarrassment.

"Be careful to step on the sheets of newspaper," Mother warned when I opened my bedroom door to go down to breakfast. "The floor's still wet."

A path of old newspaper pages led to the top of the stairway where she waited with the pail in one hand, the mop, like a knight's lance, in the other. She turned and descended ahead of me, her small head bobbing on her rather long, stiff neck with every downward step.

The scent of heavy disinfectant rose from the hardwood slats and filled my nostrils, effectively smothering the small appetite I was able to manage. I held my breath and followed her. In the kitchen my bowl for cereal, my glass of orange juice and a plate for a slice of whole wheat toast with her homemade jam was set out. Mother took out the pitcher of milk and brought it to the table. Then, she looked at me with those large round dark critical eyes, drinking me in from head to foot. I was sure I appeared pale and tired and I wished I could put on a little makeup, especially after seeing how the other girls looked, but I knew Mother would make me wipe it off if I had any. As a general rule, she was against makeup, but she was especially critical of anyone who wore it during the daytime.

She didn't say anything, which meant she approved of my appearance. Silence meant approval in my house and there were many times when I welcomed it.

I sat and poured some cereal out of the box, adding in the blueberries and then some milk. She watched me drink my juice and dip my

spoon into the cereal, mixing it all first. I could feel her hovering like a
hawk. Her gaze shifted toward the chair my father used to sit on every
morning, throwing daggers from her eyes as if he were still sitting there.
He would read his paper, mumble about something, and then sip his coffee. Sometimes, when I looked at him, I found him staring at me with a
small smile on his lips. Then he would look at my mother and turn his
attention quickly back to the paper like a schoolboy caught peering at
someone else's test answers.

"So today's your day?" Mother asked. She knew it was.

"Yes."

"What are you going to tell them?"

"I don't know," I said. I ate mechanically, the cereal feeling like it
was getting stuck in my throat.

"You'll be blaming things on me, I suppose," she said. She had said
it often.

"No, I won't."

"That's what that doctor would like you to do: put the blame at my
feet. It's convenient. It makes their job easier to find a scapegoat."

"She doesn't do that," I said.

"I don't see the value in this, exposing your private problems to
strangers. I don't see the value at all," she said, shaking her head.

"Doctor Marlowe thinks it's good for us to share," I told her.

I knew Mother didn't like Doctor Marlowe, but I also knew she
wouldn't have liked any psychiatrist. Mother lived by the adage, "Never
air your dirty linen in public." To Mother, public meant anyone outside
of this house. She had had to meet with Doctor Marlowe by herself, too.
It was part of the therapy treatment for me and she had hated every
minute of it. She complained about the prying questions and even the
way Doctor Marlowe looked at her with what Mother said was a very
judgmental gaze. Doctor Marlowe was good at keeping her face like a
blank slate, so I knew whatever Mother saw in Doctor Marlowe's expression, she put there herself.

Doctor Marlowe had told me that it was only natural for my mother
to blame herself or to believe other people blamed her. I did blame her,
but I hadn't ever said that and wondered if I ever would.

"Remember, people like to gossip," Mother continued. "You don't
give them anything to gossip about, hear, Cathy? You make sure you
think about everything before you speak. Once a word is out, it's out.
You've got to think of your thoughts as valuable rare birds caged up in
here," she said pointing to her temple. "In the best and safest place of
all, your own head. If she tries to make you tell something you don't

want to tell, you just get yourself right up out of that chair and call me to come fetch you, hear?"

She paused, and birdlike, craned her long neck to peer at me to see if I was paying full attention. Her hands were on her hips. She had sharp hipbones that protruded and showed themselves under her housecoat whenever she pressed her palms into her sides. They looked like two pot handles. She was never a heavy woman, but all of this had made her sick, too, and she had lost weight until her cheeks looked flat and drooped like wet handkerchiefs on her bones.

"Yes, Mother," I said obediently, without looking up at her. When she was like this, I had trouble looking directly at her. She had eyes that could pierce the walls around my most secret thoughts. As her face had thinned, her eyes had become even larger, even more penetrating, seizing on the quickest look of hesitation to spot a lie.

And yet, I thought, she hadn't been able to do that to Daddy. Why not?

"Good," she said nodding. "Good."

She pursed her lips for a moment and widened her nostrils. All of her features were small. I remember my father once describing her as a woman with the bones of a sparrow, but despite her diminutive size, there was nothing really fragile about her, even now, even in her dark state of mind and troubled demeanor. Our family problems had made her strong and hard like an old raisin, something past its prime, although she didn't look old. There was barely a wrinkle in her face. She often pointed that out to emphasize the beneficial qualities of a good clean life, and why I shouldn't be swayed by other girls in school or things I saw on television and in magazines.

I laughed to myself thinking about Misty's mother's obsession with looking younger, going through plastic surgery, cosmetic creams, herbal treatments. Mother would put nothing more than Ivory soap and warm water on her skin. She never smoked, especially after what had happened to her mother. She never drank beer or wine or whiskey, and she never permitted herself to be in the sun too long.

My father smoked and drank, but never smoked in the house. Nevertheless, she would make a big thing out of the stink in his clothing and hang his suits out on her clothesline in the yard before she would permit them to be put back into the closet. Otherwise, she said, they would contaminate his other garments, and, "Who knows? Maybe the smell of smoke is just as dangerous to your health," she said.

As I ate my breakfast, Mother went about her business, cleaning the dishes from her own breakfast, and then she pounced on my emptied orange juice glass, grasping it in her long, bony fingers as if it might just sneak off the table and hide in a corner.

"Go up and brush your teeth," she commanded, "while I finish straightening up down here and then we'll get started. Something tells me I shouldn't be bringing you there today, but we'll see," she added. "We'll see."

She ran the water until it was almost too hot to touch and then she rinsed out my cereal bowl. Often, she made me feel like Typhoid Mary, a carrier of endless germs. If she could boil everything I or my father touched, she would.

I went upstairs, brushed my teeth, ran a brush through my hair a few times and then stood there, gazing at myself in the bathroom mirror. Despite what each of the girls had told me and the others about herself, I wondered how I could talk about my life with the same frankness. Up until now, only Doctor Marlowe and the judge and agent from the Child Protection Agency knew my story.

I could feel the trembling in my calves. It moved up my legs until it invaded my stomach, churned my food and shot up into my heart, making it pound.

"Come on if you're going," I heard Mother shout from below. "I have work to do today."

My breakfast revolted and I had to get to my knees at the toilet and heave. I tried to do it as quietly as I could so she wouldn't hear. Finally, I felt better and I washed my face quickly.

Mother had her light gray tweed short coat on over her housecoat and was standing impatiently at the front door. She wore her black shoes with thick heels and heavy nylon stockings that nearly reached her knees. This morning she decided to tie a light brown scarf around her neck. Her hair was the color of tarnished silver coins and tied with a thick rubber band in her usual tight knot at the base of her skull.

Despite her stern appearance, my mother had beautiful cerulean blue eyes. Sometimes I thought of them as prisoners because of the way they often caught the light and sparkled even though the rest of her face was glum. They looked like they belonged in a much younger woman's head, a head that craved fun and laughter. These eyes longed to smile. I used to think that it had to have been her eyes that had drawn my father to her, but that was before I learned about her having had inherited a trust when she turned twenty-one.

When my mother accused my father of marrying her for her money, he didn't deny it. Instead he lowered his newspaper and said, "So? It's worth ten times what it was then, isn't it? You should thank me."

Did he deliberately miss the point or was that always the point? I wondered.

I knew we had lots of money. My father was a stockbroker and it was true that he had done wonders with our investments, building a portfolio that cushioned us for a comfortable, worry-free life. Little did I or my mother realize just how important that would be.

Mother and I walked out to the car, which was in the driveway. My mother had backed it out of the garage very early this morning and washed the windshield as well as vacuumed the floor and seats. It wasn't a late-model car, but because of the way my mother kept it and the little driving she did, it looked nearly new.

"You're pale," she told me. "Maybe you should call in sick."

"I'm all right," I said. I could just hear them all saying, "We knew it. We knew she wouldn't come." Of course, they would be furious.

"I don't like it," Mother mumbled.

Every time she complained, it stirred the little frogs in my stomach and made them jump against my ribs. I got into the car quickly. She sat at the wheel, staring at the garage door. There was a dent in the corner where my father had backed into it one night with his car after he had had a little too much to drink with some old friends. He never repaired it and every time Mother looked at it, I knew she thought of him. It made the anger in her heart boil and bubble.

"I wonder where he is this fine morning," she said as she turned on the engine. "I hope he's in hell."

We backed out of the driveway and started away. My mother drove very slowly, always below the speed limit, which made drivers in cars behind us lean on their horns and curse through locked jaws of frustration.

Before my father had left, he had helped me get my permit and then my license, but Mother didn't like me driving. She thought the driving age should be raised to twenty-one, and even that was too low these days.

"People are not as mature as they were when I was younger," she told me. "It takes years and years to grow up and driving is a big responsibility. I know why your father let you do it," she added, grinding her teeth. She did that so often, it was a wonder she didn't have more dental problems. "Bribery," she spit. "Even hell is too good for him."

"It wasn't just bribery, Mother. I'm a careful driver," I said. She had yet to let me drive her car and had been in my father's car only twice when I had driven, complaining the whole time, each time.

"You can never be careful enough," she replied. These expressions and thoughts were practically automatic. I used to think Mother has tiny buttons in her brain and when something is said, it hits one of those buttons which triggers sentences already formed and ready to be sent out through her tongue. Each button was assigned a particular thought or philosophical statement.

This morning it was partly cloudy and a lot more humid than it had been the last few days. The weatherman predicted possible thunderstorms later in the afternoon. I could see some nasty looking clouds looming in the west over the ocean, waiting like some gathering army to launch an attack.

"I'll be home all day," Mother continued as we drove along. "If you need me, you don't hesitate to call, hear?"

"All right," I said.

"I've done all my food shopping. I've got to work on our books."

She meant our finances. My mother had gained control of most of that fortune and prided herself on how well she kept our accounts. She attacked it with the same degree of efficiency she attacked everything else. There was a button in her brain connected to "Waste not, want not."

When Doctor Marlowe's house came into view, Mother clicked her tongue and shook her head.

"I don't like this," she said. "I don't see any good coming from this."

I didn't speak. With obvious reluctance, she turned into the driveway and pulled up just as Jade's limousine was pulling away.

"Who is that spoiled girl?" she asked, her eyes narrowing as the limousine disappeared. She hoisted her shoulders and looked ready to pounce on my answer like some alley cat.

"Her name is Jade," I said. "Her father is an important architect and her mother manages sales for a big cosmetics company."

"Spoiled," she declared again with the rock solid firmness of a doctor pronouncing someone dead. She nodded and raised her eyes. "As ye sow, so shall ye reap."

She stopped the car and looked at me with eyes that always seemed to lay the blame totally at my feet, despite the way she would mutter about and curse my father.

"When will this be over?" she demanded, gazing so furiously at the house, I thought she might cause it to explode right before our eyes.

"I guess it'll be the same time as yesterday and the day before," I told her.

"Um," she said. She thought for a moment and then turned back to me sharply. "Remember, don't let that woman make you say anything you don't want to say," she warned.

"I won't."

She nodded, her eyes still fueled by fury, remaining as bright as two Christmas tree lights. Her lips stretched and she spoke through clenched teeth.

"I hope he's sitting in hell," she said.

I wondered why I didn't.

I should, I thought. I should hate him more than she does.

I gazed at the front door of Doctor Marlowe's house.

Maybe today, maybe today I would discover why all this was so.

It gave me the strength to open the door and step out. Mother looked at me, shook her head, and drove away, her neck as stiff as ever. I watched her stop at the end of the driveway and then turn into the street and head back for home.

Then I took a very deep breath, pressed my clutched hands against my stomach, and walked up to the door to press the doorbell. When Doctor Marlowe's maid Sophie opened the door, I was surprised to see the three of them: Misty, Star and Jade, standing there right behind her, smiling, or more to the point, smirking out at me.

"We decided not to waste our time back there in Doctor Marlowe's office. If you didn't show up on schedule, we were all going to go home," Jade said, lifting the right corner of her mouth, and speaking in her most arrogant, haughty voice.

"I'm glad you came," Misty said with her habitually bubbly smile.

"Let's get started," Star added. She brought her hands to her hips and leaned toward me. "Well, c'mon in. Don't stand out there all day gaping at us like some dummy. Doctor Marlowe's waiting for you."

I stepped in and Misty jumped ahead of Sophie to quickly close the door.

"Gotcha," she said and laughed.

They gathered around me to march me back to Doctor Marlowe's office and for a few moments, I felt like I was going to my own execution.

There was plenty about myself I wanted to see die. Maybe, I thought, it was time to do it.

2

Doctor Marlowe was at her desk when we all marched into her office. She quickly finished whatever she was doing and joined us.

"Good morning, girls," she sang with that happy smile of welcome. "I didn't know anyone had arrived yet. Did you all come at the same time?"

"Where's Emma this morning?" Star asked, instead of answering her question. "She usually sets off the alarm when we appear."

Doctor Marlowe laughed. I admired her ability to never lose control, never get upset or angry at anything any of us said, especially Star, who never seemed to be tired of testing her. Of course, after having heard her story, I understood why Star was so angry all the time. And then I wondered if that wasn't really the way I should act, too.

"My sister had an early dental appointment. Everyone comfortable where you have been sitting?" she asked, glancing quickly at me. Now that I was actually here, she looked almost as nervous as I felt.

"Why shouldn't we be?" Star asked.

Doctor Marlowe's smile flickered like a flashlight with weakened batteries and then disappeared.

This morning she wore turquoise earrings and had a bit more of a wave in her dirty blond hair. It was trimmed neatly at her ears. As usual, she wore a skirt suit with a white silk blouse with pearl buttons closed at her throat.

The first time my mother had met her, she had seemed relieved that our therapist wasn't particularly pretty. For reasons I didn't quite understand, Mother was always suspicious of attractive women or else intimidated by them. There wasn't a movie star or a model with whom she didn't find fault. They were either obsessed with being too thin or conceited and had distorting priorities. Mother was proud of the fact that she rarely, if ever, looked in the mirror more than once or twice a day. She thought the world would be better without them and if she caught me gazing at myself, she would ask, "Why are you looking at yourself so much? If something's wrong, I'll tell you."

I didn't think I looked in the mirror any more than or even as much as girls my age did, but I couldn't help being self-critical and comparing myself to other girls and women I met. Doctor Marlowe's nose was a bit too long and her lips too thin, but she did have a figure I coveted. I would even like to be as tall. I always felt short and dumpy because of my own figure and height. Doctor Marlowe was at least six feet one and I was barely five feet four, and with my figure, that made me feel almost comical, distorted, despite the nice things Daddy used to say. He was practically the only one who tried to make me feel good about myself.

Was Mother right? Were those really all lies? And if they were, weren't there some lies we needed?

"Well, let's get started," Doctor Marlowe declared with a small clap. She nodded and sat and motioned for us to do the same.

There was a deep and long moment of silence, the kind that makes my heart stop and then pound. I could feel everyone's eyes on me. I actually began to tremble again, my thighs shaking. I embraced myself like someone who was afraid she would just fly apart.

"How are you all today?" Doctor Marlowe asked.

"Ginger peachy," Star said.

"Good," Misty said with a nice smile.

"I'd like to have slept in longer," Jade said. "It's supposed to be our summer holiday."

Doctor Marlowe laughed and gazed my way, her eyes soft, warm, compassionate.

Even so, a ribbon of pain stretched across my forehead from temple to temple, tightening and tightening until it felt like it was cutting through my brain.

"I think I woke up with a fever this morning," I said. "I had chills. I still have them a bit," I added and embraced myself. I rocked a little in my seat.

"Take it easy, Cathy," Doctor Marlowe said in a soft whisper. "Take deep breaths like you've done before."

I did so while the others continued to stare at me.

"I'm sorry," I whispered.

"Before I started to talk to all of you about my story, I felt like throwing up," Misty said in support.

"I did throw up this morning," I confessed.

Star frowned and shook her head.

"It's only us, Cat, not the whole country. You aren't on television on Oprah or something."

"Give her a chance," Jade ordered.

Star tilted her head a little and looked at Jade from an angle.

"Do you have some words of wisdom, Princess Jade?"

"I'm just saying it wasn't easy for any of us."

"I'm not saying it was," Star argued. "But whatever her story is, it can't be worse than any of ours, can it?"

Jade shrugged.

"I still haven't recovered from telling my own story," she said, as if we were all in a contest to outdo each other for misery.

The other two nodded in agreement.

"No one's going to laugh or anything," Misty promised with those sweet eyes.

All right, I thought. All right. They want to hear it. I'll tell them. I'll tell them everything. Then they'll be sorry. We'll all be sorry.

"My situation is a lot different from yours, and yours, and yours," I told each of them.

"How so?" Star fired back.

"For one thing, I'm adopted," I replied and quickly added, "but I didn't learn that until this year."

"Your parents kept that a secret all this time?" Misty immediately asked.

One thing about these girls, I thought, they weren't going to be bashful about asking questions. It wasn't going to be easy hiding anything from them.

"Yes."

"Weren't there any baby pictures of you?" Jade asked.

"No. Well, not before I was two."

"Didn't you ever wonder about that? Everyone has pictures of their children when they were infants."

"No. I mean, I've wondered, but I didn't ask any questions about it."

"Why not?" Star demanded.

"I just didn't. It never occurred to me that I could be adopted. I look a little like my mother. We sort of have the same nose and mouth."

"Still, you could have asked about the pictures. What kind of parents wouldn't have pictures," Jade pursued.

"I don't like asking my mother questions," I admitted. "She doesn't like me to. She grew up believing children should be seen and not heard and that's how she wants me to be."

"You're not a child," Jade said.

"Hardly," Star added with a laugh. "One look at her will tell you that."

"I'm not just talking about her bosom," Jade snapped. "Some girls physically mature faster, but that doesn't make them grownups."

"I *was* mature very early," I admitted. Maybe I wanted to stop their bickering or maybe I just wanted to get my story out.

"How early?" Misty asked leaning toward me. "I mean, I'm still waiting."

Star and Jade laughed. Doctor Marlowe held her lips still, but her eyes filled with a twinkle of amusement.

"I was still in the fourth grade when . . . when I started to develop."

"Fourth grade?" Star whistled. "You were wearing a bra in the fourth grade?"

"Not exactly. My mother didn't take me to buy a bra until I was in the sixth grade," I said.

"Well, what did you wear before then?" Star asked.

"She made me wear a sports bra, a size or so too small so it flattened me somewhat. It was made out of spandex and it felt like a straitjacket. It was really more for exercise, but she made me wear it all day. When I took it off at night, my chest was always sunburn red. I complained, but she said I had to do it because a bra for a girl my age would only emphasize my freakish appearance."

"Is that what she called it?" Jade said with a scowl. "Freakish?"

I nodded.

"I'd like to get a little more freakish myself then," Misty said. "I guess I'm going to end up having implants when I'm in my twenties."

"You shouldn't put so much emphasis on it just because men do," Jade said with fire in her eyes.

Misty gave her one of her small shrugs and turned back to me.

"What did your father say about it?" she asked.

"He didn't say anything to my mother right away. At least, not in front of me," I added. "My mother has always been more in charge when it came to matters concerning me, matters my father called 'girl stuff.' My father was always very busy. He's a stockbroker and he was out of the house early in the morning, except for weekends, of course."

"What's he look like?" Jade asked. "I mean, does he look like he could really be your father? Any resemblances?"

"I guess not. He's tall, six feet three and he's always been thin, no matter how much he ate or drank. He has very long hands. They're almost twice the size of mine, maybe three times, and his fingers . . ."

"What?" Misty asked.

I laughed.

"He used to play this game with me, itsy-bitsy spider."

"Huh?" Misty said.

"Don't you know it? You put the tips of your fingers together and you go, 'The itsy-bitsy spider crawled up the water spout. Down came the rain and washed the spider out. Out came the sun and dried up all the rain. And the itsy-bitsy spider crawled up the spout again,' " I recited and demonstrated, remembering. I guess I had a silly smile on my face. They all looked like they were going to break into hysterics at any moment.

"He used to do it with his fingers just like I showed you and then he would do it with his fingers on mine and he would crawl up and down my chest.

"I grew up thinking his fingers were really very much like spider legs, especially when he puts his hand on the table," I said remembering the image. "They look like two big spiders."

The three girls fixed their eyes on me and waited as pictures replaced pictures in my memory. I had my fingers on my chest and had turned them downward without even realizing what I was doing. My eyes closed and then snapped open and I felt myself return to the present.

"One of his fingers, the right forefinger, has a birthmark at the tip, a big, red blotch. It looks like he might have touched a hot stove or something. People who meet him for the first time sometimes ask if he had injured it and he shakes his head and holds it up like some sort of prize and explains it's just a birthmark.

"The palms of his hands are puffy and the lines are deep. In fact, he has a line so deep at the base of his left palm, it looks like he sliced it. He keeps his nails very trim. He gets manicures somewhere near his office once a week," I said. "He takes better care of his fingernails than my mother does of hers. I never saw her put nail polish on them. She's never had a manicure. Once, when I went over to a girlfriend's house and came home with my nails polished, she made me dip them in turpentine. I had to hold it in so long, it burned the skin on my fingers."

"Didn't she ever hear of nail polish remover?" Jade asked dryly. "My mother could get her a lifetime supply at cost."

"She's heard of it, but she doesn't own any. No nail polish, no need for nail polish remover," I said. I thought for a moment. "My father's nails shine. They're like ivory."

"How come you talk so much about your father's hands?" Misty asked with a wide smile.

I stared at her for a moment and then looked at Doctor Marlowe, whose eyes were narrowed and intense. How did we get into this so quickly? I wondered. Their questions had come at me like bullets. Maybe that was good. Maybe that was the best way, I thought.

I tried to swallow, but couldn't, and then I took a deep breath and felt like my father was squeezing my ribs and holding my lungs from expanding so I would keep all the secrets imprisoned in my heart. I took another deep breath to stop that all too familiar paralyzing numbness from gripping me.

"Drink some water," Doctor Marlowe ordered, jumping up and handing me a glass.

The girls all looked more frightened than surprised at my sudden reaction. They glanced at each other and then at the door as if they were considering running out of the room. They all looked sorry they had dragged me into my past so quickly. I laughed to myself.

You want to know why I think of my father's hands so much? Okay, I thought. You challenged me to tell you it all. Now you'll sit and listen even if it means you'll have nightmares too.

"Even though he worked very hard and spent a lot of time away from the house, at his firm or visiting with big clients, my father was the one who played with me. All the toys I had, I had because my father bought them. I can't remember my mother buying me any toys, not even a doll."

I shook my head and looked down.

"What?" Misty asked.

"I remember when he bought me a Barbie doll and my mother saw how it had breasts. She was so upset about it that she took the doll and smashed it to pieces with her rolling pin in the kitchen.

" 'This is disgusting!' she cried. 'How can they make toys like this for children and how can you buy something like this for her?' she demanded of my father.

"My father shrugged and said the doll was the most popular toy in the store for girls. He said the stock in the company was a good one, too.

"I knew he was right, of course. Barbie dolls were very popular and I always wanted one and all the clothes, too. I had to settle for a rag doll my father brought home the next day. My mother inspected it closely and stamped her seal of approval on it when she saw there wasn't the slightest sexual thing about it. Despite the stringy hair, it didn't even look feminine. I ended up naming it Bones."

"Why didn't your father just tell her to stuff it?" Star asked.

"My father is a very quiet man. He doesn't raise his voice very often," I said.

"But he was just trying to let you be a normal girl. Your mother is a little extreme, don't you think?" Jade pursued.

"Why is your mother so bossy?" Misty asked.

Suddenly my heart started pounding and the blood rose to my face. I looked down when I spoke. It was almost as if I could see my life, my past and all the events being projected on the floor, the pictures flowing along in a continuous stream.

"My father's not a coward, even though I can't remember too many times when he and my mother shouted at each other," I said finally.

"That's practically all I *can* remember," Jade said.

"It's her day," Star said. "We already heard about you once and once is plenty."

"Is that so?" Jade countered.

"Yeah, it's so," Star said.

Jade stared darts back at her.

"Girls," Doctor Marlowe said softly, shaking her head.

They both turned to me.

"That's not to say my mother didn't criticize my father," I continued. "I don't think a day went by when she didn't have some complaint about his drinking after work, the friends he had, the things she had asked him to do and he had forgotten or neglected. It was just that he would rarely . . . rarely challenge her. I used to believe that early in their marriage, my father decided the best thing for him to do was listen, nod, agree, accept and move on.

"Funny," I said smiling and still looking down, "but once I thought that he was wiser because of that. I had great respect for my father. He was a success in business and he seemed so well organized, contented, in control, I suppose is the word. He had an informed opinion about everything. Whenever he was challenged, he could explain his reasons and ideas. He was very good at convincing people. I guess that came from his being a stockbroker and having to sell hope.

"Dinner at our house was always educational. My father would comment about something that had happened in the government or in the economy, and most of the time, my mother and I would just listen. I mean, I would listen. When I looked at her, she seemed distracted, lost in her own thoughts. Yet, always at the end, she would say something like, 'Well, what do you expect, Howard? If you leave the barn doors open, the cows will get out.'"

"Huh?" Misty said. "What do cows have to do with it?"

I looked at her and smiled.

"My mother is full of old expressions like that. She has one for every occasion, every event."

"My granny has good expressions too," Star said.

"We already heard," Jade sang and threw her nauseatingly sweet smile at her. "It's Cat's day today, remember?" she said, enjoying her sweet taste of revenge.

Star smirked and then shook her head and laughed.

I was jealous of them. Already, I was jealous, I thought. They were at each other all the time, but I could see they also respected and in a funny way liked each other and liked to challenge and tease each other. I wanted them to like me too. Who else would like me but these girls? I worried. I could count on the fingers of one hand the friends I had had and lately, I had none. I felt like a leper because I saw the way some of the other kids looked at me in school.

It's my own fault, I thought. My face might as well be made of glass and all my thoughts and memories printed on a screen inside my head that anyone could see and read.

"I feel dirty," I muttered.

"What?" Misty asked. "Why?"

I looked up, not realizing I had spoken. It had just come out like a burp. My heart began to pound again. I glanced quickly, fearfully at Doctor Marlowe. She gave me her best calming expression.

"Did you say you feel dirty?" Misty asked.

"Let Cathy go at her own pace, Misty," Doctor Marlowe cautioned.

"She said it."

"I know. It takes time," Doctor Marlowe insisted, closing and opening her eyes softly. "You know that. All of you do," she added.

Misty relaxed and sat back.

After a few deep breaths, I went on.

"I guess I always felt people were looking at me all the time," I said.

"With a mother calling you a freak, why wouldn't you?" Jade muttered just loud enough for me to hear.

"Yes," I said. "I suppose that's true. My mother never liked me to wear what other kids my age were wearing. I had to always wear shoes, never sneakers, and my dresses were drab and not very fashionable. She complained often about the way other young people dressed to go to school, especially girls. Every time she brought me to school, she would wag her head and mutter about the clothes other kids wore. She wrote letters to the administration but for the most part, they went unanswered.

"One afternoon when she picked me up, she spotted a tiny spot of lipstick on my lip. I was in the fifth grade by then. A lot of girls came to school wearing lipstick, even though they were only ten years old. There was a girl named Dolores Potter who talked me into putting it on while we were in the girls' room together. I was embarrassed to admit I had never done it before, but she could tell and laughed because I put it on too heavily. I fixed it with a tissue and we went to class.

"I was so self-conscious about it. It was like I was wearing a neon sign. I remember every time I lifted my eyes and gazed around the room, I was positive boys were looking at me more. When the bell rang for the end of the day, I rushed into the bathroom and wiped my mouth with a wet paper towel. I thought I had gotten it all off, but there was just this one spot in the corner.

"My mother always looks at me through a microscope. She doesn't look at anyone else that way. She fixes her eyes on me and looks at every little thing. If I have a strand of hair out of place or my collar is crooked, she spots it and makes me fix it. She has this thing about me being perfect, her idea of perfect," I added. "Anyway, she spotted the lipstick and erupted. The blood rose up through her face like lava. Her eyes popped and her eyebrows rose up and without a word, she brought her right hand around from the steering wheel and snapped it against the side of my face. It felt like a whip made of fire. She was so fast, too. I didn't have a chance to brace myself. My head nearly spun completely around. I guess it frightened me more than it actually hurt, but fear can slice through your heart and bring a deeper pain.

"I lifted my arms to protect myself. My mother could lose her temper and hit me a dozen times. Where she gets the strength for someone her size, I don't know, but she sure can explode."

"You mean she still hits you?" Jade asked.

"Sometimes. Usually, it's just a slap; she doesn't hit me hard anymore and always only once."

"Whoopie do," Jade said. "How lucky can you be?"

"Next time she goes to slap you, put your fist right in her face," Star advised.

"I couldn't do that. My mother just believes if you spare the rod, you spoil the child."

"You're not a child!" Jade practically yelled at me. She looked at Doctor Marlowe. "The girl's seventeen, isn't she?" Her eyes were bright with anger, like sparklers on July Fourth. "That's the trouble with parents these days. They don't know when to stop treating us like children."

"Amen to that," Star said.

"It's not easy for my mother," I said in her defense. "The entire burden of raising me has fallen on her shoulders. She doesn't have any family support system. It's really just the two of us," I explained. "I try to be like she wants me to be. I try not to make her any unhappier."

I looked at Doctor Marlowe because she and I had discussed some of this. She nodded slightly.

"I mean, my mother is a victim, too. She doesn't mean to be cruel or anything. She's just . . ."

"What?" Misty asked.

"Frightened," I said.

Doctor Marlowe's eyes filled with satisfaction and she relaxed her lips into a soft smile.

"It took me a long time to understand that, to realize it," I said, "but it's true. We're two mice living alone in a world full of predatory cats and lots of traps."

"Is that another one of her expressions?" Jade asked.

"No. It's one of mine," I said. She shook her head and looked away.

"Did your father hit you, too?" Misty asked.

"No," I said. "He never touched me in a way that wasn't affectionate or loving," I added.

I glanced at Doctor Marlowe. Should I say it now? Should I begin to talk about the deeper pain? Should I start to explain how those fingers burned through me and touched me in places I was afraid to touch myself?

Should I talk about lips that had become full of thorns? Should I describe the screams I heard in the night, screams that woke me and confused me until I realized they were coming from inside me? Is it time to bid the little girl inside me good-bye forever and ever?

In my dreams Doctor Marlowe was standing off to the side with a stopwatch in her hand. I was bracing to begin my flight. Seconds ticked away. She looked up at me almost as she was looking at me now. Her thumb was on the watch's button.

"Get ready, Cathy. Get set."

"What if my legs don't move?"

"They will; they must. It's time. Five, four, three . . ."

She pushed down on the button and shouted, "Go! Go on, Cathy. Get out of here. Hurry. Run, Cathy. Run!"

I let go of the little hand that I held and charged forward, tears streaming down my face. I looked back only once to see a rag doll staring after me. It was Bones, but its face had become Daddy's face.

I ran faster and faster and harder and harder until I was here in Doctor Marlowe's office, surrounded by my sisters in pain.

3

"Mothers can be a lot tougher than fathers," Misty was saying. "And a lot meaner."

"What?"

I didn't really hear her. It was as if she were standing behind a glass wall and her voice was muted.

"Mothers can't hit as hard, but they can sting more with their words and their looks sometimes," she explained with a nod. She looked at Jade and Star, who just stared at her. Then, looking as if she was going to start to cry, she sat back in her chair.

"Anyway," I began again so *I* wouldn't cry, "after the lipstick incident, my mother decided to take me out of public school and enroll me in a parochial school."

"Just because of that little bit of lipstick?" Jade cried.

"I wasn't that unhappy about it," I said quickly. "I had to wear a uniform and that ended my feeling so different from the other girls because of the clothing my mother insisted I wear. No one was permitted to put on any makeup, of course, even lipstick, which made my mother happy. Discipline was strict. I knew girls, however, who snuck cigarettes in and smoked them. One was caught and expelled immediately and that stopped the smoking for a while. I got into trouble with Sister Margaret, who was basically the disciplinarian, because I went into the girls' room when two girls were smoking and the smell got into my clothes."

"So why would that get you into trouble?" Star asked.

"Sister Margaret is known for her nose, not because it's too big or anything, but because she can smell cigarette smoke a mile away. Her nostrils twitch like a rabbit's when she suspects someone.

"Anyway, later I was in the cafeteria waiting to get my lunch. I wasn't even thinking about having been in the bathroom with the smokers when suddenly I felt her hand squeeze down on my left shoulder, her fingers pinching me hard and pulling me out of the line.

" 'Come with me,' she demanded, and marched me to the office where she accused me of smoking just because she could smell it in my hair and clothes. I swore I hadn't been smoking and I started to cry, which was enough for Sister Louise, the principal, to judge me innocent, but Sister Margaret was relentless.

" 'All right, if you didn't smoke, you were right in it and certainly close enough to see what was going on. Who was smoking?' she demanded.

"The thought of telling on girls I had just gotten to know was terrifying, almost as terrifying as being caught myself. I shook my head and she grabbed my shoulders and shook me so hard, I thought my eyes would roll out. The sisters could hit you, too," I told them.

In anticipation of what I was about to describe, Star's eyes widened with anger.

"She made me put out my hands and slapped them with a ruler until the tears were streaming down my cheeks and my palms were nearly cherry red and I couldn't close my fingers."

"I'd have kicked her into her precious heaven," Star said.

"What did you do?" Misty asked.

"I told her again and again I didn't know who was smoking. 'I don't know everyone,' I lied. I closed my eyes expecting lightning to strike me or something because I was lying to a nun.

" 'Then you'll point them out,' she decided and marched me back to the cafeteria.

"The moment we entered, all the girls knew why I had been brought back. They stopped talking and looked up at me. You could almost hear them breathe. The two girls who had been smoking were very frightened. They looked down quickly, probably reciting Hail Marys at the table.

" 'They're not here,' I said.

" 'What do you mean? They have to be here. Everyone's here,' Sister Margaret snapped. She still had her hand on my shoulder and squeezed so hard, it sent pain down my spine and through my legs.

"I pretended to look around the cafeteria and then I shook my head.

" 'They're not here!' I cried. Tears were dripping off my chin by now.

"She was fuming. I thought I could see the smoke she hated so much coming out of her ears.

" 'Very well,' she said. 'Until your memory improves, you'll eat lunch by yourself in my office facing the blank wall every day.' She kept me there for a week before telling me to return to the cafeteria. The good thing was they never told my mother," I said.

"How old were you when this all happened?" Jade asked.

"I had just turned eleven. I was still in the fifth grade."

"Girls were smoking in the fifth grade?" she muttered.

"That's nothing. Kids in my school have been smoking forever," Star added.

"Terrific. Maybe Cathy's mother is right. Maybe the country is going to hell," Jade said.

"You don't know anything about hell," Star told her. "Your idea of hell is a bad hairdo."

"Is that so?"

"Girls. Aren't we getting a little off course?" Doctor Marlowe softly suggested.

Jade threw a look at Star that could stop a charging bull, but Star waved it off with a smug turn of her head and a small grunt.

"It sounds so horrible. What did your father say about your changing to a parochial school?" Misty asked. "Was he for it, too?"

"Like I said, when it came to most things concerning me, my mother was in charge. She told him what she wanted me to do, of course. It was an expense, but he just nodded as usual, glanced at me for a moment, snapped his paper and continued to read."

"Didn't he care about what you thought and wanted?" Misty followed.

I shook my head.

"Another absentee parent," Jade quipped. "Why do they bother to have children in the first place? What are we, some kind of status symbol, something to collect like a car or a big-screen television set? I'm not going to have any children unless my husband signs a contract in blood, swearing to be a concerned parent."

"You know you have to get pregnant to have children," Star teased with a coy smile. "You know that means you'll lose your perfect figure, and you'll throw up in the morning."

"I know what it is to be pregnant, thank you."

"Unless you adopt like her parents did," Star said nodding at me.

"Yes, that's right," Misty said. "It doesn't sound like they really wanted children. Why did they adopt you?" she wondered.

I turned and gazed through the window. Angry clouds had reached Brentwood and had drawn a dark gray veil over the trees, the grass and flowers. The wind was picking up and the tree branches were swaying. They looked like they were all saying, "No, no, no."

Why did they adopt me? If I had asked myself this question once, I had asked it a thousand times. My mother wouldn't reveal any answers, but I had my own deep suspicions, suspicions I had never expressed before, even to Doctor Marlowe. When I glanced at her, I thought she was hoping I would now and I thought maybe this was one reason she wanted me in this group therapy.

"I can't imagine, could never imagine my mother having a baby the normal way," I began. "I have seen my father kiss her on the forehead and occasionally on the cheek, but I have never seen them kiss like people in love, never on the lips. Mother probably would be thinking of some contagious disease if he did. Even when he kissed her on the forehead, she would turn away and wipe it off with the back of her hand. Sometimes, he saw her do it; sometimes he didn't."

"Don't they sleep together?" Star asked.

"Not in the same bed," I said. "They always had twin beds separated by a nightstand. He's not there anymore, of course."

"But even people who don't spend the night in the same bed can get together long enough to make a baby," Jade said. "I have friends whose parents even have separate bedrooms."

"What do they do, make a date to have sex?" Star asked her.

"I don't know. Maybe," Jade replied, thoughtful for a moment. She smiled. "Maybe it's more romantic."

"Oh yeah, you're married, but you got to make a date to have sex. That's really romantic."

"Passion should be . . . unexpected," Misty said with dreamy eyes turned toward the ceiling. "You've got to turn toward the man you love and have your eyes meet and then float into each other's arms with music in your heart."

"You're living in your own soap opera," Star told her, but not with her usual firmness. She looked like she hoped she was wrong.

"Maybe, but that's the way it's going to be for me and the man who loves me," Misty insisted.

Jade drew her lips up in the corners and shook her head. Then she turned back to me.

"So you don't think your mother and father had sex? Is that what you're saying?"

"They had to have had it once," I said.

"What do you mean? You just said they adopted you."

"My father told me there was almost a baby. He was alone with me one night when I was feeling very low, and he told me the story. He said my mother didn't know she was pregnant or didn't want to know. She found out when she had a bad pain in her stomach, went to the bathroom and lost the baby that was in her. She flushed it down the toilet."

"Ugh," Misty said.

"She collapsed and he had to help her to bed. She refused to go to a doctor even though she kept bleeding. My father made it sound as if she wanted it to happen. From the way he described it to me, I don't think she wanted to have sex and I think she was angry it had happened and she had become pregnant. I don't know. To this day I can't imagine them making love," I said. I guess I had a guilty look on my face. Misty widened her eyes a little and leaned toward me.

"What?" she whispered.

"Nothing," I said quickly and looked away. My heart had started racing again, beating almost like a wild frantic animal in my chest.

"Come on. We've told you lots of things we wouldn't dare tell anyone else," she urged.

"You know that's true, Cat," Star said. "We hardly have a secret left."

"You can trust us," Misty said. "Really. Who are we to talk about someone else, right?"

I looked back at the three of them. They did look sincere.

My mother's warning returned, but she didn't understand how important it was for me to get all this out. Look what keeping the ugliness inside her had done to her, I thought. I don't want that to happen to me.

"After my father had told me the story of the lost baby, I would spy on them," I confessed and quickly added, "I was just very curious."

"So? What did you see?" Star followed.

"How did you spy on them?" Misty asked.

"All our bedrooms are upstairs, next to each other. We have a two-story Spanish colonial with a deck running alongside their bedroom and mine."

"A Monterey-style cantilevered porch, probably," Jade said knowingly. "My father designed a house like that and I saw the drawings," she explained.

"Thanks for the information," Star said. "I couldn't have lived ten more minutes without it."

"If you don't want to learn anything . . ."

"Let her talk!" Misty exclaimed, excited and anxious for me to continue. "Go ahead, Cat," she urged. "I'm listening even if they're not."

"Usually, when they were both in their bedroom, I would hear some muffled conversation for a few minutes and then silence. I couldn't help thinking about it. I had read some things, knew some things."

"So you went out on the porch and peeked in their window?" Star asked impatiently.

"Yes, but only a few times," I added.

"And?" she asked, holding up her arms in anticipation.

"My mother sleeps in a nightgown with a cotton robe wrapped around her. Every time I looked in, she had her back to my father and he had his back to her. I never saw them embrace each other or touch each other or even kiss each other. I remember thinking they were like two strangers sharing a room for the night. How could they ever have made a baby?"

"No wonder they broke up. I'm surprised they were together as long as they were," Star said. Misty and Jade nodded.

"So your mother had gotten pregnant against her will, didn't want to have sex with your father anymore, and therefore, the only way they would ever have any children was by adopting," Jade concluded.

"Maybe someone else had made her pregnant," Star conjectured.

"No, I doubt that," I said.

"Maybe your father practically raped her," Misty suggested, "and that was why she wanted to lose the baby."

"You ought to write soap operas," Star told her.

Misty shrugged and motioned for me to continue.

"Why would her father remain married if he had no love life?" Jade pondered.

"Maybe there's something wrong with her father now. Maybe he's one of those men who can't have sex anymore," Star suggested. "I heard that can happen to a man. He's impotent or something," she added, insecure about the word.

"No," I said, a little too fast.

"What do you mean, no? How do you know? Have you seen him with some other woman? Is that why they got divorced?"

"That's it, isn't it?" Misty asked, smiling. "Welcome to the club."

I looked away again, took a deep breath, and then looked at them and shook my head.

"No, I never saw him with anyone else."

"So then, how can you be so sure?" Star queried. She turned her eyes on me like two tiny knives. What she saw in mine made her eyes widen as she continued to look at me.

"I know what she's saying," she said almost in a whisper.

They were all staring now, a cold look of realization moving in a wave from one face to the other, and with it, an explosion of pity, fear and disgust in their eyes.

It felt like all the blood in my body was rising and gathering at my throat. Suddenly, I couldn't swallow, but I couldn't breathe either. I guess I was getting whiter and whiter. Doctor Marlowe's face erupted into a look of serious concern. She rose from her chair.

"Let's give Cathy a short break," she suggested. "Come on, honey. I want you to splash your face in cold water and relax for a few moments."

I felt her helping me to my feet, but I wasn't sure they wouldn't just turn to air and let the rest of me fold to the floor. Like a sleepwalker, I followed Doctor Marlowe out to the bathroom and did what she prescribed. The cold water revived me. The blood retreated and I could swallow again and breathe.

"Feeling better?" she asked.

I nodded.

"You don't have to continue, Cathy. Maybe I'm rushing you," she suggested.

I considered it. How comfortable and easy it would be for me to agree and go home, return to my room and go to bed. I could pull the blanket up to my chin and shut my eyes and squeeze my legs against my stomach and wait for sleep to open a door into a happy place, someplace where I could just drift, float on warm clouds and forget and forget and forget.

But another part of me wanted to come out, to leave the room and be in the real world again. How would I ever get back to the real world if I just ran home?

"No," I said. "I want to keep trying."

"You sure, honey?" she asked.

I looked at my face in the mirror. It was still a mask. I was tired of looking at it. It was time to tear it off and take a chance on what I would find. Would I find a little girl again? Had all that had happened stopped me from growing up? How silly that would be, a little girl's face on a body as mature as mine.

Or would I simply find a shattered face, cracked like some piece of thin china, the lines running down from my eyes where tears had streaked over my cheeks and chin. How long would it take to mend that face? Would it ever be mended so that the cracks would disappear and not look like scars of sadness?

Was I pretty? Could I ever be pretty? Did I have a face that someone could love under this mask? Could I ever want to be kissed and touched? Could I dream and fantasize like Misty just had and find myself in a romantic place?

Daddy used to tell me so. He would cup my face in his hands and kiss the tip of my nose and say I was blossoming and soon all of my mirrors would reflect my beauty. When he spoke to me like that, I felt I was in a fairy tale and maybe I could be someone's princess. For a long time, he made me feel like I was his special princess, but because of that had my ability to love someone been crushed like a small flower, smashed into the earth, fading, fading, dying away like some distant star given a moment to twinkle before it fell back into the darkness forever and ever?

No, I didn't want to go home again. I had to keep trying.

"I'll go back," I insisted.

"Okay," Doctor Marlowe said, "but if you change your mind or have any problems, please don't hesitate to stop and ask to go home. I don't want to lose all the progress we've made to date. That can happen if things are rushed sometimes," she said.

"Rushed?" I laughed and the sound of that laughter seemed strange even to me. I knew it was strange and worrisome because Doctor Marlowe didn't smile but grimaced instead.

"Rushed? You know what it's like to look out the car window and see girls my age and younger walking on the sidewalk with their friends and boyfriends, their faces full of joy, their lives full of promises? I feel like an animal in a cage. I didn't put myself into that cage, either. It's not fair. I want to get out, Doctor Marlowe."

"I know, honey, and I'm going to help you do just that."

I gazed at the bathroom door.

"They all had bad times, too, but they looked so shocked and afraid back there."

She nodded.

"One or two of them might not want to stay, but somehow, I think you'll all get through it," she said. She squeezed my hand and I took a deep breath and smiled. "Ready?"

"Yes. Take me back. I want to focus on all the bad things just like you told me to do, and I want to put all my anger and strength into smashing them to bits forever and ever. Will I ever be able to do that?"

She smiled.

"I know you will," she said firmly enough to make me feel confident.

I walked out and returned to the office. I could see they had been talking incessantly about me. The expressions on their faces were so different, the hardness gone from Star, the smugness gone from Jade, and the innocence gone from Misty. We were doing what Doctor Marlowe had intended: we were changing each other as we changed ourselves. Like sisters related not through blood but through adversity and turmoil, we gathered around each other and warmed each other with our mutual pain and fear.

Together, we would help each other kill the demons.

I was anxious to go on.

4

Their eyes were full of many new questions now, questions I was still answering myself. How could all that have happened to me and right under my mother's eyes, too? How is a garden prepared and cultivated to grow black flowers full of thorns and poison? That was where I had found myself planted.

They waited patiently for me to sit and gather my thoughts. I took a small breath and began.

"When I was very little nothing seemed as important to my mother as my being able to care for myself. I was only three when she insisted I dress myself. She taught me how to run my own bath and I was given the responsibility to undress, clean and dress myself without her help. She would put out the clothes I was to wear, but she didn't stand around to help me put them on. If I didn't put something on correctly, she sent me back to my room to do it right.

"Personal hygiene, being in charge of my own body, was the most important thing to her. It was more important than anything else, school, manners, anything.

"It was hard when I got sick. I remember times when I threw up and she made me undress myself, bathe and dress myself even though I was nauseous and had cramps. I cried out for her, but she would stand outside the door and give me directions, insisting that I learn to guard and protect myself. To be naked in front of anyone, even my parents, was to be avoided at all costs."

"That's sick," Jade said. "Why would she make her own child ashamed of herself?"

"My mother doesn't think of it that way," I explained. "She thinks you should be ashamed only if someone else looks upon you. Your body is holy, precious, very private."

"No wonder your parents rarely had sex," Star muttered.

"My mother doesn't even go to the doctor because of the way she thinks," I revealed. "She's never had a gynecologist examine her and she hates taking me to any doctors. Whenever I was sick, she would try all her old-fashioned remedies first and take me only if they failed."

"Not getting herself regular checkups is so stupid," Jade said. "She could get cancer or something she might have prevented."

"What does she do when she's so sick that her remedies don't help?" Misty asked.

"I don't remember her ever being very sick. She's had colds, but she's in good health, I guess, although lately, she occasionally loses her breath and has to sit for a while almost immediately after she begins to clean. She says it's because of all that's happened and in time, it will pass.

"Anyway, I grew up with her ideas rolling around in my head like marbles pounding every time someone saw an uncovered part of me. It was especially hard in physical education class, dressing in the locker room. I never ever took a shower in school, not even in parochial school where we had individual showers."

"What did you expect would happen if someone saw you naked?" Star asked.

"I don't know. It just . . . sent a chill through me when it happened. I even imagined my mother standing there looking upset."

"You're going to grow up like her, a weirdo," Star threatened.

"No, she won't," Doctor Marlowe insisted. She turned to Star. "None of you will be weird."

"You mean weirder, don't you?" Jade said. "It's already too late to stop weird."

They all laughed. I felt a little better, stronger. I can do this, I chanted, trying to encourage myself. I can. I must face the demons and destroy them or Star will be right.

I paused, looked down, thought about how I would continue and then looked up at them.

"My father didn't have the same ideas about it all," I said, "although he behaved in the same way he did with everything else, which means he didn't argue with my mother about it. Right from the beginning, he pretended it was going to be our little secret, our special secret."

"What was?" Misty said almost before the words were out of my mouth. She grimaced with confusion.

"Give her a chance," Jade chastised.

"Yeah, stop rushing her," Star ordered.

"I'm sorry. I'm sorry."

It struck me funny how they were all becoming as protective as Doctor Marlowe.

"It's all right. I know it's hard to understand," I said, offering Misty a small smile. "I already told you that my father didn't have much to do with raising me. I rarely went anywhere with him without my mother along. He almost never attended any program at school that I participated in. He always went to bed early because he was up for the stock market so early. We didn't spend all that much time together in the evening. By the time we finished dinner and I did my homework, he was often on his way to bed. That was the routine year round."

"Didn't you ever go on a family trip or a vacation?" Jade asked.

"No, not really. A day's travel was it. My mother doesn't like to sleep in a strange bed. She says hotel rooms are never cleaned well enough and you're always sleeping in someone else's dirt.

"I recall a few times when my father went somewhere by himself, but my mother didn't seem to mind that. Then, there was a time when he took me," I said.

They all looked like they were holding their breath, but I wasn't ready to talk about that yet. I closed my eyes. It looked like red webs were spun on the underside of my eyelids.

"When I was little and left on my own to bathe and dress myself, my father would sometimes appear. That was the secret. He made it clear that I shouldn't tell my mother. We both knew she wouldn't like it and my father said we shouldn't make her unhappy. She works too hard for both of us, he explained.

"She didn't see him go into your room?" Misty asked.

"She was usually downstairs preparing breakfast or dinner or cleaning up at the time. Mother has always been so precise about what she does. She keeps to her schedule no matter what," I explained. "I almost know to the minute where she'll be and what she'll be doing. Being organized makes her comfortable.

"Even though it is so long ago, I can clearly remember the first time my daddy came into my bathroom. I was already in the tub. I didn't hear him enter the bedroom. I think he must have been practically tiptoeing. He gazed in at me and smiled and asked me if I was all right.

"I nodded and he felt the water, dipped his right forefinger in like a thermometer and wiggled it in the air, that birthmark bright.

" 'Good,' he said with a big smile, 'it's not too hot.'

"He brushed his hand over my hair and then knelt beside the tub and asked me to show him how I washed myself.

"I was always eager for him to pay more attention to me. I wanted him to hold me and hug me and kiss me. He was my daddy and I looked to him often, anticipating some warm words, some gentle touch, some loving smile. That was all so rare in my house, so when he did this, I was very happy. I mean, that's why I wasn't afraid or . . ."

"You don't have to do that," Doctor Marlowe said softly. They all turned to her, but she didn't explain.

She didn't have to explain it to me. I knew what she meant. She wanted me to stop blaming myself, stop making excuses. I nodded. When I turned back to the girls, they looked even more intrigued.

" 'I know your mother has taught you how important it is to be clean all over,' he said. 'Go on. Let me see how you do it.'

"You can't imagine how excited I was to perform for him. I scrubbed my elbows and my little legs. I washed my neck vigorously, especially behind my ears, and then I stood up and washed between my legs and behind.

"He laughed and clapped and then he left and I felt so happy about it, but when I saw him later, he looked at my mother and then back to me and winked. In front of her he tried not to act so interested in me. He practically ignored me. When I tried to cuddle up beside him on the sofa, he told me I should go to sleep and I remember feeling as if I had been slapped even though he merely lifted his eyes and shook his head. Then he went back to what he was reading.

"The only time he really showed interest in me, smiled and laughed and touched me lovingly was when he visited me in the bathroom while I took my bath and that was only occasionally at best.

"Until . . ."

"What?" Misty practically jumped to ask.

"The bumps."

"Bumps?"

"She means until her breasts started to form," Jade said with narrow, sharp eyes. She glanced at Star who nodded and then turned back to me. "Right?"

"Yes," I said. My eyes burned with tears that welled behind my lids. I swallowed back the small scream that wanted so much to come rushing out of my mouth. "Yes," I whispered, not even sure if I had said it.

"Oh," Misty said, her lips in a small circle, her eyes bright with understanding, but shock as well.

"I don't know how it was for the rest of you, but when it began to happen to me, I was frightened. I told my mother about it and she told me to stop talking nonsense.

" 'It's not nonsense, Mother. It's really happening to me!' I protested one morning at breakfast.

"My father put down his paper and looked at me with surprise, too, but he didn't say anything to help me. He just looked a little interested and then he went back to his paper.

" 'You're too young for such a thing,' my mother said throwing me a hard look. 'Girls today rush everything. You're imagining it.'

" 'No, I'm not,' I cried, tears now building in my eyes. 'I'll show you.'

"I started to unbutton my blouse and she screamed so loud and shrilly, I felt like she had sent a lightning bolt through my body. I remember I literally froze, terrified of even moving my fingers.

" 'Take it easy, Geraldine,' my father said. 'She doesn't understand.'

"I guess she realized how dramatic and horrifying she was. She became calmer and lectured me softly.

" 'We don't disrobe in any other room of the house but our bedrooms and our bathrooms,' she explained.

" 'I'll go up to my bathroom to show you,' I offered.

" 'This isn't the time for that. It's breakfast time and you're off to school. Put this nonsense out of your mind,' she insisted.

"I gazed at my father, hoping he would speak up again, but he just shook his head at me and went back to what he was reading.

"I tried to bring it up again with my mother when I returned from school, but again, she refused to listen. She insisted it was all part of my confused imagination.

" 'They make sex such a big thing on television and in movies and books today that it infects children,' she orated. She could step up on a soapbox at a moment's notice and deliver a speech about the disgusting immorality alive in the world. She didn't accidentally use the word 'infects,' by the way. My mother thinks of it as a disease, almost something you can catch by breathing near promiscuous people. She had me thinking that way. I remember holding my breath or covering my mouth when classmates said or did things I knew my mother would disapprove of."

All three girls had their mouths slightly open, their eyes wide as they listened and gazed at me with astonishment.

"I know how stupid that sounds now, but that's the way I thought.

"Anyway, a few nights later, I heard Daddy enter my bedroom and come to the door of my bathroom while I was taking my bath. As I told you before, I was about nine years old at the time which was why I was nervous and confused. My body seemed to be racing ahead. Maybe I was freakish.

" 'So what's this you've been trying to tell your mother?' he asked as he approached.

"I sat up to show him and he nodded. He studied me like a doctor for a moment and then he pressed my chest softly with those spider leg fingers.

" 'Looks like you're right,' he said nodding and smiling. 'I'll speak to your mother about it. Don't be afraid,' he told me. 'It's earlier than most girls, but it's nothing bad, nothing to be afraid to see happening.'

"He spoke so gently, so kindly, I felt relieved. Why couldn't my mother be this kind, this concerned and loving? I wondered.

" 'I can tell you're going to be a very pretty girl, a special girl,' he continued. 'Daddy's special girl,' he added. He had never said that to me before. I was very happy about it. If this would make him love me even more, I thought, then it must be good.

"A little less than a week afterward, my mother came to my bedroom door while I was doing homework. She entered and closed it behind her.

" 'All right,' she said stretching and tightening her lips until they were two pale red thin lines over her chin, 'let me see what you're talking about.'

"I just imagined my father had done what he had promised and spoken to her about it. No longer afraid or ashamed, I got up and unbuttoned my blouse to show her. She looked at me, but unlike my father, she looked disgusted by it. She had such an unpleasant expression on her face, I thought there really was something wrong with me.

" 'Is it all right?' I asked her, my voice shaking with some panic.

" 'No,' she said. 'It's far too soon. I don't like how it shows under your blouse either. I'll get something proper for you to wear tomorrow,' she promised, turned and left me standing there feeling hideous.

"The next day she bought me a sports bra, but my development continued at an accelerated pace. By the time the school year ended, I had a distinct bosom. I even had cleavage," I said.

"That's so unfair," Misty moaned. "My mother wants to buy me a Wonder Bra and here you had cleavage in the fifth grade!"

"Despite my development, my mother fought buying me a regular bra. I complained about the sports bra and she replaced it with a little bigger size, but it still pinched and squeezed. It was such a relief to get undressed every night.

"My mother wouldn't listen to any complaints. She told me to work on putting my mind off it. If I told her about a tingle or a feeling I could describe only as a tickle, she would turn crimson and scream at me for not keeping such thoughts buried in my mind. Once, she even slapped me because I mentioned it in front of my father. Then she pulled me aside and said, 'There are things decent women don't mention in front of men, ever. Hear?'

"Men? I thought. My father was a man, of course, but I didn't lump him in with other men. I remember feeling so strange about the way she had referred to him. Almost as if he were the enemy. We had to hide things from him, too, just because he was a man. What would happen if she knew my daddy's and my secret? I wondered. Daddy looked worried for a moment and then smiled when he realized I had kept it our little secret.

"Of course, I nodded after everything my mother told me and I tried to behave as she wanted me to behave, but I couldn't help overhearing classmates talking about sexual things from time to time. I had so many questions to ask, so many worries. I tried reading about it, but if my mother found any books or any pamphlets in the house, she would throw them in the garbage, even if they were library books and I had to pay for them. She declared they shouldn't be in a school library anyway, especially a parochial school.

"Once, I tried hiding a book from her. That was when I discovered my mother went through my room daily, searching everywhere for lascivious material, even under the mattress," I said.

"It sounds like you live in a prison, not a home," Jade said.

"I've felt that way, yes," I admitted.

"My room is my world. Neither of my parents would dare to invade it," she said. "We're people, too, despite our ages. It's stupid to think that just because we're under eighteen, we're some kind of lesser creature."

"Right," Misty said nodding.

"It bothered me along with so many other things. I was more emotional than ever. Sometimes, I would just lay in bed and cry. I had no specific reason for it. Tears would suddenly build and flow and I would shudder and sob. If my mother heard as she passed by my room, she ignored it. Intimate talk not only embarrassed her; it disgusted her. I felt so lost and confused. It made everything harder."

"What about your father?" Star asked. "After all, he told you that you were his special little girl, right?"

"My father was very busy at the time. He had moved to another brokerage house and was establishing himself and the clients he had brought over with him.

"Everything about our lives was routine then. One day seemed no different from the next, even the weekends blended into the week. All my premature development did was make me feel lonelier than ever. I truly did think of myself as being freakish and I tried to stop thinking about it. I tried to do what my mother wanted, but I was like a rubber band being stretched and stretched until I was about to snap."

"Didn't you have any friends to talk with?" Misty asked.

"I was terrified of personal talk and the other girls knew it. Most of the time, they teased me. Every time one of them brought up a topic related to sex or boys, I felt my ears shut and my body tighten. I usually would find an excuse to leave. I guess by my own behavior I added to the image of being freakish and weird. No one really wanted me as a friend.

"Don't think I didn't feel terrible about it. Other girls went to each other's homes. There were parties, none of which I was invited to. I rarely went to the movies. I felt like I was standing on the other side of a wall, a glass wall, looking in at the rest of the world.

"One night I sat in my tub and sobbed so hard I created waves. Mother was downstairs doing needlepoint. I heard my bedroom door open and close and moments later, there was Daddy looking in at me. He smiled.

" 'What's all this? Why are you crying, Cathy?' he asked.

"I shook my head. I couldn't explain it to myself. How could I explain it to him or anyone else for that matter?

"He saw the redness around my bosom and under my arms and looked concerned.

" 'What's this?' he asked. 'What is it, a rash?' He approached the tub and knelt down to look closer.

" 'No,' I told him. 'It's from the sports bras Mother makes me wear.'

" 'This isn't good,' he said with concern. 'My poor special little girl.'

"He rose and went to the bathroom cabinet and then he returned with some cold cream. First, he rubbed around my bosom, and under my arms with a towel, drying the skin. Then he told me to just sit back and relax as he dabbed the cold cream on and gently spread it over my chest.

" 'Good,' he whispered. 'That's good. It feels better, doesn't it?' he asked as he moved those long, spidery fingers around, under and over my bosom.

"It did feel better. When I opened my eyes, he was looking down at me with such a bright hot look in his eyes, I was both frightened and confused for a moment. Then he spoke softly again and promised to talk to my mother about the terrible thing the sports bras were doing.

"He leaned over and kissed me softly on the forehead. In my house, kisses were as rare as exotic birds. Every one I received, I cherished in my heart, I hoarded like a jewel in my treasure chest of affection. It had a long way to go to be filled.

"Anyway, if my father did speak to my mother about the problem with the sports bras, she never acknowledged it. She didn't ask or come to look. I continued to complain and on each occasion she told me what she always told me. It wasn't the proper time for me to wear anything else. If I did, it would just emphasize my awkward development and draw looks and comments that would upset and embarrass me.

"Finally, I rebelled and refused to wear the tight exercise bra. When she saw I was going to attend school with only a blouse covering my bosom, she relented and bought me a regular bra, but I seemed to outgrow them as fast as she bought them and that displeased her.

"Once, she even considered bringing me to a doctor and you already know how desperate she would have to be before she would think about doing it.

" 'Maybe there is something terribly wrong with your hormones,' she considered. That frightened me again. She made it sound like I might grow so big, I'd be in a circus. I tried to find something in the library that would explain it or tell me how to slow it down.

"In the seventh grade, we had a unit on sex education, but it was so vague and general, I didn't feel I had learned anything significant about myself. Sister Anne wouldn't permit specific questions or any question that she termed out of line. I learned more just listening to the girls talk in the locker room and bathroom, but never enough to put myself at ease.

"The only time I felt like I wasn't a freak was when Daddy came in to see me. He told me he wanted to check to be sure the rash hadn't returned and he thought it was best to dab on the cream. He always seemed to see some redness, even if I didn't.

"Once, after I finished my bath, he asked me to lay face down on the bed and he rubbed in body oil he said would make my skin softer. He put it everywhere. When I giggled because he tickled, he told me to hold my breath instead. He didn't want my mother hearing and learning our little secret."

I stopped and took a breath. I had been talking quickly because I felt if I took too long, I would stop and not be able to start again.

Just at that moment, we heard a tray of glasses tinkling and moments later, Emma, Doctor Marlowe's sister, appeared in the office doorway, carrying her usual tray of glasses, pitcher of lemonade and some cookies. Today she wore a pretty pearl white blouse with a lace collar and an ankle-length dark blue skirt. She had some makeup on, too, and her hair was brushed and neatly pinned.

"Good morning, everyone," she said. "Sorry I wasn't here to greet you, but I had a nasty time in the dentist's office. I'm going to have to have a root canal, I'm afraid," she said with a sad face. Then, she quickly smiled. "But it's not the end of the world."

The girls all stared up at her and I knew what they were thinking. Emma had a bosom nearly twice as big as mine. I knew all the jokes like 'They're so big they arrive in a room ten minutes before her.' I had heard boys say these things about me. Was this what I would look like someday?

She put the tray on the table and stepped back.

"Do you need anything else, Doctor Marlowe?" she asked her sister.

"No, thank you, Emma."

"Well, everyone looks cheery this morning, despite the nasty weather. I'll see about the lunch," she added, suddenly made nervous by our silence. She glanced at Doctor Marlowe and then hurried away.

"Dig in, girls," Doctor Marlowe said, rising. "I just want to make one phone call during our break."

She smiled at me, rose and went to her desk. Star poured herself a glass of lemonade and Misty took a cookie. Then she offered me one. I shook my head.

"I'll just have some lemonade," I said.

"Why is your mother so uptight?" Star asked. I'm sure even she was afraid to ask me any more questions about my father.

"Something must have happened in her childhood," Jade ventured. "Maybe . . . she was raped when she was a little girl," she suggested with big, teacup saucer eyes. "Was she raped?"

"I don't know," I said. "If she was, she would never tell me. She never has told me anything about the baby she lost. I already explained how she feels about even making a reference to things like that."

"She needs a therapist more than you do, or any of us do," Jade said.

"She had her visit with Doctor Marlowe, just like your parents, but she doesn't believe in therapy. She almost didn't bring me here today."

"Right, don't air your dirty laundry or something," Star said.

I smiled and nodded.

"Cat, you need some friends, and some help."

"Maybe we can be her friends," Misty suggested.

"Us? We're here because we're screwed up, too, aren't we? That's the blind leading the blind," Star said. "She needs normal friends."

"I'm normal," Jade said indignantly. "Just as normal as most anyone out there. Maybe even more normal."

Star lifted her eyebrows.

"We heard your story; don't try to convince us you're more normal." Before Jade could respond, she added, "And you heard ours. Let's not pretend we don't have problems or excess baggage, okay?"

"We can still be her friends," Jade insisted.

"Maybe she doesn't want us to be her friends." She put her hands on her hips. "You just keep sticking your rich nose into everyone's life all the time, I bet."

"You think you know all about me just because of these sessions? You don't know all about me. You don't know enough to pass judgment on me or anyone. You're the one who's being arrogant."

"Right. You're always right," Star quipped. She turned to me. "Well, you heard us talk about our problems. Do you want anyone here to be your friend?"

"Yes," I admitted. "I would like that."

Jade bit into a cookie and looked gleefully happy. Star rolled her eyes.

"Maybe you're just a lost cause. Maybe we all are. What did you call us, Misty, Orphans With Parents?" Star asked her.

"That's right."

"Okay," Star said. "I nominate Jade here to be president of the OWP."

"I second it," Misty said laughing.

"Who says I want to be president?" Jade quipped.

"You want to be the standout everywhere you go. It doesn't take a genius to see that."

Jade stared at her for a moment and then nodded.

"Okay, I accept. I'm the president," she said.

"Wait, we have to vote. All in favor raise your hand."

We all did.

"Done," Star said. "We're the OWP's and Jade is the president."

Everyone laughed as Doctor Marlowe returned. She gazed down at us and smiled.

"Did I miss something important?" she asked.

"Just an election," Star said.

Doctor Marlowe's look of confusion made us all laugh again.

I can do this, I kept thinking. I drank some more lemonade. I can do it.

5

"When I was in the eighth grade, something terrible happened to me," I continued after everyone had had her lemonade and sat back again. I glanced at Doctor Marlowe. She hadn't given me or anyone else here any instructions about what to tell and what not to tell. She looked like she wasn't sure herself what we might say and was just as interested in finding out.

"I suppose now when I look back, it wasn't as horrible as I had thought, but at the time . . . It took a while before I could talk about this after it had happened," I continued. "I kept it a secret from my parents, and actually, I still haven't told my mother about it. I knew she would find a way somehow to blame me, and I was afraid that if I told my father, he might tell her even accidentally, so I swallowed it down like bitter medicine and kept it inside even though it came up like rotten eggs almost every night, leaving me in a cold sweat and bringing me to tears of ice."

No one spoke. They hardly breathed. It was so quiet for a moment, we could hear the sound of leaf-blowers blocks away as gardeners worked behind the high walls of expensive homes. The dull, monotonous sound of their engines seemed to be the proper sound track behind a gray, heavily overcast day.

"What was it already?" Misty blurted. I saw Jade kick her and she sat back, biting down on her lip.

"Whenever I was lucky enough to have someone at school try to be friends with me, my mother usually found a way to stop it. She had watched some guest on a talk show discussing the problems with young people in today's society and she agreed with the conclusion that it was all happening because young people were a bigger influence on each other than their parents.

" 'Peer pressure is stronger than family,' she declared as if it was a major new discovery. It was practically the only time I heard her lead a discussion at dinner. She was so excited about the conclusion, she couldn't stop talking about it to my father, who looked bored, but politely listened and as usual, agreed.

"After that, whenever I mentioned another girl at school, my mother put me through a cross-examination that probably was more severe than a cross-examination during the Spanish Inquisition." I laughed. "I remember watching those court shows on television sometimes and imagining my mother in the courtroom, questioning the defendants, drilling them with biting questions as she fixed her eyes on their faces, catching every tiny revealing movement in their lips or in the way they shifted their gazes.

"You don't lie to my mother. That's one thing you don't do," I said almost proudly.

"You've got to be able to lie to your parents sometimes," Jade said.

Misty nodded vigorously. "Jade's right. It's better for them and better for you. What they don't know, won't hurt them."

"It was just the opposite with my mother," Star said. "She wouldn't know the truth if she tripped over it. She was more comfortable with lies."

"Did you lie about something or just not tell the whole truth?" Misty asked me. She smiled. "That's the way I get around things sometimes."

"I guess I did a combination of both," I said. "But not in the beginning. I was too nervous and afraid to do that. As I said, all I had to do was mention a girl's name and my mother would stop whatever she was doing and turn on me.

" 'Where were you with her? What did she say exactly? What did she mean by that? Who are her parents? Where does she live? What does she look like?'

"She would ask her questions in shotgun fashion, shaking her head and spitting out another before I had a chance to answer the one before. The more I didn't know about the girl, the worse it was. Usually, she would end by forbidding me to talk to her again and I'd have to remember to never mention that girl's name."

Jade spun angrily on Doctor Marlowe.

"How can you let her continue to live with such a monster? She hits her. She won't let her make friends. She treats her like she's something dirty. Why don't you tell the authorities?"

Doctor Marlowe closed her eyes softly and opened them with a gentle smile.

"Cathy has a great deal more to say and you should hear it all before you come to any conclusions, Jade. You wouldn't have liked it any other way, would you?"

Jade turned back to me, still fuming, her arms wrapped tightly around herself, her eyes bright with anger.

"Your mother's a Nazi," she muttered.

I didn't laugh or reply. I waited for a surge of nausea to pass and then I took a breath and continued.

"There was this girl, Kelly Sullivan, whose father works for the church in some administrative capacity. I think he manages properties or something. Her mother is in a wheelchair. She has multiple sclerosis. They live in a nice, ranch-style house only about ten minutes by car from us.

"Kelly has beautiful green eyes and apricot red hair. She's a lot smaller than me, slimmer, I should say, but most girls who were my age in the eighth grade were. She hated her freckles. There were patches of them on each check and even on the bottom of her chin, but she had a pretty face. She thought her freckles made her look like a freak and of course, I had my problem. Her parents were like my mother in that they didn't want Kelly to wear any makeup, not even lipstick. I actually thought she and I had a lot in common and for a while, I had hopes that she would be a real best friend. We often talked in the cafeteria and we shared three classes. She had other friends, but she didn't seem to me to be that popular. She was shy in school and when she met my mother, she was so sweet and polite, my mother looked at her with such approval and pleasure, I was actually jealous.

"I mean, Kelly had almost no figure yet, which my mother thought was good and normal, and Kelly was full of please's and thank you's, just the recipe for the kind of little girl my mother wanted. I had been talking about her enough for my mother to finally consent to my bringing her home with me one afternoon. I was afraid to, afraid that once Kelly met my mother and had my mother grill her with questions, she would never want to talk to me again, but I liked Kelly and wanted her for a friend and knew if I didn't have Mother's approval, I couldn't. I was very nervous about it.

"However, as I said, to my surprise Mother liked her even more than I had hoped she would. She seemed pleased that Kelly's mother was an invalid and she was especially pleased that her father was working for the church.

"Even so, my mother was very cautious and hesitant about my going to Kelly's house to study for tests together. The first time, she permitted me to go for only two hours and after exactly two hours, she was in the driveway waiting. I knew as soon as I got into the car, she would question me about every moment I spent with Kelly.

"We did study some, but we also listened to music and talked to other girls and some boys on the phone. Kelly's mother was a sweet pleasant woman and I envied Kelly for the trusting and loving relationship they had. I almost wished my mother was in a wheelchair. Maybe if she was seriously ill, she would be a more loving mother, I thought, and then I hated myself for wishing such a terrible thing."

Jade grunted and then agreed, "Maybe she wouldn't be so mean if she had to depend on you."

"Yeah," Star said. I didn't want to discuss such a thing. I still felt guilty for even thinking it.

"Kelly's father was very nice, too, and I could see how much he loved and cherished Kelly's mother," I continued instead.

"Anyway, I guess because I had gone to Kelly's house a few times and nothing horrible had happened, my mother was a little less concerned when I asked if I could go to dinner there one Friday night."

I paused and then added for Misty's benefit, "It wasn't the whole truth. I mean, we were going to eat, but it wasn't really a dinner. We were going to have pizza and Kelly had invited two other girls and some boys."

"So it was a party," Misty said.

"I guess. I had never been to a party at someone's house, so I didn't know what to call it. Kelly didn't tell me all the details right away. In fact, I didn't even know the boys were coming until that afternoon in school. It made my heart race with fear. I was terrified that my mother would find out somehow. Maybe when she drove me there, the boys would just be arriving or maybe she would take one look at my face and that lie detector in her head would ring. I tried to avoid her as soon as I got home, but she called me downstairs to recite a list of rules for my behavior.

"I sat with my hands folded in my lap as she stood before me in the living room. My father wasn't home from work yet. Sometimes, he stopped at a tavern with some of his stockbroker associates and celebrated or mourned the day's results in the market.

" 'We don't say grace before we eat every night,' my mother began, 'but we should. It's your father's fault, not mine. Anyway, don't look stupid about it and don't let them know we don't. It's no one's business. Bow your head and make sure you pronounce your amen loud and clear, understand?' she asked me.

" 'Yes, Mother,' I said eying the door and trying not to look guilty of anything.

" 'Don't stare at her mother in the wheelchair.'

" 'I wouldn't do that, Mother.'

" 'We don't adhere to proper dinner etiquette either, not that I permit you to be sloppy or impolite at the table. It's just that your father never cared for formal dining. I have everything set up in the dining room,' she told me. 'Now get up and follow me.'

"I did and I was surprised at the lengths she had gone to in order to give me instructions. She had a book of dining etiquette out and open. She had taken out every piece of silverware we owned, and our finest china with her nicest linen dinner napkins.

" 'Sit,' she ordered, pointing at my place. Then she picked up the book and held it like a Bible in her open palms. She even sounded like some kind of Sunday School teacher.

" 'You should know that the silverware is placed in the order of its use, with the implements to be used first farthest from the plate. The salad fork is placed next to the left of the plate, then the meat fork, which they might not have out, being this is Friday night, and then the fish fork which will be used first. Just to the right of the plate is the salad knife, next is the meat knife, which again, might not be there, and on the outside is the fish knife. Outside the knives are the soup spoon and, if they have it, the fruit spoon. Dessert forks and spoons should be brought in on the dessert plate, but they might have it out already. I don't know how formal they are, of course. You know what the butter plate is and how it's there for your bread. Remember not to put your elbows on the table or slurp your soup or talk with food in your mouth. Any questions?'

" 'No, Mother,' I said. I was dying inside, knowing that all we actually were going to do was open a few boxes of pizza and probably slap the pieces on paper plates, and open bottles of soda. Now I was even more terrified of her learning the truth. She might accuse me of making a big fool out of her.

"My teeth were practically chattering when it was time for her to take me over to Kelly's house. I was afraid she might go in with me, but my mother, fortunately, is shy herself, and just let me get out of the car.

" 'Call me when it's time to come home and remember, don't overstay your welcome, Cathy. Oh, wipe your mouth after every bite and always say please and thank you when you're passed anything at the table. Don't speak unless you're asked a question,' she warned.

" 'Okay,' I muttered with my head down and hurried to the front door, praying no one else would arrive before my mother pulled away.

No one did because they were already in the house. I didn't know Kelly's parents weren't home. Her father had taken her mother out to dinner.

"In fact, when Kelly opened the door for me, the music was so loud, I was afraid it might spill out and reach my mother's car even as she drove away.

"I was a little shocked. It was as if Kelly had become a different person. She was wearing a blouse tied at her waist instead of buttoned so some uncovered waist showed, and a pair of jeans with no shoes or socks. Here I was dressed in my best outfit.

" 'She's here!' Kelly screamed and the others came out of her room.

"I guess I was standing there with my mouth fallen open. Everyone laughed at me and how formally I was dressed. Everyone else was in jeans and T-shirts. I didn't know the boys, of course, and they were quickly introduced. I was too nervous to pay much attention to their full names. Michael was a tall, dark boy with light brown hair and brown eyes, Tony was a shorter boy, stout, with very light brown hair and very nice blue eyes, and Frankie was a rather heavy boy with black hair and dark eyes. Talia Morris was there and so was Jill Brewster, girls I knew from school, but not very well. I found out that Tony was Jill's older brother and he had brought his friends. Tony, Frankie and Michael attended public school.

"My second shock came when I discovered that the cups they held in their hands were not filled with just Coke. Tony had brought a bottle of rum. A cup was thrust at me immediately, and I held it like I would hold a loaded pistol when I was told what was in it.

" 'I can't drink this,' I told them. 'My mother will smell it on me immediately.'

" 'Don't worry about that. You chew some gum or gargle with mouthwash. We're very experienced with all this,' Tony assured me. 'We even drink it at school sometimes,' he added, laughing. 'Come on, join the party.' He practically forced me to sip the drink. I didn't taste the rum, but I know it was in there because it wasn't too long before I felt myself grow light-headed and a little dizzy.

"I guess I was fascinated by it all. The boys had so many outrageous stories to tell about life at their school. Compared to ours, it sounded exciting to be there every day. I sat back on Kelly's bed and listened and watched as they played music, smoked, drank some more rum and Coke, always filling my cup as well. We devoured the pizza when it was delivered. I laughed a lot and for a while, I felt so happy and good. I especially enjoyed the girls' conversation when they made fun of the sisters and our life in the parochial school. For me this was like being in another country. I was shocked by some of the things said, of course, but I tried not to show it.

"I didn't want to smoke, but they were all doing it and it seemed impossible not to do something everyone else was doing. Vaguely, I thought, my mother was right about peer pressure. It is the strongest thing, but I shook that idea out of my head or to be more honest, the rum drowned it.

"Something happened in that confused brain of mine. Suddenly, everyone looked so silly to me. I started to laugh at the way Michael rolled his eyes after sipping his drink and puffing his cigarette, taking such care to look cool and sophisticated about it. He raised his eyebrows into question marks and looked at me, and then I laughed again and it felt like a dam had broken. I couldn't stop giggling. That struck them funny and they laughed too, which only made me laugh harder until tears began to stream down my face.

"Frankie suddenly sat beside me and slipped his arm around my shoulders.

" 'I better hold her before she breaks apart. She's jiggling too much!' he cried and they all roared. It seemed no one could stop the roller coaster. He held me tighter and tighter and soon I could see the faces of the other two boys change a little. They stopped laughing and suddenly looked intensely interested in me. Kelly, Talia, and Jill drew closer to each other and watched, whispering. What were they all looking at? I wondered, and then gazed down and saw that Frankie had his hand in my blouse. One of the buttons of my blouse had come undone and he was undoing another and another.

"For a moment even I was confused about it. Then his fingers lifted the underside of my bra and exposed my breast.

" 'Let's see if everything's all right,' he declared.

" 'Stop!' I screamed and pulled away, but when I rose, I stumbled into Tony's arms, only instead of catching me, he put his hands on my bosom and held me up that way, his left hand smack over my naked breast.

" 'It's all right. Yeah,' he declared. Everyone was laughing, even the girls.

" 'My turn!' Michael said coming up behind me. 'There's enough for all of us.'

"He reached over and cupped my breasts, lifting my bra off the left side, too, and pulled me back against him. I lost my footing and slid down his body to the floor. Everyone kept laughing, but I started crying and that finally ended it.

"The girls took me to the bathroom where I threw up. They helped me clean up and kept assuring me it was all right and the boys would behave now. I had such a splitting headache, but all I could think was my mother would find out everything. I went into a crying jag.

"The boys left shortly afterward, maybe because they were afraid of getting in trouble, and things quieted down. Kelly's parents came home. Her father looked a little suspicious when he saw me sitting in practically a coma on the bed, but he didn't ask any questions, even though I imagined I looked very pale. The girls assured me they couldn't smell any rum on me. I went outside with Kelly and Talia and took deep breaths of air until I felt well enough to chance calling my mother.

" 'I hope you don't say anything about this,' Kelly warned me. 'You'll get me in a lot of trouble and you'll only get yourself in trouble, too.'

" 'You should have told me what was going to happen,' I scolded.

" 'Don't be a prude,' Talia said. 'You had a good time, didn't you?'

"I remember looking at her as if she was crazy. Boys had molested me. I had thrown up. I had a good time?

" 'No,' I said sullenly.

"I was so frightened when my mother came, I don't know how I walked out and got into the car.

" 'How was the dinner?' she asked immediately.

" 'Very nice,' I said.

" 'Did they serve fish?'

" 'No,' I said. At least that wasn't a lie.

" 'And did you behave? Did you follow all the rules of etiquette? Oh, did they start with grace?' she asked quickly before I could answer her other questions.

"I thought for a moment and said, 'Yes. It all happened the way you told me it might.'

"It was dark in the car so she wasn't able to search my eyes and see the deception. I bit down on my lip and held my breath in anticipation.

"However, she liked hearing she was right to teach me all about dinner etiquette and such and for the remainder of the ride home, she congratulated herself on being wise enough to prepare me well.

" 'Your father wouldn't know the first thing about it,' she told me, 'despite his sophistication in business. When he saw all I had done for you, he laughed and thought it was ridiculous. Now he'll see,' she said nodding. 'Now we'll see how smug he is.'

"When we arrived home, I was able to go right upstairs, claiming I was tired. She didn't question it. She was too eager to tell my father how well she had prepared me for the dinner. I crawled into bed as quickly as

I could. When I thought about what had happened, I cried. How embarrassing it was and how terrible it was that the other girls didn't come to my defense. It was almost as if I had been invited there just to be abused. When would I ever have a real friend, someone who cared about me and my feelings?

"It made me feel so dirty to recall their hands over me. I think that was a major reason why my stomach turned over and I got so sick, that and the rum. How much had I drunk? Did the girls know what the boys were doing to me and let them?"

"I wish we knew you then," Star piped up. "I'd pay them a visit for you."

"Very immature behavior," Jade commented.

"It was cruel," Misty agreed.

"The hardest thing about having something unpleasant happen to you is having no one to tell at the time," I told them. "It festers like a sore, an infection; it buzzes around in your head and your heart. I tossed and turned and fretted through nightmares for nights after that and I couldn't face the other girls at school. I knew they were talking about me, spreading stories, exaggerating, claiming I had gotten drunk and exposed myself in front of the boys and embarrassed them. Kelly avoided me and I felt even worse because of the way some of the other girls were now looking at me."

"Why would they lie about her like that?" Misty asked Jade.

"To protect themselves in case she did tell someone the truth. Right?" Jade asked Star.

"Sounds like it. I would have pulled out their tongues at that point," Star said.

"It would only make them look right," Jade asserted.

"Maybe because of the way things were at school, my nightmares continued. I had no appetite at dinner, but I had to force myself to eat so my mother wouldn't ask any questions. The hardest thing was she kept asking me about Kelly's parents, the house, things they said, and I had to make up as much as I could. I got away with it because I told my mother I had followed her directions and not asked too many questions. I kept thinking, Soon, soon she's going to realize I'm lying and the whole horrible thing will come out.

"That gave me even more nightmares. Many nights I would find myself awake, practically sitting up, listening to the scream die in my throat. In dreams I felt spiders crawling over me, dozens and dozens of them. They covered my breasts and reached as high as my chin.

"When I was a little girl and I had bad dreams, my mother would sometimes come to see me, but she never held me or kissed me. Instead, she tried to teach me how to block out unpleasantness. She told me to count until I was so tired, I would fall asleep again. Reluctantly, because I begged her, she would leave a light on in the bathroom.

"One night nearly two weeks after the disastrous party at Kelly's and all the questions and lying, I heard my door open and close and my father stood in the darkness at my bedside.

" 'What's wrong?' he asked. 'I thought I heard you cry out when I came up from getting myself a glass of milk.'

"He did that if he ever had any trouble sleeping. He once told me that sometimes numbers from the stock market keep playing as if he had a ticker tape machine in his head as soon as he closed his eyes.

"I just turned my head into the pillow until I felt his hand on my shoulder and felt him sit on my bed.

" 'Something wrong with my special girl?' he asked. I couldn't help myself. I started to cry again. He stroked my hair and waited.

" 'What is it?' he asked. 'You can tell me. Did someone do something or say something that upset you?'

" 'Yes,' I admitted in a small voice.

" 'Yes what?' he demanded. 'It's better you tell me,' he added.

"I swallowed down my tears and quietly told him what had happened at Kelly's house. He listened without speaking, but I could feel his eyes fixed firmly on me, even in the dark.

" 'Is it my fault?' I wanted to know. 'Am I bad?'

" 'No, no,' he said, and then he leaned over and put his lips to my ear and added, 'There's good touching and bad. You shouldn't be afraid of the good or be ashamed of it.

" 'Boys who grope girls are bad. It doesn't make you feel good inside, right?'

" 'No,' I agreed. He was definitely right about that, and if he was right about that, why wouldn't he be right about the rest of it?

" 'Good touching is gentle, soft,' he said and as he spoke, he showed me.

" 'Close your eyes,' he said. 'That's it. You shouldn't be afraid to sleep,' he whispered. His hands were under my nightgown and he moved his fingers softly, gently over me as he chanted, 'Be still, be happy. See, this is good touching. It's like petting a dog or a cat,' he said, 'and you know how that pleases them. See, it's pleasing you. You'll sleep now.'

"His touching didn't relax me. It felt like a tense wire was coiling tighter and tighter inside my stomach. His hands were soft, gentle, but they were moving everywhere, and it made me even more nervous than I already had been.

" 'Easy,' he said when I tried to squirm away. 'You've got to relax your body and not be afraid of good feelings.'

"I kept myself as still as I could.

" 'That's it,' he said. 'That's better. See?'

"My body felt tense. I tried to keep my eyes closed and go to sleep, but it was hard to relax with him still touching me. Finally, he stopped and stood up.

" 'Good night,' he whispered. 'We'll keep it all secret,' he promised. 'All that's happened will be part of our big special secret. Don't worry. Your mother doesn't have to know. It would only upset her anyway and we don't want to do that, do we? Cathy?'

"He needed to hear my answer. My voice cracked, but I managed.

" 'No,' I said. My heartbeat was so quick, I couldn't catch my breath.

"Moments later, he was gone and I fell into a pool of confusion, my body in a turmoil and yet, I was happy I was still able to be my daddy's special girl, happy I wasn't a bad girl in his eyes."

I paused. The three were so still, their eyes unmoving, their lips frozen.

"Well," Doctor Marlowe said after a moment, "why don't we take another break and I'll see about lunch."

No one moved; no one spoke.

"Anyone need to go to the bathroom or anything?"

"I do," Misty said rising. She looked at me. "Unless you have to go first."

"No, I'm fine," I said.

The rain had started. The wind blew drops against the window and they zigzagged their way down like crooked tears. When I looked back at Jade, she was staring at the floor. Star was gazing out the window. She looked so deep in thought it made my heart skip a beat. Their silence was louder than the thunder rolling in from the storm.

Despite feeling somewhat drained, I still thought I could do this. Doctor Marlowe had brought me to this stage in my therapy, holding my hand, consoling me and building my confidence until I thought it would be all right, but as I looked at the others, I suddenly wondered, can they do it? What nightmares and fears had I stirred in their vaults of horrid memories?

The four of us were chained together by our pain now, and the trembling one felt reached through the hearts of the next and the next and the next until we all trembled together. Was it good to share or was it cruel?

Every question raised another.

Answers taunted us with promises just like beautiful fish beneath the water, and when we reached too quickly or too deeply, they were gone in a flash, leaving us waiting, searching, hoping for another opportunity.

How could we not be afraid they would never come back, even to taunt us?

6

"I hate days like this," Jade said after a long moment of silence. "I know it hardly rains here compared to most other places, and I guess I'm spoiled, but I can't stand this dreary weather."

"I don't mind it so much," Misty said. "Unless it's day after day."

"Granny hates it because it stirs up her aches and pains," Star said.

"Too many days look gray and gloomy to me without the clouds and rain," Jade admitted.

"It's not that bad," Misty insisted. Jade didn't like to be contradicted.

"I suppose if you live like a child in a fantasy world, it doesn't matter," she said, fixing her gaze on Misty.

"I don't live in a fantasy world and I don't live like a child."

"We all do," I said and they turned to me. "I mean, if you aren't happy with things, you daydream a lot, don't you? I do," I confessed. "And you've all described doing it in one way or another, too."

"Cat's right," Star said, nodding. She glanced at Jade. "There's no point lying to each other just because everyone else lies to us."

"I spend a lot of time in my room, alone, just . . . dreaming," I told them, "a lot of time. That's what made my parents want me to see Doctor Marlowe in the first place. I hated stepping out the front door, hated going to school, just hated leaving the house at all. I missed a lot of school, claiming headaches and stomach cramps or just being too tired. It got so bad the nuns were talking to my mother about getting me a home tutor, and you know how much she would hate having a stranger in our home every day."

"Do you have a nice house?" Misty asked.

"It's okay, but it's nothing like this. We've got a good size backyard. The property's walled-in with oleander bushes growing up the walls to give us lots of privacy. My mother's always planting something that will close it in more. Mostly it's just grass and a couple of grapefruit and lemon trees. My father used to talk about building a pool. My mother would ask, 'What for?' and he would look at her as if he was giving it lots of thought and then say, 'To swim in.'

" 'It's too much work,' my mother muttered, 'and with your schedule, who's going to do it?'

"He said he would hire someone just like everyone else he knew who had a pool, but the discussion usually ended with that and nothing was ever done.

"I used to think if we had a pool, I could invite some girls over, but then I thought, what kind of bathing suit would my mother approve? Certainly not a bikini, and who would I invite anyway and suppose I found some girls who would come and they wore bikinis. Mother would ask them to leave."

"Well, if you invited friends over now, you could hang out in your bedroom, right?" Misty asked, and I wondered if she would ever want to visit.

"I suppose. You all would probably think my room was too plain. I don't have any posters or pictures up. It's probably not as big as yours or Jade's, but at least it has two big windows that face east so I get the morning sunlight. I have a pinkish gray rug and a double bed with a mahogany headboard and two posts at the foot of the bed. Beside the mirror and dresser, I have my desk, another dresser and bookshelves built into the wall. I don't have a television set or a phone in the room. My mother would never permit either. She says they're both bad influences on young people."

"It sounds like you're trapped in a cage," Jade muttered.

"Oh, our house isn't that small. We have a good size living room with a fireplace and large panel windows that face the west so there's lots of afternoon sunshine. Mother hung thick drapes to block it out when she wants to. The kitchen is big. My mother likes to cook and bake. I wouldn't call her a gourmet cook like you have, Jade, but she's good at making traditional meals and pies. That was one thing my father always complimented, her food. He was a meat and potatoes man."

"So he married her for her cooking and money, is that it?" Jade asked dryly.

"Didn't they fall in love first?" Misty followed quickly.

"I never actually came out and asked either of them when or how they fell in love. I guess I never felt they had and the little I did learn about their past convinced me I was right. They didn't date and have a romance like your parents or Jade's. My mother's father actually met my father first. He started to invest with him. He either mentioned my mother or introduced him to her one day and that was how they got to know each other.

"My mother didn't have a job and never went to college. When I asked her why not once, she told me there wasn't anything she wanted to be. She was an okay student, but not very ambitious, I guess. I think it upset my grandfather. From the little my mother has told me, I don't think they had a good relationship because he was so critical of her, telling her she would be a spinster and amount to nothing if she remained at home, just helping her mother with the housework and the meals.

"Sometimes, I got the feeling she got married to stop my grandfather's criticism. It wasn't exactly an arranged marriage, but my grandfather seems to have had a lot to do with it. She keeps her wedding album practically hidden away on a shelf in the living room. I used to look at it occasionally. She doesn't look bright and happy in her wedding pictures; it's more like she's going through the motions, doing something that has to be done, but something without passion and excitement. It doesn't look like a special day for her.

"It would have to be something very special for me," I said. "I mean, you should just glow in your wedding pictures, don't you think? The photographer shouldn't even need flashbulbs because your face is so lit up, right? I'd love to be fulfilled and loved by someone who made me so happy I glowed."

Misty laughed. Jade smiled and shook her head, and Star raised her eyebrows and nodded.

"No," I continued considering their questions more, "I don't think my parents ever felt that way about each other or had time for love, not the way you talked about your own parents and their romances," I told them. "When I asked my mother where they went on their honeymoon, she told me they just went straight home.

" 'There was plenty to do to set it up,' she said, 'and there was no point in wasting money on some overpriced vacation where they charge you twice the price for everything you can get at home.' "

"If she thinks like that, she'll never go anywhere," Jade said.

"She doesn't. Don't you remember what Cat told us about taking trips?" Star pointed out.

"Have you lived in the same house all your life?" Misty asked.

"Yes. My mother is not one who likes change, even small changes like wallpaper or rugs, much less a move to another house. Lots of times now, I wish we would move. The house seems stained with bad memories for me, and as long as we're there, I can't help but imagine my father is still there."

"Did you ever ask her why they adopted you?" Jade asked. "I know you told us that you didn't think they had sex much, if at all after your mother lost the baby, but it still doesn't explain why they would adopt you, or anyone for that matter."

"No. Like I told you, my adoption was something I discovered just recently, after . . . after other stuff happened. It's hard for my mother to talk about it right now."

"Hard for her to talk about it?" Jade cried with indignation. "They always act like they're the ones who are suffering, like we can endure the pain because we're young. Nothing scars us; nothing really hurts us. We'll outgrow it, even betrayals and broken promises. Hard for her? Your mother hasn't got a right to be more upset than you. Don't let her get away with it," she advised. "Ask her anything you want and insist on an answer. You deserve it."

"Yeah, if she refuses to tell you what you want, threaten to wear lipstick and eye shadow," Star suggested.

Misty laughed and I smiled, and we were all laughing when Doctor Marlowe returned. She looked very pleased.

"Well, I hope you all are hungry. As usual, Emma has gone overboard with lunch."

They all looked at me to see what I wanted and what I would say.

"I guess I am hungry," I said.

Anyway, I thought, I'll need my strength if I'm to go on with my story.

Lunch was truly a break for us. I think they needed it as much as I did. We talked about everything but our home life and our parents and the things that had brought us here in the first place. However, I wasn't anywhere as up-to-date as any of them when it came to movies and music.

"I don't know how you listen to that hip-hop," Jade told Star. "It's so monotonous."

"It is not. You haven't given it a chance. That's why you say that. Who do you like?"

"I like Barry Manilow," Misty admitted. "I do," she insisted, "and I've even been to three of his concerts."

"What about you, Cat?" Jade asked me.

"I guess I like everything or whatever I get to hear, that is. My mother hates me listening to any music too long. She thinks it hurts my schoolwork."

"Get earphones and she won't even know when you're listening," Star suggested.

Doctor Marlowe sat off to the right eating and listening to us without comment. I wondered if the others ever got the feeling we were all under some giant microscope, all being observed and studied. Maybe someday we would get together somewhere else, without therapists or parents, and be free to talk about all this, free to talk without anyone looking at us and studying us.

Or maybe when today ended, we wouldn't see each other ever again. Maybe just the sight of one of us would bring back all the bad memories and they would look for ways to avoid the rest of us, especially me, I thought, especially after I'm finished with my whole story.

I almost didn't feel like going on when lunch was over and we returned to the office. Why not leave it at this? I wondered. I had already gone further than I had expected. Wasn't Doctor Marlowe satisfied?

One look at her face told me no, told me she wanted me to tell them the worst, if not today, then maybe tomorrow, and if I didn't, it would fester and irritate inside me, just as I had told them it would.

They waited for me to begin again. I sucked in my breath and started.

"When I was in the tenth grade, my school sent a letter home with every high school student announcing that the school was sponsoring an annual dance with an all-boys parochial school. The dance was described in detail, when it would start, what food would be served, what we were permitted to wear and not wear, and how well it was going to be chaperoned by the sisters. There was some statement about the importance of healthy, clean social activities and how the dance was an important learning experience for young people. This way we would have something decent to measure the wrong sort of activities against. Parents were actually encouraged to permit their daughters to attend.

"My mother wasn't happy about it, but she was trapped by the fact that the school she admired was promoting it. I recall my father finally offering a firm opinion about something involving me.

" 'The way this is described,' he pointed out after dinner one night, 'it will actually be another learning experience. I should think you'd want her to be in a controlled, healthy environment for something like this, Geraldine.'

"My mother pressed her upper lip over her lower and stared at the school dance announcement as if it were a warrant for my arrest rather than a social affair.

" 'She'll need a new dress,' she said in a discouraging tone of voice.

" 'So? Get her a new dress,' my father said.

"I sat there practically holding my breath. He winked at me and I felt wonderful. My heart was in a pitter-patter just anticipating the preparations.

" 'The styles these days are so . . . awful. It's hard to get anything decent,' my mother complained.

" 'I'm sure you can find something, somewhere, Geraldine,' he told her, refusing to give in like he usually did. He could see how important this was to me and he was playing my knight in shining armor.

"My mother looked at the announcement again and then at me. I could see she was relenting.

" 'I suppose you'll want to wear lipstick, won't you?' she asked me.

" 'All the girls her age do,' my father said quickly. 'On occasion, there's nothing wrong with it, Geraldine. As long as she doesn't overdo it,' he added.

"I couldn't believe how firmly he was coming to my aid, speaking up for me.

" 'Girls get into trouble so easily these days,' my mother muttered. 'One small thing leads to another and then a bigger thing and before you know it, they're pregnant.'

" 'Oh, I suppose you and I can make sure that something like that doesn't happen to our special little girl,' he said glancing and smiling at me again. When he said, 'special little girl,' my heart skipped a beat and I think I even blushed.

"My mother's eyebrows rose but fortunately, she was staring at him and not me.

" 'Is that so, Howard?' she said. 'You mean you're finally going to take some real responsibility for her?'

" 'I know I've been busy and left a good deal of this to you, Geraldine. I've been remiss on that score, but I'll do my part now that Cathy is getting of age.'

" 'Of age for what?' my mother pounced.

" 'Oh, meeting people, getting out more, learning the ways of the world,' he said calmly.

" 'She's better off not knowing the ways of this world,' my mother insisted.

"They talked about it a little more. My father volunteered to drive me to the school and pick me up after the dance. Finally, she reluctantly agreed even though she added that she thought I was still too young for such a thing."

"And did she agree to permit you to wear lipstick?" Jade asked with a coy smile.

"A little," I said. "Although, she kept the tube in her room after we bought it."

"Where? In the safe?" Jade asked.

"Practically," I said smiling. "The hardest thing was finding a dress she liked. We went to so many department stores, but nothing was right. Finally, she found this small store out in the valley. I think it was more like a costume shop. The hem was low enough to satisfy her. It reached a little below my ankles, and the collar went halfway up my neck. It looked like something from the 1800's. It was too big, too, but she thought that was fine. She found shoes that matched and I had what she considered my new party outfit.

"When I looked at myself in it, I nearly burst into tears. I was sure I would be ridiculed. It had puffy sleeves, lots of lace, and big black buttons on this emerald green heavy cotton material. She had me put it on and model it for my father, who sat there with his eyebrows hoisted.

" 'Looks like she's in a play or something,' he said. 'It's practically a costume. Is that the sort of party dress a girl would wear today?'

" 'It's perfect,' my mother insisted.

" 'I feel stupid in it,' I declared, encouraged by my father's reaction. 'When I walk, I can hear the material swishing around me. It's too loose and I'll choke to death in this collar if I try to eat anything,' I wailed.

" 'It's perfect,' my mother repeated. 'Proper and perfect.'

" 'No boy is going to want to dance with me wearing this,' I complained.

" 'Is that what you're worried about? How many boys will dance with you?' my mother asked.

" 'No, not how many,' I moaned. 'Any.'

"I was nearly in tears about it. I wanted to go to the dance very much. I saw it as my chance to make new friends and maybe to have a social life, too, but I was terrified that wearing that dress would make me look like a buffoon.

" 'Why can't I get something more in style?' I cried.

" 'The styles today are downright pornographic,' my mother said. 'You saw that from the little we viewed in the department stores. And besides, you read the dance announcement and rules. Most of the things on sale in the stores wouldn't be permitted anyway. Be happy you have something decent,' she insisted and left it at that.

"I went upstairs to sulk about it, and later, my father came to my room. He asked me to put on the dress again and I did. Then he stood back, studied it for a moment and stepped forward to unbutton the collar almost down to my cleavage.

" 'That looks better,' he said, 'but don't do it until after you get to the school. You're becoming a very pretty young lady, Cathy, do you know that?' he asked and I felt myself blush all over.

" 'No, I'm not,' I said. 'I'm too big and I don't have any nice features.'

" 'Sure you do,' he said. 'I'm just sorry I haven't had more talks with you about what you should expect now that you are mixing with boys. I'm glad the dance is still a week away. There's a lot I want to tell you, show you, explain to you. Most parents throw their children out to the wolves, especially their daughters, and then wonder why they get themselves into trouble. Your mother thinks the answer is to keep you here under lock and key, but I know the answer is to make you smart and aware so nothing comes as a surprise.

" 'Doesn't that make more sense to you?' he asked me and I nodded because it did sound right.

" 'Tomorrow is a holiday and the market's closed, too. I'll spend some time with you in the afternoon when your mother goes food shopping, okay? I'll help you prepare for the birds and the bees.'

"I had no idea what he meant, but I nodded. He stood there staring at me for a long moment and then he smiled, came forward and kissed me on the cheek.

" 'Don't you smell good,' he said. 'What is that, the bath oil I bought you?'

" 'Yes,' I said. He put his nose against me and inhaled so hard, I thought I might be drawn up his nostrils. Then he planted another small kiss on my neck, patted me on the hip, and left the room.

"You probably wonder why I remember so many details. That was because my father was so confusing to me. Sometimes he acted as if I was invisible and sometimes, he would stop and stare at me so hard, I couldn't help my heart from thumping. This was one of those times."

I paused and gazed down at the floor for a moment. I could feel their eyes on me and then I caught them looking nervously at each other. Doctor Marlowe had templed her fingers beneath her chin and rested her elbows on her knees as she waited, too. Lunch tumbled in my stomach, but I swallowed back any gagging.

For me it was like making a big, wide turn in my story. The worst was yet to come and I knew it, and from the sound of their silence, I knew the girls were aware of it, too. They looked worried for me. They looked like they really cared.

"The next day I hadn't forgotten what my father had said, but I was very occupied with my schoolwork and thinking about the dance. At school all the girls were talking about it. Most of them had been to dances like this before and many knew a number of the boys who would be attending.

"I sat to the side in the cafeteria and listened to the older girls talk about it, trying to learn as much as I could so I wouldn't appear like such a fish out of water when I attended. When I heard some of the girls describe what they were going to wear, my heart sank. Most were going to dress in clothes my mother had vetoed. Everyone but me would be in style.

"I had already been plagued by nightmares in which I arrived at the dance and the whole party stopped as one girl and boy after another looked my way. Even the sisters looked amused at what I wore. Then, they all broke out into hysterical laughter and I ran out of the building into the night, tears streaming down my reddened cheeks.

"I was coming to the conclusion that I shouldn't go to the dance, that it would be worse for me afterward. All my chances to have any sort of normal social life, to make friends, to be invited to anything else, would be washed away the moment I entered that decorated gymnasium, I thought. I decided I just wouldn't go. I was sure my mother would be happy about that decision."

"Damn," Star muttered.

"But," I said, "I didn't have to make that decision."

The girls all widened their eyes and waited.

"After my mother had left the house, my father came to my room. He knocked and entered and under his arm was a big box.

" 'What's that?' I immediately asked.

" 'Part of our special secret,' he told me. 'You better not tell her about this, or I'll be drawn and quartered at sundown the day after your dance,' he warned and put the box on my bed. He stepped back.

"I just stared down at it.

" 'Well, open it and look!' he cried and laughed.

"I approached it slowly and took off the cover. There in the box was a new dress, a real dress, green velvet with a knee-length skirt and spaghetti straps and some beads on the right side. It was the most beautiful dress I had ever seen. He even bought me shoes to match it!

" 'How can I wear this, Daddy?' I asked, astounded. 'Mother won't let me.'

" 'She won't know. You'll put on the dress she made you buy and after we leave the house, we'll pull over and you'll put on this dress,' he said nodding at the box. 'You won't have a mirror to check yourself out, but I'll be your mirror,' he offered. 'Put it on. Let's see how right I was about your size and such,' he added.

"He stood there with his long arms folded under his chest and waited. My heart was pounding. Changing in front of him was truly doing something forbidden, but I was too excited about my beautiful new dress to care.

"I quickly unbuttoned and removed my blouse, took off my skirt and slipped into the dress. He came behind to zip me up and then he turned me toward the mirror.

" 'Like Cinderella,' he said. 'Look how beautiful you are now.'

"I was actually frightened by my own appearance. The dress fit a bit snugly, especially the bodice, and there was just the suggestion of the beginning of my cleavage. Would the nuns turn me away? Wasn't Daddy afraid of that?

" 'Perfect,' he said instead. 'That's a dress.'

" 'What if Mother hears about this?' I asked him.

" 'It's a green dress, too. Besides, she won't hear about it. Where does she go to be able to hear such things? Well?'

" 'Oh Daddy!' I cried. Tears were filling my eyes. 'Thank you.'

"I gave him a hug and he kissed the top of my head and held on to me for a long moment.

"Then he held me out, at arm's length, looked me over, nodded and smiled.

" 'Now,' he said, 'it's time for your lessons.' "

7

" 'Keep the dress on,' he ordered. 'Everything should be as close as possible to how it is going to be at the dance.' He thought for a moment. 'We need some music, too. Yes, that's it. We'll turn your room into the school ballroom.'

"He snapped on my radio and found a station.

" 'How's that?' he asked about the music.

"I shrugged.

" 'I guess it's okay,' I said. I hadn't been to a school dance before, so I had no idea what sort of music would be played, especially at a parochial school dance."

"No hip-hop, I bet," Star said.

"No," I said. "They censor the words in the songs. They wouldn't even play Madonna."

"Some dance," Star muttered.

" 'Okay,' Daddy said. 'Let's start at the beginning. You come to the dance and like all the girls, you gather together, talk about everyone's clothes and hairdos. Now,' he added with a wink, 'they'll surely be talking about you. And in a nice way, an enviable way,' he quickly added.

" 'As soon as the boys see you, especially how you look now, you'll be approached by one or more and asked to dance. Be polite. Don't turn anyone down outright unless he's particularly disgusting,' he said and I smiled.

"Who else but my father would think me pretty? I wondered, even in this great dress.

"My father looked like he read my thoughts.

" 'I don't want you underestimating yourself, Cathy. Don't seem surprised and so grateful when a boy asks you to dance. In fact, hesitate for a moment as if you're deciding whether or not he's worthy of you.'

" 'Oh Daddy,' I said. 'I don't think I can do that.'

"After all, I thought, I had never yet been asked to dance by any boy ever. Even if the first looked like Frankenstein, I'd surely say yes quickly.

" 'I want you to make them wonder,' " he said firmly. 'It's important that you establish self-respect in their eyes immediately. Okay,' he continued, 'I'm the one asking you to dance. Look like you're thinking about it. May I have this dance, Cathy?' he pretended. 'Go on. Do what I said. Just a quick glance around as if you're checking to be sure no one else is waiting in the wings. Go on. Do it,' he told me and I pretended too, feeling foolish, but doing what he wanted anyway. 'Good,' he said. 'Now a small smile, a nod and step forward.'

"I did as he told me and he held out his arms. He listened to the music for a moment.

" 'This is one of those dances we can actually dance together,' he said with a laugh. 'I'm sure the nuns won't permit anyone to dance any closer than this,' he said putting his hand on my waist and holding my other hand up. We moved around my room. 'That's good,' he said. 'Fine. However, you should expect some boys might still try to take advantage when the nuns aren't watching so carefully. They'll move you a bit closer like this and their hands may move off your hip like this and slide over your rear end. See,' he said.

" 'What do I do?' I asked quickly.

" 'Step back and then say, "Watch your hands if you want to dance with me." Make sure you say it like you mean it, okay?'

"I nodded. I was very nervous now and worried. Was this all going to happen? How did Daddy know so much? I wondered as well.

" 'Do it,' he said.

"I stepped back. 'Watch your hands if you want to dance with me,' I repeated. He shook his head.

" 'Firmer. Mean it,' he told me and I did it again, trying to sound serious.

" 'Okay. That's better,' he said. 'Good,' he continued.

" 'What if the boy doesn't want to dance with me anymore?'

" 'Good. You've eliminated an idiot.

" 'Now, however, if you get to like one particular boy and he seems to like you, too, he might ask you to sneak out of the dance with him. What are you going to say?'

" 'I don't know,' I said, unable to even imagine such a scenario. 'No, I guess.'

" 'That's what you *should* say.' He held his gaze on me and a small smile formed in the corners of his lips. 'But you might be tempted. He might be a very good looking boy or popular,' he warned, lifting his voice.

" 'I won't do it,' I promised.

" 'Nevertheless, whether it happens at this dance or the next, it will happen someday, Cathy. It's natural no matter what you promise now. You're prettier than you think and boys will be boys. You're going to want to go and I'm not saying you never should. I just want you to be prepared when you do eventually give in to your inner voice,' he said.

" 'Inner voice?'

" 'Every man and every woman has one. It's usually silent, but at the right moment, at the right occasion, it speaks up. It demands to be heard and you can't stop it. In fact, you might not want to,' he said. 'There are things that are going to occur which will make the voice louder, stronger inside you until finally, it's the only voice you hear. You will no longer hear your mother's voice or even mine.

" 'You've got to be prepared for that,' he told me. 'If not, then what your mother said the other day at dinner will happen. You'll get yourself into trouble. You don't want that, do you?'

" 'No, Daddy,' I said.

"I remember it was as if a frightened little bird had somehow gotten caught in my chest. It fluttered about, its wings grazing my heart, my lungs and my ribs. I felt weak. My legs were trembling. Daddy looked so serious, so worried. How dangerous was all this?

" 'Good,' he said. 'Then we'll do something to prevent it, but like everything else, Cathy, we better keep this as our special secret. Your mother just won't understand. She has different ideas about these things, unrealistic ideas, I'm afraid. I'm not trying to get you not to love her, but you know what I mean, don't you?'

" 'Yes, Daddy,' I said.

"He smiled and then he stepped up to me again and turned me around to look into the mirror.

" 'You are not a little girl anymore,' he said. 'You are a real young lady. Your body is armed, loaded, ready to explode, take off, soar. I'm sure you have already felt some of this. I'm sure,' he added with a tiny smile, 'you have already heard the inner voice, especially in dreams. Am I right? Don't be ashamed or afraid to tell me,' he pursued.

" 'Yes,' I said in a whisper. I wasn't really sure what he meant, but I thought that was the answer he expected and needed. He smiled and brought his face closer to mine.

" 'It's all right. Don't be afraid,' he said. His face looked almost as flushed as mine felt.

" 'All right, let's go to lesson number two,' he decided, stepping away. 'Pretend I'm the boy you like, the one you have been hoping would pay attention to you. Now he has and like I said, he tells you to meet him in the hall.

" 'Pretend to go to the girls' room,' he said in a different voice. He even stood differently and smiled differently. 'They won't know the difference, Cathy. C'mon. You go first and I'll follow. Then, instead of going to the girls' room, meet me just outside the school door. We'll go to my car for a little while. No one will even miss us,' he added.

"It was funny playing this game with him, and yet it was also exciting for me, just like I was in a soap opera or something.

"He stepped closer to me, looked to the side as if checking to see if we were being watched, and then slipped his hand into mine and gently played with my fingers for a moment.

" 'C'mon,' he said. 'I want to be alone with you for a while. Everyone's watching us here. We can't really talk and there are so many things I want to tell you, Cathy. Please. Just for a little while, okay?'

"I could hardly speak. I was afraid to say no, and Daddy was right: there was another voice inside me, tiny but there, a voice encouraging me to go, suggesting that it might be a lot more fun.

" 'Don't disappoint me, Cathy. Please,' he pleaded.

" 'What should I do?' I cried in desperation.

"Daddy stared at me so seriously.

" 'Either go or say no,' he said back in his daddy voice. 'What will it be? You want to go, don't you? Don't you?' he pursued.

" 'A little, I guess,' I admitted.

" 'Okay,' he said. 'That's all right. You're being honest. I'd rather that than you pretend otherwise. We'll just have to move faster to the next lesson,' he said and turned for a moment as if he was thinking and planning.

" 'Where can we go? Where can we go to practice and learn?' he asked himself aloud. Then his face brightened and he turned back to me.

" 'I know.'

"He reached out and took my hand and we left my room. I thought we were going to go downstairs, but he turned and headed toward his and my mother's room.

"I didn't go into my mother and father's room very often. She kept that door closed all the time, too. I really didn't have much reason to go in there. She did all the cleaning in there. I could help only with the downstairs, the living room, den, dining room and kitchen, as well as my own room and the bathrooms, of course.

"I couldn't remember a time when I was in their bedroom just with Daddy. It felt so strange, almost as if I had gone to an unfamiliar place.

" 'Let's see,' he said standing inside the doorway and looking over the room. 'Yes, that's it. My bed will be the car.'

"He changed his posture and his whole demeanor again and then turned back to me with that eerie smile.

" 'Cathy,' he said. 'I knew you would do it. I knew you would come. I knew you liked me just as much as I like you. Maybe it's even more than that. Like is for kids and we're not kids anymore.

" 'It was so crowded and noisy in there anyway, wasn't it? This is better. C'mon. No one will see us in my car,' he added and pulled me toward his bed.

"He pretended to open a car door and slide in.

" 'Backseat has more room,' he told me as he sat on his bed. 'C'mon, get in.' He beckoned and reached for me and I sat on his bed, too.

" 'Close the door, silly,' he said.

" 'What?'

" 'The car door, Cathy. Close it.'

" 'Oh,' I said and even though I felt a little foolish doing it, I pretended to reach out and pull the door closed.

" 'Would you like a cigarette?' he asked me.

" 'A cigarette? No, I don't smoke,' I said.

"He smiled.

" 'That's good,' he said. 'We wouldn't want anything bad to happen to those beautiful lungs of yours, would we? Relax,' he said putting his arm around me and pulling me a little closer to him. 'We don't have those frustrated penguins staring at us now, making us feel like we're doing something dirty.'

"It was so strange to hear Daddy talk like this, but when I looked at him, his face was so different: the way his lips turned up in a strange smile, the glint in his eyes, everything made him look like someone else. Someone scary.

" 'You're very pretty,' he told me. 'You've been keeping it a good secret, but I always thought there was a pretty girl hiding in there,' he said. 'The other girls are so stuck-up and stupid, but you're not. You're a real girl, Cathy, the kind of girl I could like a lot. I mean that. I really do.'

"I admit I loved hearing Daddy say these things. They were words I had dreamed being said to me many times. It was as if Daddy had gotten into my head and listened some nights and overheard that inner voice he spoke of before, the voice that told me I'd do anything just to be loved.

"Suddenly, he kissed me on the neck. It was such an unexpected kiss; I felt weak and anxious at the same time.

" 'You're delicious,' he continued, nibbling on my ear. 'Just as delicious as I had imagined.'

"While he did this, I didn't realize his hand had slipped off my shoulder. Suddenly, I felt the zipper moving down as he kissed me on the neck and then the side of my face, moving over my cheeks. I think I actually got numb all over.

"He got the zipper almost all the way to my waist and then began to slip the straps off my shoulders, nudging my dress along with them. Everything he did surprised me and the shock of it all paralyzed me.

" 'You like me too,' he said. 'Tell me you like me too. C'mon say it. Say it, Cathy,' he chanted.

"I did. I couldn't help doing everything or anything he asked. Was this what really would happen? I wondered.

"He didn't take my new dress all the way down to my waist. As soon as he had it away from my breasts, he turned me to him and kissed me full on the lips. My eyes popped open. His fingers had unfastened my bra and seconds later, he leaned on me until I fell back on the bed. I could barely breathe. I wanted him to stop—it was so embarrassing.

"I think I made some sort of noise of protest and suddenly, he pulled back, sat up and stared down at me. His face and his neck were all red. He looked like he was having difficulty catching his breath.

" 'Okay,' he finally said, back to his daddy voice. 'Let's stop and review everything. What just happened to you?'

" 'I don't know,' I cried. 'It happened so fast!'

" 'Exactly. That's how boys work. They don't ask permission for each and every touch and kiss. One thing follows another until here you are half naked and onto the next step,' he said.

" 'There's more?'

" 'Yes, much more,' he rattled. He ran his hands through his hair and looked at my mother's bed for a moment. 'Okay,' he said without turning back to me. 'Dress yourself quickly and we'll go over this. The whole point is for you to learn and be prepared.'

"I did what he said and waited. After another long moment, during which his face returned to a more natural shade, he turned back to me.

" 'What mistakes did you make?' he asked.

" 'I don't know,' I said.

" 'You don't know? How can you not know?'

" 'It all happened so fast, Daddy, and I didn't know what you wanted me to do,' I moaned at his angry expression.

" 'All right, all right,' he said calmly. 'First, you got into the car too eagerly. Any boy who saw that would expect you would be cooperative; otherwise, why get into the car?'

" 'To talk, I thought.'

" 'Boys don't really want to talk. Maybe a little afterward, but not at this point. Talk is just a kind of bait to get you to come out to the car. You can come out and you can get into the car, but you should set the rules quickly. As soon as you got into the car and I kissed you, you should make it clear you'll go no farther,' he explained. 'You didn't even put your hand on mine to get me to hesitate or stop. Any boy who saw you behave that way would think he could go faster and farther.

" 'Now,' he continued, 'you have to decide how far you can go without losing control, understand?'

"I nodded.

" 'Good,' he said standing. 'Good.' He glanced quickly at the clock. 'That's all we have time for today. Your mother should be coming home any moment. You better take off the dress and put it back into the box. I'll keep it in the trunk of my car,' he told me.

"We both knew my mother might find it no matter where I tried to hide it.

"I returned to my room and did what he asked. Then he took the box and went out to his car. It was hidden away before my mother returned.

"I felt terribly confused and upset and guilty about everything that had happened, but I knew if she found out what my father was doing for me . . . and to me, there would be hell to pay in my family. Some lies, as you said before, Misty, are necessary," I added and sat back.

Once again, they were all just staring at me. Jade was the first to fill the silence.

"You didn't know you were an adopted child then, so you still thought he was your real father, right?" she asked.

"Yes, that's right."

"Well, didn't you think it was . . ."

"Disgusting?" Star offered.

"Yeah, disgusting," Jade seconded.

"No, not right away," I said. "I didn't know what to think. When he was touching me it made me scared and upset. But I thought he was very nice to want to help me, to care about things like my dress and do what other girls' mothers might do for them. And, the things he was *telling* me about boys was very helpful. My mother would never talk about these sort of feelings. I told you how she reacted to the Barbie doll. It made her sick to even have sex suggested to her.

"Afterward, I told myself that Daddy didn't want anything terrible to happen to me and yet he still wanted me to be a normal girl and have fun like other girls my age, something my mother didn't seem to want.

"No, I didn't hate him then. Not then," I practically whispered as my eyes filled with tears.

"Okay, Cathy," Doctor Marlowe said softly. "It's okay. You and I knew this might be their reaction in the beginning, right? Cathy?"

I turned to her and glared. For a moment I was very angry at her for bringing me here and getting me to tell all these things. Slowly, I felt my blood cool down.

"Cathy?" she said.

"I'm okay," I snapped back at her. I stared down at the floor. "I just thought he didn't want me to become a bad girl," I muttered.

"Why wouldn't she think that?" Misty piped up. "He was always very nice to her and he tried to buy her nice things. He seemed to care more about her than her mother does."

"I'm sorry," Jade said. "I didn't mean to make you feel bad or guilty or anything. I'm sorry."

"Me too," Star said. "It isn't your fault you're here. That's for sure."

I was quiet, thinking.

"Yes, it is," I said. "It's my fault; it's my mother's fault and it's my father's fault."

I looked up at them.

"I wanted to be loved, to be wanted. There were other voices inside me, screaming at me, but I kept them smothered. I thought maybe Daddy would make me a special girl. Maybe I'd become as sophisticated as some of the snobs at my school. Maybe the boys would really like me and maybe I could be the most popular girl there. I'd surprise them all, I thought. With Daddy's help, I'd surprise everyone, even myself.

"Why can't I be beautiful? I'm tired of being a freak and feeling odd and different and hiding myself. I'm tired of being ashamed of who I am and what I look like. Daddy made me feel pretty and mature and he would make me better than them.

" 'Shut up,' I told the voices inside me that told me what we were doing was wrong. 'Keep still and don't dare try to stop me, not now, not ever.'

"Maybe I was bad then. Maybe I was just as bad as he was. I went to sleep that night anxious, and yet excited about the dance and what boys I might meet there."

I looked up at Doctor Marlowe.

"Maybe that's why," I said referring to the big question we had left hanging between us after all my sessions with her to date. "Maybe this is the reason why I don't hate him as much as my mother wants me to hate him, as much as everyone wants me to hate him."

She nodded, a soft smile on her face.

I looked back at the girls.

Yes, I thought, this is good. I'm glad I'm here. I'll go on no matter what I see in their faces and in their eyes.

8

"As usual, by the time I rose and went down to breakfast the next day, my father had already gone to work. I had had very strange dreams all night. They were full of startling colors and strange places and faces. I remember seeing myself walking through a field of multicolored clouds that then floated away to uncover a field where arms and hands appeared to be growing out of the ground like stalks of corn. I twisted and turned, avoiding them. They reached out toward me as if they had eyes as well as fingers and I had to move and spin to avoid being seized.

"I guess I literally turned and twisted in my bed too, because when I woke, I actually ached all over, especially right here in my waist and in the back of my legs," I explained showing them.

"I was afraid my mother would take one look at me that morning, see how upset I was, and fire a slew of sharp questions, but she was occupied with her electric stove. Something was wrong and she was complaining about the way modern appliances simply created more complicated problems.

"Still, I felt strange after what Daddy and I had done, and I probably would have felt even more anxious about it if it wasn't for a conversation I overheard at lunch. Debbie Hartley was talking about her newest boyfriend Alex Lomax, she was complaining about him, actually. Debbie is one of the most popular girls at school. Everyone believes she has had the most experience with boys, so when she says something about dating or some boy, the girls are all glued to her every word as if she was spouting gospel. I was no exception.

"I sat just within listening range and tried to act as if I wasn't interested, but she began by describing how Alex had tricked her into going for a ride in his father's new Cadillac the night before and then parked in some deserted dump, knowing all along that his intention was to get her into the backseat, 'Where,' she said, 'he surprised me by producing a condom!'

"My ears perked up. It was almost the same situation Daddy had envisioned.

" 'He had the nerve to assume that when I told him before I wasn't ready, I meant we didn't have protection,' Debbie declared. 'Of course, he tried everything, telling me how much he cared for me, how he couldn't sleep because I was constantly on his mind. Then he tried kissing me on the neck, nibbling my ear, acting as if I was nothing more than some car engine he was trying to get started.'

" 'What did you do?' Judy Gibson asked her.

" 'I told him if he didn't back off, I'd kick him where he would remember it until his dying day,' she said with fury in her voice. 'Imagine, using as an excuse my saying I wasn't ready. Boys deliberately misunderstand things you say or misinterpret things you do just to get you to do what they want,' she proclaimed. The girls nodded and bobbed their heads simultaneously like puppets on strings.

" 'So you're not going with him to the dance?' Betty Anderson asked her.

" 'Of course I am. He's cute, isn't he? I can handle him. He'll behave now, but you've got to show them who's in control fast or . . .'

" 'Or what?' Judy asked breathlessly.

" 'Or you'll be pushing a baby carriage in the Beverly Center mall,' she predicted.

"All the girls around her nodded again in unison, all wide-eyed. My heart was racing. Daddy was teaching me the right things, I thought. If all these girls, who supposedly were far more experienced with boys than I was, were this vulnerable, what could I expect?"

"I bet that Debbie Hartley was full of jelly beans," Star said. "She was just trying to be a big deal in front of her sheep."

"You think so?" I asked.

"Why else would she put down her boyfriend in front of them like that?"

"Star's right," Jade said. "I know girls like that, too. They are usually making it up to look like they are more experienced. Unless she's just a sex tease, of course, and likes to torment every boy she dates," she added.

"Maybe," Star said, "but I think we're probably right about her anyway."

Misty said nothing, but nodded with a knowing look on her face.

How I wished I was experienced enough to recognize these things as well as they could, I thought.

"Nevertheless, it was on my mind the remainder of the day. I couldn't stop thinking about it all, even when I got home and started my homework. Daddy came home late that night and my mother complained about the stink of booze on his breath. He did look like he had drunk more than usual. His eyes were a little more bloodshot and he had this devil-may-care smile on his face as she chastised and lectured him.

"He didn't say anything special to me, but at dinner, I caught him looking my way occasionally and winking. Of course, I checked to see if my mother had caught us conspiring each time, but she was occupied with the meal and with reminding my father about her great-uncle Willy who had become an alcoholic from his daily drink with the boys and ended up dying in the gutter, penniless. It was one of those family stories that takes on the power of a legend. My father was never very impressed with it and once told her that her mother probably made it all up.

"That set her off on a tirade against his family, whom she called white trash. Daddy never defended them no matter what she said. As I grew older, I wondered why, but he always retreated from my questions with the statement that they were all 'A bunch of lunatics.' According to him, it was better to pretend they didn't exist, that they never existed.

"After dinner my father fell asleep in his chair reading and my mother continued her complaining, only now, directing it to me.

" 'See what a waste of energy it is to get yourself drunk,' she pointed out, nodding in his direction. 'It's better you never put your lips to any alcohol.'

"I thought about what had happened at Kelly's after I had begun to drink the rum and considered that she was probably right about that.

"Anyway, I went up to my room for the night. I heard her go to bed before Daddy and then, after I had bathed and gone to bed myself, I heard his footsteps on the stairs. He paused at my door. I held my breath and then I saw the door open slowly. He slipped in and closed it behind him.

" 'Cathy? Are you asleep?' he whispered.

" 'No, Daddy,' I said. 'I just got into bed.'

" 'Good,' he said and approached the bed. He sat at my feet for a moment. I could hear him breathing hard as if he had run up the stairs. Then he reached out and lay his hand, palm down, on the small of my stomach.

" 'Are you still excited about going to the dance?' he asked.

" 'Yes, Daddy,' I said.

" 'Good,' he said. 'Well then, it's time to go on with our lesson.' He rose to sit closer to me. 'Remember where we were. You like this boy and you want him to like you,' he said quickly. 'Now boys can do something that is so unexpected and surprising to you, you'll get confused and lose your control,' he told me, which was almost exactly what Debbie had told her girlfriends at school.

"I heard what sounded like the rustle of clothing and a moment later, he lifted the cover and slipped into bed beside me.

"When I was a little girl, he had done this once. My mother was busy downstairs and he came into my room and slipped into the bed and held me and stroked my hair and petted me as he talked about things we would do together someday. I used to long for him to be like that again.

" 'Now remember where we were when we left off,' he whispered in my ear. 'You're in the backseat of his car and he has kissed you and told you he loves you and needs you and wants you to love and need him, and you like all that. You want all that. Then he moves quickly,' Daddy said and put his hand where it was on my thigh the day before.

"I held my breath, waiting for him to tell me what I was supposed to do. When he didn't speak, I thought he was waiting for me to move his hand away, but he moved it to that very private place between my legs before I could do anything.

" 'When he touches you here, it's different,' he said. 'It makes that inner voice louder, right?

" 'Oh Cathy,' he said in that pretend voice before I could respond. 'You feel so good.'

"Then, without warning as he had promised, he turned himself and I felt his hardness against my inner thigh. He was right about it surprising me. I couldn't speak; I couldn't move. It was more than just a shock. It turned me to stone.

" 'He'll want you to touch him, Cathy. You should know what it's like for him so you will know what to expect. Here,' he said bringing my hand to him. 'See what happens to him. See?' he said.

"He held my hand there and I felt his heart beating through my palm.

"I cried out and turned away quickly, burying my face in the pillow.

" 'That's all right,' he said. 'That's good. That's the way you should be, but now you know what to expect. That's good, isn't it? Isn't it?' he asked again until I nodded my head. 'Good,' he said. 'Good,' he chanted, but he sounded a little frightened too.

"He rose and I heard him dress and start for the door.

" 'Good night, Cathy,' he said. 'That was tonight's lesson. There's just one more step to go,' he added as he opened the door and slipped out.

"I couldn't stop crying and then I became angry at myself. Why was I crying? Look at what Daddy had done for me. In minutes I was ahead of the other girls who would probably learn all this while it was happening and wouldn't know what to expect. I was more sophisticated than Debbie Hartley. Stop crying. Stop being a baby. Stop being immature, I told myself.

"Damn, Cat, didn't you know how wrong it was?" Star asked.

"I thought it was good!" I protested. "I didn't know. I had no one to talk to about it all. Daddy was nicer to me than ever!" I cried, tears now building aggressively under my eyes and pouring over my lids to streak down to my chin.

"Easy, Cathy," Doctor Marlowe said. "We've talked at length about this. You don't have to be ashamed. You don't have to blame yourself. The girls understand," she added looking at them.

Misty nodded.

"Is he in jail at least?" Jade asked.

"No," I said.

"Why not?" she demanded.

"Let Cathy tell you everything at her own pace, Jade. If she wants to go on, that is," Doctor Marlowe said.

The girls sat back and looked at me anxiously. They didn't look angry so much as they looked frightened now. I was beginning to feel like I was the strongest of us all.

"I'll go on," I said.

Misty leaned forward and touched my hand. She smiled and I took a deep breath.

"Daddy was very busy the next two days. Something dramatic had happened in the stock market and he missed dinner on Wednesday night. On Thursday, however, he surprised both my mother and myself by telling us that he had to go to Santa Barbara to meet with an important client on Friday. He would leave late in the afternoon, so we could go along. He suggested we stay overnight and have dinner at a nice restaurant on the beach.

" 'It's a great town, great stores. You'll have a good time,' he told my mother.

"Of course, she had her expected reaction. Santa Barbara was so close. Why was it necessary to stay overnight in an expensive hotel where strangers slept? It started her off on one of her favorite topics: her theory about why there was so much disease in the world. She believed it was due to travel, to people spreading germs and viruses. She was especially critical of air travel, claiming the germs were circulated for hours and hours in a plane. She had never been in a plane for just that reason, and she would certainly not go to Santa Barbara and stay overnight in some hotel.

" 'Oh, too bad,' Daddy said and then turned to me and asked if I would want to go with him. 'It's a business expense,' he said. 'The client is actually going to pay for it. I can get us a suite.'

"I looked to my mother but she seemed uninterested in my answer. I don't know if she thought I was going to be like her and refuse or if she didn't really care what I decided. Daddy looked at me with eyes that told me he really wanted me along.

" 'We'll be home early enough for you to prepare for the dance,' he added, then looked at my mother and winked at me.

" 'Okay,' I said.

" 'Good,' he said quickly. 'I'll swing by after you come home from school and we'll head out to beat the traffic. Sure you won't join us, Geraldine?'

" 'Of course, I'm sure,' my mother said.

"Didn't she realize what was going on?" Jade asked quickly, her face flaming bright red with fury.

I shook my head.

"It was so far from her thoughts, she couldn't even imagine it," I told her.

"I bet she feels really bad now," Star said.

"She does but she blames him the most, of course," I said. "And me, too."

"Forget about blame. What happened? Did you go with him?" Jade asked.

"Yes. I was very nervous all the next day. The talk at school was all about the dance, of course, and some of the girls were asking me what I was going to wear. When I described the dress my father had bought, they looked envious. It made me more confident and even proud and more appreciative of Daddy.

"When I got home, I packed a small bag for overnight. My mother acted as if she had either forgotten or hadn't paid enough attention to understand I was going. She didn't try to stop me, of course. Why would she?

"All she said was, 'Make sure you take a bath in the morning and wash away all the germs you'll get on you sleeping in someone else's sheets. Wear as much as you can to sleep, too,' she advised.

"I promised I would and a little while later, Daddy arrived to pick me up. Shortly afterward, we were on our way. It was the first time we ever went anywhere alone overnight. I was naturally nervous and excited.

" 'I have a surprise for you,' he said after I got into the car. 'Check the backseat.'

"I saw three boxes from a department store.

" 'What is it, Daddy?'

" 'Look for yourself,' he said with a laugh and I reached over the seat and brought the boxes forward into my lap. First, there was a small box full of cosmetics: lipstick, eye shadow and makeup. Then he had bought me more clothes, clothes my mother would surely forbid. There was a soft pink cotton sweater, a pair of black Capri pants and black square-toe flats.

" 'Oh Daddy,' I said. 'Where can I wear this? Not to school, you know. Mother would be furious.'

" 'No, it's just for today and tonight. We'll keep it all beside your dress in my car trunk for another time. I know what your mother would say, too,' he added, raising his eyebrows. 'But she's just out of touch with things today.' He smiled at me and then leaned over and kissed me on the cheek. 'Go on,' he said, 'climb into the back and put it on.'

" 'Now?'

" 'Sure. Let's arrive in Santa Barbara in style,' he said, laughing.

"I was so excited about it, I did what he suggested. The sweater was a lot tighter than I would have liked and it had a deep, V-neck collar. There was no hiding my bosom in this, I thought, and the pants were tight, too.

" 'I don't really know how to put on makeup, Daddy,' I said, but I put on the lipstick anyway.

" 'That's okay,' he said. 'I wanted you to have it. I want you to have self-confidence, Cathy. Your mother has gone about all this in the wrong way. But we're fixing things,' he added, 'right?'

"I was so thrilled with what was happening, I agreed quickly. When we stopped at a gas station, I hopped out and went to the bathroom to look at myself. I couldn't believe the change. It actually frightened me. Was this really me?

"Daddy looked so pleased. The gas attendant was staring at me hard when I returned to the car.

" 'See that,' Daddy said. 'See the way that young man was ogling you? You are attractive, Cathy. Never think you're not,' he said.

"How good that made me feel. I felt like hugging him and thanking him. He cared about me. Nothing else seemed to matter for the moment, nothing."

I glanced at Doctor Marlowe. She looked displeased. I could hear her coaching me: Stop trying to explain yourself. Stop trying to find excuses. It wasn't your fault.

Nevertheless, I thought, Mother was right. How could it not have been some of my fault? I still believed that, even now, even as I told the story of what happened that night.

"A little while later, we pulled into the motel. It was right near the ocean.

" 'Where are you meeting your client, Daddy?' I asked him.

" 'I'll call from our room,' he said, 'and see what he wants me to do.'

"The room he got for us wasn't a suite. It was just a room with a king-size bed.

"He saw the surprise in my face when we entered together.

" 'This is the room with the best view,' he said. 'The bed's big enough, right?'

" 'I guess so,' I said hesitantly.

"Never before in my life had I ever slept in a bed with anyone, not even as a child. My mother always made it clear to me that I couldn't come crawling into her bed or my father's. If I was afraid or just needed to be held, I had to smother those feelings.

"Daddy called his client and left me at the motel while he went to see him. There was access to the beach behind the complex and I took off my shoes and walked barefoot in the water as the tide washed ashore. I kept thinking how Mother would complain that I would track in sand or catch some disease on my feet. It made me laugh and I was suddenly filled with this great sense of freedom. It was as if Daddy had snuck me out of the castle, out from behind the high walls and chains of rules. Here I could soar, laugh, splash and be devil-may-care.

"It was a beautiful afternoon, with just a few wispy clouds across the horizon. I threw myself on the beach and stared up at the blue sky, dreaming of floating up into it. The sand was so warm and cozy. I must have fallen asleep for a while because suddenly I heard Daddy's laugh.

" 'There you are,' he cried. 'I thought you might have run off with that gas station attendant.'

" 'Oh Daddy,' I said. 'He wasn't really looking at me that way.'

" 'Like hell, he wasn't!' Daddy exclaimed. In our house my mother hated when he said hell or damn, not because she was so religious. She just thought it was crude and a bad influence on me. Out here with the vast ocean before us, the wind blowing through my hair, the sky so blue, nothing, no rules, mattered.

" 'Well,' he said, 'I'm free now. What would you like to eat? Why don't we have seafood? We're at the ocean,' he said. Everything sounded exciting to me.

" 'Should I change back into my other clothes?' I asked.

" 'Absolutely not,' he said. 'I want everyone to be jealous of me.'

"He reached down for my hand and we walked back to the motel together, where he showered, shaved and dressed while I watched television. We went to a very nice restaurant on the wharf and I had lobster and then we shared a dessert, something called a mud pie, which was a wedge of vanilla ice cream smothered in hot fudge. Again, I could hear my mother chastising us for eating such a rich dessert.

"Before we returned to the motel, we did what he had promised: we went into the town and visited some of the quaint shops. He bought me some inexpensive but interesting artistic jewelry, a necklace and a ring. He said they would go well with my new party dress, the one he had bought, of course.

"It was one of the happiest and nicest days I could remember. When we returned to the motel, I assumed we were going to sleep. I got ready for bed. Daddy watched television, sitting in a chair, and his eyes closed. I never felt as contented so I was confident that I would have only good dreams.

"Some time after I had fallen asleep, I woke in the dark room because I felt him beside me.

" 'It's time for your last lesson,' he whispered, his lips touching my ear.

"My heart began to pound.

" 'What, Daddy?'

" 'Girls who do go too far are like swimmers who have gone beyond the buoy out in the ocean you saw today. The waves have taken control. Despite what they want now, they are lost in the rhythm and can only wait for it to end.'

"As he spoke to me softly, he ran his hands over me, lifting my nightgown.

" 'Daddy,' I moaned. 'This is wrong!'

" 'You have to know what this is like,' he insisted. 'And it's not wrong. It would only be wrong if I were your *real* daddy.'

"Not my real daddy, I thought. What did he mean? The shock in my eyes made him stop.

" 'You're finally old enough to know the truth, Cathy. Yes, you're adopted, but even though you were adopted, we've always loved you. Still, don't tell your mother I've told you. It was something we were supposed to do together someday. Don't worry about it. You're my special girl, remember.' He moved his body over mine and kept whispering in my ear, 'My special girl. My special girl.'

"It hurt, but I don't know what hurt more: what he was doing or finding out the truth about myself. I was spinning with such confusion, it all seemed like a whirlwind of nightmares. I cried and cried and in the morning, I saw the blood. There was some on my nightgown. He told me I had to throw it away. If I didn't, my mother would wonder and the most important thing, always the most important thing, was keeping our special secret.

"I wasn't very talkative the next morning. For a while, the shock of all that had happened took my attention away from what he had told me. Daddy tried to cheer me up. He talked about other places we would visit, now that I was old enough and could be independent. A few times, I thought I would ask more about my adoption, but I couldn't bring myself to form the words.

"We got back on the highway and headed for home. Again, he tried cheering me up by talking about the dance and how much fun I was going to have. I fell asleep for most of the trip and didn't wake up until we were pulling into our driveway.

" 'Everything all right?' he asked me before we got out.

"Everything all right? I thought. You told me I was adopted and after what we did, everything is supposed to be all right?

" 'Yes,' I lied and hurried into the house.

" 'Did you take your morning bath?' was my mother's first and only question the moment she saw me. She didn't ask a thing about the day, where we had gone or what we had done. I told her yes and went up to my room.

"I looked into my mirror and didn't recognize the girl I saw there. I couldn't shake off the feeling of being dirty. I still feel like that once in a while, but learning I was adopted, that I had a mother and father that I had never known left me feeling even more empty inside. Shattered . . ."

"You can stop now, Cathy," Doctor Marlowe said.

I gazed at her and shook my head.

"No," I said. "I can finish."

She smiled at me.

The three girls, my sister Orphans With Parents, weren't smiling. They were the ones holding their breath now.

I wanted to say, "It's all right. Everything's going to be all right."

But I had no idea if it was or ever would be.

9

"**I** think something died inside me that night at the motel."

I looked at Doctor Marlowe and smiled.

"Some people think it was innocence. The little girl was gone, swept away abruptly.

"I felt so tentative about myself, so uncertain. Rather than my now being armed with a new, mature confidence, I felt like I was blindfolded, walking on a tightrope, unsure about every step, anticipating some great fall. With that feeling came the loss of all the excitement that I had felt building in me about the dance. I wasn't even interested in going anymore. I felt sick, weak, drained of my emotions.

"I lay on my bed and stared up at the ceiling for hours with my eyes wide open, thinking of nothing that I can recall.

"Daddy was the only one to check on me. Mother wasn't doing anything to encourage my going to the dance, of course. When he saw I was just moping about and he realized how late it was, he came up to see why.

"He knocked lightly on my door. I didn't respond and he opened it and peered in.

" 'What are you doing? Don't you have to get ready?' he asked.

"I was afraid to let him know what I was feeling so I complained about being a little nauseous and tired. He came into my room and closed the door behind him.

" 'That's just stage fright,' he said with a smile. 'All girls have it on their first date or social event, Cathy.'

"I didn't agree or disagree. I just turned my head and stared at the pillow.

" 'It's not important anymore,' I muttered.

" 'Not important anymore? Of course, it's important. Cathy, you've got to go now,' he insisted. 'If you don't, your mother will blame it on my taking you to Santa Barbara. She'll start to rant and rave about disease and dirt and all that. We'll never be able to go anywhere again without her bringing it up and complaining. You won't have a minute's peace if you stay home. Believe me.

" 'Besides,' he said, 'I got you that wonderful dress and those shoes and you have the jewelry to wear. You're going to be the belle of the ball. Don't miss this, Cathy. C'mon, sweetheart. Why have I spent all this time with you? All the lessons,' he added. 'After your experience, I'll spend time with you again and we'll talk about what more you need to know, okay? Cathy?'

"I felt my stomach churn and I had to swallow and swallow to keep from having to throw up.

" 'Okay, Daddy,' I said. 'I'll start to get ready.'

"I just wanted him away, wanted him to stop talking.

" 'Good. I know just where to pull over between here and the school for you to change into the real dress waiting for you in the car trunk,' he said. 'I'm taking my camera and I'll snap a few shots of you so we can have something precious to remind us of our special secret.'

"He came over and touched my hair and stood there looking down at me. For the first time, I felt myself cringe inside. I was afraid he might sense it, too, but he didn't.

" 'You're so pretty. My special little girl,' he said, leaning down to kiss me on the cheek before he left, closing the door softly behind him.

"It still took a great deal of effort for me to gather enough enthusiasm to bathe, do my hair and dress, but I did. I moved like someone just going through the motions, someone in a daze.

"However, when I put on that dress my mother had bought and insisted I wear, I stared at myself and just started to giggle and giggle. It was like a dam had broken. In fact, I was a lot like I had been at Kelly's house after I had drunk too much rum. I couldn't stop laughing. Tears rolled down my cheeks. My chest and my ribs ached so much, it actually frightened me, but I couldn't stop.

"I tried holding my breath. That didn't work either. My lungs just burst, leaving me gasping for air. My legs gave out and I sat on the bathroom floor. My sitting there with the skirt of that dress all around me oozing green struck me even funnier, I guess, because I laughed harder. It was maddening. My peals of laughter were interspersed with dry heaves. My entire insides felt like they were in rebellion. I thought my whole body might come up and out of my mouth, including my lungs and my heart. It would all spill out on the floor."

"Ugh," Misty cried.

"Yes," I said nodding. "My thoughts were disgusting, but I couldn't stop that either. I'm actually leaving out half of it," I told her.

"Forget that. What did you do?" Jade asked. She looked like she understood the madness that had taken control of me, like she'd felt it herself before and she wanted to know how I had handled it. She was leaning forward, practically ready to lunge off her seat at my response.

"I tried to stand by reaching up to the sink and pulling myself to my feet. When my hand slipped off the ceramic, I broke into another fit of hysterics. It was as if the bathroom was coming alive and every part of it, every fixture, was trying to avoid me like I was contaminated or something or maybe, shocked by what I looked like in the 'perfect party dress.'

"My laughter seemed to come from a lower and lower place in my body now. It rolled up in small, thunderous peals, flowing through my throat and echoing in my mouth and my ears. I was on all fours, crawling, and that made me laugh harder. Everything I did, every thought I had, every breath I could take, brought a new surge of hysterics.

"I was afraid it was never going to end. It was like having the hiccups and doing everything possible to stop them, but nothing works, know what I mean?"

They all nodded quickly, especially Jade.

"I crawled up to my bedroom door, the door that was always supposed to be closed. That struck me funny, too: always supposed to be closed. I might die in here before I can get to the door, I thought, but my mother would think that's fine. It was proper.

"I reached the knob and turned it, falling back as I did so. There I was on my back on the bedroom floor, my arms out, looking up at my ceiling again. I was laughing loudly now. My whole body trembled so much, I thought I must be shaking the whole house.

"Yet, neither my father nor my mother heard me. My mother was running the vacuum cleaner downstairs. I turned myself over on my stomach and I crawled out of my bedroom. My laughter stopped for a few moments and I caught my breath and thought it might be over. Whatever it was might be done, but when I reached the top of the stairway and looked down those steps, I started to giggle again.

"I reached out and put my hands down on the next step and then I began to slide, laughing as I did so. My mother must have finally heard something strange. She flipped off the vacuum cleaner and listened and then went into the living room where my father was watching television.

" 'Turn that down,' I heard her say. I was halfway down the stairs on my stomach. He did what she demanded and they both listened.

"Moments later they were at the foot of the stairs, looking up at me, both their faces so twisted and confused by the sight of me, which of course, struck me funny.

" 'What are you doing?' my mother screamed. 'You're ruining your new dress. What are you doing?'

" 'I'm going to the dance, Mother,' I said. I slid down another step or two. 'I know you're not happy about it, but I'm on my way,' I added and I laughed and laughed until I missed a step with my hand and tumbled to my right, over on my shoulder and then my whole body seemed to rise and float as I did a somersault, landing on my back and crying out.

"In seconds I was at their feet. They both looked so surprised and shocked. I wanted to laugh again, but the pain was too sharp.

" 'My God,' my mother said bringing her hand to her mouth, 'what's wrong with her? Is she . . . drunk?'

"She knelt down to smell, twitching her nose like a squirrel. I closed my eyes on her face, choked on a chuckle that was caught in my throat, and passed out.

"When I woke up, I was in an ambulance on my way to the hospital.

"And you know what? I was still wearing that ridiculous party dress," I said. "I guess I babbled quite a bit, revealing enough to draw the paramedic's attention and concern.

"At the hospital emergency room, they put me through some X-rays and examined me before they gave me a sedative. I slept through the remainder of the night and when I woke in the morning, my mother was sitting at my bedside staring out the window. She had her chin resting on her open palm and her elbow against her body. She looked so thoughtful and for a moment, so much younger than she was. Actually," I said glancing at Doctor Marlowe, who knew it all of course, "I didn't recognize her."

"Didn't recognize your own mother?" Misty asked. "Why not?"

"At the time I didn't even recognize myself," I replied.

Misty scrunched her nose and her eyebrows dipped toward each other.

"I don't remember this part well, but my mother does. She knows every moment of it by heart and recites it from time to time, reminding me what I put her through."

"Huh?"

"Let her talk," Jade stammered, her hands clenched into fists and resting on her knees. Misty sat back quickly.

" 'Where am I?' I asked my mother.

"She dropped her hand and turned to me. Her face aged back to where it should be in seconds.

" 'You're in the hospital,' she said. 'You passed out at home. They gave you tests and found nothing wrong with you, but you said things.'

" 'What things?'

" 'I don't know everything exactly, something about lessons, and now you're . . .' She looked around the room. 'You're on the mental health floor. You're here for observation and there will be a doctor, a psychiatrist, and maybe someone else coming to speak to you. It's horrible. It's all just so horrible.'

" 'What is?' I cried.

"She shook her head and sighed deeply. I studied her and tried to remember, but it was as if a thick concrete wall had fallen around my memory.

" 'Who are you?' I finally asked her.

" 'What?' she said stepping back. 'What did you say?'

I looked around the room and then at her.

" 'I don't know why I'm here,' I said.

" 'What are you talking about?' She stared at me. 'What are you doing?' she asked, her voice shrill. 'I'm going to get your father,' she added as if it was some kind of threat.

" 'My father?' I asked, a little frantic. Butterflies had begun to flutter in my chest and I didn't know why.

" 'He's downstairs in the cafeteria. He's having coffee and something to eat. Do you want to tell me why you're acting like this? Do you want to tell me what all this means before these strangers start to ask you questions?'

" 'I don't know,' I said turning away from her. 'I can't remember anything.'

"She stood up and hovered over me for a few moments.

" 'I don't know what's wrong with you. I was going to let you go to the dance. I bought you a dress for it.'

" 'A dress? Yes, I remember a dress.'

" 'It's ruined,' she said. She shook her head. 'What are you doing?'

"I was scrubbing my arms and my breasts, wiping something away.

" 'I don't know,' I said and looked around the room again. 'Am I supposed to be here? What am I supposed to do? Can't you tell me who I am?'

" 'Oh dear,' she said and turned. She looked like she wanted to flee.

At the door she paused to look back at me. 'I don't know why you're doing this,' she repeated and left.

"I just closed my eyes and I fell back to sleep and when I woke again, I was alone in my room.

"I lay there quietly, my mind so full of blanks. I struggled to remember, fought with every letter, every word that flowed through my mind. It was very scary. I felt like everything was just inches from me, but I couldn't reach anything. I felt like I was dangling. There was nothing below and nothing above me.

"Finally, a kind-looking older man in a white lab coat came in with a young nurse at his side. He introduced himself as Doctor Finnigan and the nurse as Mrs. Jenner.

" 'Why am I here?' I asked him. 'I can't remember my name either.'

" 'You've suffered a traumatic experience,' he began. 'From what we can tell, it's not a single, explosive experience. You're not physically hurt in any way, but you've still suffered severely enough to cause a condition of generalized amnesia. These things don't last. Don't worry,' he assured me. 'I would like to try some hypnotism,' he concluded.

" 'Hypnotism? You're going to hypnotize me?'

" 'I think it might help. It won't hurt you in any way,' he promised.

"He did have a very kind face, soft blue eyes and gently curved lips.

"He asked me to concentrate hard on this small disc he took out of his lab coat pocket and began to spin, and then . . ."

"What?" Misty asked.

"I don't know. I woke up confused again, only this time, I felt as if I was coming out of the darkness into the light. I must have been sleeping because it was much later in the day. Mrs. Jenner was there. She asked me how I was and I said, 'I'm fine.' I told her I was hungry and she laughed and went to get me something to eat.

"Doctor Finnigan returned, too, only I didn't remember him immediately. However, I remembered everything else. It came back to me in waves and waves of pictures and thoughts. He introduced himself again.

" 'Why am I in a hospital?' I asked him.

" 'What do you remember last?' he replied.

" 'I was getting ready for the dance. I . . . was looking at myself in the mirror, I think,' I told him and he smiled and said that was good. I was getting better quickly, which was what he had expected. I asked for my parents and he told me my mother would be coming up to see me any moment.

" 'What about my father?' I asked him.

" 'Do you want to see him?' he asked me. He studied my face carefully.

" 'No,' I said.

"He nodded.

" 'You're going to be all right,' he promised, squeezing my hand.

"Mrs. Jenner brought me my tray of food and as I was eating, my mother arrived. She stood outside in the hallway with the doctor and they talked in very low murmuring voices for a while. I finished eating before she came in. Then Mrs. Jenner took the tray and left Mother and me alone.

"She looked very sick, pale, her eyes bloodshot. I can't remember ever seeing my mother cry. If something bothered her that much, she would go off to be by herself. She stood by my bed now and the tears slipped out of the corners of her eyes like fugitives sneaking down her cheeks.

" 'Horrible,' she muttered. 'It's so horrible. He doesn't deny it.'

" 'What?' I asked her. 'Who?'

"She took a deep breath and shook her head. She seemed to suck her tears back into her eyes, straightened her body, filling her spine with steel again, pulling her shoulders up.

" 'Let's not talk about it now,' she commanded. 'Let's never talk about it.'

"Of course, that was not to be." I gazed at Doctor Marlowe. "Talking about it became very important. We've traveled a long way, right, Doctor Marlowe?"

"A very long way, Cathy."

"Are we home yet?" I asked her. I was trembling a little.

"Almost, honey," she said. She looked at the other three who were sitting quietly. "You're all almost there," she said with a smile.

I nodded and took another deep breath.

"I remained in therapy for a while, working with Doctor Finnigan. By the time I returned home from the hospital, Daddy was gone. Like your mother, Misty," I reminded her, "my mother had tried to purge the house of everything that would remind us of him. She didn't go so far as to sell or give away his favorite chair, but she didn't just clean out his closets and drawers. She sanitized them. She scrubbed the house as if his essence, the very memory of him, was something that could be vacuumed up, scrubbed away.

"Unlike you, Jade, I didn't have to be involved in much of the legal stuff. I knew my mother had started the process of getting a divorce, of course, and I knew that lawyers had met and settlements had been concluded to her satisfaction.

"Like your daddy, Star, mine was gone suddenly, almost as if some wizard had made him disappear. I know it was part of whatever was decided that he would never have any contact with me again. It wasn't something I easily accepted or believed. To this day I sometimes expect him to appear, to come walking up the stairs, to knock on my door and open it and smile at me and ask how his special little girl is doing.

"It would be like everything that has happened was just a bad nightmare.

"But then, my mother is always there to remind me it was no dream." I looked at Doctor Marlowe. "That's good and bad, I know. I have to face the demons to destroy them, to rid myself of them," I recited.

She nodded.

"But it would be nice to bury them forever."

"You will," Doctor Marlowe promised.

"Why wasn't he arrested? Why didn't he go to jail?" Jade wanted to know.

"First, my mother didn't want all the notoriety. Even today, not that many people know the real reason for their separation and divorce. Second, I don't think I could stand having to tell this story in a courtroom, even if it was only before a judge.

"I did meet with a judge and a representative of a child protection service to conclude custody questions. For a while I thought they might take me away from Mother, too, that maybe they thought she was really more directly responsible. I suppose it was hard for them to believe she was so . . ."

"Dumb?" Star asked.

"Blind," I corrected. "Mother is comfortable in her own world."

"You might as well be away from her," Star muttered.

"I can't say I don't love her or need her. She's the only mother I've ever known."

"I still don't understand why she wanted to adopt you in the first place," Jade said.

"I know. That's something I have yet to learn. There's much I have yet to learn. She's suggested to me that there were rumors about my father and his sister and maybe that was why his family was so distant. She never talked about it before because it was too disgusting to even form such words with her lips, much less utter them."

"Why would she marry someone like that?" Misty asked.

"I don't think she knew about the rumors before she got married," I said. "It's like I'm just learning about my own family now, like doors are being opened to rooms I never knew existed. I'm unraveling a roll of secrets almost daily. Some of it I want to know, and some I wish I never knew."

Jade nodded.

"My mother was always reluctant to talk about any of this, as you know. Lately, I think she has realized her own need to get stuff out, although it's still not easy to get her to do it. I think she's also afraid of what it might do to me. To her credit, I think she wants me to get stronger and stronger, but she wants it to be something we keep in our own house, in our own world."

I sat back and suddenly, I felt so tired I couldn't keep my eyes open.

"Well," Doctor Marlowe said. "I think we should stop. We've gone about as far as or actually even further than I had hoped we would."

"I guess we can each stop feeling so sorry for ourselves," Jade said. "Is that it?"

"In a way. The most important thing is none of you should feel alone, lost, so different you think you are the only one who has been singled out for what happened in your lives. There are other people, many people who will understand.

"Each of you is special. Each of you have a great deal to recommend you and to make you feel good about yourselves. You're all attractive, intelligent young women and you will overcome all of this difficult and sad history."

"Thanks to you," Misty said.

"No," Doctor Marlowe said looking at all of us, "thanks to yourselves. I'll be seeing each of you again, separately, but I don't think we're going to have to go on and on much longer. You've all made very significant progress. You've made the big turn," she said, smiling.

She glanced out the window.

"Look, the sun's breaking out. Jade, you can get back to that summer vacation you're supposed to be enjoying."

"Right," she said. Then she smiled and nodded. "Right."

Doctor Marlowe stood up and we all rose. We could hear music coming from upstairs, something from an opera.

"I've heard this in the school music suite," Misty said. "Isn't it Gianni Schicchi?"

"Yes, very good, Misty," Doctor Marlowe confirmed.

"I'll get you tickets to our school concerts this year," Misty told her. "It's not quite the opera, but it's close!"

"Thank you. Emma would like that. Good-bye, girls. Have a good week. Until I see you all again," she added and reached out for each of us to squeeze our hands.

When we opened the front door, we could see that today my mother was the first one who had arrived. She sat impatiently, nervously. Her eyes darted toward us and then away. I could almost see her knuckles turning white as she clutched the steering wheel.

All three looked at her. Then Jade turned to Star.

"I guess it isn't easy for anybody," she said. Star offered a reluctant grunt of agreement.

Doctor Marlowe closed the door behind us.

"Anybody want my phone number?" Misty asked.

"I'll just take everyone's," Jade said. She smiled at Star's look of surprise. "I'm the president of the OWP's. I'll call you all when it's time for us to have our first real meeting. Maybe I'll have a brunch or something."

She gave us her number. My mother kept giving me looks.

"I've got to go," I said. "Thanks for being good listeners."

"I guess we can all say that to each other," Misty said.

"You've got that right," Star added.

Jade fixed her eyes on my mother again and then suddenly, she started ahead of me, toward my mother's car.

"What's she doing?" Star asked but followed. We all did.

Oh no, I thought, if she says something horrible . . .

"Hi, Mrs. Carson," she said. "You've got a very nice daughter. Have a nice day," she added. Then she threw me a sly smile and sauntered toward her limousine.

"That girl," Star said muttering. She looked at my mother. "Hello," she said. "She's right. See you, Cat," she told me and started for her grandmother's car.

"Bye," Misty said to me. "We'll see each other again. I'll bug Jade until she does what she promised."

"Okay."

"Hi," she sang toward my mother and waved. Then she hurried toward the waiting taxicab.

I opened the car door and got in.

"What was that all about?" my mother asked, a look of astonishment on her face.

"I don't know. Nothing much, I guess," I said.

"How did it go in there?"

"All right."

"Aren't you going to tell me anything?"

She still hadn't started away.

"There isn't anything you don't know, Mother. The question is, are you going to tell *me* everything?" I asked.

She fixed her eyes on me while they grew small for a moment and then she nodded and we drove away, the others right behind us, like a parade or maybe . . . a funeral.

After all, we had buried enough sadness to fill a good-size cemetery.

Epilogue

Mother and I didn't talk about anything significant for a few days afterward. I understood that like me, Mother was trying to find her way through all this. Sometimes, it seemed as if tall weeds and vines had grown from the floors and ceilings in our house and we were hacking our way through to reach each other. I remembered how much importance Doctor Marlowe placed on patience and understanding. I, of all people, knew how bad it was to force someone to open the doors to dark rooms.

Mother attacked her housework and all her chores with a vengeance, searching for something to fill every waking moment so she wouldn't have to stop and think and remember.

It was hardest during our meals. When she finally had everything on the table and we had nothing left to do but sit and eat, there would be that terrible, deep silence. If I looked at her, she would start to rattle off orders, telling me about things she wanted done in the house and then quickly following that with a list of things she needed to do herself.

"He wasn't all that much help around here," she muttered one night. "I had to do most everything that concerned this house myself anyway."

That was her first reference to my father since I had returned from the final group therapy session at Doctor Marlowe's. I offered to be of greater help to her and she promised she would give me more to do. She thought I could handle more responsibility.

She definitely needed more help. Every once in a while, I would notice her stop whatever she was doing, place her hand against her chest and close her eyes. She looked like she was waiting for her heart to start beating again.

"Are you all right, Mother?" I asked.

She hesitated, took a breath and nodded.

"I'm fine," she said. "As fine as I could be under the circumstances."

"Maybe you're working too hard, Mother," I said.

"I'm fine," she insisted and walked away quickly.

Finally, one night I came downstairs and found her sitting in the living room, gazing out the window. She was in the rocker and she was moving herself back and forth gently. I could see she was so deep in thought, she didn't even realize I had entered the room. I sat across from her and waited. Her eyes moved very slowly until she saw me and then they widened and brightened.

"How long have you been there?" she asked.

"Just a few seconds," I said.

"I didn't hear you come in." She sighed. "Looks like it might rain again. I think we're getting a leak in the roof over the pantry. I'll have someone check it tomorrow."

"Mother, there was a question that kept coming up in my group therapy."

"What question?" she fired at me.

"A question I have had in my own mind for a while now. I don't want you to get angry at me for asking it, but it's important to me."

"I hate questions," she muttered. "Ever since what happened happened, that's all the world's been full of for us, questions."

"People have to have answers, Mother. I need answers just like anyone."

"Answers can make for unnecessary trouble. Sometimes it's best not to ask questions," she said.

"No, Mother," I pursued. "It's never better to bury your head in the sand."

"Is that what that doctor taught you?"

"No. I taught it to myself. If I had asked some questions and if you had . . ."

"All right," she said. "All right. Let's get this over with. What question?"

I paused and she looked away as if to make it easier for me.

"Why did you adopt me?"

"What?" She turned back to me. "What kind of a silly question is that?"

"It's not a silly question, Mother. Was it because you lost a child and didn't want to try to have another?"

"What? Who told you I lost a child?"

"Daddy."

"It was another one of his lies. He was just trying to get you to feel sorry for him and blame me for everything wrong in this house."

"That wasn't true?"

"No."

"I thought it was. Being a mother has never been easy for you, and I couldn't help feeling that all the time."

"Blaming me. I knew it."

"I'm not blaming you. I'm asking you to be honest with me. I need to know everything. I'm old enough now, Mother. I've been forced to grow up quickly," I added.

She glanced my way, her eyes filling with pain.

"Why does everything have to be explained all the time?"

"I have a right to know about myself, Mother. I'll never get better if you don't help me. It might even help you," I added.

She stared at me, looked out the window and rocked. I didn't think she would say any more. I expected I would just go upstairs and leave her in silence as I had done so many times before.

"My mother," she said suddenly, "got pregnant at forty-four. It was a very big surprise to my father." She looked at me.

I was afraid to speak, afraid she might stop.

"Soon after she announced she was pregnant, your father came into our lives. He was always a sly one, looking for some opportunity. My father was just as sly in some ways. He drew him in like a spider, giving him bigger and bigger investments to handle.

"Howard proposed to me and my father . . . my father came to me and practically begged me to marry him. My mother left for a while and gave birth to you and Howard and I adopted you," she said quickly. "I guess it was all part of the deal. I guess you could say my father sold you and me to Howard in a neat little inheritance-wrapped package. And don't think your father didn't throw that back at me when this all happened," she added with fury in her eyes. "He threatened to tell everyone about your birth, our marriage. It was pure blackmail. Otherwise, I would have seen him put in some jail cell and had the key thrown away."

"My grandmother was really my mother?" I asked incredulously.

She spun on me.

"You wanted to know everything. Now you know. You see why God told Adam and Eve not to eat of the Tree of Knowledge? Sometimes, you're better off in ignorance."

I stared at her.

"We're . . . sisters? Is that what you're telling me?"

She took a deep breath and looked out the window again.

"Half-sisters. Toward the end of his days, my father told me he was convinced he wasn't your father."

"Who is my father?"

"I don't know," she replied quickly, almost too quickly.

She turned to me.

"So now you know all this. Are you going to be better for it? What are you going to do with the knowledge, Cathy?"

"I don't know. It will take time to digest it," I said, swallowing hard.

"You want my advice? Bury it. That's what I did."

"Did you? Did you really ever bury it or did you let it bury you?"

She studied me and then her eyes narrowed.

"So, what are you going to do now? Are you going to hate me more for keeping the truth from you?"

"I don't hate you," I said.

"Are you still going to call me Mother?"

"I don't know how I can start doing otherwise," I said.

She nodded. Then she turned and looked out the window.

"I'm tired, Cathy," she said. "Let's let each other rest," she pleaded.

"Okay," I said and left her rocking, staring into the night, staring back through her own troubled memories.

Her revelations didn't make me feel any better. In fact, they made me feel even more alone, even more like someone just drifting. What did I have to look forward to now? I wondered.

I thought about the other girls. They were like me that way, too. They were drifting.

Maybe we would get together someday.

Maybe we *could* all be friends.

Would that be so crazy?

"No," the lost little girl inside me cried. "It would be wonderful.

"It would be like a few wildflowers who found their way into their own private garden."